THE
QUEEN'S GAMBIT

A Leonardo da Vinci Mystery

THE
QUEEN'S GAMBIT

Diane A. S. Stuckart

BERKLEY PRIME CRIME, NEW YORK

THE BERKLEY PUBLISHING GROUP
Published by the Penguin Group
Penguin Group (USA) Inc.
375 Hudson Street, New York, New York 10014, USA
Penguin Group (Canada), 90 Eglinton Avenue East, Suite 700, Toronto, Ontario M4P 2Y3, Canada
(a division of Pearson Penguin Canada Inc.)
Penguin Books Ltd., 80 Strand, London WC2R 0RL, England
Penguin Group Ireland, 25 St. Stephen's Green, Dublin 2, Ireland (a division of Penguin Books Ltd.)
Penguin Group (Australia), 250 Camberwell Road, Camberwell, Victoria 3124, Australia
(a division of Pearson Australia Group Pty. Ltd.)
Penguin Books India Pvt. Ltd., 11 Community Centre, Panchsheel Park, New Delhi—110 017, India
Penguin Group (NZ), 67 Apollo Drive, Rosedale, North Shore 0632, New Zealand
(a division of Pearson New Zealand Ltd.)
Penguin Books (South Africa) (Pty.) Ltd., 24 Sturdee Avenue, Rosebank, Johannesburg 2196,
South Africa

Penguin Books Ltd., Registered Offices: 80 Strand, London WC2R 0RL, England

This book is an original publication of The Berkley Publishing Group.

This is a work of fiction. Names, characters, places, and incidents either are the product of the author's imagination or are used fictitiously, and any resemblance to actual persons, living or dead, business establishments, events, or locales is entirely coincidental. The publisher does not have any control over and does not assume any responsibility for author or third-party websites or their content.

First Edition: January 2008

Library of Congress Cataloging-in-Publication Data

Stuckart, Diane A. S.
   The queen's gambit : a Leonardo da Vinci mystery / Diane A. S. Stuckart.— 1st ed.
      p.   cm.
   ISBN-13: 978-0-425-21923-2
   1. Leonardo, da Vinci, 1452–1519—Fiction.   2. Murder—Fiction.   3. Milan (Italy)—Fiction.
I. Title.
   PS3619.T839Q84   2008
   813'.6—dc22   200703565

PRINTED IN THE UNITED STATES OF AMERICA

10   9   8   7   6   5   4   3   2   1

To my husband, Gerry. He knows why.

ACKNOWLEDGMENTS

Like most books, this one would not have been written without the help and support of several people. Thanks to Martin Greenberg and Denise Little of Tekno Books for the original concept and for being brave enough to hand it over to me. Thanks to my writing friends—Carol, Kathryn, and Paula—who offered encouragement and showered me with all things Leonardo. Special appreciation to my aunt, Mary Ann Panevska, who kindly translated various passages from Italian to English; any misapplication of that information rests with me, and not her! And, finally, all manner of praise for my husband, Gerry, who cooked supper every night for a month without complaint while I was on deadline. Love you all!

THE
QUEEN'S GAMBIT

1

While I thought that I was learning how to live, I have been learning how to die.

—Leonardo da Vinci, *Codex Atlanticus*

MILAN, PROVINCE OF LOMBARDY, 1483

Crimson flowered against the alabaster brocade, the vivid hue spreading and dulling to claret along its petal-like edges. A splattering of cordovan had laid a random pattern around that ruby bloom, as if a paint-dampened brush had been flicked a time or two in its direction. My artist's eye approved the contrast of whites and reds displayed to advantage against the verdant lawn. Were I to re-create this scene upon my easel, I might add a handful of bright spring leaves against the weighty fabric, perhaps sketch a pearly dove atop the nearby boulder.

Certainly, I would have forgone the sleek dagger whose handle protruded like some grisly silver stamen from the center of that bloody blossom.

I had ample time to analyze the composition of the unsettling still life, given that I was the first to find the dead man. He lay sprawled here within the high-walled garden that was but a small enclave amid the vast grounds of Castle Sforza. The palace was the ancestral home of the acting duke of Milan, Ludovico Sforza, also known as Il Moro for his dark complexion and by other appellations far less polite because of his unscrupulous manner. Of course, Ludovico was duke in name only, given that he had wrested the title from his infant nephew a few years previously and had not yet been formally designated as such by the pope.

The castle was now my home, as well, though my rank was not nearly as lofty. Indeed, as apprentice to the duke's master engineer and artist, Leonardo the Florentine—also known as Leonardo da Vinci—my place in the castle hierarchy was on level with that of stableboy. Along with a score of other youths who had shown greater than usual talent with a brush, I toiled from dawn to dusk in the Master's workshop. There, I inventoried samples of fabrics, mixed pigments, and cleaned palettes . . . and, on some fortunate occasions, even put color to fresco or panel under the great man's tutelage.

Luckily for the day's festivities, however, it had not been a stableboy but me—the apprentice known to all as Dino—who made the grim discovery. Otherwise, an alarm would have been raised within seconds. Within minutes, everyone from the lad who cleaned the piss pots to the duke himself would have crowded into the garden to view the body. Such an outcome surely would have put a damper upon the game of living chess being played upon the castle's main lawn this very afternoon.

The amusement had been a last-moment addition to the week's activities in honor of the duke's current guest, Monsieur Villasse, the French ambassador. At stake was a friendly wager between the two men regarding a painting to which both had laid claim. Rather than settle the matter in a way that might give offense to either party, Ludovico had decreed that they would play a game of skill for the rights to ownership of the treasure.

The discussion had taken place the previous morning in the Master's workshop. The duke and the ambassador stood in the center of the rough wooden floor, facing one another like a pair of sword-wielding antagonists. Both were dressed in a similar fashion, with their slashed satin doublets of reds and blues and golds trimmed in matching velvet and worn over parti-colored tights. The duke wore a soft beret of bejeweled crimson velvet, that delicate cap emphasizing the coarseness of his dark features. The ambassador's high-crowned hat was of a deep blue that contrasted to advantage against his soft gray hair and dark eyes.

Both men's finery provided a stark contrast to the Master's simple brown tunic over dark green hose, garb similar to what we apprentices wore. He stood a short distance from the pair, seemingly unconcerned with this interruption to the day's work as he favored them with a polite smile and let the two nobles speak between themselves.

The other apprentices and I huddled behind some half-finished panels a respectful distance away, pretending not to listen even as we strained our ears to catch a few words.

"Chess, perhaps?" the ambassador had suggested in his heavily accented Italian in response to Ludovico's pronouncement. He wore an agreeable smile. Doubtless, he pictured the pair of them bent over a cozy board before the fire in the main hall, moving delicately carved ivory figures while drinking fine wine.

Il Moro, however, had more grandiose ideas.

"Chess, yes, but let us indulge in something a bit more extravagant," the duke responded. "Legend has it that two noblemen from Venice once wooed the same fair young woman. Rather than settle their dispute with swords, they held a living chess match, with members of their respective courts taking the part of the pieces. The victor of the match also won a new bride."

He paused to indicate the object of their wager, the comely female form painted upon a recently finished panel that sat upon an easel before them. "Since we also battle over a woman, why do we not settle the matter in the same fashion?"

"An interesting idea, Excellency," Villasse said with a shrug. "But is it possible to arrange such an event with so little notice?"

"Certainly. You have met my court artist and engineer. He can create such an amusement overnight. Can you not, Leonardo?"

Peering past concealing panels, I saw the Master move toward them, his innate grace obvious even in the few steps he'd taken. He stood several inches taller than both men, his lionlike mane, dark with a faint russet tint, rippling to his shoulders. With his handsome, bearded face and confident bearing, even in his simple garb he appeared to me more regal than either of the other men. His pleasant expression never changed, though I had worked under his stringent tutelage long enough to recognize the slight flicking now of his fingers that was a sign of disdain or impatience . . . often both.

"Certainly, Excellency," came his smooth reply as befitted a man who knew who his benefactor was. Since the Master was in charge of the court's pageantry, which included all manner of galas and festivals, such royal whimsies were not uncommon to him. That did not make their accomplishment any less difficult, however. "All preparations will be complete for a living chess game at noon on the morrow. I presume you shall want courtiers as your playmen?"

While the duke made a few commands neatly presented as mere suggestions, Vittorio, the youngest of the apprentices, leaned closer to me, his unruly blond curls bouncing. Eagerly, he whispered, "Do you think this chess match will give the Master a chance to display his mechanical lion?"

"Perhaps," I murmured back with a smile, for I understood the youth's excitement.

The Master had recently created a marvelous metal creature that he'd allowed us apprentices to see demonstrated before any public unveiling. Through some complicated method of pulleys and weights, the brass lion could open its mouth to emit a roar, while its breast opened to spill forth a dramatic bouquet of fresh flowers. I, too, had found it a most wonderful invention and hoped to see the beast perform before the court one day soon.

But the lion did not make an appearance at this event.

Rather, under my Master's direction, the duke's gardeners had toiled beneath torchlight to sculpt a portion of the parade ground just within the main gate of the quadrangle so that its grass resembled an immense checkered board. An army of royal valets, tailors, and seamstresses had worked the night through, as well. Their job was to assure that the courtiers who were to take on the personages of the various chess pieces would be dressed in the appropriate elaborate garb—black or white—that represented their fictional stations.

My task, along with the rest of the apprentices, was to remain by my Master's side at all times, ready to perform one job or another.

I should not have been surprised that he had completed all arrangements for the festivities by midmorning. Where earlier had been a broad expanse of lawn, colorful tents and tables and benches now gave the grounds a carnival-like air. A gilded royal box had been hastily constructed for the duke, so that he and the ambassador could rest in comfort while the game went on. A second box would seat various of the noble family, along with members of the court and favored guests such as the visiting archbishop of Milan. On display nearby was an elaborate gilded easel draped in black and white silk, upon which sat the oil portrait that would be the victor's prize. Two of the apprentices stood guard, lest one of the spectators venture to peak beneath the cloth for an unauthorized look.

In what would prove to be an interesting bit of irony, Leonardo had made a change to the cast of players upon the chess field. Instead of the traditional standard-bearers on either side of the queen and king, he insisted that those players would be garbed as bishops. A much more interesting costume, he claimed; besides which, that was how it was done in the English court. Such a substitution mattered little to us servants, ignorant as most of us were of the game that was the nobleman's purview. For myself, at that time I knew only enough of the pastime to name the various pieces.

When the flourish sounded at noon, the playmen took

their individual squares amid the grassy chessboard. Both the topiaried lawn and the stark costumes of the players had drawn an approving cheer from the spectators gathered to witness this most unusual event. The Master had been well pleased by the reaction. While he would claim his satisfaction was in serving Ludovico, we apprentices all knew that he enjoyed the adulation of a crowd, even if that praise came indirectly.

The duke controlled the white pieces, which I learned had allowed him the first move. Assisted by a team of advisers, he and the ambassador conveyed their wishes to the gentleman who Leonardo had appointed master of the game. That dignified personage—a slight, gray-bearded member of the duke's personal staff—sat in a smaller box lavishly draped in black and white silk. He, in turn, called out the plays for all to hear.

Each move was conducted with appropriate spectacle and a flourish of horns, so that the travel of a playman from one square to another might take several minutes to complete. Indeed, the black knight's move to the board's center had occupied the greatest portion of an hour, for it included the dramatic arrival of a snorting black stallion that served as mount for the ride of three squares' length.

Two hours into the match, only a handful of plays had been accomplished. Still, the novelty of the living chess game had been sufficient to keep everyone's attention. Had I been less sleepy from the long night before, I might have taken equal interest. As it was, I joined several other of the apprentices behind one of the hastily erected screens of painted hedges that served to mark off the playing field from where the spectators sat. There, I closed my eyes for just a moment . . . and like the rest, promptly fell asleep.

All too quickly, an intermission had been called. The prolonged fanfare that announced it rudely awakened us from our slumber, while the players dispersed to take refreshment. The interval was doubtless a particularly welcome respite for the four gentlemen who, as the white and black castles, wore wood and fabric frameworks representing siege towers as their costumes. I dutifully rejoined my fellow apprentices to wait at the ready for any command from the Master.

The trouble commenced when another trumpet blast from the royal musicians signaled a return to the game, and a white bishop had not retaken the field with the other players. Another delay was called. As I was standing closest to the Master, I received the first task of locating the missing man.

"Quickly, Dino, search the grounds for him, and do not tarry!" he commanded of me, while sending two other of the youths, Paulo and Davide, to investigate the castle.

I had tried the obvious places first—the banquet tent, the privies—but without success. Finally, I'd thought to try this garden, even though its gate was firmly latched. Had I not been following the Master's orders, however, I would never have dared to peep inside a place from which all but high-ranking members of the court were banned.

The walled garden was close enough to the playing field that I could hear sound drifting from the spectators impatiently awaiting resumption of the entertainment, but the enclave was surprisingly private for all that. Perhaps it was the thickness of the damp stone walls, or the hint of breeze wafting through the twisted olive trees and spreading palms that dotted the garden. The scents of blooming roses and lilies hung about me, their warm perfume far more enveloping than the harsher aromas beyond the walls. Certainly, the gentle trickle of water into a long, low stone trough filled with pink and yellow water lilies added to the tranquil air and further muffled outside sound.

Little wonder that garden served equally well both as a place of escape and as the perfect site to commit murder. For murder it most surely was, given that the knife that I'd previously described protruded from the unlucky man at a spot midway between his shoulder and neck. Moreover, the blow that had killed the courtier must have had some strength behind it, for it had pierced a heavy brocaded mantle worn over a tunic and chasuble.

"Saints' blood," I whispered, using one of the stronger invectives I had learned from my fellows. I crossed myself reflexively, the tracing of fingers less a prayer than an
instinctive warding off of evil. Thus steeled, I stepped closer
and knelt in the damp grass in an attempt to determine the
man's identity.

He was the person I sought, for he wore the snowy vestments of the wayward white bishop. His borrowed miter—
the tall peaked hat traditionally worn by high-ranking
clergy—lay beside him, doubtless having tumbled from his
head as his assailant struck him down. A white wooden
cross almost as tall as he lay in a similar state of abandonment. Given the copious spill of blood and his unnatural
stillness, I swiftly determined that the ersatz bishop was
long past any assistance that the royal physician could sup-
ply. Thus, I weighed my next move.

You might think from my calm assessment of the situation that I was used to finding murdered courtiers, but such
was not the case. To this point in my fairly brief life, my experience with dead people had been limited to a handful of
relatives and neighbors, none of whom had expired by any
unnatural means. Finding a corpse that had met a violent
end had indeed been a shock. Only by deliberately viewing
the scene as one to be painted had I managed not to flee the
garden in abject terror. Now that the first alarm had passed,
however, my greater concern was notifying the Master.

I rose on unsteady legs, the knees of my dark blue hose
soaked through now from the damp grass. Only then did it
occur to me that whoever had done this foul deed might still
be about, watching me from a gloomy corner of the garden.
My life could be in equal jeopardy!

Abruptly, the garden's placid atmosphere took on a
threatening air. The low trickle of water became an ominous
mumble of unseen voices, while the soft flower perfume became but a tawdry mask for the baser smells that now em-
anated from the dead man. The insects buzzing about his
corpse hummed far louder than the hint of breeze, and the

cool shadows now seemed but a haven for some vicious, un-known enemy.

With frequent backward glances, I managed my retreat from the garden unscathed, praying as I hastily closed the gate after me that I would never have to return to it. I paused long enough to jam the latch into place with a stick to dis-courage anyone else from accidentally stumbling upon the se-cret that the garden contained. Satisfied that I had procured a few moments' more time, I rushed off to find the Master.

He was pacing alongside the grassy chess field, while the spectators and playmen milled with equal restlessness. Seeing me return unaccompanied, he rushed toward me, his russet hair floating like a capelet behind him.

"Dino!" he roared, "what is taking you and the others so long to complete a simple errand? We cannot resume play mi-nus a bishop. Where is the conte, His Excellency's cousin?"

The dead man is cousin to Il Moro?

I felt myself blanch. Though my only connection to the man's murder was in the unfortunate role of the one who had found his body, I was well aware of the noble penchant for blaming the bearer of bad news. The duke, in particular, rel-ished punishing minor infractions with a heavy hand. Though I was but a witness after the fact, I could well suffer some un-pleasant consequences for having been the one to discover his relative's brutal slaying.

The Master must have seen something of my distress upon my face for, as he halted before me, he commanded in a kinder tone, "Tell me, my dear boy, what do you know of the conte's fate?"

"Dead," I whispered. "Murdered."

Another master would have been shaking me, demand-ing explanations, but not Leonardo. He rubbed his chin with his thumb and forefinger, as if contemplating my words. Then, betraying his surprise by nothing more than a lifted brow, he gestured the most senior of the apprentices, Constantin, to his side.

"I fear I must provide some assistance to our missing white

bishop. Go tell the master of the game that these instructions come from me. He should call the jugglers and musicians to the playing field and have them commence with a few more minutes of entertainment . . . preferably a diversion that features fire or something equally enthralling. Once the bishop is fit for play, the match will resume with no further delay. And should Paulo and Davide return in the interim, tell them that they are to rejoin the other apprentices."

"You may depend upon me," the boy replied, his reedy voice deepening with importance as he puffed his narrow chest and pulled himself up to his full height. He made a swift bow and trotted toward the box where the master of the game was seated.

That accomplished, Leonardo returned his attention to me. "I will want to know all, but for now explain nothing until we are out of earshot of the spectators. Just lead me to the conte."

I had taken a swift step toward the garden, when he stopped me with a strong hand upon my thin shoulder. "And we shall try not to draw attention to ourselves, Dino, shall we not?"

I nodded and set off at a more moderate pace through the crowd, the Master following calmly behind me. A few who knew his work called out to him as he passed, and he acknowledged them with a smile and a few words of assurance. Only when we reached the garden did his benign expression change to one of grim resolve.

"All right, boy, tell me where the conte is, and what you know about his fate."

"H-He's in there," I replied, gesturing toward the closed gate, which I was relieved to see still was barred as I had left it. "But I can tell you little more than that. He was already dead when I found him—stabbed—and no one else was to be seen. As there was nothing I could do for him, I returned to you right away."

"You did as you should," he replied, giving a small nod

of approval as he eyed the stick I'd used on the latch. "Now, I must see the conte for myself and assess the situation."

It took all my resolve to follow Leonardo back into that frightful garden and close the gate behind us. I allowed myself the briefest of fantasies that perhaps this had been some feverish imagining of mine, and that the garden would prove empty. But, of course, that was not to be. The crumpled form dressed in white bishop's raiment still rested upon the grass where I had left him.

Leonardo knelt and, with the casual air of a farmer inspecting a butchered lamb, rolled the dead man onto his back. The conte's head lolled carelessly to one side, and I winced to see his dull, half-closed eyes and the way his tongue protruded slightly from between his lips. I could see now that the man's hands were stained in his own drying blood, doubtless from when he had clutched at his wound in a futile attempt to stanch the gory flow.

I gulped back a sudden rise of bile, imagining the conte's last moments. Surely there had been a moment of surprise at the attack, and then great pain . . . and finally, fear, as he must have known his wound was mortal. Had his killer stood coldly by and watched him die, I wondered, or had he fled the instant the deed was done?

Sympathy for the murdered man rushed through me, and I allowed myself a better look at him. Slender of build, with pale skin and fashionably styled hair the color of a wren's wing, he would have cut a fine figure at court. He had been a young and relatively handsome man in life—certainly, more comely than his older cousin—but death had laid an unkind hand upon his features, blurring them into thickness.

Seemingly untouched by the sight, the Master felt at the man's throat and at his wrist, then shook his head. "As you said, it is too late for him," he observed.

Returning the corpse to its original position, he went on, "However, the body is still limp and only slightly colder than one would expect of living tissue. And see how I can

press his flesh"—he demonstrated with a forefinger to the
dead man's exposed calf—"and it does not retain the impression. Beyond this, we know the conte was still alive when the
intermission was called, so we can say with certainty that he
has been dead for no more than an hour. As to the cause behind his demise, that answer is obvious, do you not agree?"

I gulped again and nodded. Soon after joining the Master's workshop, I had heard whispered rumors from the other
apprentices that Signore Leonardo had learned his anatomy
by studying the dead . . . human remains, as well as beasts.
They said that he had even carved up bodies simply to observe their inner workings. Seeing the cool interest with
which he now studied the corpse before him, I could well believe such tales.

"If we are to discover who has done this deed," he went
on in the same composed tones, "it would be useful to know
whose knife is buried in the Conte di Ferrara. The handle
appears to have some carving upon it, as may the blade. Perhaps an examination of it will tell us where it originated, if
not to whom it belongs."

I braced myself to watch him pluck the knife from the
luckless man's body, but to my relief he left the weapon
where it was. Instead, he gracefully rose—how was it that
the knees of *his* stockings were not dampened at all?—and
turned back toward me.

"We shall wait for that, however, until His Excellency
has been notified of what has transpired. I fear I shall have to
summon him from the playing field and bring him here. I
will need you to stand guard over the conte for me until we
return."

I stood speechless for a moment. I had vowed upon first
leaving it that I would never return to this garden, yet
here I was again in it, not many minutes later. And now,
when I would have gladly fled the place a second time, my
Master was asking me to remain here alone with a murdered man!

"Come now, dear boy," he went on, flicking his fingers in

that well-known sign of impatience at r
"There is nothing to fear from the dead, and]
that whoever is responsible for the deed is
someone discover his guilt. Surely you are a brave enoug..
fellow for this task . . . or should I summon one of the serving wenches to stand watch in your stead?"

That last question spurred me to action, as surely he
knew it would, though perhaps not for the reason he intended. I squared my shoulders and lifted my chin proudly.
"Do not worry, Master, I will make certain no one disturbs
this place until you return with the duke."

"Good. I will return shortly with His Excellency. Let us
just hope that this bad business does not reflect poorly upon
us."

I waited until the Master had latched the gate after him
before dropping my brave front and scurrying to the wall,
intent on putting as much distance as possible between the
conte and me. I huddled with my back pressed into the
stones, safe from anyone—dead or alive—sneaking up behind
me. For good measure, I made the sign of the cross again and
whispered a swift Paternoster. The Master was right that the
dead could not harm anyone; still, I was less certain of his assurances that the person who had so brutally struck down the
conte was long since gone. Surely this had not been the work
of some random assassin . . . or had it been?

Fortunately, this was not my dilemma to solve. Very
soon, I would be well out of the situation. To distract myself
in the meantime, I reached for the pouch at my belt and
withdrew my most valued possession.

It was a small stack of paper that I had obtained from a
rag seller soon after arriving at the castle. I had traded the
man an old tunic for the precious sheets, which I then had
painstakingly bound with a bit of found cord into the form
of a book. Upon those gloriously blank pages, each night I
dutifully documented in minuscule script the most important lessons of my apprenticeship.

I had begun what I called my notebook in emulation of

the Master. I had watched in amazement as, day after day, he filled copious pages of notes, those loose bits of paper of varying sizes containing all manner of jottings. Written as the words were in an odd, reverse hand, I could not easily read them. Still, I had admired the tiny sketches that illustrated numerous passages, marveling how with but a few strokes of his pencil he captured the wing of a bird in flight or the form of a man laboring. My thought had been that something of his genius might lie in the fact that he constantly put his ideas to paper. In doing the same, myself, perhaps some of that genius might rub off on me. If not, then my scribblings would serve as a secondary record of the Master's doings. Even if I never became a famous painter in my own right, I still might gain a bit of success that way.

Finding the note I sought along the corner of one page— like the Master, I used every empty space and even wrote new lines crosshatched over old—I reviewed my list of various greens to see how many of those shades I could spy within this garden. The task was not an idle one; rather, it was but one of many exercises that the Master had instructed all of us apprentices to perform during our leisure moments while under his tutelage.

"If, for example, I were to ask you to explain the color blue, I would expect you to name a score or more of different variations within that family," he had told us. "Moreover, you should be able to fully describe each one. And, of course, you must be able to mix each of those tints upon your palette."

Upon occasion, he would permit a more senior apprentice to add a bit of paint in one of those hues to a work in process, but only after that youth could demonstrate he could properly conjure the suitable color. A fortnight earlier, I was allowed to add a few brushstrokes of sapphirine to a painted angel's robe, much to the envy of my fellows. I had blushed with pleasure when the Master then produced a bit of that color, which he had earlier mixed, and proclaimed that my rendition of the shade was quite comparable to his.

I had reviewed a dozen of the more basic tones such as emerald, ivy, and olive, and had moved on to more subtle hues as verdigris and beryl, when I heard the latch turn. I stuffed the notebook back into my pouch and jumped to my feet, reaching the conte's body as the gate swung open, and the duke strode in, trailed by half a dozen of the royal guard. He gestured those men to remain at the gate, then nodded for the Master to follow him.

I pulled off my cloth cap and made a bow, backing away deferentially at Il Moro's approach. He paid me less heed than the buzzing flies, however, sweeping past me as if I were not there before halting before his cousin's prone form.

Had I been expecting a show of grief, I would have been sorely disappointed. Glancing up past my lowered lashes, I saw the duke nudge the dead man with one elegantly booted foot. Then, with a sound of disgust, he turned back to the Master.

"Pah. What a fool Orlando was to allow himself to be murdered this way." He shook his head, anger further darkening his swarthy features. "As you may have heard, Leonardo, I had only just made the conte my ambassador to France. He was to journey to Paris in a fortnight and further discuss with King Louis those matters touched upon during Monsieur Villasse's visit here. This is quite an inconvenience to me and to my plans for Milan. I have cousins enough to spare, but no more ambassadors at the ready."

"Unfortunate, indeed," the Master replied in a respectful tone. "I can only imagine the difficulty this has caused you. Do you suspect, Excellency, that your cousin was murdered because of his role in your diplomatic corps?"

"It is possible. However, we should not limit ourselves to a single conclusion without more evidence."

He flung his red velvet mantle over one shoulder and leaned over the body. In the swift gesture of a man accustomed to handling weapons, he pulled the knife free from his cousin's shoulder, releasing a spatter of blood. With the same practiced moves, he examined the darkened blade for a moment before flinging it so that its point was buried in the earth at his feet.

I watched the weapon quiver there for a moment like a startled serpent and then gazed back up at the duke. His expression was forbidding, consumed mostly by anger; still, I sensed some other emotion playing upon his countenance, as well. Disbelief . . . perhaps a bit of fear?

An odd reaction for so cold a man, I told myself. His even more pitiless brother had been assassinated several years earlier, leaving behind a widow who had assumed the role of regent on behalf of her young son. Rather than allow the proper succession, however, Il Moro had callously wrested that position from her and the rightful heir, taking control of the court. Surely it was no coincidence that the Sforza coat of arms prominently featured a winding grass snake upon it. If anyone should be familiar with the ofttimes deadly politics of the royal palace, it should be he.

But with the duke's next words, I suddenly understood his apprehension.

"Whoever the slayer was, he did not bring his own assassin's tools. That knife has my crest upon it. In fact, I believe it came from my own table."

2

The royal game is a battle in miniature . . . and life in miniature.

—Leonardo da Vinci, *The Notebooks of Delfina della Fazia*

So saying, Sforza brushed his hands together as if eradicating any hint of connection with the murder weapon. Whatever that flicker of other emotion across his cold features had been, it now vanished as he returned his attention to the Master.

"We must uncover the guilty party in this matter," he decreed, "and in that I will require your help. If Orlando's death was not a simple murder, but an assassination, the ramifications could be significant."

Leonardo nodded. "I agree, Excellency. But surely you would want your own men, and not an outsider such as myself, to expose the truth."

"That is precisely why I want you, because you are an outsider."

The duke's coarse features settled into a look of scorn. "Until I know the reason for my cousin's death, I cannot trust anyone among my court to proceed on my behalf. The men who executed my brother were among his trusted advisers. Thus, the culprit in this instance might be one of my own men . . . perhaps even a member of my family. No, it must be you who discovers the killer's identity and learns if I am next upon his register."

"Then I am honored by your trust, Excellency," the Master replied with a bow. "I will begin my investigation immediately and shall have an answer to you as soon as possible."

The duke, meanwhile, gestured to the leader of his guards. "Remove the Conte di Ferrara to his quarters. Stand guard outside his door, and do not let anyone else in to see him, not even his wife. If anyone asks, explain that the conte has been stricken by a contagious pox. Neither you nor your men are to disclose any word regarding his death until I issue a formal proclamation tonight."

He paused, his lips twisting cruelly. "Be assured that, if the news makes its way through the castle before that time, the consequences for those who spoke shall be severe."

"A sensible plan, Excellency," Leonardo smoothly interjected while the guards exchanged anxious glances. "The longer we delay in making the news of his death known, the more confident his killer will be that he has gotten away with the crime. But if I might make a suggestion, perhaps your men should take care to conceal the conte's body before they carry him into the castle."

At the duke's crisp nod of agreement, the Master addressed the leader of the guards. "Perchance you might obtain one of the linens from the banquet tables near the playing field?"

That man snapped a command to one of his underlings, who rushed from the garden. He returned a few moments later with a length of cloth only lightly spotted with grease and wine. With more efficiency than reverence, the guards wrapped the corpse, splotches of crimson oozing through the makeshift shroud to further stain the white linen. Only when the guards had carried their burden from the garden and closed the gate behind them did the duke again address the Master.

"I have every confidence in you, Leonardo, but know that I

do expect this nasty business to be concluded within a few days." Il Moro paused and gave him a wolfish smile. "And now, let us return to our chess match. I cannot afford a forfeit, as I intend to take that painting of yours as my prize."

With those words, the duke took a few steps in the direction of the gate, only to pause and turn his attention to me. I hurriedly bowed my head. It was the first time since he had entered the garden that Il Moro had looked in my direction, and I could not help a small shiver of fear as I found myself subjected to his obsidian gaze.

"As I said, the consequences for anyone who speaks of this matter before I do shall be severe. I am sure you will keep that in mind, Leonardo."

Though he spoke to the Master, I knew his words were for me. Not daring to glance up, I hunched a bit deeper into my cloak and kept my gaze firmly fixed on the ground until the duke had departed the garden in a swirl of crimson velvet. The Master waited until his benefactor was far from earshot before giving a small sigh.

"Well, Dino, it seems we will have our work cut out for us, discovering the identity of the conte's murderer. I suggest we begin our investigation now, before word of the killing becomes common knowledge and our advantage of surprise is lost."

"We . . . our?" I echoed uncertainly, Il Moro's warning still loud in my ears. "Begging your pardon, Master, but are you saying that you want me to help you?"

"But, of course." He gave me a satisfied nod. "While mine will be the intellect that will piece together the evidence we uncover, there are mundane tasks that will need to be performed by someone of lesser skill. Moreover, I will need someone such as you who can mingle among the court unnoticed. As a mere apprentice, you will be ignored in a manner that I, as Leonardo, would not be."

It was hardly the most flattering of portraits that the Master verbally painted of me, but a small thrill of excitement began to build in me at the notion, superseding my previous fear. Only moments ago, I had been but a lowly apprentice, one of a score who trained in the Master's workshop. Now I would be working directly with the great Leonardo and assisting the Duke of Milan in a secret mission. How many other youths could claim such an honor?

"Do not stand about daydreaming, Dino," he scolded, interrupting my moment of self-importance. "Quickly, we must also return to the playing field. We need a replacement white bishop in the game."

He scooped up the forgotten miter and cross from where they had fallen and strode from the garden, with me half running to keep up.

"Where will we find someone to take the conte's place?" I asked as I trotted alongside him toward the milling band of spectators. "Surely whoever you ask will first want to know why he cannot continue the game."

"That is precisely why I have chosen someone who knows of the murder and who can be trusted to keep silent about it."

He halted and looked at me. "Make haste and find Luigi the tailor," he commanded, to my astonishment. "Tell him I have decreed that he dress you to the part of the white bishop immediately. We should have sufficient bits of garments remaining that he can construct a similar costume with little effort. As soon as you are attired, take the field in the proper spot."

"But surely someone will notice that I am not the Conte di Ferrara," I weakly protested.

By way of response, the Master thrust both the cross and the peaked hat that he was holding into my hands. "The substitution will not be immediately obvious," he said. "In costume and at a distance, you might be mistaken for the duke's cousin, as you have the same slender physique, with pale features and dark hair, as the conte. But, upon closer inspection, it will be eminently evident that you are not he. Thus, you must make careful mental notes as to people's reaction when they discover our deception."

As I had remained rooted where I stood in my surprise,

Leonardo caught me by the elbow and began walking me toward a striped tent not far from the playing field. It was there that the tailor in question was stationed should he be required to make repairs to the costumes during the course of the chess match.

"Those with no knowledge of the conte's fate will simply be curious as to why you have taken his place," the Master continued. "Should the assassin still be about, however, his first worry when he spies you is that his victim survived the attack. He will take pains to get close enough to determine whether or not you are indeed the duke's cousin. This is the person for whom we are searching. Be aware of anyone who pays you greater attention than the situation warrants. I will also be watching the field for such a reaction."

"But, what if—"

He cut me short with a gesture. "Should your piece be chosen to move, the master of the game shall instruct you what to do. And remember, if anyone questions the substitution, tell him nothing other than that you were informed the conte is unable to continue, and that the duke's master of pageantry instructed you to take his place. Is that understood?"

"Yes, as you wish," I replied in resignation.

We had reached the gaily beribboned tent where Luigi now was peering out, a curious look upon his pudgy face. His attention, however, was all for Leonardo; as the court's master tailor and valet, he considered himself well above most of the castle staff, including the master of pageantry's apprentices. I suspected he also considered himself superior to the Master.

"Ah, Signore Leonardo, I am at your service," he began in oily tones. "Is there a problem with one of the costumes? Or is another of your many tunics in need of repair?"

"In a manner of speaking."

Before the tailor could protest, the Master gestured away that man's two young helpers who were seated outside the tent stitching away at some linens. Then, all but shoving me into the tailor's flabby arms, he curtly informed Luigi, "I have given my apprentice instructions for you regarding the chess match. Follow them to the letter."

So saying, he turned on his heel and started toward the box where the master of the game sat. Luigi sketched a bow in his departing direction before dragging me into the stuffy confines of the tent. Once inside, however, his pretense of civility vanished.

Favoring me with a disdainful look, he released his sweaty grip on me and demanded, "Very well, boy, what does the great Leonardo require of me now?"

"I am to be the new white bishop," I replied, perversely warming to the role now that its re-creation inconvenienced the unpleasant tailor. "The Conte di Ferrara is unable to continue play, and the Master said I was to take his place. He says this must be accomplished immediately, as the game cannot continue without me."

"I am used to dressing royalty, not servants," the man proclaimed, his second chin atremble as he flung his arms heavenward. "And am I to create an identical costume from nothing? Why did someone not think to demand the costume back from the conte? By Saint Michael, I am surrounded by incompetents."

Still muttering, the tailor snatched the cross and miter from me and then began pawing through the stacks of garments piled upon a table toward the rear of the tent. While he searched, I gazed about in interest, astounded by the wealth of fabrics crowded into that small pavilion.

Stretched between each pair of the tent's support posts were heavy cords, from which hung fur-trimmed velvet mantles and slashed silken tunics, parti-colored hose and sweeping woolen gowns. Indeed, I was encircled by garments enough to clothe the entire population of the castle! For the purposes of the day's chess match, however, every article of attire was white or black, or else a combination of the two colors. The repeated contrast from dark to light made the tent's fabric walls seem to pulse, and I had to shut my eyes for a moment lest I grow dizzy.

"Here."

At the sound of the tailor's peeved voice, I opened my eyes in time to see him shove an armful of snowy garments in my direction. I managed to grab them before they tumbled onto the layering of green wool rugs that formed the tent's floor.

Luigi's pudgy features twisted into a smirk as he watched me stagger beneath the unaccustomed weight. "Your master is fortunate that I had sufficient vestments remaining to match those of the other white bishop. Now, remove your tunic and put on your costume so I can make any other adjustments needed."

"No!"

My vehement response made his bushy black eyebrows momentarily vanish beneath the greasy fringe of hair covering his forehead. Blushing, I quickly amended, "What I meant to say, Signore Luigi, is that I prefer to keep my own tunic on beneath the bishop's vestments."

"Suit yourself," he replied with a sour look, "but don't blame me if you find yourself uncomfortable after an hour under the sun. Now, put those on before your Signore Leonardo wonders at the delay."

With the master tailor's help, I swiftly donned the series of tunics and mantles that made up the white bishop's garb. By the time he had settled the towering miter upon my head and put the cross back into my hands, I had a new-found respect for the clergy and royalty who regularly wore such heavy raiment.

Luigi stepped back to assess my appearance, his fleshy lips pursed in disapproval. "Your master should be grateful that my talent with the needle is such that I can make even a mere apprentice look respectable. See for yourself."

He indicated the polished brass mirror that hung near the tent entrance. I glanced at my reflection and gasped at the stranger who stared back at me. The tailor was right. In this fine garb, I could pass for nobility; indeed, I could easily be taken for a clergyman as which I was disguised. Moreover, the fleeting resemblance between the Conte di Ferrara and me was more pronounced now, so that it was unlikely anyone would notice the change of bishops at a distance.

"Many thanks, Signore Luigi," I told that man. "I am certain the Master is grateful for your service to him."

The tailor contented himself with a snort and turned his back on me, making a show of rearranging the neatly hanging garments around him. Leaving him to his sea of black and white fabric, I hurried from the tent and in the direction of the playing field.

A cheer went up as I took my place in the queen's bishop's square among the other white-garbed players. The trio of jugglers who had been tossing flaming torches abruptly gathered them up and, trailing smoke and fire, rushed off the field. I glanced toward the sidelines, where the master of the game sat. Leonardo stood beside him, and he gave me the faintest nod before gesturing at the royal musicians. A fanfare sounded, accompanied by even louder applause as the master of the game rose.

Raising his hands for silence, he called, "Black shall now make the next play."

From there, the game continued at the same sedate pace as before, with each subsequent play a small spectacle in itself, more so when one piece captured another. My initial nervousness at being there among the court's nobles began to fade as I realized that no one upon the playing field was paying me any heed. We were spaced far enough apart that, had any of my company been so inclined, quiet conversation would be difficult over the sound of the spectators and periodic trumpet blasts from the musicians. Indeed, the other playmen appeared merely bored and uncomfortable standing at constant attention within their individual squares in their borrowed garb.

I allowed myself an inner smile of satisfaction at the realization. It seemed that the privileges of nobility were offset by the burdens of duty . . . in this case, following the duke's whim for a game of living chess. I suspected that none of these courtiers dared risk offending Il Moro by declining the invitation to participate in the event. Perhaps the role of apprentice was not a bad thing, at all.

Very soon, however, I began to succumb to the same bored discomfort as the men around me. My character had not yet been called to move, leaving me little to do but stand in my square and shift from foot to foot as unobtrusively as possible. And, reluctant as I was to admit it, the ill-tempered Luigi had been right to warn me against wearing my tunic under the bishop's costume. The open playing field with the sun above was far warmer than the garden had been, so I found myself growing increasingly uncomfortable beneath the layers of heavy fabric.

Worse was the bulky miter, so large for me that it balanced upon my ears. Unlike my simple woolen beret, the towering headpiece had a tendency to slip with any movement, so that I feared it might topple off should I make a sudden move or let my attention waver for a few seconds. Rather than risk such embarrassment, I had to remain as still as possible. As for the cross, while it would have made an excellent stick upon which to lean, I followed the other bishops' lead, balancing it on the ground before me and holding it upright by the crosspiece.

The one positive aspect of my location was the fact that I did have an excellent view of the imposing structure before me that was, for now, my home.

Coming from a small town, I had been awestruck by my first sight of the magnificent castle fortress that bordered Milan's city walls. The red-bricked stronghold spread in a vast quadrilateral cornered by two immense cylindrical towers of gray stone at the front and two square stone towers to the rear. From within the castle grounds, which took more than half of the enclosed space, I could look up to see the twin rows of arched windows cut along the inner walls. In times of war, soldiers would man their posts there; in more peaceful times, the rooms and corridors served as storage places and housing for additional tradesmen and servants.

Past the sprawling grounds lay the magnificent main

palace. There were the lushly appointed ducal quarters where Il Moro and his family lived, as well as the kitchens, stables, and servants' halls. The main entry through the fortress gates lay behind me, a huge arched doorway cut from the multisto- ried square clock tower that rose almost twice again as high as the stronghold's walls. Had I the opportunity to ascend the stairway within that tower and wind my way up to its crown- ing cupola, I would be able to see miles of fields and rolling hills in all directions . . . maybe even spy the town from which I'd come.

"White queen's bishop, travel two squares on the diag- onal."

That call from the master of the game, followed by a loud fanfare, abruptly pierced my ennui. I was being instructed to move!

I gave a nervous glance about me, not certain if I should proceed or wait for further instruction. I could see the path left open for me when the white pawn to my right hand ear- lier had moved forward a space, so my destination was appar- ent. But even as I hesitated, a trio of young pages dressed as altar boys in white linen and carrying lit candles almost as tall as they were trotted from the sidelines in my direction.

They, at least, appeared to have been coached in their role, I saw in relief. Lining up in front of me, they waited for an- other trumpet blast. Then, to the notes of a familiar hymn of worship, they began a slow walk in imitation of the opening processional for Mass. Gathering my own dignity, I followed at a similar pace toward the square that was my bishop's des- tination. Once there, the candle-bearing youths circled me half a dozen times before again departing the field. A polite round of applause followed.

While the field of players around me narrowed, I moved twice more. Once, quite excitingly, I even captured the black knight, who engaged me in mock battle until my cross finally defeated his sword. But in the very next move, the black queen—a wizened dowager of the Sforza family whose swirling midnight attire heightened the chalky pal-

lor of her disapproving features—swooped down on me like
a vulture to carrion.

I had almost forgotten my reason for being there when I
found myself standing nose to forehead with her—the old
woman was a good head shorter than I—and I saw the suspicion in her narrow black eyes.

"You are not my grandnephew. Where is Orlando?"

"He was unable to continue, and Signore Leonardo asked
me to take his place," I managed, more startled than I cared
to admit by the old woman's unexpected accusation.

She spat upon the manicured ground. "Worthless boy, he
has brought this upon himself!" With surprising strength
for one so frail, she promptly gave me a hearty shove over
the boundary of my allotted spot.

I staggered a bit and had to clutch at my swaying miter,
while the spectators clapped and cheered on the old woman's
antics. Having figuratively defeated me, she stood with regal
grace in the center of that grassy square I had but recently
occupied, inclining her head in all directions in acknowledgment of the applause.

Leaving her to her moment of glory, I straightened my
headpiece and, cross in hand, marched with solemn dignity
to the sidelines. There, the other captured pieces stood com-
miserating with each other and freely toasting their status
with wine. I was swallowing a welcome draft of it when the
Master appeared at my side.

"Very well, Dino, what have you to report to me?" he
murmured.

I shook my head and replied in an equally soft tone,
"Nothing of import, I fear. Only the black queen appeared
to notice I was not the conte, and that is because she happens to be his great-aunt. She appeared surprised that I had
taken his place and asked where he was."

The Master gave a thoughtful nod. "That would be the
Marchesa d'Este. She is an evil-tempered creature, from what
I hear, but I think we can safely assume she is not physically
capable of the deed. And, as you have said, she expected to

see the conte, which would not be the case had she been his murderer."

Rubbing my newly bruised shoulder, I was prepared to disagree with his assessment of the marchesa's strength, but the sound of discord upon the field distracted me.

Another two moves had occurred in rapid succession following my departure from the game, with this current play involving both black queen and white. The black-robed marchesa appeared to be struggling with the white queen, a young woman who, despite the look of genteel alarm upon her fair features, seemed determined to complete her assigned capture of her protesting counterpart.

I glanced over at Leonardo, who allowed himself a small smile at the sight. Shrugging, he told me, "This is not my affair, my dear boy. It is a matter for the master of the game."

Barely had he spoken the words than that gray-bearded gentleman rose from his seat in the main box and made his way onto the playing field. An animated conversation between him and the two queens promptly ensued, while the spectators began calling words of encouragement to that suddenly beleaguered gentleman. He had not earned his high place among the duke's advisers without good cause, however, for a few minutes later, he escorted the now-mollified marchesa toward the sidelines. The triumphant white queen, headdress askew, resolutely took her place in the contested square to another round of applause.

The play proved to be checkmate, for the French ambassador's black king could not elude capture with an answering move. The master of the game returned again to the field to confirm the duke's victory, his announcement bringing cheers . . . the loudest of them, I suspected, from the remaining players on the field who had spent the past few hours all but motionless there. Black pieces and white each gathered on our respective side of the field again, while the duke and the ambassador met at the center and exchanged bows. Monsieur Villasse's expression was one of pleasant acquiescence; Il Moro's features reflected a baser look of triumph.

The Master had already brought the easel to the field's center, the painting upon it still covered. With a flourish, he whipped off the length of black-and-white silk to reveal the finished portrait of a pensive young noblewoman cradling a snowy ermine. The spectators applauded a final time as the Master ceremoniously handed the painting to Ludovico.

The duke and ambassador exchanged bows again and then departed the field to the sounds of a concluding fanfare. The players and spectators, meanwhile, made their way to the tables and tents, which had been replenished with an even more sumptuous bounty of food and wine. I allowed myself a sigh of relief and plucked the miter from my head. With luck, the Master would allow me to shed the bishop's vestments now that the game was ended.

I could see a glimpse of his russet brown mane bobbing through the throng. Before I could head in his direction, however, I felt my arm gripped from behind. Startled, I dropped the miter and swung about to stare at a handsome, golden-haired woman of middle years.

Her ice blue eyes in a sharply carved face were wide in surprise, so that I guessed she was as alarmed by the sight of me as I had been by her assault. Abruptly, she loosed her grasp. "Pardon," she breathlessly exclaimed. "I fear I was looking for the other white bishop."

She dashed off before I could stop her; still, I had the presence of mind to scoop up my miter and follow her through the crowd, using the wooden cross to clear a path when the throng pressed too tightly. I ended my chase a few moments later when I saw her rush up to my counterpart in a similar white vestment. The second white bishop turned to her with an expression of pleased surprise, and the pair walked off toward the vintner's tent, arm in arm. Relieved that this encounter had been but a case of mistaken identity, I again went in search of the Master.

He found me first. "Quickly, Dino, while everyone is occupied, let us return to the site of the murder to continue our investigation."

"Might I first remove my costume?" I hopefully inquired.

He shook his head. "Not quite yet, I fear. I am not ready to surrender those vestments back to our friend, Signore Luigi. They may be required later in our investigation."

I sighed and swiped at my damp brow as I followed him back to the garden. The afternoon's festivities had grown increasingly merrier in proportion to the amount of wine that continued to flow. I allowed myself a longing look back at the banners and tents and laughter. When would an apprentice ever have another chance to take part in such gaiety, and alongside members of the court, no less?

Stiffening my resolve, I put aside thoughts of the revelry and turned my attention to the more serious matter at hand. I had been witness to the duke's command that the Master find the conte's assassin, and I knew that Il Moro would not tolerate failure in this matter. If I could assist the Master in any fashion, it was not simply my duty . . . it was my true desire. Beyond that, having been the one to find the murdered conte, I felt some small connection to him. I could not in good conscience let his murder go unsolved.

After making certain no one was watching, we slipped through the heavy wooden gate and back into that quiet enclave where the Conte di Ferrara had spent his final moments. The afternoon was growing short, and the shadows within the garden stretched even longer than before. Enough time had passed since my discovery of his body, however, that my unease at being in that tainted spot had lessened, even if it had not entirely disappeared.

As always, the Master seemed unaffected by such mundane feelings. Briskly, he told me, "The first thing I would have you do is lie in the identical spot and in the same position as we found the conte."

I eyed that bit of lawn with some misgivings. Unsettling as it had been to discover a dead man, it would be far more disconcerting to take my repose upon the very ground where he had breathed his last. But what other choice did I have? At least the conte's borrowed vestments had soaked up most of the blood, so that the grass where he had lain appeared untainted by any sanguineous humors. Still, I could not help a shiver of distaste as I prepared to comply.

"Wait."

The Master bent toward the forgotten murder weapon, which still protruded from the spot where the duke had flung it. Plucking the knife from the dirt, he brandished it so that the still-bloody blade glinted in the garden's half light. Then he pointed it in my direction.

"As I said, I shall want you on the ground," he said with a slight smile, "But first, I fear that I must murder you."

3

. . . let the line of the blood be discerned by its color, flowing in a sinuous stream from the corpse to the dust.

—Leonardo da Vinci, *Manuscript 2038*

Murder me?

I stared at the Master in disbelief. Had my beloved teacher been imbibing to excess at the vintner's tent, or had the shock of the conte's murder simply driven him mad? Reflexively, I took a step back, at the same moment that the Master gave a cheery laugh.

"Really, my dear boy, you did not truly believe I meant to harm you, did you?" he asked, lowering the knife again as I sheepishly dropped my gaze. "Perhaps I should have worded it thusly, that we must try to re-create the killing of the conte. To do so, I need your help."

He scanned the grass, then nodded as if satisfied at what he saw. "First, you must stand in this very spot." He took me by one shoulder and moved me a dozen paces in the opposite direction, positioning me beside the large boulder. "Now, you must turn your back to me."

Confused, I complied, glancing over my shoulder at him as I did so. The Master stood with the knife clutched in his left hand, which he favored, before shaking his head and transferring it to his right.

"We shall assume," he said, raising the weapon head high, "that the killer is among the vast majority of men in that he favors his dexter hand. Now, Dino, I will make as if to stab you. Look away, and remain very still."

I managed not to flinch when I felt the blade tip touch the spot between my shoulder and my neck. Chill waves seemed to emanate from the tainted metal, but I assured myself it was my imagination that conjured such feelings. It remained fixed there for an interminable time while I heard the Master behind me muttering about angles and force and arcs. Finally, the pinprick of pressure was released.

"Very well, I have seen what I need to see. Now, slowly, move to the spot where the conte fell."

I did as he bade, noticing now as I did so a few spatters of blood atop the grass. With more careful scrutiny, I could see that they continued in a faint trail to the very place where I'd discovered the body. I halted there and looked up at the Master, wide-eyed.

He nodded. "Very good, Dino. I see you have determined that, while the gentleman died at the spot in which you were standing, he was stabbed there beside the boulder. We are making progress in our investigation already. Now, fall to the ground and align yourself as you found the conte."

Obediently, I crumpled to the ground, feeling somewhat disrespectful at mimicking the dead man's role even as I understood the need. The bishop's vestments were a hindrance, wrapping about me as I flailed my way into the remembered position, so that I longed for the freedom of my simple tunic. The Master must have shared my impatience, for he intervened.

"No, not quite right," he declared, reaching down to move one of my arms farther from my body, and then to twist one knee at a different angle. "There, that is it. Try not to move. I must examine you from all sides."

I lay as still as possible while he circled me half a dozen times, pausing occasionally to bend and peer at one angle or another of my body. The scrutiny made me uncomfortable, and not just because I was portraying a dead man. Since coming to the castle, I had become quite adept at keeping myself a good arm's length from the Master and my fellow apprentices to avoid any inadvertent physical contact. Given my situation, I could not risk anyone getting too close, yet now not only was the Master standing but inches from me, he was prodding and moving me about like a slab of clay.

Fortunately, the Master's attention was focused less on my physique and more upon the problem I represented. After a few minutes of examination, he halted and gestured me upward. "You may arise, Dino. I have learned what I wanted to know."

"And what is that, Master?" I ventured as I scrambled to my feet and dusted bits of grass and dirt from the borrowed vestments.

Knowing his secretive nature, I was not surprised when he answered, "I have learned that it is unwise to settle upon a solution to a problem before you have all the evidence at hand. We are finished in the garden for the time being. You may return the costume to Signore Luigi and go about your usual duties."

I left Leonardo idly examining the murderous knife that he still held and made my way from the garden, miter and staff tucked under my arm. While I would be glad to rid myself of the unwieldy costume, I found myself disappointed that my role in the investigation was over . . . as was any opportunity to rejoin the other players for the balance of the afternoon's festivities. In my lavish attire, I felt the equal to any member of the court. Of course, I knew there was more to being a noble than simply dressing the role. Only someone like Leonardo, with his breadth of knowledge and air of supreme confidence, could successfully bridge the two worlds. That ability was one reason for his success at court. Doubtless, it would be the key to solving the mystery of the conte's death, if indeed such a resolution were possible.

But surely my ability as a mere apprentice to fade into the background like a tapestry on the wall could serve equally well in gathering information!

I returned to the tailor's tent and stripped off my bishop's costume, leaving the garments with one of Signore Luigi's apprentices, as that dour man was not to be found. Returned to my usual garb, I made my way back through the merry crowd, enjoying the freedom of movement my clothes provided, which I had begun to take for granted these past weeks. Nearby, I glimpsed my counterpart white bishop in conversation with two of the black pawns. The woman who had mistakenly accosted me and then gone off with him must have found herself a new partner, for she was nowhere to be seen.

The ersatz bishop seemed not to miss her company, for he was enthusiastically gesturing to his new audience with the goblet he held while pausing every few words to drink from that same cup. His libation of choice was red wine, I judged, for crimson drops liberally splattered his snowy cassock, their number growing with every swallow. The sight reminded me of the conte's fate. I shivered despite the late afternoon sun and swiftly distracted myself by picturing Signore Luigi's sour face when he discovered the abuse the other bishop's garments were taking.

I made my way back to the workshop, intending to rejoin the other apprentices for our evening meal. Vittorio, however, was the only one of them about. He was busy sweeping the wooden floor—as the youngest of our number, he had the humblest tasks assigned him—and the shower of dust in the air made me sneeze.

He glanced up at the sound and grinned. "Sorry, I was in a hurry to finish up and join the others. They've already gone off to the kitchens to eat. Why weren't you with them?"

"I was assisting the Master," I told him, earning a shrug in return.

That vague explanation was enough for any of us apprentices. We all knew that one could never guess at what odd task Leonardo might assign us on a particular day. It could be something as simple as wandering the castle grounds in search of various specimens of yellow flowers . . . or as unsettling as playing the role of a dead man in hopes of learning the identity of his killer. Of course, I mentioned nothing of this last but settled on a wooden bench to wait for the younger boy to finish his chore.

Broom bristles flying like a cock pursued by a hawk, Vittorio moved down the length of the workshop. In his enthusiasm, he barely avoided the row of cloth-covered panels that held a number of works in progress. Opposite those lay a long, narrow table upon which lay the various tools of our trade: bundles of animal hairs for crafting brushes; pots of minerals for producing various colorants; bowls of fresh eggs, the yolks of which would be mixed with pigment to create the tempera paint we used. On the far side of the table lay bare panels waiting to be sanded and then covered in a layer of white gesso, which readied them for painting. Shelves on the wall behind the table held plaster casts of various body parts—arms, feet, hands, and even noses!— that we used for reference when living models were not available.

Both the table and the rough wood floor bore testament to our zeal for our tasks, for splashes of every shade found in nature dotted their surfaces. The vibrant paint mosaic enlivened our humble surroundings, the most notable feature of which was the brown wool blanket that hung at one end of the workshop, partitioning off the section where we apprentices slept.

I reached for a brass mortar and pestle and idly pounded into red dust the bit of hematite it held. Part of my training as an apprentice was to master all these tasks necessary to running an artisan's shop such as ours. Though seemingly simple enough responsibilities, I swiftly had learned that they required as deft a hand as was needed to create a portrait. My fellows and I had ample time to practice those crafts, however, for our workshop was always busy. In addition to the war machines and sculptures Leonardo designed for him, Il Moro had made clear that every room and hall in his palace would be filled with colorful renderings of saints and sinners, alike. The duke's grandiose wishes kept us apprentices fast at work every day of the week. Thus, in the hours between morning and evening vespers, we toiled nonstop, save for when we paused to sup at ten of the morning and five of the afternoon. And, of course, there were always a few final tasks to complete before retiring to our pallets for the night.

Vittorio and his broom had reached the end of the room. Using a discarded bit of board, he scraped up the mound of debris he had accumulated and flung it out the workshop window. "All finished," he proclaimed in satisfaction. "Come on, Dino. Let's go eat."

We grabbed up our bowls and knives and headed out the back door of the workshop into a small courtyard that led to the kitchen and nearby servants' quarters. Unlike the lush lawns and gardens of the main courtyards, the ground here was little more than broken stone and hard-packed earth. We were not far from the stables, so that the familiar, redolent odor from them mixed in with the sharper aromas of woodsmoke and rotting food from the kitchen. Near the garbage heap was an alcove that sheltered battered tables made from boards and barrels, along with rows of rough wood benches. This was where we apprentices and the other servants took our meals.

Constantin and the other youths were seated there, supping on a mutton stew that was, I suspected, more stew than lamb. I followed Vittorio to the door outside the kitchen, where one of the girls was ladling out bowls to the castle staff. We went to the end of the line to wait our turn. Too bad I had not been able to keep my bishop's costume awhile longer, I wistfully thought, for a glimpse into the smoky kitchen told me that the nobles would be feasting on quail and venison tonight.

I reached the front of the line and held out my bowl. "Hello, Dino," the dark-haired servant girl greeted me with a coy smile as she ladled out my portion. "Do you remember me? I'm Marcella. I've just started here in the kitchens. Perhaps we can be friends."

"Of course," I muttered in return, feeling myself blush as I ducked my head and hurried away, bowl in hand. This was one thing I'd not been prepared for in my role as apprentice to Leonardo: fending off the attentions of the serving girls. I had already been forced to quash the hopes of one particularly forceful young woman who worked in the laundry by claiming a prior attachment to a girl in my home village. Should Marcella continue to show more than a friendly interest, I would have to tell her that same story.

I settled myself next to Constantin, who unfortunately had taken note of that brief exchange. "What's the matter, Dino, are you frightened of women?" he good-naturedly taunted as I felt my blush deepen. "The servant girls all seem to like you because you are so pretty. If I were in your boots, I would play the situation to my advantage."

"Me, too," Vittorio chimed in with a wide grin. "Why, look, she actually gave you a bit of meat in your stew. She must like you a lot."

"She's just being friendly," I muttered, dismayed to discover as I stirred my bowl that indeed it was brimming with bits of mutton. The other youths began laughing and nudging one another, their humor increasing as I looked up to see Marcella smiling broadly at me. I swiftly dropped my gaze and applied myself to the stew.

One of the other apprentices, Paulo, set down his bowl and leaned forward, the expression on his ruddy face suddenly serious. "Never mind this," he said, his voice dropping to a conspiratorial whisper. "Remember how Davide and Dino and I were sent to look for the missing white bishop during the chess match today? Now, it turns out that one of the duke's family is dead . . . maybe that very man!"

"Dead?" Vittorio echoed, the word ending in a squeak as Paulo clamped a hand over the lad's mouth.

I bit back a gasp of my own. How had the news already

broken free, especially after the duke's dire warning? Perhaps one of the guards had spoken. But whom would Il Moro blame for the transgression? I prayed it would not be me.

Paulo, meanwhile, gave him a quelling look that made the other boy's eyes widen in consternation. He looked around to see whether or not Vittorio's exclamation had been heard beyond our table. When it appeared it had not, he lowered his hand from the boy's lips.

"I heard from the valet who heard from one of the house servants that Il Moro's men brought a body into the royal family's quarters by the back way," he went on. "It happened not long after the chess game was delayed for so long. They say he had a sudden case of the pox."

He looked about the table, his gaze ending upon me. "Dino, you were gone long after Davide and I returned to wait with the Master. Tell us, what do you know?"

"Nothing. The Master sent me on another errand, which is why I did not come back."

My words were not quite a lie; still, I swiftly took another bite as an excuse to say no more. While gossip flew through the castle on raven's wings, at least the story was nothing more than the tale the duke himself had concocted to forestall the truth. It seemed we other players in this bit of deceit had escaped the consequences with which Il Moro had threatened us.

My denial, however, did not go unchallenged.

"I don't believe you," one of the older apprentices, Tommaso, retorted. "In fact, I heard from one of the apprentices to Luigi the tailor that you brought him back a white bishop's costume after the chess game was over. And one of the jugglers claimed that the white bishop who returned to the game after the intermission was not the same one who left the field."

"Sounds suspicious to me," Paulo added as a wave of alarm began to sweep me. "Come, Dino, tell us what you know!"

"Wait." Constantin's reedy voice took on the air of authority as befitted the most senior of our number. Scowling

in Tommaso's direction, he went on, "If Dino does know
something, you can be certain he has been instructed by the
Master to keep silent. What happens outside the workshop
is none of our affair. We are here to learn from Leonardo and
nothing more. So let us speak of something else."

I heard the muttered protests of one or two of the other
youths, but Constantin's words prevailed, and the conversation turned to a proposed fresco that the Master was planning.
I shot Constantin a grateful look and set myself to finishing
the rest of my stew. By the time I'd emptied my bowl, it
seemed Paulo's gossip had been forgotten. I slipped away
from the table, careful to avoid Marcella's glance as I headed
back to the workshop.

The setting sun had left that room in murky gloom, and
I lit a dozen candle stubs to banish the worst of it. By then,
the other apprentices were filtering back to the workshop in
small groups. No one needed to assign tasks, for we all
knew what must be done before we retired for the night. I
joined Vittorio and Davide in sanding a small pile of newly
made boards.

An hour later, Constantin decreed that the evening's
work was complete, so that we were free to do as we wished
until we retired. Most of the apprentices gathered in smaller
groups to play dice, wagering pebbles and bits of glass, as
none had any coin to speak of. As the atmosphere in the
workshop grew more boisterous, Tommaso grabbed up his
battered lute and began plucking a lively air, his stubby fingers a graceful blur along the instrument's wood neck.

I did not join them but settled myself on the corner
hearth where the remains of an earlier blaze still smoldered.
Using a bench as a makeshift table, I pulled out my notebook from my pouch and set to recording a few notes from
the day's events.

This was my usual routine, and rarely did I feel the need
to measure my comments, save when dwindling space on a
page demanded it. Tonight, however, I chose my words with
care lest someone else ever happen upon my papers. Just a

few words—garden, bishop, knife—and but single initials to identify those figures who had partaken in the day's drama. It was enough that I would be able to recall the incident in total at a later date but not so incriminating that someone else reading the passage might discern what actually occurred.

The guttering of candles dictated when our evening's merriment would cease. As we already had consumed most of the week's allotment of tallow, the end came fairly soon. I had just finished a tiny sketch of the garden, with landmarks including the final resting spot of the ill-fated conte, when the candle nearest me died with a small hiss in a puddle of wax.

"Time for bed," Constantin declared to the exaggerated sighs and moans of the others. I suspected from some of the evening's earlier comments, however, that everyone secretly would welcome their beds this night, given that we'd spent most of the previous night up helping prepare for the chess match.

Tommaso ended his song with a dramatic flourish, while Paulo and Davide pocketed their respective sets of dice. I carefully stowed my pages away in my waist pouch again and followed the others to our makeshift quarters behind the woolen blanket.

That barrier of cloth screened off a surprisingly spacious anteroom beyond the main workshop. Along its walls lay a series of shallow alcoves that must have once been used for storage. Now, however, each niche sheltered a narrow wooden pallet cushioned with a bit of straw that served as a bed. Of course, those recesses were not deep enough to accommodate the entire length of the pallet, so that fully half of each bed protruded into the room's center, leaving little space in which to walk. Still, the alcoves offered an illusion of privacy almost unknown to those of our station. I had managed to claim the one in the farthest corner, giving me an even greater measure of seclusion.

Indeed, if not for the fact we were tucked away in our

alcoves each night like so many boxes and barrels, I might never have been able to keep up my deception as long as I had!

I waited until the other apprentices had settled in their own spots, and Constantin had snuffed the final candle. The sole light was provided by a pallid moon shining through narrow windows high on the anteroom's outer wall. It was sufficient illumination that I could make out the outline of my hand held right before my nose, but nothing more. Certain my movements could not be seen by any of the others, I sat cross-legged upon my pallet and reached beneath my tunic to unwind the tightly drawn length of cloth that served to flatten my breasts beneath my male garb.

Now I took my first deep breath since dawn when I, Delfina, had donned the constricting fabric that concealed my female attributes and allowed me to pass as the boy, Dino. It was a ritual I performed each morning, well before the other apprentices arose from their respective cots. Then I reached a hand to my hair, giving in to a moment's vanity as I lamented its loss. While once it had spilled in thick raven ripples all the way down to my hips, now it was cropped in boyish fashion that barely grazed my shoulders. I allowed myself a small sigh at the thought. In some ways, that particular sacrifice had been the hardest change to make.

But losing my hair and subjugating my womanhood in order to masquerade as a young boy was a small price to pay for the chance to study painting with the great Leonardo . . . an opportunity that would have been denied me as a female.

Of course, it had taken more than merely putting on boy's clothing and cutting my long tresses to convince people that I was male. To help the illusion, I had consciously lowered the timbre of my voice to sound less feminine. I also claimed my age as several years younger than I was, so that my beardless cheeks and softer features did not draw undue attention.

True, I had been the butt of much good-natured chiding

for days after my arrival, when I refused to undress or answer nature's call in front of the other apprentices. But interest in my perceived excess of modesty had long since faded, so that no one remarked upon it anymore. And, fortunately, we apprentices were not allowed to flaunt our nether regions with scandalously short tunics, as some of the nobles were wont to do. And while those gentlemen displayed their male appendages every time they climbed a step or mounted a steed, my knee-length overgarment meant there was no chance of someone noticing I lacked that bit of male anatomy.

But I found that what made my masquerade relatively simple was the fact that people see what they expect to see. I claimed myself as a male; thus, so long as I did nothing to disturb the illusion, I would be accepted as one.

Carefully folding the length of cloth out of sight under the bed, I exchanged my boy's garb for a simple nightshirt and slid beneath my blanket, eager for sleep after last night's long hours spent assisting the Master. Slumber proved elusive, however, as questions concerning the dead man in the garden haunted my thoughts.

Who had killed him, and why? Had his death been a result of a moment's heated passion or an action of deliberate calculation? How could the Master and I possibly discover the person responsible for the deed, when it seemed the only witnesses were the dead man and his killer? And did anyone mourn the conte's passing . . . or, like the duke, would the rest of his family view his murder as little more than an inconvenience?

I stifled a groan, mentally cursing the fate that had drawn me into this vile web. It should have been Paulo or Davide who had made the grisly discovery. Knowing the Master's obsessive nature, I was certain he would not rest until the crime was unraveled, especially now that the duke had charged him with the task. This likely meant that I, too, would see little sleep in the interim. Equally unsettling was the fact that my involvement in the investigation would likely mean I would spend excessive time alone in his presence.

As but one of many apprentices, I thus far had escaped anything more than cursory examination by him. Alone with the Master, I would be subject to closer scrutiny. A man with Leonardo's vast powers of observation could well see through my masquerade unless I was extraordinarily careful.

Now my visions of the dead conte were replaced by dramatic scenes of Leonardo discovering my true nature and banishing me from his workshop . . . indeed, from the castle itself. If that happened, I would have nowhere to go. Certainly, I could not return home again, given the circumstances of my departure from it several weeks earlier.

To be sure, I had not deliberately set out upon this adventure as apprentice to Leonardo, nor had I any desire to make myself a man instead of a maid. Rather, both adventure and disguise had been thrust upon me by circumstances.

I had felt the first true inklings of discontent one morning as I struggled to haul home a bundle of newly laundered linens. My two younger brothers, meanwhile, were spending a leisurely day learning carpentry alongside my father, Angelo della Fazia, who was a master of that trade.

I realized how fortunate my brothers were, in that they had their paths in life laid out for them. Once they passed their apprenticeships, they would join a guild and one day become masters, themselves, later acquiring wives and children. Their choices were few, and yet their prospects were promising. My future, however, lacked any such clear-cut landmarks, now that I had strayed from the accepted course for a woman of my moderate station.

Certainly, my unconventional situation was neither approved nor encouraged by my mother, Carmela. Having already moved a step up the social ladder by her marriage to my father, she had hoped to further advance her position by marrying off her only daughter to a man of even greater status. She had her eye upon a wool merchant, perhaps, or else a banker. Then she could smile in satisfaction when she and her friends discussed their respective offspring, pointing out how well I, her daughter, had married. But, to her unending vexation, negotiating a successful union had proved more daunting. Indeed, I was long beyond the age when I should have been wed, given that my eighteenth birthday had just passed.

My solitary state was not from lack of trying on her part. From the time I reached my twelfth year, my mother had paraded me before any number of likely candidates in hopes of catching their eye. A few halfhearted offers had been made over the years, but none acceptable to her. It was not because I was unpleasant to look upon; indeed, I had been told by many that I resembled my mother who, with her luminous green eyes and sleek dark hair had been deemed a beauty in her own youth. But my obsession since girlhood with paints and brushes had alarmed the more wealthy potential suitors.

Had I limited myself to meek depictions of posies, my aberration might have been overlooked, even approved. Unfortunately, word had spread throughout our small town that Delfina della Fazia could paint as no female should, rendering dramatic images of saints and warriors with a talent that drew equal parts praise and censure. And no man of reputation wanted a spouse who attracted such unseemly notice.

My mother had tried to forbid my painting, but I had an ally in my father. An artist in wood, he understood my need to create and decreed that I should be allowed to pursue that calling if I so chose. That was one of the few times that my mild-mannered sire exercised his right as head of the household over my mother, and she blamed me for that transgression.

The matter had come to a head when, a few weeks before I left my home for good, a friend of my mother's had glimpsed one of my works in process, an interpretation of Christ's temptation. Keen of eye, the good lady had noted the resemblance between one of the minor demons in my painting and

one of the town's more influential gentlemen, Signore Niccolo, a corpulent man of middle years well-known for his
petty evil. Word of this insolence had spread throughout the
township, so that the merchant in question demanded to see
the painting himself.

Luckily, I had foreseen such a turn of events. Barely had
the woman left our house when I had revised the painting to
reflect a more generic countenance for that demon. And, for
good measure, I added that gentleman back into the scene
but portraying him as one of Christ's defending angels, instead. Thus, when that panel was revealed to the irate man,
my father had been able to convince him that the entire incident had been but a misunderstanding. Indeed, the merchant
had been so pleased with his depiction as a servant of the Lord
that he had offered to buy the painting from my father on the
spot.

That would have put an end to the situation, save that
the following day he sent an offer of marriage to me by way
of my father.

A sound intruded upon my memories, abruptly bringing
me back to the present. Amid the soft sighs of sleep that cho-
rused around me, I heard the flutter of cloth as the curtains
that separated the apprentices' quarters from the workshop
momentarily parted. Then came the muted sound of footsteps upon the rough wood floors. I recognized the footfalls
immediately, for the Master often walked among us at night.

Indeed, Leonardo had the unfortunate habit of summoning one or another of the apprentices long after the rest of the
castle was abed to join him walking about the grounds.
Whispered speculation was that his purpose was licentious,
but in my own experience I had found this was not so. A
handful of times, I had been the one roused from sleep to
serve as his nighttime companion. Once, I simply had trailed
him through the darkened gardens while he pointed out the
various constellations twinkling in the night sky and specu-
lated on the possibility of men building flying machines that
would take them to the stars. Another time, he'd used me to

help dig a miniature version of the castle moat in a patch of dirt outside the workshop . . . this, so that he could try out the various configurations of a small-scale model of a convertible bridge that he was designing for the duke.

The truth was that the Master slept but little, for his restless mind seemed always consumed with projects new and yet to be finished. Yet genius did not rob him only of sleep. It seemed also to cheat him of that most basic of human needs, that of companionship. For whom could he converse with as an intellectual equal, given that even the cunning Il Moro could only partially comprehend the depths of a man such as he? It did not help matters that Leonardo exuded an air of self-confidence in his everyday dealings that bordered upon seeming arrogance. The result was that most people either held him in such awe that they trembled to speak in his presence, or else they dismissed him as a lunatic because they were unable to understand his detailed explanations of engineering or anatomy or the theory of painting.

Yet even a man possessing his great knowledge still required interaction with his fellows. I knew, as surely as if he had told me, that it was during the dark hours when sleep eluded him that his loneliness seemed the most painful, wrapped as it was in night's solitary embrace. Such was the reason he solicited us apprentices to join him in his nocturnal wanderings, to stave off that emptiness.

Tonight, however, it was something other than loneliness that brought him to our quarters. Thus, I was dismayed but not surprised when his lanky shadow drifted across my cot, and I felt a touch upon my foot.

"Come, Dino, surely you are not sleeping?" he whispered, giving my lower limb a shake. "Have you forgotten that we have an investigation to conduct? Now, dress yourself quickly and meet me outside the workshop."

"Tonight, Master?" I murmured through my yawns, weariness emboldening me to question him. "Would it not be better to wait until the sun is up again, rather than attempt to work by candlelight?"

Leonardo snorted, the sound loud enough to startle Tommaso, who was sleeping across from me, out of his rhythmic snoring for a few breaths. "You need not worry about candlelight where we are going, my dear boy," he softly replied, "for I am taking you to a feast."

4

Alas, how is it that violent death unleashes in even the dullest of men that most unseemly of all human emotions, avid curiosity?

—Leonardo da Vinci, *The Notebooks of Delfina della Fazia*

A few minutes later, I made my way outside the work-shop, where Leonardo paced the dirt walkway like the great cat whose image his name invoked. The half moon that clung to the distant hills provided light enough so that I could see he no longer wore his usual workmanlike garb. Instead, he had donned a short gown of emerald satin trimmed in black velvet over parti-colored hose. The broad sleeves of his gown were slashed and also laced, stylishly revealing glimpses of his white, laced doublet beneath. A black velvet cap clung to his shaggy mane, adding a finishing touch.

Dressed as he was, he could easily pass for a noble, I thought in admiration, feeling shabby by comparison in my same tunic and hose. Indeed, he wore the fashionable garb with the careless air of a man accustomed to finery. I wondered briefly if he had grown up among such luxury and abandoned it for his art, or if his ease was simply born of the same innate grace that seemed part of his genius.

Not noticing—or else not deigning to acknowledge—my stare of appreciation, he gestured impatiently for me to follow.

He did not look back to see if I complied but started at a swift pace toward the main wing of the castle. I swallowed a yawn and trotted after him, already dreading whatever plan he might have up his voluminous sleeve. But as Signore Luigi was nowhere in sight, I felt confident that this particular adventure would not require any sort of costume on my part.

Unfortunately, I would be proved wrong.

We halted outside the kitchen, where earlier I had taken my evening meal with the other apprentices. The door was open, and the firelight from the many hearths needed to sustain the collective stomach of the noble household made that long room bright as midday. Warmth billowed out into the cool night air like a bull's hot breath, and I took a step back. While the kitchen might be a comfortable place on a chilly winter's morning, most other times it likely was a hellish furnace in which to work. Tonight, with the late evening's feast following upon the afternoon's merriment, the kitchen servants had many hours of labor ahead within that inferno, producing platter after tureen of sumptuous fare for the castle's noble residents and their guests.

I gave a silent prayer of thanks that I was an apprentice to a great painter and not bound to a cook or a baker . . . though, to be sure, that role would have been open to me only in my boyish guise. I had found here that, even in these modern times, women rarely were deemed strong enough to take on the formidable task of working a noble kitchen. Indeed, the flirtatious Marcella was one of the few females I had seen working there.

Most of the unskilled kitchen workers were boys who drew water, scrubbed pots, and tended to fires, while the young men with more training took on such jobs as kneading bread and plucking fowl. Those who were sufficiently presentable could eventually make their way up to the rank of porter, tasked with rushing the finished dishes to the dining hall, as well as carving and serving and pouring. While that was one of the more enviable roles in the kitchen hierarchy, neither was it one for the faint of heart or weak of limb.

The Master paused at the kitchen door, his expression one of cool consideration. Then, with a characteristic flick of his fingers, he turned to me. "This, my dear Dino, is where we shall begin the next phase of our investigation. A great number of possible suspects will all be gathered in the main hall to partake of tonight's banquet. The duke has advised me that he has not yet made the news of his cousin's death public. Indeed, even his own family members know nothing of what has happened."

"But, Master," I spoke up, "I have already heard the rumors—"

"Rumors that someone succumbed to a pox. Yes, the castle is fertile ground for such gossip, but fear not, the secret is still safe. The duke intends to make an announcement of the murder sometime during the festivities. We must be at hand to see who among the party is surprised by the news, and who is merely feigning his shock."

I frowned. "So you are certain that the murderer is a member of the court, and not someone from without?"

"It is but a matter of simple deduction, my dear boy," he replied, reaching beneath his sleeve to withdraw a sleek metal blade that gleamed with ominous familiarity. "We have determined from the crest upon it that the murder weapon came from the duke's own household. A professional assassin would surely have brought his own tools upon such an assignment and would not have left behind so blatant a piece of evidence of his crime. This"—he gave the knife that had killed the conte a dismissive tap of the blade—"is designed for skewering bits of fowl and beef, not men. It is a weapon of opportunity, not of efficiency."

And, yet, the knife in question had performed the task quite effectively. I swallowed uneasily at the memory. Still, his reasoning was sound enough, and I nodded my agreement.

Satisfied, Leonardo returned the knife to his sleeve. "And now, Dino, I must once more call upon you to play a role. We should not be too quick to assume the guilty party is a member of the nobility. He could as easily be a kitchen boy as a barone. Thus, while I am seated at the banquet table with the other guests, I will need you to mingle with the kitchen help. Have you ever thought to try your hand at being a porter?"

POURING wine from a heavy metal vessel into a goblet at a distance of several feet without spilling any takes a steady hand. Filling the same goblet as it dipped and swung about while its owner recounted an exciting tale to his tablemates took an even greater skill than I possessed. Unfortunately, I did not discover this deficiency until I all but baptized a portly young knight who insisted upon additional libation but refused to part with his cup long enough for me to fill it properly. Mumbling abject apologies over the splashes of red that now decorated the sleeve of his ivory gown, I clutched my half-empty pitcher to my chest and fled.

Luckily, the gentleman in question had already imbibed sufficient wine so that he was only halfhearted in his efforts to berate me for my lack of dexterity. "Spray me again, boy, and I'll have your hide nailed to the guardhouse!" he roared after me, while his fellows merely laughed at his misfortune.

Suitably chastened, I made my way back to the kitchen. Perhaps I would have better success handling something a bit less liquid, I told myself, and prudently exchanged my pitcher for a platter of sweetmeats. Tray firmly in my grasp, I rejoined the stream of porters winding down the corridor toward the distant dining hall. Here, along this passage connecting the two wings, the air was slightly less stifling than either of those two places. I paused halfway so I could swipe the sweat from my face with my sleeve, lest I draw undue attention by my flushed face and streaming brow.

As I had guessed, the kitchen was indeed a sweltering place in which to work. Fires blazed in all manner of hearths, from those large enough to accommodate a bull upon a spit, to simple boxlike ovens where delicious breads baked. Each fireplace served a different purpose, depending on which area of the immense room it was located. One section of the kitchen produced nothing but pastries and confections; another one roasted, boiled, and baked all manner of beast and bird; still another was responsible for making butters and cheeses.

Here, too, everything was stored. Dry and wet larders each groaned with a village's worth of foodstuffs and spices, while separate sculleries accommodated the collections of silver and pewter needed to serve the immense meals. No space in the kitchen was wasted, not even the ceilings, from which braids of vegetables and sacks of dried meats hung like baubles. Below the kitchen's footing of rough-cut stone—a far easier surface to clean than the old-fashioned dirt floors covered in rushes—lay a cellar where casks of beer and wine were stored. Of course, I had merely heard about the place. Only a few privileged members of the kitchen staff actually had access to it.

As the kitchen masters were prone to brag, their hot, fragrant domain operated with the same efficiency as Il Moro's army. Indeed, it was the great number and diversity of its laborers that made my surreptitious joining of the staff a far easier task than I had anticipated. My promotion from Leonardo's apprentice to kitchen porter had been accomplished by the simple expediency of pilfering a spare blue and white tunic, which I belted over my own garb, and grabbing up a wine pitcher.

As for being recognized as an imposter, of that I had little fear. So many young men were employed in the kitchen that I was sure their masters could not be certain of every one of their names and identities. Feeling more confident now in my role, I was halfway down the twisting corridor, when a single word drifted to me from the murmur of voices ahead.

"Blood."

I almost dropped my platter in surprise as I sought the source of that unexpected and gruesome syllable. Twenty paces ahead of me, two young porters—each hauling a basket of breadstuff almost as large as he—were earnestly talking as they preceded me toward the dining hall. Mindful of my role as Leonardo's spy, I strained my ears to hear more of their conversation. I knew that the duke had not yet announced the news of his cousin's assassination. Could these youths have some secret knowledge of it beforehand?

I quickened my pace as best I could without making my actions overtly apparent. So engrossed were they in their discussion, however, that the pair did not seem to notice my presence when I drew within a few steps of them. What I heard next heightened my suspicions.

"—went as planned," the older-looking of the pair was saying, his full lips abruptly twisting into a sneer. Husky and red-haired, he appeared the sort always ready to engage in a fight. His hands were clenching his basket so tightly that they had gone white. "I suppose we were fortunate that it happened."

"Did anyone see you enter or leave?" the other boy asked in seeming concern. Taller than his companion, he was quite a bit thinner, as well, with coarse black hair that fell over his brow no matter that he shook it from his face.

Listening to this exchange, I felt my heart begin to beat faster. Perhaps the Master had been right, and the conte's murderer was not necessarily a member of the noble class. I held my breath, waiting for the other youth's reply.

He shrugged, the motion sending a fist-sized loaf of bread tumbling unheeded from his basket. "I don't think so. But someone is bound to stumble across him anytime now, and then the search will be on."

"Maybe we should hide or just run away," the second boy suggested, fright now evident on his face.

His companion shook his head. "We can't. We're not finished with our work yet."

We had reached the bend in the corridor that opened into the dining hall, when the first youth noticed my presence. He halted and swung about so abruptly that I had to juggle my platter to keep from colliding with him.

"Y-You!" he sputtered, the fury in his tone palpable

enough to make me take a reflexive step back. "What are you doing, listening in on a private matter?"

"I wasn't listening to anything," I protested, assuming a tone of innocent indignation that belied my sudden nervousness.

The young man standing before me was not so young as I first had thought him, and he was far more muscular than I'd realized. Moreover, he and his oversized basket were now blocking my way. Trying for a conciliatory tone, I went on, "I was told to bring this tray to the dining hall. I can hardly help it if you were going in my same direction."

"Yea, but you can help sticking your nose into other people's business," the black-haired youth spoke up, standing shoulder to shoulder with his friend and glaring in menace.

What would have happened next, I dared not guess, but I was saved from any potential harm by the sudden appearance of one of the kitchen masters rushing into the corridor.

"What are you boys doing, just standing there?" he demanded, his round face glowing with sweat and distress. "Quick, into the hall with that food! You know the duke does not tolerate delay."

I gave silent thanks for the man's unwitting intervention. If these two had any role in the conte's murder, surely they would not hesitate to do me harm if they believed I had found them out. For the moment, however, I was safe. Reluctantly, my possible assailants did as the kitchen master instructed, but not before the red-haired youth muttered over his shoulder, "We'll be looking out for you, so you'd best keep your mouth shut."

I made no reply but trotted off toward the far end of the hall, swiftly distributing the sweetmeats among the guests while doing my best to hide myself among them. Once I'd emptied my tray, I abandoned it behind an unoccupied chair and found refuge for myself behind the same white stone column that an elderly gentleman was using to take care of some pressing personal needs. I moved a prudent distance from him while still keeping hidden. From here, I had a clear view of the dining hall and the duke's guests.

Broad tables extended from the doorway and down the room's length in a double row. That arrangement, in turn, butted up against a larger table placed crosswise upon a dais at the far end of the hall, not far from my spot of conceal-ment. The entire grouping formed a long, two-pronged T, with perhaps half a hundred guests crowded along either leg of it and ranked in order from minor nobles to relatives of the duke. Those of greatest status sat closest to the raised table where Il Moro presided, flanked by his immediate family and his guest, the French ambassador. My concealing column was not far from that spot, so that I had an enviable view of the goings-on there. I already had glimpsed the Master seated in one of those coveted spots near the head table. While he appeared to be in animated conversation, I knew his keen gaze must have been taking in every one of his fellows.

I also noted something more disturbing: the fact that not every seat at the duke's table was occupied.

Several places away and to the right of Il Moro, a plate and a footed cup—both untouched—sat before an empty chair. To one side of that vacant spot perched my nemesis from the chess game, the ancient, black-gowned Marchesa d'Este; to the other sat a plain-faced young woman with hair dark as my own, and with eyes wide and light brown. Robed in a sleeve-less, pink brocade surcoat worn over a gold-embroidered che-mise of an even paler pink, she appeared but a few years older than I.

I knew with sudden certainty that the chair between the unlikely pair would have been reserved for the Conte di Fer-rara. As for the young woman, I guessed her to be the conte's wife, the Contessa di Ferrara. She apparently had no knowledge of her husband's fate, for her unremarkable fea-tures were set in mild amusement as she attended to her wine cup. The marchesa, too, appeared undisturbed by her grandnephew's absence but applied herself to her meal with a heartiness that belied her sparse figure.

I turned my attention back to the other guests, vigilant now for any signs of remorse or fear. But the guilty party—if indeed he was among this number—was concealing his culpability quite well. Here, too, the likelihood of overhearing an incriminating bit of conversation was far less than in the outer corridor. The voices of so many, interspersed with the inevitable clatter of all manner of dishes being served simultaneously, made for a din every bit as loud as a marketplace on an early morning.

Too, the room lacked the usual tapestries that might have softened the clamor. Instead, at the duke's direction, Leonardo had begun a series of frescoes for the hall that would have put any such wall hangings to shame. Sections of the great room now blazed with colorful depictions of beleaguered mortals, somber saints, and dazzling celestial hosts set amid rolling countryside settings reminiscent of the scenery beyond the castle walls.

The mood among the guests reflected far more cheerful a mode than those scenes. While pouring wine earlier, I had overheard numerous favorable comments regarding the living chess match that had been the afternoon's entertainment. I had made careful mental note of that praise so I could tell it to the Master at a later time. To be sure, I'd had a few unsettling moments as I moved about the guests, when I realized I was serving one or another of my fellow chessmen. I found, however, that they did not recognize me in my current role . . . most likely because none spared me or any other porter more than the briefest of glances.

It was an interesting situation in which to be. On the one hand, I found myself relishing the power of my servant's anonymity; on the other, I could not help but be appalled by such a dismissive attitude. But the Master had charged me with an important role this night, so that I had little time to dwell upon such indignities.

With that in mind, I glanced about for the porters whose conversation I earlier had overheard. Neither appeared to be among the two score of youths in blue and white tunics busy serving the guests. They must have returned to the kitchens . . . assuming, of course, they had not instead fled the castle. I frowned. I did not know either youth's name, but their countenances were emblazoned upon my memory. Surely I would recognize them should I see them again. And, given the snippet of conversation that I had overheard, I was certain the Master would want to question them regarding the conte's murder.

Even as I was debating returning to the kitchen in hopes of learning their identities, a murmur arose from the duke's table. The sound swiftly spread down the hall, and I could hear the change in the timbre of the surrounding conversations as all heads curiously turned in that direction. Then Il Moro stood and grandly raised a hand, the gesture serving as efficiently as a trumpet blast to silence his guests.

In response, the same kitchen master who had inadvertently intervened earlier on my behalf gave his porters a similar signal. The small regiment of young men dispersed to the hall's four corners to stand at attention. I left my temporary refuge and moved swiftly to join the nearest group in anticipation of the duke's words.

"I am pleased to see you are enjoying yourselves here at my table tonight," the duke began, his tone verging upon something like geniality. That lapse into softer emotion immediately raised my suspicions, and I leaned closer to better hear his words. "As you know, our purpose in gathering is to honor our visitor, Monsieur Villasse, the French ambassador. He is here as emissary from our good friend, King Louis, in hopes of forging an alliance between our two countries."

Il Moro continued in similar fashion for some moments in fulsome praise of the French and their king, adding a few disparaging words against the Venetians, with whom Milan was conducting a halfhearted war. His words drew sounds of polite approval from the gathered nobles and a tight smile from the ambassador, who I judged did not quite return the duke's purported affection. Or perhaps he simply had not yet forgiven Ludovico his loss at the chess match earlier. I noticed now that the game's prize, the painting of the young woman with her ermine, was displayed upon an easel behind the duke, the exhibition doubtless a deliberate reminder of who had been the victor of that contest.

The duke went on to commend the participants in the chess match, sparing special praise for the Master's efforts in conjuring the entire affair out of thin air in a matter of hours, as it were. Leonardo smiled and gave a modest nod acknowledging the congratulatory words, though I rather suspected he would have preferred some tangible reward to this public tribute.

Il Moro's next words, however, sharply recalled to me the reason for my presence here in the hall. "Unfortunately, the afternoon's entertainment was spoiled by an unpleasant incident," the duke continued, his earlier hint of affability replaced now by sternness. "By now, some of you have heard how my cousin, the Conte di Ferrara, was taken ill during the game. I regret that I must tell you . . . must tell his wife, my dear cousin Beatrice . . . that this is not what happened."

He glanced at the plain-featured young woman whom I had rightly pegged as the Contessa di Ferrara. She paused, holding her wine cup in mid sip, to stare at the duke, surprise and then uncertainty twisting her pale mouth. I gnawed at my own lips in sympathy. Would he leave the crowd now to take her aside and privately tell her of her husband's murder, or could he be so cruel as to break the news of her widowhood to her before the rest of the court?

Not surprisingly for a man who was callous enough to supplant his late brother's son as duke before the lad was ever old enough to reign, Il Moro chose the latter course. "The reason my cousin Orlando does not dine with the rest of us," he intoned, "is that he was cruelly struck down in my gardens by an assassin earlier today, and is this night lying dead in his quarters."

A collective gasp echoed through the hall, punctuated by cries of protest and surprise. As for the contessa, she gave a violent start that splashed her wine from its cup. The deep red of the grape spread across her gown's bodice in grotesque if unwitting imitation of the blood that had stained her husband's robes. After that one reflexive reaction, however, she seemed to freeze in her chair, as if she, too, were caught in death's grasp. The ancient marchessa sat equally still, save for the abrupt and seeming involuntary twitching of her head, as if she had been set upon by a sudden palsy.

Ludovico, meanwhile, was gazing about the hall with what I could only interpret as an expression of satisfaction at the chaos his announcement had engendered. He raised his hand again, waiting for silence to fall once more before he went on, "We do not yet know the name of the villain who killed my cousin. Indeed, we do not even know if he was one of us"—he paused for a heartbeat and glanced down the table at the French ambassador, who looked suitably distressed—"or if perhaps he was an assassin sent from some other court. No matter, we will soon discover his identity, and he will pay with his life for his crime."

The ambassador abruptly leaped to his feet, toppling his own wine cup in the process. "I assure you, Excellency," he sputtered in his heavily accented Italian, "that the people of France had no hand in this terrible matter. His Majesty, King Louis XI—as well as his son, Charles—had planned all manner of honors for the conte during his visit, which now sadly never shall be. But do not doubt that our Christian Majesty will be outraged to hear what has happened. He and all of France will offer what assistance we can to help you find the vile killer of your cousin."

"That will not be necessary. I have my own man who is tasked with solving this crime. But for now, I wish to let everyone know exactly how my cousin died."

So saying, he pulled from his belt the same knife that had been used to murder the counte. He raised it so that the blade glinted beneath the glow of lamps and torches that illuminated the long hall. The action drew a gasp from the women, while the men leaned forward and muttered uneasily among themselves. Some, like the portly knight I previously had splashed with wine, even brought a reflexive hand to their hip where their sword would have hung had they been dressed for battle instead of supper.

"I fear it was not a pleasant death that was visited upon the conte," the duke went on with a thoughtful look at the weapon he held. "Indeed, I daresay it was painful, though I can assure his beloved wife that his suffering did not last long. Such a wound as he suffered would inevitably prove fatal in but a few minutes. If you will but observe . . ."

He turned toward the painted wall behind him and, for the second time that day, abruptly flung the blade so that it sliced through the air like a diving falcon. A heartbeat later, the knife quivered where it protruded from high on the plastered wall, its tip buried in the breast of one of the Master's freshly painted, white-robed angels who gazed with raised hands upon the frescoed scene of struggling mortality depicted below him.

At the sight, the contessa uttered a piteous shriek and slumped in her chair. Her sound of grief was echoed by any number of other ladies of the court, several of whom rushed to the fainting woman's side, while others swooned in their own seats, or upon their partners' shoulders. Yet even as the outcry grew, a far more unnerving sound pierced the night.

It took me an instant to recognize it as a woman's callous laugh. Chilled, I turned swiftly toward the direction from which the sound still echoed, frantically searching for its source. Abruptly, my gaze was drawn to a familiar figure . . . the same golden-haired woman who had mistaken me for my counterpart white bishop following the chess match earlier in the day. She sat midway down the far table, her lavish gown of pale blue and gold echoing the faded azure of her eyes and the stark yellow tint of her stylishly coiffed locks beneath an elaborate veil. Now, her handsome features were twisted into a pale mask of mirth, her red lips stretching wide as the harsh sound continued to pour from them.

Then her pale gaze locked with my horrified stare, and an even more frightful peal of laughter rent the air as she stood and pointed directly at me.

5

It is as great an error to speak well of a worthless man as to speak ill of a good man.

—Leonardo da Vinci, *Forster Bequest MS II*

I caught back a gasp, my gaze darting frantically toward the Master to gauge his reaction to this unforeseen turn of events. His attention seemed fixed elsewhere, however, so I glanced about the room, anxious to see who else had taken note of the infernal creature. To my surprise, no one save I seemed to be paying her any heed. It was as if she and I existed separately from everyone else in the hall. She seemed to demand that I rejoice with her in the dead man's fate, and I simply stared back as I absorbed the horror of her behavior.

Tearing my gaze from hers, I gave my head an uncomprehending shake. Why did no one other than me find something amiss in this woman's frightful display of amusement amid the general dismay? Surely the duke should summon his men to hold her so that she could be questioned regarding the murder, or at least be banished from the hall for her callous behavior in the face of the Contessa di Ferrara's fresh grief.

But even as those thoughts flashed through my mind, the woman's laughter changed, became instead a cry of alarm. And she was not pointing, I saw, nor even looking in my direction. Instead, her hands were flung heavenward in apparent grief while the gentleman beside her attempted to console her. Indeed, now that my first shock had passed, I was uncertain if the sounds that had come from her had ever been laughter, at all.

I ran a hand across my flushed face. Caught up as I was in the Master's hunt for an assassin, could I simply have imagined I was witnessing some guilty behavior? Perhaps Ludovico's dramatic display with the knife had unwittingly aroused in me some hitherto unknown female tendency toward hysteria, with the lapse momentarily clouding my usually clear judgment.

I did not have time to wonder more about it, however, for the duke lifted his hand again for silence. As the guests began to settle themselves, I was relieved to see that the contessa's chair was empty now, someone apparently having had the decency to escort her from the hall during the momentary turmoil. As for the marchessa, she had regained her place as well as her composure and was once more addressing her meal as if the announcement of her grandnephew's murder had never happened.

"Be seated," the duke commanded those of his guests who were still milling about the hall. "I know my dear cousin, Orlando, would wish you to carry on with your merry evening and save your mourning for later. Eat and drink your fill."

He paused to let his gaze roam the crowd, his dark visage growing sterner. "But be warned. Until the Conte di Ferrara's killer is found, no one shall enter or leave the castle grounds unless I allow it. My guards are posted at the gate and along the walls to assure my orders are followed. Anyone attempting to circumvent my command will be presumed to have had a role in the conte's assassination and will be punished accordingly."

This time, the murmur that followed Il Moro's announcement was quieter and tinged now with an undercurrent of angry suspicion as the guests began to eye one another darkly. I suspected their concern was less with determining which of their number, if any, had committed the murder, and more with resentment over their enforced captivity while the crime was being solved. Most of the nobles had villas of their own in the outlying countryside and had come to the castle for but a day and a night's entertainment. Any longer an absence could prove a hardship for their households . . . not to mention, for their wardrobes.

And what if the assassin were not found for days, or even weeks, assuming he was ever found at all? How long could the castle support so many extra mouths, given that each guest would have brought along a small retinue? I pictured the castle's magnificent kitchens all but stripped bare in a week and wondered if Il Moro realized that was one possible repercussion of his literal barring of the castle gates.

If he did, the scenario did not appear to concern him. Indeed, the duke had returned to own his meal and seemed to be carrying on a pleasant conversation with the obviously discomfited French ambassador. The kitchen master, meanwhile, gestured for the porters to resume their serving. I found an abandoned wine pitcher and snatched it up, needing an excuse to make my way to where Leonardo sat so I could tell him of the two porters and their suspicious words. As for the mysterious woman, I would mention her, as well, but leave him to pursue any conversation with her, as she would never deign to speak to someone of my station. Beyond that, I would learn if the Master had himself noted anyone worthy of investigation.

My progress toward him took a bit longer than I expected, however, accosted as I was with cry after cry of, "Boy!" and the waving of empty wine cups. It seemed that the duke's guests were determined to make the best of their involuntary stay by consuming even more than the usual portion of strong drink. I used the opportunity to listen to what was being said about the conte, now that his fate was known, but caught only bits and pieces of conversation.

"Fine enough sort . . . bad at dice, but a good horseman."

"Think anyone will want to console that wife of his?"

"Surprised it took so long . . . thought he'd find the point of a blade before now."

By the time I made it to the place where Leonardo sat, I had concluded that the court both mourned the conte's passing and was callously unsurprised at his fate. Barely a mouthful of wine remained in my pitcher now; still, I made a show of pouring it into the Master's half-full cup as I leaned close enough to whisper, "I have made some small progress in our investigation. Shall I tell you what I have learned, or speak with you later?"

He did not immediately answer but instead put the vessel to his lips and took a deep draught of his wine. His black velvet cap had slid askew, and his russet hair looked as if he had been running his long fingers through it; moreover, his strong features beneath his neat beard were tinted now by emotion or else the effects of drink. Indeed, he appeared ruffled in spirit as well as appearance, so that I wondered if the duke's dramatic display with the knife had displeased him. His reply, however, was couched in composed tones, even as the murmured words took me by surprise.

"I believe our investigation has reached an end almost as soon as it has begun. You see, my dear Dino, I believe I know who committed this heinous offense against the conte."

My eyes opened wide at this announcement. Before he could further elaborate, however, a curly-haired youth edged between us and proffered a platter of tiny roasted fowl nestled upon a festive bed of ferns and primroses. Leonardo's reaction to the interruption was immediate and unexpectedly passionate.

"No, no," he protested, his mouth twisting with the same sort of disgust that another man might display at being presented a plate of carrion. With a single long finger, he pushed aside the offering, saying, "I do not feast upon my fellow creatures. Take that abomination from me, and bring me a bit of fruit."

The lad stuttered an apology and rushed off with his rejected course to do the Master's bidding. Had I not been preoccupied, I could have warned the youth beforehand of Leonardo's odd habit of refusing to consume the flesh of fowl and beasts. While I did not profess to understand that inclination—I had never yet rejected a properly prepared portion of meat—I had no doubt his concern for dumb creatures was a true conviction and not a simple affectation. Indeed, I had heard tales oft repeated of the Master that he would purchase caged birds in the local marketplace, only to set the tiny, feathered creatures free again. And I had myself seen him forcibly halt one of Il Moro's soldiers from beating a ragged stable cur for some perceived canine offense.

My concern now, however, was not for Leonardo's dining habits. "You know the assassin?" I whispered back in amazement. "Tell me, Master, who is he?"

"I prefer not to say until I have more proof, but do not trouble yourself. He does not yet realize that he is now the hunted one, rather than the hunter. So long as he believes himself undiscovered, we have nothing to fear from him."

His tone was preoccupied, and I saw the pensive look he gave toward the frescoed wall behind the duke. The knife remained embedded in the plaster, and I suspected the Master's dismay now was less for the conte than for his damaged work of art. He sighed. "Dino, my boy, you have performed admirably tonight. You are free to return to your bed now. We shall speak more of my findings in the morning."

"As you wish."

I gave a quick bow to hide my disappointment and, pitcher in hand, departed the hall. While I understood his need for caution before making such an accusation against any man, I had hoped to be taken more into the Master's confidence regarding our investigation. I comforted myself that this omission was less a reflection upon our differences in station and more due to the fact that a man of genius such as Leonardo did not easily share his musings with lesser mortals. I had no doubt that, had Il Moro been the one questioning him as to the assassin's identity, he would have been equally as reticent with the duke.

I paused as I reached the corridor to make certain that my two earlier adversaries were not lying there in wait for me. Even if they had no hand in the conte's death, it seemed that at least one had been involved in some nefarious scheme of which I now had unwelcome acquaintance. Should they ever happen upon me again, they might well proceed with their unspecified threats against me. And while growing up with brothers left me with some rudimentary knowledge of defending myself, I knew I would be no match for these two.

The corridor bustled with other porters, but not that pair; neither did I spy them among the crowd in the kitchen. Perhaps after their unplanned encounter with me they were avoiding the kitchen, as well. Careful not to draw undue attention, I carried my empty wine pitcher to a spot conveniently near a doorway, where a trio of wine casks pulled from the cellar for this particular feast was stacked. Taking momentary refuge behind this wood pyramid, I divested myself of my porter's garb and slipped out the doorway into the courtyard beyond.

Cloaked now in star-pricked darkness and inhaling draughts of cool night air, I felt stripped of more than the burdensome blue and white tunic. Here in the shadows, I could breathe freely for a few moments, not worrying that someone would discover my porter's masquerade or, worse, pierce my apprentice's disguise to reveal the female beneath. Neither did I have to remain alert lest someone summon me for one chore or another. And while the conte's murder still weighed upon me, I could more easily remind myself that solving the crime was the Master's task and not mine.

I did not bother to stifle my yawns as I made my way back to the workshop. Late as the hour was, however, I was not alone in my wanderings. I could hear the echo of soft voices and shuffle of footsteps upon the dirt that edged the back entrances to the nearby stables. Louder was the crunch of gravel beneath shod feet as others made their swift way along the main paths that quartered the castle grounds. High atop the castle walls, I could see the shadows of Il Moro's soldiers momentarily darkening the narrow openings in the parapets as they patrolled the perimeter of the estate. Of course, they were up there every night, those castle guardians in their dark doublets and trunk hose who spent as much time at dice as they did keeping watch. Given the duke's orders, they doubtless would be more diligent than usual this night in their rounds. I suspected, however, that anyone truly wishing to scale the surrounding walls could do so were he fast enough and silent enough.

I suppose I should have felt uneasy making the walk alone back to the workshop, but I did not. True, a murderer presumably still walked free somewhere here upon the castle grounds, but he had already claimed his victim. He would have no reason to risk capture by killing for a second time in one day, and for no good reason . . . unless of course, his reason was addled, and he murdered strictly for the sport of it.

That possibility, though admittedly an unlikely one, abruptly dispelled my sense of safety and spurred my feet to swifter action. I was out of breath by the time I reached the workshop door. Though greater darkness lay within its walls, here I was safe, for my fellows would spring to my assistance should someone unaccountably be lurking in the shadows.

Mindful that they slept, I tiptoed down the long expanse of wooden floor. My fingers brushed the edges of the heavy worktables as I made my way more by feel than by sight, guided as well by the none-too-gentle snores that drifted from the curtained alcove. I was anxious to add my own snores to that chorus. Dawn was not far away, and my yawns now nearly rent my face in two. I had little hope that the Master would take pity on me and allow me an extra few hours' rest, given that he likely would awake refreshed with even less sleep than I would have had this night.

I found my cot with little incident save a stubbed toe suffered when tripping over the broom that Vittorio apparently had not put away when he finished his sweeping. Quietly rebuking him with a few colorful words I'd earlier heard from some of the kitchen staff, I gratefully climbed beneath my blanket. I dared not unwind the concealing length of cloth about my chest, fearing I might sleep too deeply and not waken early enough to retie it on me before daylight fully pierced our gloomy alcove. Thus, though Morpheus beckoned, I was unsettled enough that I found myself resisting his embrace.

As I lay there uncomfortably in the dark, I could not help but return to that thread of thought that I had abandoned when the master summoned me a few hours earlier. I recalled now that other embrace I had but recently fought . . . that of the specter of marriage.

As expected, my mother had been overjoyed to learn that the wealthy Signore Niccolo would deign to take to wife someone of my advanced years and unconventional behavior. For myself, I had wondered at the man's motives. At the time, I could come up with no reason save that he desired further angelic renditions of himself. With a merchant's thrifty eye to a bargain, he likely had decided marriage to an artist was far cheaper than acting as patron to someone such as Leonardo or Signore Donatello. Or, far less likely, it could have been that he had caught a glimpse of me upon leaving our house that fateful day and abruptly been smitten from afar. But no matter the reason he desired me, I would not consent to the marriage.

I had informed my parents of my decision and was met with understanding by my father. As for my mother, she raged at me for my ingratitude at refusing so magnificent an offer, the sort of which likely would never come again. Still, she had been calm enough by nightfall. I took to my bed that evening confident that she would not press the matter, given that my father had sided with me.

I learned the next morning, however, that my faith had been misplaced. I awoke to find myself locked in the tiny third-story chamber in which I slept.

"And there you shall remain, Delfina, until you come to your senses," Carmela had declared through the keyhole in response to my shouts for assistance. "Such foolishness that you will not marry Signore Niccolo . . . pah!"

As she held the only key, my father could obtain my freedom only by wresting it from her, which he was loath to do. Instead, he counseled me through the door to remain calm. "Your mother will regain her senses in a day or two," he assured me, "and then we will inform the signore of our decision. For now, just indulge her in this madness."

My brothers were equally complicit in my incarceration, sheepishly standing guard lest I try to flee when my mother twice a day unlocked the door long enough to bring me food and water. "Mother is right," my younger brother, Georgio, advised me in a mournful voice. "You can't spend the rest of your life here painting. If you don't marry the signore, what is to become of you?"

It was a question that I had asked myself more than once over the years. My father was a master of his trade, and my mother had brought a small dowry to their marriage, so that our home was comfortably large enough for both a workshop below, and two stories of living quarters above. Unlike most of our neighbors, we had only our immediate family beneath our roof. My grandparents on my father's side, whose house this once had been, were deceased, while my mother's parents lived with her older sister. But our comfortable situation would change when my brothers married a few years hence. A least one of them would surely bring his new family into the house, so eventually there would be no room for me.

I had ample time in which to search for my answer as the predicted day or two of my detention stretched to three days, and then four. The solution finally came on the fifth day, as I opened my window to dump the contents of my chamber pot onto the cobbled street below me. I'd emptied the vessel and was poised to pull the window closed again, when a prosaic yet promising sight caught my attention.

At a neighbor's house across the way, someone had hung a bit of laundry to dry. The garment was a man's simple tunic, but as it fluttered gently upon the breeze, it seemed to take on a life of its own. I watched its silent dance, my artist's mind filling in the image of a young, slim figure . . . a youth with dark hair who made his carefree way down the street. And then, abruptly, I realized that I was picturing myself belted into that man's tunic, my hair cropped so that I resembled a boy.

The revelation so startled me that I almost let the chamber pot crash onto the street. I avoided that small disaster, however, and swiftly closed the window. Uncharacteristically faint, I sat upon my bed and clutched my hands to still their sudden tremble as a plan came to me, full-blown. I could do it, I told myself. It was the perfect solution, allowing me to avoid marriage to Signore Niccolo while letting me pursue my life's dream.

"Tell Papa that I wish to speak with him," I called through the keyhole to my other brother, Carlo, whose turn it was to serve as guard. A few minutes later, I heard the key scrape in the lock. The door opened just wide enough for my father to squeeze through before swiftly shutting behind him.

"Do not indulge her for more than a minute, Angelo," came my mother's stern voice from outside the door as the key turned in the lock again, imprisoning him in the room with me.

He gave a helpless sigh and then smiled sadly at me. "I suppose we best speak quickly. Tell me, daughter, have you reconsidered marriage to the signore?"

"I have."

My statement brought a look of surprise to his broad, weathered features. Choosing my words carefully, as I knew my mother would be listening beyond the door, I went on, "Papa, you know I would not have had to worry about marrying had I been born male. I could have become an apprentice to a great master of painting and pursued my art. But in order to find someone to take me on, I would have had to leave here and make my way to Milan."

I paused and gave him a significant look. "Of course, that would have been a simple enough journey for a boy," I told him, as if he did not already know that. "You understand, don't you, Papa? A girl could not make such a trip alone, nor could she find a master to take her on, but a boy could."

My father's look of surprise had faded into an expression of uncertainty, his gaze searching my face for further explanation. Lowering my voice, I repeated, "A girl could not do such a thing, but a boy could. Of course, he would be sad to leave behind his family, but think how happy he would be doing what mattered most to him. And no one would wonder at seeing a boy traveling alone, even one who looked so young. Don't you agree it is a shame, Papa, that I was not born a boy?"

His uncertain look abruptly was replaced by understanding. Raising his eyebrows, he slowly nodded.

"It is true, Delfina, that a boy could do such things," he agreed. "In fact, I have heard that the famous painter, Leonardo the Florentine, is even now staying in Milan with the duke at Castle Sforza. It is said he has a large workshop and numerous young apprentices working for him. Learning from a man such as Leonardo would be a wonderful opportunity for you . . . had you been born a boy, of course."

"Had I been born a boy," I echoed meaningfully. "But since I am but a meek female, you can tell Mama that I will consent to marry Signore Niccolo."

A delighted cry came from the other side of the door. "That is wonderful news," Carmela exclaimed, unlocking the door and flinging it open.

Her smile as she rushed to hug me held the sort of warm approval that I had not seen from her since I was a girl. I returned her fond hug, blinking back sudden tears as I realized it had been years since she had expressed anything other than dissatisfaction with me. I had forgotten what it was like to have my mother's unconditional love, had pretended for far too long that I did not notice the air of silent disappointment that always wrapped the two of us like some ragged cloak we were forced by circumstances to share. And now that we seemingly had cast aside that well-worn garment, I was poised to disappoint her again.

I withdrew from her arms rather stiffly, though I managed a smile. "I am pleased that you are happy with my decision, Mother. But do grant me one small favor. Please wait another day before you inform the signore of my answer."

She frowned a moment, and I feared she might refuse me this. Another day, and I would be gone, with no harm done save that my father would have to send a polite missive of refusal to Signore Niccolo. But if word of an engagement were to be made public, my subsequent abandonment of my future bridegroom would bring embarrassment to my family. And while this would not change my plans, I was loath to leave my parents and brothers in such a situation.

To my relief, she brightened. "Well, I suppose it cannot hurt not to look too anxious. But first thing tomorrow, your papa shall send word to him."

With that settled, she began a brisk recital of all the details that would have to be dealt with to prepare for the wedding. I perched upon the edge of my bed and listened silently as she paced purposely about the small room. My father, meanwhile, had smilingly excused himself, but not before we exchanged knowing glances as he paused in the doorway. I had found myself smiling, as well, albeit a bit sadly. Still, I was certain that I could depend upon my sire to help with my plan.

My confidence had not been misplaced. That night, when I returned to my room after the evening meal, I found tucked beneath my blankets an old tunic, jerkin, and trunk hose that had belonged to my younger brother.

I had taken a moment before I snuffed my candle to write out the brief note that I would leave behind. I had mentally composed a poignant missive earlier in the day, but when the time came to put the words to paper, the rehearsed sentiment seemed suddenly false and overblown. I gnawed my pen uncertainly, searching for inspiration. Finally, I settled on a few terse phrases, which, if not excessively fond, were far more truthful than any florid farewell.

I must leave. Do not worry about me. I shall send word on occasion.

Delfina.

Tucking the note away for later, I undressed and burrowed beneath my covers. I managed a few hours of fitful sleep before arising again well before dawn. By light of a small candle, I gathered up the few items I would take with me and then silently pulled on my borrowed attire.

Certainly, it was clothing grand enough for a young apprentice. The tunic, though worn and slightly behind the fashion (indeed, it was but a single shade of deep blue, with no puffs or slashing of its sleeves) was still quite serviceable. The scarlet trunk hose was more the style, being the same bright shade that many of the young men wore. I fumbled a bit with the unfamiliar garment but was soon dressed. Thus attired, I felt myself blush in the darkness at the daring sensation of freedom—nay, almost nakedness—that I felt at not being wrapped in yards of skirts. It would doubtless take a bit of time before I could wear such clothing without feeling quite exposed to the world.

Unfortunately, another problem outweighed my embarrassment. Even with my chemise serving as shirt beneath it, and the plain brown jerkin tied over it, the borrowed tunic clung to my female curves in a manner that made my sex evident. I thought a moment before pulling those garments off again and swiftly tearing another chemise into a series of long strips. Those lengths of cloth I methodically wrapped over my breasts as if I were binding a wound, until I had flattened the offending features into obscurity.

The effect when I resumed my tunic was far better than the first time. Satisfied, I belted the garment with a strip of leather to which I tied the heavy cloth pouch that would hold a few coins and trinkets. Another larger sack would hold a change of linen and other personal belongings. Then I turned my attention to the final item that would have to be addressed before my transformation was complete.

While I had never been vain about my appearance, I must confess I had always nurtured an unseemly bit of pride over my abundant dark locks. Unbound, my hair rippled down my back and all the way to my hips in raven waves so thick that I could easily cloak myself in nothing else and still retain my modesty. Most times, however, I wore it in a thick plait, which I might twine with ribbon or wrap into various complicated configurations about my head. Since I had just arisen from bed, the heavy braid lay meekly over one shoulder.

I grimly took hold of the sleekly bound tresses with one hand, while holding in the other the small knife I had earlier secreted in my clothes chest for just this purpose. Then, wincing in anticipation, I began cutting.

The task was completed in moments. I clutched the severed braid to me, momentarily feeling as faint as if I had cut living flesh. Perhaps my feeling of lightheadedness had been literal, for without the unaccustomed weight of all that hair, I felt as if I could move about with the ease of childhood. I laid the beribboned hank upon my bed and then brought my candle closer to my mirror to inspect my handiwork.

Even cloaked by shadows, that costly oval of tinned glass revealed my image with shocking clarity. Except that it was not I, Delfina, reflected there. Rather, a wide-eyed, dark-haired youth only a handful of years past childhood met my startled gaze. He looked like a finer-boned copy of my two brothers . . . a pretty youth, but with a firm set to his mouth that belied any weakness. As for the wrapping around his chest, should anyone take note of that affectation, they would dismiss it as but a poor youth's attempt to copy his betters with their padded tunics that gave their figures a more manly profile.

I found myself smiling in amazement, and excitement began to well within my tightly constrained breast. I could do this, I told myself. To be sure, I would have to be on guard at all times, particularly when relieving myself or taking the occasional bath, but otherwise it was merely a matter of abolishing the overt feminine from my daily behavior. My brothers would prove good role models, for I would have to but mimic their actions and manner of speech to pass myself off as a boy. The final touch for this masquerade would be assuming a more masculine appellation. But what should I call myself?

"Dino," I whispered to my reflection, impulsively dubbing myself with a name that echoed my own closely enough so that I could comfortably answer to it. "I am Dino, someday to be a magnificent painter . . . perhaps even a rival to the great Leonardo."

Speaking the words aloud suddenly made the dream seem a possibility, so that I was anxious now to begin my adventure. I reached for my cloak and then hesitated at the sight of the length of cut hair curled like a sleeping feline upon my blankets. I could leave the braid as a token of sorts for my mother, but she would then guess what I had done to disguise myself. And as I knew she would surely send my brothers out searching for me, I could not allow her so blatant a clue as to my fate.

I grabbed up the braid and left the note in its place, then pinched out the candle and made my silent way downstairs to the kitchen. There, a few coals from the evening's meal still glowed upon the hearth. I stirred them, awakening a blaze of orange flames that danced hungrily before me. I hesitated, my gaze caught by their restless movement. Then, taking a steadying breath, I resolutely sacrificed my final symbol of womanhood to the fire.

The acrid stench of burnt hair assailed my nostrils as the

braid was consumed in a ravenous little blaze that seemed to light the entire room. Once the final traces of my vanity had crumbled to ashes and the sated flames resumed their previous slumber, I made my way to the larder. While I had my choice of many tempting foods, I contented myself with appropriating more simple fare . . . a small loaf of bread and a chunk of cheese. I was not sure how long my journey would take, but this way I would not go hungry.

From beyond the kitchen's shuttered windows, I heard the faint crow of a cock too impatient to wait for the sun's first light to begin his morning serenade. It was time to set off, so that I would be well upon my way by the time my absence at the breakfast table was noticed and anyone went in search of me. Of course, I would have to wait until dawn for the town gates to open to begin my journey in earnest, but in the hour or so still remaining before sunrise I could surely find myself a snug barn in which to wait.

I unlatched the front door—with luck, my father would be the first to rise, so that no one would remark upon the fact that it was no longer barred—and slipped out into the night. A faint breeze cooled my suddenly flushed cheeks, though it could do nothing to slow the swift beat of my heart as I turned for a final look at the house where I had spent my entire life. I pictured the people inside, my parents and my brothers. Though I knew my father would defend me to them, I wondered what the rest of my family would say when they realized I was gone. Would they mourn me or dismiss me with good riddance? More important, if I ever returned, would they welcome me back or turn me away at the door?

THE same question now worried at me as I lay upon my cot waiting for sleep. But it did no good to dwell upon what was past, I scolded myself, especially since I was not the only one of my fellows to have left a family behind to take on the apprentice's role. Indeed, Vittorio, Constantin, and most of the others had traveled even farther than I to join the Master; moreover, several of them were many years younger than my true age. Better I should worry about a few hours' rest than giving way to self-pity.

I squeezed my eyes tightly shut, ignoring the single tear that slipped from beneath one lid to dampen my cheek. At least tomorrow, this business of the conte's murder should be put to rest, if Leonardo was indeed correct in his conclusions regarding the assassin. Then I could cease my nocturnal investigations and return to my role as student to the Master.

Comforted by the prospect, I let myself be lulled by the soft chorus of boys' snores around me. Just as I finally succumbed to sleep, however, an unexpected thought drifted along the edges of my final waking consciousness. It was not a disturbing enough idea to prevent me from burrowing deeper beneath my blanket as I gave a final yawn, but the notion did follow me into my dreams.

Which is perhaps why my slumber was made restless with visions of myself being pursued by a black queen through the dark halls of Castle Sforza.

6

The master is to the apprentice as the father is to the son, save that master and apprentice come together by purpose, and father and son, by chance.

—Leonardo da Vinci, *The Notebooks of Delfina della Fazia*

"Even though white has no color in itself, it takes on tinges of the colors against which it is set, both in nature and upon the painted panel. Thus it is with our archangel's robe."

Leonardo gestured with his brush at the winged figure upon the frescoed wall whose breast had been pierced by Il Moro's knife the night before. "Since he floats upon the heavens, the folds of his garment that are exposed to the sun rising behind him will reflect that same dazzling light," he went on. "The rest of that cloth will be dyed with the faintest hint of blue from the atmosphere around him. Color and reflection . . . that is why no competent painter will ever render any object an unadulterated white. So mix your colors, Dino, that we might put our heavenly host back to his former state of glory."

I nodded gravely, my attention on the last of the raw egg yolks that I had liberated from their shells. Handling this one as gently as I would the chick that it should have become, I rolled the orange orb between my palms to remove the remaining film clinging to it. Once the yolk was dry, I pinched its rubbery sac between finger and thumb, as if I were the legendary Achilles' mother dangling her child above the River Styx. With equal care, I used a clean wooden splinter to pierce the yolk, letting its contents bleed into the polished mouth of an upturned shell that served as a small bowl.

Half-a-dozen shells filled with liquid yolk sat before me upon the same long table that, the night before, had spilled over with every delicacy. Now, however, its highly polished surface served as a makeshift workbench upon which my painting supplies were arranged. I turned to the small containers of finely ground pigment—among them lapis, verdigris, and hematite—that I had already prepared. The colored powders were being warmed atop a tiny, coal-fueled brazier the Master had designed just for that purpose, as he claimed the tempera mixed more smoothly when the pigment was heated. I knew I had to work swiftly, for the paint, once prepared, dried in but a short time.

A few minutes later, pigment and yolk were mixed, the resulting gluey substance thinned with just enough warm water so that the color would flow from the brush. Now it was my turn to stand aside while the Master, his previous night's finery put aside for his usual brown tunic, folded back his left sleeve and began repairing the marred fresco.

I watched with awe untainted by familiarity as his brushes—some of hog's hair, others tipped with weasel fur—flashed across the scar in the painted plaster. He began with white and then switched brushes to pick up a hint of sky blue, applying it in the faintest of strokes. From there, he moved through my small rainbow of paints, sometimes taking them in their original state, but just as often mixing splashes of different colors upon a wooden palette to form a new hue. While his method might have appeared haphazard, I knew it was not. Had he been tasked with re-creating these shades, he would be able to recall the exact number of brushstrokes of each color that had gone into mixing each new tint he had created.

I had learned early on in my apprenticeship that the technique he now was using was called *fresco secco* . . . painting with egg tempera upon dry plaster, a method traditionally used to repair or touch up an existing fresco. The original scene upon this wall, however, had been accomplished in the usual manner known as *buon fresco*. Rather than using traditional paints, the artist instead would dissolve pigments in water and apply the color to a layer of wet plaster. It was an exacting technique. No more an area of wall could be readied with plaster than could be painted within half a day's time, for this method required that the color be absorbed into the plaster as it dried. When, a few hours later, every bit of moisture was gone from the surface, the pigment became part of the very plaster, rather than simply being paint laid atop it.

I had also learned that such limitations meant the fresco had to be designed so it could be divided into many days' worth of segments, or *giornata*. Properly planned, they would blend naturally into each other, with the finished work appearing seamless. I'd seen how the painting started at the top, with the Master working upon a scaffold near the ceiling and systematically moving his way each day closer to the bottom of the wall, so that one day's work would not accidentally besmirch the prior day's painting. This particular fresco, I knew, was composed of two and twenty segments, meaning that was how many days it had taken to complete it.

I had been among the several apprentices who, every morning, had prepared the wall for painting. A thick layer of rough plaster had already been applied to the entire area, along with a tracing of the complete fresco to be painted. Our job was to lay a thin, smooth top coat to the section to be completed that day. Once the fresh plaster was applied, our next task was to transfer that day's portion of scene that we had just plastered over back onto the wall. That was accomplished by first tracing the outlines of the drawing—a work that the Master previously had rendered upon paper—with a tool that pricked holes in the paper, making a stencil of sorts. While the taller boys held the drawing to the wall, it usually fell to me to use a bag filled with finely ground charcoal to dust along those lines. That black dust passed through the pinpricks and left behind the outline of the figures to be drawn over in red ink and later to be painted.

It was the Master who applied most of the fresco; however, he occasionally rewarded our hard work by letting one of us paint a cloud or a tree branch or some other minor portion of the day's scene. I let my gaze drift proudly to a section of the fresco low upon the wall that depicted a minor saint resting beneath a shade tree, a bucket lifted to his lips. The nearby well from which the painted figure might have drawn the water to quench his thirst was my creation. I had beamed with pride when Leonardo reviewed it before my fellows.

"See how Dino has added a fallen stone here, and moss upon those rocks there. He has given his well a look of age, an air of neglect. And so we wonder, is our saint the first man to drink from it in a long while? Has the well keeper moved away, or has he simply grown lax in his duties? Our young apprentice has illustrated how, properly rendered, even the most minor detail of a painting can raise questions in the viewer's mind."

I smiled again as I remembered this unusual bit of praise from the Master. Of course, the most important thing was that my work was a fair copy of his style. That had been the most difficult part of my apprenticeship, subjugating my own manner of painting while I—along with the rest of the apprentices—learned to draw in Leonardo's own technique. This way, we could assist him on large projects such as the frescos, and yet our hand would not be noticeable against his work. Had I been as young as most of my fellows, I would have had an easier time of it, for I would not have had to undo as many years of practice. But I had always been a quick study, and it had been an exciting challenge to try to mimic the Master's seemingly inimitable brilliance.

I returned my attention to his progress. While the *buon fresco* would be far more durable a painting method, the *secco* was much easier and more forgiving of any errors . . . this in addition to allowing the painter the ability to incorporate other variations in the work while applying the color. Indeed, the Master was making changes to the archangel even as I watched. Where before his hands had been lifted in praise, they now were folded at his chest in prayer. A heavenly glow rose from his fingertips, illuminating the area over his heart as if to better show the pureness of his being.

"There," Leonardo abruptly pronounced in satisfaction and put down his brush. "The duke's unfortunate bit of vandalism is now repaired. What do you think, Dino?"

"I would not have believed the fresco could have been improved upon," I truthfully answered, "but I confess I do prefer this version of your archangel. Now, he looks more—"

"Pious?" he supplied with a grin as I searched for the proper word. "Perhaps to you he does, but to my eye, he now appears rather smug, as if he could intervene with God on man's behalf but chooses not to do so. But perhaps you will be so kind as not to advise the duke that is the true theme of this fresco, a repudiation of the belief that man is not worthy to address his Creator directly. My theory—assuming, of course, that there is a God—is that men of every station have His ear at all times, should they bother to address Him. I believe the duke is under the impression that the painting depicts man's inevitable separation from God save in those few cases where He is interested in listening."

"Oh," was the only response I could summon. I was aware that Leonardo's religious beliefs were unorthodox, to say the least. This did not stop him, however, from accepting commissions for the traditional scenes of saints and sinners . . . though apparently he was not averse to adding his own personal if subtle interpretation to such works.

While a bit shocked at his lack of devoutness, his words recalled my painting where the unfortunate Signore Niccolo went from demon to angel with a few judicious strokes of my brush. It was comforting to know that even an artist of Leonardo's stature could be subject to the whims of patronage . . . and that he could find ways to circumvent such censorship, should he so desire.

But the Master, never long to focus on any particular task, had already lost interest in the fresco. Instead, his brow furrowed, he picked up the knife that he had pulled from the wall before beginning his work. His long fingers handled it less like the utensil it was and more like the weapon it had been used as in the case of the conte. Then, abruptly, he plunged its point into the tabletop, causing me to start and almost spill the container of ground hematite I was putting in an open box with the other supplies.

I recovered my grip on the small bowl before any of the expensive mineral could tumble out, and swiftly packed it away. Leonardo seemed not to have noticed the near mishap, however, as he seated himself at the table and stared pensively at the still-quivering knife.

I recalled his unexpected statement of the night before, that he knew who had killed the conte. My curiosity, which I had managed to keep in check these past hours, now was revived by the sight of the murder weapon. I stowed away the last of the brushes in my wood box and waited for him to speak. When no explanation was forthcoming, however, I ventured, "Master, you told me last evening that you knew the identity of the conte's murderer. Will you reveal his name yet?"

"I cannot do so, not at this point. You see, my dear Dino, knowledge and proof are two different birds." He flicked his fingers as if frightening away those figurative feathered creatures. "I may be certain I know who the assassin is, but I cannot as yet offer any evidence to show how I came to that conclusion. Should I bring Ludovico my suspicions now, with no proof to bolster them, he would dismiss me as readily as he would a town beggar."

"Then we must uncover that truth," I stoutly declared. "Tell me, what would you have me do to help?"

"I would first have you put away the brushes and pigments, and then you may meet me at the small green just beyond the stables."

I sketched a bow and hurried out with my box, leaving the Master still seated at the table. At least this would not be another nighttime errand, I thought in relief as I stifled a yawn. How much worse it would have been had the Master not graciously advised Constantin that I was to be allowed an extra hour of sleep past dawn this morning. That bit of favoritism, while welcomed by me, had drawn a few pointed looks and whispers from the other apprentices when I finally joined them. The murmurs had resumed when Leonardo called me aside to assist him in repairing the fresco, leaving the others behind with the day's mundane tasks. I had thought their reaction but the usual grumbling, until I made my way back to the workshop again.

"The Master's pet returns." Tommaso greeted me with a smirk, executing a mocking bow as I struggled past him with the bulky box. The other apprentices looked up from their tasks, expressions eager as they waited to see if I would answer the other youth's challenge.

Cognizant of my male masquerade, I knew I must reply in kind or risk suspicion. "The Master may favor me, but only because my talent is greater than yours," I shot back with a matching curl of my lip as I headed toward the storage shelves. "Should your small skill improve, perhaps you will earn greater notice, as well."

"I paint as well as anyone here," Tommaso retorted in a stung tone, his pale cheeks reddening. He glanced around at his fellows for support. "Davide, Paulo, do you not agree?"

"You paint well enough," Paulo conceded with a grin, "but Dino is exceptionally talented. What do you say, Davide?"

All eyes turned to that youth, who was known among the apprentices a diplomat and a peacemaker. He thought for a moment; then, in measured tones, he replied, "I think they both are fine artists, but perhaps Dino better understands the Master's approach to technique."

"Ha! I understand the Master as well as Dino, as well as any of you!" Fists clenched, Tommaso stomped over to where I crouched, returning the pigments and brushes to their places. "Apologize for what you said."

I rose and planted my hands on my hips, meeting his gaze . . . not a difficult task, for we were of a size. "I am sorry you were offended. Now, leave me be, for the Master has requested that I return to him immediately."

"I know why he favors you," Tommaso said with a sneer. "It's because you are as pretty as a girl. I've heard the Master likes pretty young boys." Before I could react, he reached out and pinched me hard upon the cheek.

I slapped his hand away and glared at him in outrage. "That's not true. The Master has always treated me as a father, and nothing more. You are vile in your suggestions."

By now, the other apprentices were gathering around us. I could hear their murmured comments, some agreeing with me, others conceding they had heard whispers of such proclivities. Cheek throbbing, I turned my angry gaze on those doubters.

"If the Master has ever laid an inappropriate hand upon any of you, I challenge you to speak now. If not, I suggest that you find something better than foul gossip with which to occupy your time. Perhaps Constantin can put you to some more productive task."

Constantin, who had been busy attending the application of gold leaf upon a series of panels in the far corner, had finally broken free of that work to stride across the workshop to attend to our argument. Now, he pushed through the cluster of apprentices to glare down at Tommaso and me.

"Enough of this! Tommaso, I need you to mix another pot of gesso. Dino, if the Master is waiting on you, I suggest that you take your leave right now." He rounded a baleful look on the remaining apprentices. "As for the rest of you, back to work, lest I ask the Master's permission to take a stick to you."

The rebuke had its intended effect. Limiting themselves to muttered protests, the other boys shuffled off to resume the tasks they had abandoned, leaving Tommaso and me alone with Constantin. I gave the latter an apologetic look, even as I deliberately put a hand to my bruised cheek to remind him I was not the aggressor. "I will be off to attend the Master now."

He gave a curt nod that suggested he understood the situation, but all he said was, "Your only task is to do as Leonardo requires. Tommaso will take care of whatever chores would have been yours today."

I shot a sidelong look at that youth, whose expression still reflected barely contained outrage directed against me. What I had done to incur his ire, I could not say. All I knew was that, as I made my way across the workshop toward the door, I could feel his heated gaze against my back. Now, in addition to the two porters from the night before, it seemed I had gained another enemy.

I determinedly put aside that bit of unpleasantness as I started for the green. The morning was well advanced, and the day a fair one. Beneath an azure sky, the castle grounds bustled with greater than usual activity as a result of Il Moro's decree that none of his guests might yet depart. Sumptuously gowned noblewomen and their finely garbed servants were taking in the gardens, while their equally grand spouses practiced with swords upon the paved segments or exercised their restless steeds. The rumble of voices interspersed with the clash of hoofbeats echoed far louder than usual within the quadrangle, bringing to mind the town square on market day. Yet, for all that bustle, the mood was somber, the conte's unsolved murder lying like a finely made shroud upon the court.

I found Leonardo on the far side of the green, seated on a stone bench and scribbling from right to left, as was his wont, upon a sheet of paper. He looked up at my approach and gestured me to sit beside him.

"I am compiling a series of lists to assist us in our investigation." He indicated a page lying between us, which he'd covered in that same mirror writing. "This first, I composed last night following the banquet. It is a record of those who attended or took part in yesterday's festivities. I have crossed through the names of those whom I can personally attest did not leave the field of play during the time the duke's cousin was murdered."

I scanned the roll, which I saw in amazement contained perhaps two hundred names, mine and the other apprentices, included. To my relief, ours were scratched through, as were the greatest number of the rest. Even so, a substantial enough number remained as possible suspects; moreover, the list did not include most of the castle servants, whose humble station did not preclude the possibility of a murderous heart.

Leonardo frowned, his next words echoing my thoughts. "Of course, while that narrows our list of potential assassins on the field, it does not take into consideration the great number here at court who did not take part in the festivities. Still, it is a start," he said and tucked away the list in his tunic. "Now, tell me who you observed last night at the banquet, and who aroused your suspicions."

I swiftly related the tale of the two porters whose seemingly incriminating conversation I had overheard. He listened with interest; however, when I finished, he shook his head. "I have no doubt that those two were involved in some nefarious scheme, but I do not think they had a hand in the conte's death. Had they actually killed a nobleman—especially a relative of Ludovico—they would have been long gone from the place, rather than risking an undoubtedly painful execution should they be found out. Who else did you observe?"

"There was another person of interest . . . a noblewoman, by her dress and manner."

I went on to describe my encounters with the woman whom I had mentally dubbed "the bishop's lady." Although I was reasonably certain now that her outburst following the duke's announcement of his cousin's death had been spurred by grief and not glee, something in her reaction still disturbed me. But as I recounted my observations of her actions aloud, the case against her sounded increasingly dubious.

The Master listened thoughtfully, however, nodding when I had finished my recital.

"I believe the woman you speak of is the Contessa di Malvoral, wife to another distant relative of Ludovico. Her husband is quite older than she, and, if I recall correctly, he had been the duke's original choice of his ambassador to France's king. Perhaps now the Conte di Malvoral will have another chance at the post."

"And that could be a reason for him to have killed Il Moro's cousin," I exclaimed, sensing possible vindication as I jumped to my feet. "That would also explain his wife's behavior, as she must have known what he had done. Tell me, Master, is the Conte di Malvoral the man you suspect of the crime?"

"Yes, he is, along with several others."

That caveat came with a wry shrug, so that my excitement abruptly drained from me. I resumed my seat and frowned at him, puzzled. "I don't understand. I thought you said last night that you knew who murdered the conte."

"I know who the likeliest suspect is, but I have yet to rule out all the others. I have also learned from years of my various experiments that it is folly to remain wedded to a theory before one has sufficient proof to justify the union. That is the reason for my second list."

He indicated the paper balanced upon his knee, and I

leaned closer for a better look. He had divided the page into two columns. Painstakingly reading backward, I saw that the first was headed by the word "Reason," while the second was entitled, "Occasion."

"We will start with our first category," he said, gesturing to the left column. "I would say we could safely assume that the conte, just as all those others who fall to an assassin's hand, was murdered for a specific reason. If we can discover that reason, we will find the person responsible. You have already suggested that the conte might have been killed for gain, and that Malvoral—or perhaps someone else—benefited from his demise. So tell me, Dino, why else would one man murder another?"

"Revenge," I promptly offered. "Anger, perhaps, or even hate. Maybe to prevent him from doing or saying something that would affect the killer."

"Very good." Leonardo nodded as he jotted down my suggestions. "What else?"

"Maybe he owed someone money and refused to pay. Or maybe someone owed him and preferred to murder rather than repaying his debt."

I hesitated, searching for more reasons in recalling the various comments I had heard as I made my way among the tables last night. The announcement of his death had seemed shocking news to the assembly, but not everyone mourned his passing equally. By my reckoning, he had friends and enemies in equal part.

I returned to the original theory the duke had put forth upon learning of his cousin's fate. "Il Moro seemed to think the reason he was murdered was that the conte was his ambassador to France. Perhaps someone from our court or theirs sought to forestall that alliance with the French king."

"Certainly, that would be a prime motive for such a crime," the Master agreed, making his note. "But let's not forget defense of one's self. Perhaps the conte was not the original victim but the aggressor, and his murderer had simply sought to preserve his own life." He frowned and added, "Though we found no evidence that the conte had a weapon of his own."

"Unless the other man took it away with him?" I suggested.

Leonardo lifted a brow. "An excellent point, my dear Dino. You are indeed well-suited to the task of solving mysteries."

He made another note while I ducked my head, feeling my cheeks redden at yet another compliment. To be sure, such praise from the Master made up for my previous sleepless night! With a few more strokes, he finished that list and then moved his pen to the other side of the page labeled "Occasion."

"Now that we have our list of possible reasons," he continued, "we must determine who among the court could lay claim to each motive. But we must limit that list to those who would have had the opportunity to commit the crime during that half of an hour that the conte was missing before you discovered him."

We spent the next several minutes discussing the possibilities . . . or, rather, Leonardo reviewed seemingly the entirety of the court, writing down a handful of names while I simply nodded gravely at each decision. Of course, I was at a disadvantage, given my humble station at the castle. Indeed, I knew none of the nobles by sight or name, save the duke. The master, however, seemingly knew every inhabitant of the court, from Il Moro down to the humblest boy in the kitchen.

When he finished, the original list was thoroughly lined through and crosshatched over—all done in Leonardo's distinctive backward hand—so that the document appeared to my eyes quite illegible. He, however, gave a satisfied nod.

"I believe we have a good start," he said, folding the page into neat quarters and tucking it inside his tunic along with the first list. "We shall need to conduct some discreet conversation with everyone upon this page within the next day. If we do not find the assassin quickly, I fear Ludovico may face an uprising among his nobles should they be confined here on the castle grounds much longer. But first, we have another task to perform. What is the hour?"

Not waiting for my reply, he pushed aside the flowing sleeve that covered his right arm. I stared at the square metallic box perhaps two fingers in height that was tied to his lower forearm by a length of leather. He raised his arm to peer more closely at the odd device, and I saw in surprise that he wore what appeared to be a miniature version of a tower clock.

He glimpsed my expression of amazement and quirked a brow. "I see you have noticed one of my latest inventions. It is a time-keeping device designed to be carried about so that one can always keep track of the passage of the day. I call it a wrist clock."

"And does it really work?" I asked a bit doubtfully.

For myself, I had always been content with listening for the chimes of the clock upon the tower, or the sound of church bells ringing the Angelus, or else checking the position of the sun, itself, to keep up with the hour. It had never occurred to me that one might wish to carry time, as it were, upon one's person. What could be the need?

"We are within a few seconds of it being three of the afternoon," he replied. Barely had he spoken than we both heard the clock tower strike three times. My doubts immediately were supplanted by admiration, and I could not help a small gasp of awe.

"And yes, my dear Dino," he added, sounding a trifle out of sorts, "my wrist clock does work. I will concede, however, that the original version was far less successful, given that it operated with weights, as does a standard tower clock. Such design will not always function properly while it is strapped to an arm, which is prone to move about. To solve that difficulty, I am currently experimenting with tightly wound strips of metal instead of weights. But that is a matter for another day. The conte's funeral will be commencing within an hour, and we have work to do."

He stood and reached beneath the bench, pulling forth a burlap sack that I had not noticed until that moment. Its contents clanked and bulged against the rough covering, but I could not guess what the bag might contain, even when Leonardo unceremoniously thrust it into my arms.

"Follow me, and quickly," he commanded as I struggled to my feet while juggling the unwieldy bundle. "We must make our way to the churchyard."

He took off at his usual swift pace, with me attempting to keep up with his long strides. We were headed for the main gates, I saw in surprise, and I wondered how we would contrive to leave the castle grounds in the face of Il Moro's earlier decree. But, as was so often the case when the Master was in charge of matters, my fears quickly proved groundless.

The guards' aggressive stance as they moved to block the gate lasted only as long as it took them to recognize that the man before them was Leonardo. They bowed deferentially, and I surmised that the duke had previously given them orders that his court engineer, alone of his retainers, was free to depart the grounds if he so wished. When the Master returned their gesture with an impatient flick of his fingers, they promptly straightened and made haste to open the man-sized door cut into heavy wooden gates, bowing again as he walked through it.

As for me, I was summarily ignored. I knew, however, that should I have attempted such a departure on my own, my treatment would have been far different.

Once beyond the castle's sun-baked red walls, I felt the oppressive air that had wrapped the court since the conte's murder fall from me like a forgotten cloak. I took a deep breath, savoring the warm smell of the countryside . . . the scent of rich, warm soil; the delicate perfume of fruit trees and wildflowers; and even the faint, sharp smell of manure from the distant herd of cattle. Here, the air was free of the usual heavy aromas of wood fires and cooked onions that were characteristic of the castle. The sky outside the castle walls seemed a richer blue, as if it had been painted in the luminous oils that the Master favored over the usual bright yet more delicately hued tempera. Even the soft clouds along the horizon were puffier, whiter, than when viewed from behind the battlements, though in the distance a darker band of clouds approached, indicating we might be in for a storm.

We reached the burial grounds a short time later. I had heard rumors that the duke eventually intended to move his familial burial plot to the Convent of Santa Maria delle Grazie, which lay at some farther distance from the castle. The Master had intimated that he would be the one to decorate the chapel's walls, and that his plans for the monks' dining hall included a fresco representing the Lord's final meal. For now, however, the Sforza dead continued to join their ancestors here, within sight of the castle that would have been their home in life.

I never failed to find a churchyard anything but dismal, even during daylight hours. This cemetery was as doleful as any . . . overgrown with sickly cedars and junipers, brightened here and there with a neglected clump of nasturtiums or spill of thorny rose canes, its sloping surface roughly terraced with rock hewn from that same low hill upon which it had been constructed a century earlier. Leonardo, however, hummed a gay tune as he threaded his way along the uneven graveled paths through the lichen-scabbed monuments toward the largest edifice within the cemetery walls.

It was the tomb of the Sforza family, an imposing structure of rough-cut red stone cornered with larger blocks of pale limestone that resembled the Sforza castle itself. The family crest with its ominous serpent coat of arms was carved above the heavy wooden doors, which had already been pried opened in anticipation of receiving the crypt's newest occupant. The lit torches bracketed on either side of the opening did nothing to dispel the gloom within.

"You still have the bag?" the Master asked unnecessarily as he glanced my way. "Good. Now, make haste. We must set up our equipment before the mourners arrive with the conte."

Then, as casually as if he were entering a great hall, he grabbed up one of the torches and gestured me to follow as he started down the damp stone steps leading into the tomb.

7

Happy will be those who give ear to the words of the dead . . .

—Leonardo da Vinci, Manuscript I

I gripped the bulky sack more tightly and, reciting a silent prayer, followed Leonardo into the yawning mouth of the crypt. Carved steps led down into a large, columned antechamber that hung heavy with stale air tinged with decay . . . the lingering scent not surprising, given that generations of Sforzas must have been laid to their final repose within the cavelike walls.

The flickering torch revealed glimpses of grand sepulchers where the highest-ranking nobles were encased in carved rock, as well as the niches and plain slabs upon which family members of lesser status were laid wrapped in silk or linen cloth. While many of the bodies had long since crumbled into proverbial dust, several more recent dead continued to wear rotting burial garments upon equally tattered bone and hair and flesh, the wizened forms likely still recognizable to those who had known them in life.

I paused beside the nearest column, trying not to shudder as I took in the long-departed host of nobles around me. Did they resent this intrusion into their slumber, or were they long departed from this place, leaving nothing behind but remnants of their discarded human form? While Scriptures taught the latter, my own lingering doubts about the hereafter made me grateful for the Master's nonchalant presence in such a place.

The light from the crypt's open doors, though it was a welcome beacon back to the world above, spilled only a few steps downward into the darkness. High above, narrow windows let in just enough fresh air that the noxious vapors of death would disperse outward, and allowed mere slivers of sunlight into the tomb. Even this bit of illumination faded long before it reached the stone floor, so I felt as if I waded about in a cloud of lampblack.

Uneasily, I swatted at the cobwebs that wrapped themselves around me. With little illumination from either windows or entry, that left only the uneven light from the torch, which the Master now set into another iron bracket upon the nearby windowed wall. I paused to look around me and promptly regretted doing so. The restless flames spread a wide enough glow but threw about dancing shadows that, to an imaginative sort, made the dead look as if they stirred upon their stone beds.

As I was one of that fanciful number, I let out a small shriek when fingers that I was sure must belong to a deceased Sforza abruptly clamped upon my shoulder. The hand gave me an impatient shake, and I turned to see the Master's face behind me in the gloom.

"We do not have time to tarry," I heard him say over the hammering sound of my heart. "Quickly, bring the bag here beneath the torch."

Silently chastising myself for my folly, I hurried to comply. He took the sack from me and untied it, then reached into its depths. As I stared curiously, he drew forth what first appeared to be a large copper basin. A closer look revealed that the object more closely resembled the broad open mouth of a court musician's trumpet, save that a copper strip had been attached to its rim, running halfway along one edge before curling back down again along its inner surface.

As I tilted my head to look at it from another angle, the strange device suddenly called to mind something else. Confused, I looked back up at the Master. "Why, this appears to be the ear of some metal giant."

"Very good, my boy," he replied in approval. "You have correctly discerned its intent. This is a mechanism designed to amplify the sound of a distant voice, when listening to that same voice from nearby is not prudent. Thus, our task here shall be to act as a dead man's ears."

"But I do not understand," I truthfully replied.

Leonardo gave me a pitying look. "It is quite simple. Those who carry a burden of guilt rarely are able to shoulder it for long. They soon require absolution . . . if not from their confessor, then from their victim. We shall set up this device here within the tomb, and then wait without. Once the mourners have concluded their business, we shall see who might return to the tomb to unyoke themselves before the dead man, and perhaps even confess to killing him."

He turned the strange ear over to show me the hooks and links by which it might be hung from a spot upon the wall. In this particular case, it would be positioned within one of the narrow windows above us.

"I shall attach a short tube here"—he reached into the sack and withdrew a length of copper pipe, which he connected to the back of the device—"and that shall protrude from the window. Once the hearing mechanism is situated, we shall return outside and add additional lengths to that tube. Now, take this, Dino," he said, handing me the copper ear, "and I shall lift you to the window so you may hang it."

With brisk efficiency, he gathered the pitiful remains of some past Sforza from the slab beneath the window and carefully put them to one side, then hopped atop that raised platform and pulled me up to join him. Making a stirrup of his hands, he motioned me to step foot there. As I clung with one hand to the metal basin and with the other braced myself against the wall, he lifted me in a single easy move that hinted at strength far greater than his graceful figure would suggest.

"Make haste," he urged as I struggled to balance, "yet be certain the ear is securely attached. While I doubt anyone will notice it hanging there, they will not be able to avoid doing so should it tumble from its perch and hit them upon the head."

Aware of my vital role in this plot, I lifted the ear into place, threading the copper tube through the window so that it protruded into daylight. The hooks made easy purchase into the rocky crags, so that within a few moments I pronounced the mechanism properly set.

He lowered me again with that same efficiency of movement, so that I landed quite lightly before him. Then, for reasons I could not fathom, as I stood there inches from him, I felt my cheeks reddening there in the dark. A sudden lightheadedness swept me, and I swayed.

The Master caught me by the arm. "Take care, boy, lest you tumble from here and strike your head," he calmly warned me. "I would hate to have the Sforzas claim so promising an apprentice from me."

Still gripping my arm, he lowered me to the safety of the crypt floor and then lightly leaped down to join me. I swept a hand across my forehead and took a deep breath. "My apologies, sir. I fear the evil humors here within the tomb muddled my head for a moment."

"Then we shall give you fresh air. Come, take up the bag and let us quit this place."

So saying, he grabbed the torch from its bracket and led the way from tomb back to the land of the living. I gratefully gulped down the clear air and then literally shook the dust of the crypt from my shoes. Leonardo, meanwhile, had returned the torch to the outer bracket and was peering at his wrist clock.

"The mourners will soon be here," he announced, just as the faint strikes of the distant clock tower announced the next hour. "Let us finish assembling our device and then take our places behind the tomb."

I noticed now that the crypt was partially built into a portion of a small hill, its rounded peak at a level with the rear of the tomb. The window from which the pipe from our device protruded was halfway between the hill and entry. While I held the sack, the Master rummaged in it, pulling forth various shapes of similar tubing, which he affixed together. By the time he attached one end to the metal ear, the remaining pipe snaked down the crypt and along its edge, leading up to the growth of hedge that anchored one corner of the tomb into the hill.

"We shall position ourselves there, so we have view of the entry as well as an ear within," he declared as he reached inside the now-slack bag for a final piece. Motioning me to follow, he scrambled up the incline and slipped behind the greenery. He caught up the tube and then attached to it a curved section that ended in a smaller version of the original oversized ear.

"This is what we shall use to listen to what is said. Put this to your ear, Dino, while I briefly return underground so we may test its efficacy."

I did as instructed. At first, the only sound was the same faint murmur that one might hear when playfully attempting to listen to the ocean from a seashell. Then, abruptly, the Master's voice rang quite clearly in my ear, so that I nearly dropped the earpiece in surprise.

"Dino, can you hear me?"

Recovering myself quickly, I lowered the piece and spoke into the tube. "I hear you quite well, Master," I answered in awe before putting the device to my ear again.

Once again, his voice was uncannily clear as he replied, "Then you have done your job properly. Wait, and I shall rejoin you momentarily."

A few moments later, he had climbed back to our spot

behind the concealing greenery. Now we could hear a murmur of distant voices speaking, which rose and fell upon the
light breeze. "That is prayer. They are nearly here," Leonardo
said in satisfaction.

He stretched himself at full length upon the ground, where
I joined him, the listening tube positioned between us. From
our higher vantage point, I could peer between the leafy
branches to see a procession winding its way from the nearby
chapel through the churchyard's main gates. The conte's body,
draped in white and covered in blossoms and greenery, lay
upon a bier shouldered by members of the royal guard, those
on each of the four corners carrying lighted torches in their
free hands.

Behind the bier walked the conte's heavily veiled wife,
and then the duke and his family. Other members of the
court followed, their number interspersed by groups of
young altar boys carrying candles and sweetly singing some
hymn I did not recognize. Leading the mourners was a retinue of finely robed priests who marched as smartly as any of
Il Moro's soldiers. They surrounded an oddly familiar figure
dressed in white robes, a miter upon his head, and a large
cross raised before him. My eyes widened, and I turned to
stare at Leonardo.

"Ah, I see the archbishop himself is conducting the service," he murmured with a satisfied nod. "And it appears all
of the court is in attendance, as well. Doubtless they saw the
funeral as a welcome opportunity to escape the castle grounds
for a time."

As the procession drew still closer, we lapsed into silence
and simply observed. Of course, the number was such that
only those at the very front of that column could draw close to
the crypt. Thus, those remaining farther behind broke ranks
to settle against convenient monuments and exchange subdued gossip. We were close enough that I could hear the archbishop's prayers, the familiar ritualized Latin that served every
occasion from baptism to death. The family listened with stoic

demeanors as befitted their station. If the contessa had spent her night wailing in grief, no one could know, for her heavy veil hid any telling sign of pale cheek or red eyes.

A concluding "Amen" from the priests as the archbishop gave his final blessing signaled the end of the service. While the mourners silently watched, the guard carried the conte's body down into the tomb.

As they vanished within those walls, the Master motioned me to listen with him at the earpiece. Leaning closer, I could hear the ringing of their boots upon the stone steps and the further shuffle of footsteps. I pictured them as they presumably made their way to the conte's waiting bier, where they would lay his body for his final rest. Next came a murmur of voices and a nervous laugh, followed by an admonition from one of the guards.

"Watch what you're doing! You almost dropped the man. Now, show some respect and settle him on there properly."

"He's settled, and none too soon for me," another voice grumbled. "Christ's footprints, with that bad blood between him and the rest, I'd have wagered we would have been carrying him here long before now."

"Careful how you speak of the dead," a thin voice spoke up.

I could almost see the speaker rapidly crossing himself to protect himself from any ill omens. From his fearful tone, it seemed that whatever bad blood the other man had hinted at was indeed a matter of some gravity. The Master and I both leaned closer to the listening device, eager to hear more about this apparent discord between the Conte di Ferrara and some other unknown men that could well have some bearing upon his untimely murder.

Unfortunately, the remaining guards must have already been conversant with that particular bit of gossip, for no further explanation was forthcoming. The warning merely drew a snort from yet another of the men who cryptically replied, "It's not the dead you have to worry about around here; it's the living that concern me."

"Orlando is well protected, at least. Such a waste, to leave so fine a blade to rust here in the dark," another voice glumly proclaimed.

The shuffling footsteps recommenced, and then the sound of boots upon the stone stairs. The guards came blinking back into the sunlight, the now-empty bier swinging lightly between them. The four torchbearers extinguished their flames, though leaving the pair of torches burning on the outer walls of the crypt, itself. The other two guards, meanwhile, solemnly closed the tomb doors behind them, causing a protesting squeal of ancient hinges that ended in a solid thunk as the two doors reconnected, and the heavy latch fell into place again.

At that, the funeral party began to disperse. The family and courtiers made their way toward the cemetery gates, where wagons and carts waited to return them to the castle. In a surprisingly solicitous move, the duke escorted his cousin's widow from the tomb himself. Once, he bent and murmured something to her. If she replied, she did so with no tilt of the head, with no answering gesture. Instead, she kept to her regal pace that had served her thus far. My gaze followed her veiled figure in unwilling fascination as I tried to imagine her thoughts at the loss of her husband.

Grief . . . despair . . . remorse.

Perhaps, even relief?

Why that last possible sentiment had occurred to me, I was not certain; still, I dutifully tucked away the notion for further study later and turned my attention to the archbishop. He had never made it as far as my town's humble church, so that I had never seen the man before the day of the chess match and now this funeral.

Neither had I heard ill about this particular bishop, who had served since before I was born, though others who preceeded him had drawn the ire, if not contempt, of their flock. But His Eminence Stefano, Cardinal Nardini apparently limited himself to a reasonable number of servants, spent more time on matters of religion than of state, and managed to keep his mistresses and illegitimate offspring—if, indeed, he had any—well hidden from the outside world. And he appeared from my vantage point to exude an air of dignified piety appropriate to his exalted station in the Church.

There seemed a painful irony in the fact the conte had been costumed to resemble that illustrious clergyman when he met his end, and now the true archbishop was presiding over his burial. Signore Luigi had done his job well, I thought in grudging admiration, for the vestments that the tailor had hurriedly created for the chess match were almost as sumptuous as His Eminence's own lavish garb worn this day. Indeed, any of those mock bishops would have looked as at home in the pulpit as they had upon the chess field.

Flanked by his holy retinue, the archbishop moved with an old man's stilted gait back toward the chapel, where his equally elegant closed wagon waited to return him to the castle. The conveyance was worthy of his station, drawn by a matched team wearing the archbishop's insignia upon their bridles. I watched him make his halting way into the carriage, after which one of the priests closed the carved door after him. He would ride alone, I knew, while the other clerics followed behind in their more common wagons, and the monks journeyed back on foot.

"Finally, this business is ended. Now we wait and see who returns to visit the conte," the Master softly declared as the last of funeral party departed the gates, leaving the two of us alone with the singing larks and the dead.

He sat up and took the empty burlap sack that had contained the hearing device, folding it into a neat square. Then he stretched back on the ground again and tucked the cloth beneath his head like a pillow, his russet hair spread in neat wings on either side of his face.

"Keep fast watch, Dino," he instructed, shutting his eyes and crossing his arms over his chest, "and wake me should anyone return to the tomb." A few moments later, his soft snore was the only sound other than the larks that enlivened the empty churchyard.

I suppressed a small grin, wondering if I had discovered the Master's secret for being able to subsist on but a few hours' sleep a night. The other apprentices and I had long since noticed his tendency to disappear from the workshop for an hour or more several times throughout the course of a day. Perhaps some of those absences were not to attend to work-related matters, but opportunities for a nap.

I found myself giving way to a sympathetic yawn as I ruminated upon how pleasant it would be to sleep a few minutes here beneath the sun's dying warmth. Not that I would care to slumber away in such a place after dark, I reminded myself, the unsettling notion dispelling my momentary weakness. Besides which, the Master had tasked me with a job to do, and I had no wish to fail him.

Propping myself on my elbows, I instead fixed my gaze on the cemetery gate, waiting to see if one of the mourners had concealed himself within the chapel and would now make himself seen. Why the Master was so certain that someone would return here, I could not guess, but I had long since learned that his intuition was usually proven well-founded.

When several minutes passed and no one made his way back to the crypt, I found myself growing restless. If I had not been charged with keeping watch, I would have pulled out my ever-present notebook to record bits of the day's most interesting happenings. That writing would have to wait until the evening, however, when my stint as watchman was over. For the moment, I could distract myself only with my memories.

I could see from my vantage point a bit of the road along which Leonardo and I had traveled to the church. The sight reminded me of my journey to the great city of Milan. The streets of my town had still been dark when I started out, and the gates still closed, for my travel had begun well before dawn.

Upon leaving my father's house, I had taken temporary refuge in a stable not far from the main walls, snuggling down in an empty stall to wait for the sunrise. Just as now, I had dared not shut my eyes lest I sleep and miss my cue, that being the rumble of the first wagons making their way into town. Once I heard that familiar sound, I had brushed off the inevitable straw from the old cloak that had served as my blanket and slipped away long before my fellow stable mates— three pale mares and a snoring donkey—roused themselves from slumber.

Though I expected any instant for someone to clamp a heavy hand upon my arm and stop me, no one paid me any heed as I strolled out of the open gates and onto the narrow road leading toward Milan. And why would anyone have noticed me? To all outward appearances, I was but another youth leaving home for the lure of the magnificent city over the hills.

Inwardly, however, I trembled with self-consciousness in my boy's garb, feeling almost indecent with my cropped hair and trunk hose. Yet the intoxicating freedom of movement slowly won me over, so that soon it was all I could do not to skip along the path, so light did I feel. Even the belt wrapped around my waist beneath my tunic seemed like a feather, though it was heavy with the florins that my father had given me the night before I had begun my journey.

"You'll need money," he had whispered to me during the few minutes that my mother had left us alone near the hearth. "Your new master may require pay for your place with him . . . and if not, you will still need a bit of coin, as an apprentice's wage is meager, at best."

He had paused to give me a sharp look. "I wonder, girl, have you truly considered what you are getting yourself into? An apprentice's lot is not an easy one. You'll be up at dawn and to bed well after dark. You'll be put to work at any sort of menial task your master wishes to give you, and likely it will be weeks before you even lay a brush to a panel or wall. And should you refuse a chore, you will be shown the door . . . that is, if you are not whipped, first."

He shook his head and put a hand to his forehead, his

expression abruptly more distressed. "Ah, me, am I making a terrible mistake, letting my only daughter embark on such a journey?" he asked in soft despair. "Suppose someone discovers your disguise . . . what would become of you then? Your apprenticeship would be at an end, and no decent man would ever have you. Why, you might end your days on the street, as a washerwoman, perhaps."

Knowing that being condemned to such an ignominious livelihood was, in truth, but a step up from being a woman of easy virtue, I could not fault my father for his concern. The thought had occurred to me, as well, but it was a risk I was willing to take.

"I understand, Father," I consoled him. "This adventure will not be an easy one, but we both know that this can be my only opportunity to learn my craft. We have no great painter here in our small town, and even if we did, he would surely be loath to take on a female as apprentice. Should Leonardo let me into his workshop, I promise that I shall work hard."

"Very well." He nodded and reached into his jerkin to pull forth a small leather bag, which jingled musically. "I suspect that, even should I try to stop you, you would set out on your own without my blessing. So, let me do what I can for you," he said and quickly slipped the heavy pouch into my hands.

When I would have protested, he shook his head. "I would have had to scrape up far more for your dowry," he murmured. "Just be sure you hide it well upon your person. Remember always to keep a single florin in your purse, but never more than that lest someone see your coin and think to rob you. Keep your eyes open, child, and once you are upon the road, try to find some likely traveling companions so that you are not alone in your journey. Unless the weather is poor, or the roads uncommonly crowded, you should be walking but one day and half of another until you reach the city."

"Do not worry," I assured him as I tucked away the small

bag. "I shall be safe enough in my disguise, and I shall heed all of your advice. Leonardo will surely take me on . . . but if not, I will find another job at the castle and continue to petition him until he changes his mind. Either way, I shall be certain to send you word of my situation."

"Then it is settled," he replied, and pulled me to him in a rare hug.

"What is settled?" came my mother's voice as she returned to the room, her gaze bright with interest as she took in the tender scene.

With a guilty start, we ended our unaccustomed display of affection and stepped apart. My father gave me a formal nod and then turned to my mother. "Do not worry, Carmela, I am but telling our daughter what she should expect in her new life. There will be much that is different, and she must be prepared."

"Pah, that is a mother's duty," she replied in exasperation and marched over to me. Taking me by the hand, she pulled me onto the small stool beside the hearth and then sat upon the chair opposite me. "Now, forget everything your father has just told you," she grandly commanded as she waved away her husband, "and let me explain what you will need to know."

It was a conversation I had hoped to avoid. Involved as I had been with my own plans, however, I was caught unawares and so could do nothing but sit and take in her words. I had listened with surprise and some alarm to certain of the things she said, including the more earthy details of what she called one's wifely duties.

"Take what enjoyment you can, but do not expect overly much," was her frank summation of that particular role. As for the rest, she was equally blunt.

"Most important in a marriage is that you show your husband respect, that you let him think that he is the one in charge of the household," she said with a dismissive sniff that made it clear she considered no male equal to such a task. "Never handle any of his possessions or snoop about in his papers, at least, not so that he can guess what you have been about. And always remember that it matters not that you may be more intelligent than he. Your role as wife is to act submissive, no matter that doing so chafes as keenly as a monthly cloth."

While I blushed a little at that last indelicate reference, her sour view of the married state only strengthened my resolve to avoid that particular entanglement. Still, I could not help but feel sorry for her, caught as she was in that very web that I would soon escape. When I tried to express something of that to her, however, she shook her head and smiled a little.

"Pah, it is different with your father and I. He is one of the few men about who is intelligent enough to understand the advantages of having a clever wife; thus, he does not resent my role in our marriage." She shrugged. "He is talented enough at his woodworking, I will give him that, but it has been I who has managed all his plump commissions and who found him the rich patrons who have rewarded him handsomely over the years, so that we can afford now to pay your dowry."

That last reference to those nuptials that, unbeknownst to her, would never be said had sent a small wave of guilt through me. I had comforted myself with the notion that perhaps my mother would spend some of what would have been that matrimonial prize upon herself. My eyes opened by her blunt talk, I could see now that she had run our small household with the same ruthless efficiency as Il Moro ran his duchy, and that doing so had taken no little effort on her part. She, far more than Signore Niccolo, deserved the fruits of those years of hard work.

So caught up was I in my memories that it took a moment for an unexpected sound from the listening device to dash away my reverie. I stiffened in surprise, and then cautiously put the metal cup to my ear. Had I simply imagined that I'd heard a faint noise echo from it? But how could that be?

I scanned the cemetery grounds for some sign of an intruder, though I was certain that Leonardo and I were alone in the churchyard. While my thoughts might have momentarily wandered from the task at hand, I had kept my gaze carefully fixed upon the tomb's entry the entire time. I had seen no one approach. Still, a soft sound had come from within the crypt itself.

"Have we visitors, Dino?" the Master softly asked, one eye flickering open.

I gave an uncertain shrug. "I've seen no one about, save ourselves," I replied in an equally low tone, "and yet I would have sworn I heard . . . something . . . make a noise inside the conte's tomb."

"Indeed?"

He was fully awake now, rolling onto his stomach to spare a sharp look at the crypt's entry. We were positioned behind and slightly to one side of the stone monument, so that our view, while not entirely unimpeded, was clear enough to tell that the crypt doors were still closed as the guards had left them. Moreover, had someone managed to open them without our noticing, we certainly would have heard the sound of the hinges.

Wordlessly, Leonardo snatched the listening device from me and held up one finger to keep me silent as he put the metal cup to his ear. His gesture was unnecessary, however, for I could barely draw a breath as I waited for a repeat of that sound.

And then it came again, a moan loud enough that I could hear its frightful echo myself, though the listening device was at the Master's ear.

"The conte has returned from the dead!" I gasped out in alarm, while a cold chill slid like a sliver of winter's ice along my spine. Even Leonardo looked momentarily nonplussed before shaking his head and favoring me with a stern look.

"Contain yourself, boy. I assure you, the dead do not return to life. If, indeed, that sound did emanate from the deceased man, it was strictly a natural phenomenon resulting from the inevitable buildup of humors in the corpse."

Barely had he offered that explanation, however, than the plaintive wail repeated itself.

I felt myself blanch, and I feared for a moment that I might actually swoon. As for the Master, his stern expression darkened even more, if possible, and with an oath he tossed aside the listening device.

"This matter bears further investigation," he proclaimed and leapt to his feet. "Come, Dino, do not cower there like a girl. It is time we find out who—or what—is inside that tomb with the conte."

8

Victory and death are similar in many ways. Each is both a conclusion and another beginning.

—Leonardo da Vinci, *The Notebooks of Delfina della Fazia*

L eonardo used a twisted bit of wire he pulled from his pouch to make short work of the large lock that held the hasp in place across the crypt doors. We pried open the heavy doors again, and the resulting metallic shriek of rusty hinges was almost as unnerving as the otherworldly wail that we had heard from the tomb's depths but a few moments earlier. Then, for the second time that afternoon, I followed Leonardo down the hewn stone steps into the Sforza family crypt.

Had I been alone, I would have long since fled the churchyard in terror, headed for the safety of the castle gates. But as the Master had commanded me to accompany him, I had no choice other than to comply. Not that I would have cared to remain alone outside the crypt while he went inside, I reminded myself. The sun was fading in earnest now, and it would soon be as dark without the tomb as it would be within. The prospect of waiting by myself in a shadowy churchyard was as unnerving as entering a crypt that held some unknown horror. Exhorting myself to bravery, I slipped past the gaping doorway and continued down the steps.

I am not ashamed to admit that I clung to the hem of
the Master's tunic as we descended into the chamber. He
had grabbed up one of the remaining torches outside the
doors to again illuminate our progress, but its flame had
burned down to a portion of its earlier brightness. Thus, the
meager glow lit nothing beyond a few inches in front of us,
adding an element of physical danger to any unnatural aspect of our investigation.

For the moment, however, the only sound within the tomb
besides the flame's gentle hiss was the soft shuffle of our shoes
upon stone. We had reached the chamber, and Leonardo raised
the torch to spread the weak light farther. Shadows danced off
the recumbent forms of the nearest dead Sforzas, but the rest
were lost to the darkness, save for one whose fresh white linen
faintly reflected back the torch's wan flames.

We moved closer to the rock slab where the Conte di Ferrara had been laid not many minutes earlier. His form beneath
the filmy lawn was unmistakable, as was the burgeoning odor
of decay from his corpse that the fragrant flowers and pungent
greenery could no longer disguise. I covered my nose with my
free sleeve while still keeping a firm grasp upon the Master.
While the conte was most assuredly dead, that did not necessarily mean that he had departed this realm.

Seemingly unperturbed by the stench, Leonardo brought
the torch nearer to the dead man's shrouded form and leaned
in for a closer look, meaning that I was all but standing
upon the man, as well. I kept my gaze off to one side, however, not wishing another look. I could recall too clearly how
he'd appeared when I first found him, the life but recently
drained from his veins. I needed no further memories to
haunt my dreams!

"I do not think the sound we heard came from him,"
Leonardo softly stated as he straightened once more. "The
humors have risen within his flesh to a point that his lungs
can hold no vestiges of air that could be released in such a
manner. We shall have to uncover another explanation."

He raised the torch again and began a methodical walk

through the rows of columns and slabs, examining every group of mortal remains that inhabited the place. I kept as close on his heels as I could, trying not to gag from the surrounding miasma of death even as I kept a sharp watch on the floating rectangle of light above that was the open crypt door. Its previously comforting yellow brightness had faded to a dull pewter glow, an indication that the setting sun now barely clung to the horizon.

In not many more minutes, that dying orange orb would slip behind the distant hills completely, leaving us in darkness unrelieved save for our flickering torch. As for the slitted windows high above, their narrow depths were already draped in shadows, so that they may as well have been shuttered for all the light they allowed. I dared not wonder what might happen should the torch's meager flame gutter out while we were still within the belly of the crypt, throwing us into total darkness.

By now, we had examined perhaps half the bodies—or what little was left of them—yet had found nothing that hinted at the origin of the sound we had heard. My earlier terror had subsided into a more manageable fear, and some of my natural curiosity had returned. I reminded myself I likely never again would set foot in a noble tomb such as this and, thus, should take care to observe everything about me. If nothing else, my impressions might make an interesting subject for a painting one day, should I tire of painting mere saints and sinners.

It was at that point, of course, that the hideous moan softly echoed once more.

I gave an answering shriek, swiftly smothered by one hand as I grasped with the other at the Master's arm, nearly causing him to drop the torch. "There it is again," I gasped out unnecessarily as he struggled to keep the flame steady. "Please, let us leave while we still may."

"Nonsense," he muttered back. "Someone—or something— is with us in this crypt, and we shall not leave here until we discover its identity."

Burdened by the growing darkness and my relentless grasp upon his tunic sleeve, he slowly moved in the direction from which the low cry had come. Had it sounded yet again, I doubted I would have heard it, so loudly was my heart pounding in my chest. Still, despite my fear, I could not flee and leave Leonardo to face this unnatural terror alone.

I had noted on our first excursion into the tomb that niches were carved into the wall at three different levels, allowing for a good number of dead to be stacked like bundles of cordwood upon each stone shelf. It was in the farthest corner of the crypt that we spied the body tucked into one of the middle niches. Unlike the other remains that were little more than bone, this sturdy corpse appeared to have been installed but recently among the dead. Once again, the flickering torch seemed to lend an uncanny hint of movement to the body, as if it were struggling to free itself from the stone.

A soft crunching beneath our feet stopped us short. Leonardo lowered the torch so that the stone floor was faintly lit, and we promptly saw the source of the sound.

"Bones," he confirmed as I skittered to one side to avoid stepping again upon the remains of one of Il Moro's distant relatives.

Indeed, it appeared most of an entire skeleton lay scattered before us the aged frame now little more than shards. The damage was far greater, I knew, than any we could have caused with a few misplaced footsteps. It was as if someone had ruthlessly swept the vestiges of some long-departed noble from one of the niches, not caring when the dry bones shattered like discarded pottery upon the ground.

"But who would do such a thing?" I whispered, appalled. Of course, I knew that such resting places were often reused after the passage of many years, but only after the original bones had been carefully gathered and respectfully deposited elsewhere. No such consideration had been given to these sad ruins.

By way of reply, the Master pointed his torch in the direction of the nearest niche and the shrouded form within. "I do not know yet who did it," he softly replied, "but the reason why is quite obvious. Someone needed this particular alcove for another body. Yet there has been no recent death among Ludovico's relatives other than the conte."

He thrust the dying torch at me. "Hold this, while I see who is lying here in some other man's place."

While I watched in horrified amazement, he dragged the wrapped form from its hollow in the wall, carefully laying it upon the cold stone floor. I could see now the dark stain upon the fabric near its head, and my confusion grew. Who would swathe a body without properly cleaning it first? But I had little time to wonder over that for, grasping the free end of the winding cloth, the Master promptly began to unwrap the still form.

It took but a moment to reveal glimpses of a familiar blue and white parti-colored tunic . . . the same sort of porter's tunic I had worn the night before while serving in the duke's dining hall. A thrill of dread ran along my spine. I leaned closer with the torch, waiting for a glimpse of the face that belonged to the youthful-looking figure before us and wondering if I would identify him from my brief stint in the kitchen.

A final twist of the cloth revealed a deathly white countenance whose forehead and cheeks were liberally streaked with dried blood, so that the features were nigh unrecognizable. Choking back a gasp, I knelt beside the Master as he probed the still form before us much as he had examined the dead conte the day before. Even I could tell, however, that the boy had met a violent end, likely at someone else's hands. But why would they have taken pains to wrap his body and hide him in this crypt? Why not toss him in the river, or leave him on the hillside, or simply bury him somewhere outside the castle grounds?

"What's this?"

With a frown, Leonardo abruptly halted his examination

and sat back on his heels. He reached into his tunic and pulled forth the familiar murder weapon that had most recently resided in the dining hall wall. Then, before I could ask what he intended, he grabbed up the boy's limp hand and swiftly pricked one finger with the point of the knife.

A dark drop welled where the knife had pierced flesh.

"The dead do not bleed," he pronounced in satisfaction and tucked away the knife again.

Not quite believing what I had just seen and heard, I swung my frightened gaze from the boy back to him. "Do you mean he still lives?" I choked out, the torch trembling in my hands. "Then, quickly, we must help him!"

"And so we shall. But, first, I must finish my examination before we attempt to move him again."

Barely had he begun, when the boy lying before us stirred, and his eyes flickered. A soft moan issued from his parched lips, the same mournful sound that had drawn us back into the crypt. But as the cry died away, he subsided into such stillness that I was certain he now had breathed his last.

"Fear not, Dino, he still lives," Leonardo grimly answered my unspoken question, "but for how much longer, I do not know. He has sustained what should have been a lethal blow to the head, and it is nothing short of a miracle that he has clung to life this long. Had we not been drawn back into the crypt by his moans, he most certainly would have been dead by morning. But even should we manage now to get him back to the castle alive, it still is likely he will not survive the night."

I only half heard the Master's words, however, for I was studying the boy's face. For the moment when his features held some hint of animation, he had appeared vaguely familiar. And then it came to me.

"Why, he is one of the porters who accosted me in the hallway last night," I exclaimed, swiftly turning to Leonardo. "Remember how I told you about them, how they were acting in such a suspicious manner?"

"Indeed? Then I wonder if his cohort is the one who did

him in, or if he also sleeps somewhere within this crypt." He rose gracefully, torch in hand. "I must take our small flame and finish checking the tomb in case both boys were victims, and not just the one. I fear, Dino, that you must wait here with this lad while I do so."

"Don't worry, Master, I am not afraid," I assured him, surprised to find out that was true.

In fact, my previous trepidation was slowly being replaced by outrage . . . this despite the fact that, only the previous evening, I had viewed the same youth now lying injured before me as an enemy. How could anyone so callously attack a mere boy, then wrap him like a corpse and lock him away to die most horridly in a crypt? What terror he might have suffered, had he ever wakened enough to realize exactly where he was! While it might be too late now to save the youth, at least I could offer him the comfort of my company in what might be his last minutes.

I settled myself as comfortably as I could, taking the boy's cold hand in mine as I watched the Master make his rounds of the ever-darkening crypt. His search appeared quite thorough, the faint light moving high and low along the tomb walls as he swiftly examined every opening in the stone. The guttering torch gave out just enough light to illuminate his upper body, the glow reflecting against his russet hair and turning it to gold. One corner of my mind found some small amusement in the way he appeared to float through the darkness like one of his nimbused saints he was fond of painting.

More important matters, however, occupied the greatest part of my thoughts. I spared another glance at the crypt's open doors, barely able now to distinguish the shadows without from the shadows within. Another problem presented itself with the fall of night. How would we manage to carry an unconscious boy along a rough, dark road all the way back to the castle gates? And, just as importantly, how would we manage to smuggle him past the guards . . . assuming they would be as accommodating letting us return to the castle grounds as they had been to let us leave them?

My grip on the boy's hand tightened, and I was relieved to feel his fingers reflexively grasp mine. "We shall get you out of here," I softly assured him, "and perhaps you will be able to tell us who has injured you so grievously."

Leonardo, meanwhile, had finished his rounds and returned to where I waited. "The other is not here," he flatly stated, handing me the torch. "Come, we must make haste and bring this boy back to the castle."

He bent to lift the youth, then hesitated and swiftly stripped off the boy's telltale blue and white tunic. He bundled both that article of clothing and the discarded winding cloth into the same hollow where we had found the boy lying.

"There," he pronounced. "Should the would-be murderer return to check on his work, it will appear upon a quick glance that a body still resides upon the shelf. And without his outer garment, our young charge will not be as easily identified as a member of the kitchen staff when we bring him through the gates."

So saying, he lifted the youth onto his shoulder and motioned me to precede him. Torch aloft, I quickly led us through the darkness toward the faint glow at the top of the stone stairway. We made our exit not a moment too soon. Barely had we gained the final rough step that took us out of the crypt and into the growing dusk of the churchyard when my torch gave a final sputter and extinguished itself.

I paid little heed to this sudden lack of illumination, however, so busy was I drinking down the clean, sweet air beyond the tomb's foul confines. Leonardo settled his unconscious burden against a nearby gravestone, and I helped him once more push closed the heavy doors of the crypt. He closed the lock he'd left dangling and then reshouldered the injured boy.

Our exit from the churchyard was equally swift. By now, charcoal swatches of clouds patched the gray sky above, bringing sunset to an end with greater than usual speed. Not only would we have the dark to contend with on our return journey, but perhaps a storm, as well.

Relief swept me as I spotted outside the churchyard walls a small, two-wheeled cart that had been left behind by the earlier mourners. The Master gave me an approving nod as I claimed the crude conveyance. We settled the young porter as comfortably as we could upon it, and each of us took a side and began to push our way back toward the castle.

The cart took no little effort to keep steady upon the path, but our progress was far swifter than had we attempted to carry the unconscious youth upon our backs! Here in the half light of dusk, I could better see evidence of the trials he had endured. The caked blood upon his face had once flowed quite freely, so that surely its loss had served to weaken him beyond the blow he'd suffered. A layer of gray dust enveloped him, for the fine powder that was equal parts crumbled rock and powdered bone had penetrated the layer of cloth that had wrapped him as he lay within that alcove. That, alone, would be cause for concern, even had he not already been gravely injured. Who knew what sort of dormant maladies he had been breathing in that place of death!

We made good time down the uneven path, even while slowing our pace over the particularly rocky patches lest we further harm our injured charge. Once or twice, he gave a muffled moan, but beyond that did not rouse from his unnatural sleep, for which we were grateful. The darkening skies were kind, as well, for I did not feel the first few drops of rain upon my bare head until we finally reached the castle gates.

Two burly soldiers who had been ensconced within the guard post stepped forth to challenge us as we approached. "Who goes there?" came the familiar demand from the one in the lead, his words accompanied by the businesslike clang of a sword being half drawn from its scabbard in demonstration of the guard's readiness.

Leonardo stepped from the shadows. " 'Tis I, the duke's master engineer," came his impatient reply. He gestured toward the cart upon which the unconscious boy lay. "One of my apprentices suffered a mishap while we were attending to an important project for His Excellency. Do not leave us standing here in the rain. We must bring the boy to the surgeon as quickly as possible."

"Of course." The guard snapped to attention and turned to his fellow, who was peering curiously at the cart. "Why do you tarry? Can't you see it is Leonardo who addresses you? Quickly, let him through."

The second soldier straightened. "How was I to know who it was?" he protested, shooting the Master a suspicious look before sauntering back to the gate. "You know we have orders not to let anyone in or out."

Still muttering, he threw open the same smaller passage we'd come through earlier that permitted foot traffic to move in and out of the castle grounds while the immense gate itself remained securely barred. He stood to one side as we maneuvered the cart through the narrow opening, and I could feel his gaze upon our backs as he shut the heavy wooden door after us.

The sun had set in earnest now, so that our only illumination came from scattered windows and doorways along the castle grounds. With darkness came a cool wind that tossed a few errant raindrops so that they splattered my face with an uncomfortable chill. Thunder rumbled now in the distance, and I knew it was but a matter of minutes before the clouds split open and drenched us all.

"Shall we not carry him to the surgery?" I asked in confusion. For Leonardo was rolling the cart in the opposite direction from the barber's shed near the stables where the surgeon normally plied his trade.

The Master made a sound of disgust. "I have seen that surgery, and it is not a fit place for even those who are whole of body. I shall take him to my quarters, instead. Be off with you, and summon the man to meet me there."

His command was fittingly punctuated by another clap of thunder. I did not wait for an accompanying lightning bolt but rushed toward the main wing of the castle in search of the duke's physician. If fortune held, he would still be in his room and not on his way to the hall where the higher-ranking retainers took their meals well apart from the castle's lesser staff.

As it was, I quite literally stumbled across the man as I ducked into the open passage that ran the length of the wing. He was a short, balding man whose thin legs seemed barely able to support his globe of a belly; still, he wore his dignity with the same gravity as he wore his long robe of forest green.

"Leonardo, eh?" the physician sourly grunted, dusting himself off while I straightened my own disheveled tunic and explained who had sent me. "I do not understand why the duke puts such stock in a mere artist. And what does the great Leonardo require from me?"

I hurriedly told him my mission. When I finished speaking, he grunted again and shook his head. "Ha, I am surprised he would deign to call upon my services, since he considers himself far more versed in the matters of the human body than I am. Now, hush your babbling, boy . . . I have not said I will not come," he went on when, fearing a refusal, I started to protest. "Wait here, and let me get my tools."

He turned back down the passage and entered a closed door. After what seemed an interminable amount of time—though likely it was but two or three minutes—he stepped out again, this time carrying a small wooden chest. He thrust the container into my arms and gave an impatient nod. "Come, boy, take me to your master, so we may be done with this."

Staggering a bit beneath the box's weight, I started for the workshop with as swift a step as I could manage. The surgeon kept pace with me, his robe billowing in the cool breeze that was bringing the storm. As I rounded the corner of the main workshop where the other apprentices and I performed our daily tasks, I could see now the faint glow of a taper in the window of the building beside it.

This was the Master's private quarters, where he stayed when not ensconced in his other workshop in the city. Here, he had both a place to sleep and a separate workshop into which none of us, to my knowledge, had ever been admitted. In this place, he carried out the more elaborate experiments for Ludovico, designing various modern combat machines and contraptions to be used by Il Moro's personal army. Whether they were more practical than the Master's brass lion, none of us knew, though rumors persisted of boats that could travel underwater and bridges that unfurled themselves across rivers.

The chamber that the surgeon and I entered was small and modestly furnished with a simple bed and a large table flanked by two benches, and a second, smaller table covered with books. Shelves lined one wall, holding everything from bowls and cups to books to some sort of animal skull. It was well lit with several lamps, a requirement for a man who spent most of the night awake and at some task or another. As for his private workshop, it likely was reached by means of the second door at other side of the room . . . a door that unfortunately was shut.

Leonardo had laid the unconscious youth upon the larger of the tables, which he'd fashioned into a makeshift bed with a pallet of blankets, and was ministering to him there. A basin beside him was filled with dark water, and beside it was a cloth stained equally red. He had cleaned the blood from the boy's face, and the sight of the patient's unsullied features confirmed that he was indeed one of the two porters from my previous night's encounter. I had no chance to study his features, however, for the surgeon pushed past me to address Leonardo.

"I presume you have already made your own examination?" he sourly asked without preamble. "Tell me, Signore Leonardo, what is your diagnosis?"

"The boy has suffered a blow to the head, likely administered by some blunt object, and occurring some hours ago," the Master coolly replied. "As to any other injury, I cannot say at this point, but it is apparent he is grievously injured and in dire need of immediate treatment, lest he expire on the spot."

"Very well, let me take a look at him."

While the surgeon rummaged in his chest, Leonardo turned to me. "Dino, you have done all you can for the moment. Why don't you go to the kitchen and see if you can manage to find yourself some supper, as I have caused you to miss the evening meal with your fellows. When you return, I will let you know if I require your services any further."

I knew better than to protest. And, as I saw now in the surgeon's hands what appeared to be a hammer and chisel, I did not relish remaining there to witness whatever was to come. Thus, I made a swift retreat through the same door through which I had entered.

The rain had begun now in earnest, so that by the time I reached the kitchen door, my hair and tunic both were plastered to me. I shook my head like one of the stable curs, sending water flying in all directions. I likely made a pathetic sight, I thought with no little chagrin as I scraped the mud from my shoes.

But perhaps I could use my disheveled state to my advantage, I decided, suddenly hungry now as the appetizing aroma of roasted beef—a dish destined for the nobles' table—drifted to me. I huddled in the doorway, shoulders hunched against a chill that was not entirely feigned, and waited for one of the cooks to spot me.

"Dino, is that you?" a pert voice demanded. "Whatever are you doing, standing there and dripping rainwater all over the floor for me to mop up?"

Momentarily confused—who in the kitchen knew me by name?—it took a moment for me to recognize the sturdy dark-haired serving girl who flounced over to where I shivered in the doorway. When she planted her fists on her ample hips and grinned up at me, I recalled her as the young woman who had shown an undue interest in me . . . or, rather, in Dino.

"H-Hello, M-Marcella," I stuttered and felt myself blush,

which only amused her more, for her grin broadened. "My Master sent me to the kitchen to find some supper. He said it was his fault that he kept me out too late to join the other apprentices for the evening meal."

"At least he shows a bit of concern for you, which is more than one can say about most of the masters around here," she said with a meaningful look at one of the cooks who was busy by the hearth berating a pair of his luckless charges. "Wait there behind the casks"—she indicated the same barrels that I'd hidden behind the previous night while doffing my porter's disguise—"and I will see if I can find you a bowl and a bit of bread."

I hid as instructed, using a towel I found there to dry the worst of the rain from me while I waited to see if she might make good her promise. While I felt a bit guilty at the deception—would she as eagerly have risked the ire of her master for Delfina's sake?—I was not noble enough this night to put aside the possibility of a full belly in exchange for a clear conscience.

Several minutes later, Marcella returned, and I could see through the gap between the casks that she was carrying a dish covered by a bit of linen. Glancing about first to make sure she was unobserved, she slipped behind the barrels to join me.

"Here," she said with a grin and proffered the bowl. "You'll find this more tasty fare than what you apprentices normally sup upon."

I pulled back the cloth and gave a sigh of satisfaction as I saw the small feast she had pilfered for me. In addition to a generous slice of the roasted beef that I had smelled, she'd added a bit of sausage and cooked onion, and an apple tart. I'm not ashamed to say that I made swift work of the meal, which was the most sumptuous I'd had since I had been at the castle.

"Ah, it pays to have a friend in the kitchen, does it not?" she asked with a saucy wink, seating herself beside me as I finished the final crumbs. "Perhaps that will persuade you to visit me more often."

So saying, she sidled uncomfortably close to me, so that I had to stand abruptly or else have her in my lap. She huffed a little at this blatant rejection of her overtures, her smile twisting into a pretty pout. "And here I thought you liked me," she complained as I tried to hide my alarm. "What's wrong, am I not pretty enough for you?"

"You're a very pretty girl," I truthfully choked out while wildly searching for some acceptable excuse that would discourage any further attempts at a closer friendship while not offending her. "It's just that I am so busy with my apprenticeship that I don't have time for anything else. Besides, I'm not sure our Master will allow us to associate with anyone outside the workshop."

"You mean, Signore Leonardo?" She gave a dramatic sigh. "He is quite the handsome gentleman, is he not? Surely a man such as he would not discourage a bit of romance."

I mentally gave that comment a doubtful snort. To the contrary, I would have wagered that the Master would dismiss her notions of romance as a waste of time that could be better spent helping him with some project or another. Increasingly uncomfortable with the direction in which our conversation seemed headed, I sought to change the subject while perhaps advancing the Master's investigation.

"I fear that everyone in the kitchen is not as friendly as you are, Marcella," I told her in a placating tone. "You see, last night I had an unpleasant discussion with two of the porters while I was carrying out business for the Master."

I briefly described the encounter and told her what the two youths looked like, while conveniently omitting the fact that this had occurred while I was myself disguised as a porter and indulging in a bit of spying for Leonardo. She gave a considering frown, making appropriate sounds of protests when I related how the pair had threatened me. Then she shook her head.

"That sounds like Renaldo and Lorenzo," she declared in disapproval. "They go everywhere together. Lorenzo is the tall, skinny one with black hair. He's probably the one who made all the threats, though Renaldo is more likely to carry them out."

I gave a considering nod. Based upon her description, the youth we had found in the crypt was Lorenzo, which meant it was his companion, Renaldo, who was still to be accounted for. "So, have you seen either of them today?" I asked as casually as I could.

She shook her head again. "Last time I saw them was last night, and only for a few minutes. I would keep my distance from them, Dino, if I were you," she went on in an earnest tone, abandoning her previous flirtatious air. "They are always fighting or off gambling with the guards or scaring some of the younger boys into giving them their food and their pay. And most of the girls are afraid to be caught alone with them, too. I've heard the kitchen master threaten to turn them out any number of times, but I think he is worried what they would do."

Any sympathy I'd had for the injured Lorenzo was rapidly evaporating with this litany of his faults. It seemed he might have brought this disaster upon himself by his own deeds; still, I could not let the attempt upon his life go unpunished if it were in my power to discover the culprit. But from Marcella's account, any number of people might have reasons to wish him harm, with none of them having anything to do with the conte's murder. Renaldo might have met with the same unfortunate end as had his companion . . . that, or else he'd prudently fled the castle to avoid such a fate.

Aloud, I merely said, "I will heed your advice and avoid them. But for now, my Master is awaiting me, so I had best return to the workshop."

"Are you sure you can't stay a bit longer?" she asked, her flirtatious manner returning as she reached out coy fingers to stop me.

I pretended not to know what she was about as I deftly avoided her grasp and instead slipped my empty bowl into her waiting hand. "Thank you again for supper," I told her quite sincerely, even as she shot me a vexed look. "Perhaps we can chat longer tomorrow."

"Perhaps," she replied, sounding only slightly mollified.

I made my swift escape from the kitchen, grateful to see that the rain had stopped while I'd partaken of my supper. I could not avoid getting wet a second time, however, for the puddles the shower had left behind still covered much of the courtyard. My trunk hose were damp all the way to my knees by the time I had splashed my way back to the small room beside Leonardo's quarters. He was waiting there for me in the dimly lit doorway, his tall shadow spilling across the cobbled walk.

Even before he spoke, I could surmise from his expression that the situation had changed for the worse. "I fear I have bad news, Dino," he said, confirming my intuition as he gestured me inside the room.

The pallet where the injured porter had lain was empty once more, the blankets rolled to one side and the floor around it littered with bloodied rags. The physician and his wooden box were gone, as well. Though I could not mourn his loss, the sight of his makeshift deathbed still sent a cold chill through me. I crossed myself and offered up a swift prayer that the departed Lorenzo was being dealt with as fairly as he deserved in the next world.

"The surgeon was not able to save the young man," Leonardo went on. "Normally, I would fault the man for a lack of skill, but the injury was severe enough that even a physician of some talent could not have preserved his life. The best we were able to do for him was assure that his fate was not unknown, that there will be some record of his passing."

"And what will become of him now?" I wanted to know.

The Master lifted a wry brow. "He will be returned to the same churchyard in which we found him, though his final resting place will be rather less grand than the tomb of the Sforzas. Unfortunately, for the moment we do not have a name to chisel upon his stone."

"But we do," I exclaimed, and swiftly related what little I had learned from Marcella about the two youths' identities.

When I finished, Leonardo gave me an approving nod. "Well done, Dino. Your cleverness has advanced our investigation, for I cannot but help think these two murders are related. And that is not all."

He paused and reached into his tunic, withdrawing a small white object that he balanced in the palm of his hand. "Take a look, my boy. Now we know the identity of the young man whose life was taken . . . and perhaps something more. For, if I am not mistaken, your friend Lorenzo managed to leave behind a clue as to the identity of his murderer."

9

We know well that mistakes are more easily detected in the works of others than in one's own . . .

—Leonardo da Vinci, *Manuscript 2038*

I stared in puzzlement at the small figure Leonardo held. Half again as tall as the width of my palm, it was carved of some white stone similar to marble that seemed to glow beneath the lamplight. Its chiseled lines were vague—or perhaps simply worn smooth with time and handling—so that although it hinted a human form, it could as easily be but a pleasing shape.

"While the surgeon went to summon his assistants to remove the young man's body," he explained, "I made a cursory check of his garments hoping to find some clue as to his identity. While doing so, I spied a pouch tied to his belt. It occurred to me that it might contain something of interest to our investigation, so I confiscated it before the surgeon returned."

He reached into his tunic with his free hand, withdrawing a small leather purse similar to the one I wore on my own belt. He tossed it to me.

"As you can see," he went on while I untied the leather cord and peered inside, "the boy's remaining possessions are what one would expect . . . a few florins, a pair of dice, a scrap of cloth with a saint's figure painted upon it, a crumbled bit of tart. But this carving was an unforeseen find and something quite out of the ordinary to be carried about by someone of his station. What would you say it is?"

"I am not sure. Some sort of religious symbol?" I hazarded a guess.

My answer drew an exasperated look from the Master. "Really, Dino, I would have expected better of you. A statue, yes, but one of particular significance, under the circumstances. Can you not see that it is a chess piece? But which one it is, that is the question we must answer."

He motioned me over to the small table in the corner where the lamp gave off a small but steady light. Gesturing me to take a seat, he settled himself upon the bench opposite from me.

"As your knowledge of chess is limited to your participation in Il Moro's ill-conceived match, let me explain to you a few things about the game," he said and set the figure upon the tabletop before me.

Assuming the same lecturing tone he used with us apprentices when explaining a new painting technique, he continued, "Chess has been in existence for many centuries, originating in the Arab lands. This diversion of kings and nobles has been the subject of paintings and poetry and sermons. A game can be played to pass the time pleasantly, or to decide a wager, or even to settle a war. Often, it is but a pleasant mental exercise . . . other times, it becomes a true battle of wits . . . and on other occasions, it may even serve as a metaphor for romance. Most importantly, just as with any activity that has endured for any substantial length of time, its play has gone through numerous transformations over the years."

"Do you mean that the rules change?" I asked, interested despite myself but wondering where this homily was leading.

He nodded. "Indeed, the manner of play has evolved over time, including how many spaces and in which direction the various pieces may move. But those pieces, themselves, have also changed from country to country and age to age. You will recall for our chess match how I substituted the figure of the English bishop for our traditional standard-bearer. But that is not the most dramatic change that has been made to the pieces. Do you know, Dino, that the chess queen was not always a queen . . . and, in fact, was not originally female?"

Not waiting for my reply, he went on with his explanation. "In India and the Arab lands, where the game originated, the piece we know as the queen began life as a vizier. This would be a male figure representing the court's counselor to the king. It was not until the game took a foothold in the Western countries that the vizier metamorphosed into the royal female that is familiar to us. And it is only of late that her role in the game has changed. Once, she was weak, limited in her movements. But the more modern manner of play allows her free rein of the board, so that she is now perhaps the most powerful of all the pieces."

"So this chess piece of Lorenzo's is a queen?" I asked in some confusion.

He reached for the figure and turned it about, so that I could see it appeared the same from either angle.

"Perhaps . . . or perhaps not," he replied. "As I told you, the game had its start in the land of the Arabs, whose religion forbids the realistic depiction of human figures. Thus, their chessmen were but abstracts of the characters for which they stood. I suspect from its material and manner of carving that the chess set from which this particular piece came had its origin in Spain, which is heavily influenced by those who follow the law of Islam. And so the figure may be a representation of the traditional vizier. Or, again, it might be a queen."

My interest growing, I reached for the carved figure on the table before me. Perhaps it was the blurring of the masculine and feminine within the piece that drew me to it, reminding me of my own current role. Or perhaps it simply was the pale aura of the stone and its smooth lines. What-ever it was, my fingers closed over the figure, and I found myself seized by a sudden urge to keep it with me.

Had the ill-fated Lorenzo been attracted to it in much the same way and simply stolen the piece for himself?

Before I could suggest such a notion, Leonardo abruptly stood and began to pace about the small room, his long fingers flicking in that familiar gesture. "And lest we forget the other possibility, we return to our friend the bishop. You see, Dino, the queen is not the only piece in the game to have changed dramatically from its original source. The bishop did not begin life as a clerical figure, or even as our standard-bearer. In fact, he was not human, at all, but a beast . . . an immense tusked creature from the Eastern realms known as an elephant. But, with time, the beast evolved into a man. And, as with the queen, that meant he would be represented in an Arab chess set in only the most vague of forms."

He halted in his pacing and spun to point a long finger at me. "So tell me, Dino, is the chess piece you hold a queen or a bishop?"

I reluctantly set down the figure and shook my head. "I fear I do not know . . . and I confess myself thoroughly confused. What difference can it make if it be queen or bishop?"

"My dear boy, have you not been listening to me?" he shot back in some asperity. "The conte's death was no simple murder, nor was the porter's. In fact, the entire situation is fraught with far too many coincidences that have a basis in this noble game of which we speak."

He strode toward me and began ticking off the points upon his elegant fingers. "First, the conte was murdered in the course of the chess game, while dressed as a bishop, no less. Second, the chess match was held at the behest of the French ambassador, who might be considered the vizier to the king of France. Third is the matter of the Contessa di Malvoral. While she is not a queen, she is a female member of the nobility who, by your own reports, behaved most oddly upon hearing news of the conte's death."

Halting before me, he finished, "And finally, we have our young porter, who you overheard discussing some unknown if nefarious scheme, and who was left to die under most unusual circumstances alongside the murdered conte. On his person at the time of his death was a chess piece, which we can safely guess does not belong to him. Surely he carried it about as a clue, and now we must decipher its meaning to discover the name of the assassin."

It all sounded quite logical, the manner in which the Master laid out his reasoning before me, save for one thing . . . I had no doubt that the departed Lorenzo knew even less than I of playing chess. Certainly, an untutored porter would not choose so symbolic a way to point to his murderer, even had he known the meaning of the pieces.

It was far more likely that this last was indeed a coincidence. Chances were that, in the course of his duties, the boy simply had happened upon some room in which a chessboard was laid out and felt the same compulsion, as had I, to hold this piece in his hand. The only difference was that he had taken the impulse a step further and stolen her away.

Her.

Strange, but some intuition told me that this piece was indeed the queen and not the bishop. Giving in to that fancy, I picked her up again and ran my fingers along her comforting form, willing her to reveal what truth she knew. The events of the past few days rushed through my mind: finding the conte lifeless in the garden; taking part in the chess match; the supper in the great hall, where the duke announced his cousin's death; the conte's burial presided over by the archbishop himself; and, afterward, our finding the unlucky Lorenzo entombed in the crypt of the Sforzas.

As I viewed these memories with a keen inner eye, another would-be explanation regarding the conte's murder abruptly occurred to me. It was a possibility so surprising that it was all I could do not to gasp as if I had been struck a blow. It was all so obvious . . . why had we not seen it before?

I was loath to disagree with the great Leonardo, and yet I
was convinced that I was correct in this matter. The question was, could I convince him, as well? I took a deep breath
and carefully asked, "Is it possible, Master, that the conte
was murdered by mistake?"

He lifted a brow by way of reply. "Anything is possible,
my dear Dino," he said after a moment's consideration. His
tone was sharp, yet I heard a note of interest in his voice.
"Let it never be said that I am not open to all possibilities.
Pray, tell me your theory."

Swiftly, I repeated my thoughts regarding Lorenzo and
the improbability of his being sufficiently versed in the
game to use a chess piece to point to his killer's identity.
When the Master merely nodded at me to continue, I proceeded to explain the notion that had just now struck me.

"You will recall, Master, that you said the bishop is not the
usual piece one would find in a game of chess. This must
mean that few people would have expected to see such a figure upon the playing field the other day. Yet, on the afternoon
of the conte's murder, there were no fewer than four bishops
there . . . five, if you count the archbishop, who we saw seated
in the box with Il Moro's other honored guests."

I paused, wondering if I were about to make a grave mistake yet knowing I must persist. Taking a deep breath, I
went on, "What if the assassin murdered the wrong man?
What if the actual victim was to be the true archbishop? It
could be that the killer simply mistook the duke's cousin for
His Eminence when he happened upon him in the garden,
all because of the bishop's costume, which Signore Luigi so
cleverly re-created."

The Master made no immediate response but stood in silence staring at me, so that I feared he was about to de-
nounce me as a fool, or worse. And then, as I was poised to
retract my words as but a momentary lapse into folly, a slow
smile spread across his face.

"Dino, you put me to shame. While I was busy concoct-
ing elaborate scenarios, you have looked to the obvious. It is

indeed possible that the conte's murder was but a misstep on the part of the assassin, though this would then beg the question as to why anyone would want to kill the archbishop. But I do believe we now have another avenue of investigation before us."

So saying, he strode over to the door and threw it open. "I will require some time in which to contemplate this new state of affairs. You may go now, Dino. We shall speak again in the morning."

I could not help a momentary sense of pique at being so summarily dismissed upon the heels of what might be a momentous revelation. Still, I hurried from the room lest he change his mind and keep me there all the night testing theories. It was likely he would be awake until dawn attempting to solve the mystery, his urgency fueled by the passing of yet another day with no answer for his patron. Il Moro was not known for his patience, and doubtless he would soon be summoning Leonardo for a resolution to the matter of his cousin's death. Should no murderer yet be identified, the duke's patience could well pass its breaking point . . . a frightening prospect, to be sure!

The main workshop was but a few steps away, and I slipped in through the side door so as not to call attention to myself. The other apprentices had finished the day's chores and were gathered as usual beneath the lamplight for a bit of recreation. Constantin gave me a friendly nod, but most of the other boys appeared not to notice my return, or else spared me only the slightest interest before returning to their various amusements.

Only Tommaso gave me his full attention, looking up from his dice game to fix me with a baleful glare that followed my progress to my usual spot by the hearth. I pretended not to notice his angry regard, even while I wondered again what I had done to deserve his ire. Resolving not to let his behavior interfere with my duties to the Master, I seated myself on the rough stone and reached into my pouch for my notebook.

It was only then that I realized I still had hold of the chess queen. Guiltily, I opened my palm and stared down at the pale figure. Since the Master had all but tossed me from the chamber, I suspected he would not want me to return tonight, even if he had already realized that I had inadvertently walked away with one of his clues in our investigation. If he needed it before morning, he knew where to find me; otherwise, I would keep it safely in my possession until the next day.

"And what's that, a present from the great Leonardo?"

I looked up with a start to see Tommaso standing before me, fists planted on his hips while a sneer lent a cruel cast to his blocky features.

I swiftly closed my fingers over the chess queen and favored the stocky youth with a matching look of disdain. "Not that it is your concern, but it belongs to one of the porters I know. He asked me to hold it in safekeeping for him while he is away."

The explanation, while not that far from the truth, did not mollify Tommaso. Leaning in more closely, so that I could smell the onions upon his breath from his earlier supper, he retorted, "I think you're lying. I think the Master gave that to you as a token. Let us see what you are worth to him." Then, before I could react, he grabbed my wrist with one hand and began pulling at my fingers with his other, trying to make me release my hold on the piece.

I leaped to my feet and used my free hand to latch on to the fingers that were prying at mine, attempting to break his grip even as I struggled to keep my balance. "Let me go!" I demanded, aware that I was overmatched but determined not to give in. When he ignored my words, I redoubled my efforts and took it a step further, landing a kick squarely in his shin.

He yelped but continued the assault, and I felt my grip begin to weaken. Once again, our quarrel had attracted the attention of our fellows. Forgetting their conversations and their games of chance, they had rushed as one toward us.

"Hit him, hit him," the chorus began, though whether their encouragement was for my opponent or for me, I did not know. Above their chanting I could hear the voice of

Constantin demanding that we cease our struggle. I would have gladly complied, save that I was not the aggressor, and I feared what would happen should Tommaso manage to seize the chess piece from me.

Abruptly, he released his grip and swung in my direction, landing a blow squarely on my chin. The impact dropped me to my knees. I blinked rapidly, swaying while trying to dismiss the sudden black veil that seemed to have dropped over my eyes. Vaguely, I was aware of the jeers echoing around me, and the fact that the youth had succeeded now in wresting the chess queen from me.

My anger surged. Though still dizzy, I lunged forward and grabbed him at the knees as he was backing away, the pilfered figure held high above him in triumph. My meager weight was still substantial enough to knock him off balance, and he promptly tumbled flat upon his face. My moment of victory, however, lasted but an instant. Swift upon the sound of my attacker thudding gracelessly to the floor was the unmistakable crack of shattering stone as the chess queen flew from his grasp and landed some distance beyond us.

That small sound and my horrified gasp were sufficient to silence the other apprentices. They fell back a respectable distance from us, save for Davide and Paulo, who rushed to drag the groggy Tommaso back to his feet, and Constantin, who hurried to help me up.

"The rest of you, back to your games, or else to your beds," he growled. Then turning to me, he asked, "Are you hurt, Dino? That was quite a blow he dealt you."

"I'm fine," I weakly replied. Indeed, though my head still was ringing, it was a small matter compared to the broken chess queen. How would I explain her damage to the Master? And, if the piece truly had been a clue, what would its loss mean to solving the conte's murder?

By now, the other youths had dispersed and were quietly involved in their earlier activities . . . all save Tommaso. He sat at one of the workbenches, a bloody cloth clutched to his mouth. I was hard-pressed to spare him any sympathy, given that he'd brought his injuries upon himself and, in the process, perhaps destroyed what could have been an object of value.

After once more reassuring Constantin as to my health, I picked up a candle and went in search of the chess queen. Perhaps I would be lucky, and the damage to her was minimal, so that she could at least be pieced back together.

Light held low, I searched the shadowy corner of the workshop where I judged the figure to have landed. Finally, the meager flame reflected upon something gleaming softly white. Relieved, I bent beneath a table to find the top half of the figure which, save for its missing portion, appeared otherwise intact. But where was the rest of it? I continued my search, the candle clutched awkwardly in one hand and broken piece in the other as I crawled along the rough floor.

"Here, Dino, let me help you."

The muffled voice belonged to none other than Tommaso. Still pressing the rag to his mouth, he squatted down beside me and eyed the piece I held. "Is it very badly broken?" he wanted to know.

I shot him a suspicious look, not trusting this change in manner. Expression contrite, he went on, "I didn't mean for it to break, I just wanted to see what you had. Maybe we can fix it if we find all the pieces."

"Maybe," I answered shortly, not yet inclined to forgive.

Shuffling forward on my knees, I moved the candle back and forth in an attempt to make as methodical a search as possible. Tommaso inched alongside me, breathing heavily through swollen lips. Several minutes later, as it seemed our search would prove fruitless, he abruptly called, "Look, there's another bit of it."

Raising the candle in the direction he pointed, I glimpsed a pale glow reflecting back at us from beneath a shelf. I lay at full length upon the floor and reached an arm under a wide section of rough planking that held dozens of long-abandoned molds. My reach was not long enough, however, no matter how I stretched my fingers.

"Let me try. My arms are longer," Tommaso offered. Not waiting for my reply, he lay beside me and thrust his arm beneath the shelf. A moment later, he was seated upright again, that other piece clutched in his hand. I scrambled to a seated position, as well, and lifted the candle so we could better see our find.

He held up to the flame what appeared to be the remaining half of the queen. Seeing it, I sighed in relief. It seemed fortune had intervened, and the figure had broken into but two pieces. Perhaps it could be repaired, after all.

Tommaso, however, was frowning as well as he could with lips swollen to twice their size. He shook his head. "I don't think the piece is damaged, after all," he declared and ran a finger around its edge. "See how smooth and even the break is, and the way there appears to be a lip of sorts? And, look, see how it is hollow? I think it is meant to come apart."

I gave an answering frown and held my portion of the chess piece to the flickering light. Now I could see that indeed it was a clean break, so clean that it could not have occurred at random. "Perhaps you are right," I said and handed it to Tommaso.

He gently eased the lower half into the upper. To my surprise, the pieces joined neatly together again. Grinning, he handed the now-restored queen back to me, and I examined it closely. The seam between the halves was all but invisible, so it appeared the figure had never been broken apart.

"But this is wonderful," I exclaimed, smiling in delight. "I feared the piece might be damaged beyond repair. Thank you."

"You should not have to thank me. Remember that I dropped it in the first place." Tommaso stared glumly at his hands. "I didn't mean any harm. It's just that I thought . . . that is, I wondered why . . . ."

"You wondered why the Master would give me a gift, and not you," I finished for him. "I told you that the figure is not mine, and he did not give it to me. He merely showed it to me to see if I knew what it was. I must return it to him in the morning." I hesitated, and then asked, "But suppose he had given it to me, Tommaso. Why would that matter to you?"

"Because it would mean he favors you now," he burst out, "and before you came, I was the one he liked best."

The declaration—whether or not it was true—hung between us for a few moments as I wondered how best to respond to him. I had spent enough time in the Master's immediate presence that I fancied I had some understanding of his nature. While I had to admit being flattered by his recent attention, I suspected his choice of favorites tended to be based upon who was most useful to him at a given moment, rather than on any more sincere emotion. And, for the time being, it seemed I was proving my usefulness.

Reflexively, I played with the chess figure as I pondered the situation. It was not that I doubted that Leonardo cared for his students; it was simply that I knew a man of his genius viewed life differently from the rest of us mortals. And, unfortunately, it seemed that Tommaso might have interpreted any attention from the Master as having some deeper meaning than it did.

I promptly forgot about Tommaso's wounded feelings, however, as I heard something now moving within the chess piece. Worried, I handed him the candle. "It seems like there is something has broken inside the queen, after all. Hold the light still, and I will take another look at her, now that we know her secret."

So saying, I twisted at either half until I was able to separate both pieces again. As I pulled the queen apart, I saw a metallic flash that was the candle flame reflecting off something, followed by the unmistakable clink of a small object landing on the floor beside me.

Tommaso did not wait for my word but quickly moved the light to one side, searching with me for whatever it was that had fallen from the hollowed chess queen. It took me but a moment to spot it; a tiny brass key. I picked it up and stared curiously at it.

"Odd that we did not see this before, but it must have been wedged tightly within one of the halves," I said in surprise. "I wonder, what can it open?"

"A jewel chest," Tommaso promptly suggested. "My father is a goldsmith, and I have seen many small caskets that are unlocked with a similar key. Whatever it holds must be precious, indeed, for its owner to hide away the key like that."

"Perhaps you are right. Who would think to search a chessboard for the key to a jewel box? But as the chess queen is not mine, what she holds is not my concern, either," I lied, doing my best to hide my sudden enthusiasm.

Carefully, I returned the key to its hiding place within the upper half of the chess queen and fit the two pieces back together again. Tommaso could not know it, but his rash action might have led us closer to the conte's murderer . . . that, or it would send us down an unrelated path. No matter, I would show my find to the Master first thing in the morning and let him judge what to do with the tiny key.

I tucked the chess queen safely into the pouch at my belt and then thrust a conciliatory hand at Tommaso. "Shall we put aside our quarrel now? Truly, I am doing only what Leonardo asks of me. I have no wish to become his favorite over you."

"Very well." He took my hand, though I could sense some remaining reluctance in his manner, and he did not quite meet my gaze. "Our quarrel is forgotten."

"Then let us rejoin the others, before Constantin grows worried and searches us out. Perhaps we have time for a few tosses of the dice before the candles burn down for the night."

Dusting myself off, I scrambled to my feet and started back toward the hearth, where the other apprentices were gathered. Tommaso followed more slowly. For the rest of the evening, he was careful to speak politely to me, but he continued to avoid looking in my direction. I did not press him for more, deciding it was sufficient that I did not have to fear another confrontation with him, at least for this night. I did not yet have an ally in him, I knew, but perhaps he was no longer my enemy.

But later that night, long after we had all retired to our pallets and a chorus of youthful snores wafted through the hall, I could see that he was still awake. He sat cross-legged upon his cot, his stocky figure an even blacker shadow against the surrounding darkness. Once, I fancied I heard a sigh, though whether it was of resignation or anger, I could not tell. I did not know if he stayed awake the night through, however, for I soon fell into a deep sleep of my own.

All I knew was that, when Constantin roused us all at dawn, Tommaso's bed appeared not to have been slept in, and he was nowhere to be found.

10

O, what truths are revealed when we hold a mirror to ourselves.

—Leonardo da Vinci, *The Notebooks of Delfina della Fazia*

Tommaso's disappearance caused a stir among the apprentices that next morning. At first, we assumed he simply had arisen early on some errand, perhaps at the Master's bidding. Upon further investigation, we found that all his personal belongings were missing from the box at the foot of his cot. Constantin, in particular, was distressed, likely fearing he would be blamed for this defection. Thus, he approached me, anxious to know if the youth had given any indication that he planned to leave.

"You were the last to speak at length with him, Dino. Did he fear we would turn him away because of your fight last night?"

"I think not," I told him, even as I instinctively put a hand to the bruise on my chin. A glance at my wrist showed a series of fingertip-sized bruises encircling it, evidence of Tommaso's strong grip. Wincing a little, I added, "We agreed to end our quarrel, but he did remain awake long after the rest of us. Perhaps something else was preying on his thoughts beyond our disagreement."

"This is bad business," Constantin replied with a shake of his head. "I heard rumors from one of the kitchen girls that two of the porters also are missing. It does not bode well, especially when Il Moro has forbidden any to leave the castle grounds."

Knowing what I did of at least one porter's fate, I could not disagree with the sentiment, though I dared not offer more than vague platitudes.

"I am sure Tommaso is fine," I replied. "He may be of hot temperament, but he seems well able to take care of himself. He did mention his father last night. Perhaps he took a sudden longing for home and decided to return there without telling us."

"Perhaps," Constantin agreed, though his features showed clear doubt. His expression promptly transformed into one of alarm when he heard the workshop door open and Leonardo, munching upon a fresh pear, walked in.

The Master, however, seemed far less concerned than did his head apprentice over the loss of one of his charges. "He did not have the fire in him to become a great painter," Leonardo coolly dismissed the absent Tommaso, "or else he would have remained among us. Now, summon the others . . . we begin work today on the final fresco in the dining hall."

While Constantin and the others began gathering the plaster and necessary tools, the Master took me aside. "I have another role for you this day, Dino," he told me, tossing aside the remainder of his pear, "but first, do you still have our chess queen?"

"Of course," I exclaimed, though I had all but forgotten her in the excitement of searching for the missing Tommaso. Eagerly, I pulled the figure from my pouch, adding, "But it appears she has secrets of her own. Last night, we discovered quite by chance that she is made from two pieces, and is hollow within. And, inside her, I found this."

With an effort, I pulled the piece apart again and shook the key from its hiding place into my palm. Leonardo gave an approving nod as he examined it and then motioned me over to a nearby shelf. Rummaging among various boxes, he finally pulled forth a bit of beeswax, which he softened in his hands. That accomplished, he took the key and pressed it into the wax, then carefully pried it free again.

"As you can see, a perfect mold of your key. I will cast a duplicate, which we may then use once we learn what it is meant to unlock. In the meantime, we shall return the original to its hiding place, so that the owner will never know the chess queen's secret was discovered."

Once the halves were restored to a single piece, he tucked both that figure and the wax mold into the pouch at his waist, then returned his attention to me.

"We have much to do today. You will recall our list of those persons most likely to have some connection to the conte's murder." He reached into his tunic, withdrawing the familiar folded sheet of paper from yesterday, with its cross-hatched columns. "I intend to speak with them today, but I would like you present, as well, so that you may give your impressions to me afterward. But it would draw suspicion were you to accompany me dressed as an apprentice. You must be thought to be my manservant. And so, before we set out, we will pay another visit to Signore Luigi."

"AH, Signore Leonardo, do you bring me another of your tunics to mend?" the tailor exclaimed upon seeing us. "I do not know why I put such effort into them, when inevitably each is eventually returned to me with any manner of rips and tears."

"Fear not, my wardrobe is intact this day," the Master replied with a careless shrug. "Unfortunately, the same cannot be said of my apprentice, Dino. I require certain tasks of the boy that call for him to be dressed as if he were page to Il Moro himself. Can you accomplish such a feat by noon of this day?"

We were in Signore Luigi's small shop within the city walls and not far from the castle's main gates. The tailor was one of the few who had been allowed to leave the castle grounds, for Leonardo had successfully pleaded his case with the duke the morning following that particular proclamation. He had accurately pointed out that Luigi's whereabouts could be accounted for throughout the chess match, given that he was in constant attendance upon one or another of the players. Il Moro gave his leave, after remarking that removing the corpulent tailor from the court meant the kitchen's dwindling stores would last a bit longer.

The tailor's workshop was a larger and far neater version of the tent assigned to him during the chess match, though instead of nothing but black and white, the place was awash in color. Here, bolts of rich fabrics—silks, velvets, brocades— were stacked ceiling-high upon rows of shelves. Those rolls formed along one wall a patchwork rainbow of greens, golds, reds, and blues, those brilliant hues interspersed with more sober black and purple and white. A table to one side held boxes of ribbon in flamboyant shades I would be hard-pressed to create in tempera, while another bin held lace and linen, and another, various bits of fur meant for cuffs and collars.

Luigi pursed his fleshy lips and scrutinized me as if I were something he had found upon the sole of his shoe. I kept my own gaze lowered, praying he would declare the request impossible. The risk of discovery would be too great were he to clothe me as the Master wished.

Unfortunately for me, the tailor's pride won out over his disdain for me.

"But of course, Signore Leonardo," he finally said with a tight smile. "With florins enough, anything may be done . . . even transforming this shabby apprentice into a respectable page. Leave him alone with me for an hour or two, and I can assure you that you shall be pleased with the result."

"I will expect you back at my quarters once you are finished here," Leonardo told me, and then spent a moment discussing with Luigi how I should be clothed, and how much he was willing to pay for the same. I heard little of that conversation, however, concerned only with my immediate future.

For I was about to be turned over to the tailor's mercies, perhaps made to undress before him. The prospect put me in a state very close to panic. I had managed to avoid all but minimal disrobing while being costumed during the chess match, but I doubted my excuses for not removing my tunic would hold a second time. Yet I knew I could not go against the Master's wishes in this matter.

A few moments later, he departed, leaving me alone with the tailor. Once again, absent the Master's presence, Luigi's expression of oily benevolence vanished and was replaced by a sour look. "You are fortunate, boy, to have such a generous patron. As you doubtless heard, I have been instructed to dress you in a manner that befits mingling with the nobles. I do hope Signore Leonardo is getting his money's worth from you."

The suggestion, delivered with a lewd wink, would have been offensive enough had he known my true gender. But given my male role, it was far more insulting, both to the Master and me. Carefully controlling my rage, I drew myself up to my full height and looked the tailor squarely in the eyes.

"Your insinuation is without merit," I replied in a cold voice. "Master Leonardo's conduct toward me is no different from the behavior of any conscientious master toward an apprentice. He provides the training, and he expects only that I work hard to learn my trade. Any kindness he shows is strictly out of charity, and he expects no repayment of any sort. And so, signore, I will have your apology on behalf of us both for your words."

"Y-You will have m-my apology?" the tailor stuttered in outrage, his chins quivering as he shoved his face into mine and waited for me to cower or otherwise retract my bold speech. When I silently stood my ground, he finally took a step back and allowed himself a small bark of a laugh.

"Very well, young apprentice," he retorted with a sniff, "since you have so eloquently stated your denial of my charge, I shall concede that I was mistaken and offer you and Signore

Leonardo my apologies. Now, let us be done with our business together, so that I never have to set eyes upon you again."

So saying, Luigi returned to his worktable and reached into a small chest sitting atop it, pulling forth a length of cord that was knotted at regular intervals along its length. Holding it in one hand, he slid his other beefy thumb and forefinger along the cord to smooth any twists. Then, with a humorless smile, he advanced upon me again.

"Come, boy, I must take your measure so I can dress you to Leonardo's satisfaction."

Knowing what was to come, I stumbled back out of reach. "Surely that won't be necessary," I protested, instinctively crossing my arms across my upper body in a protective manner. "I'm certain that I can find something among these fine garments that will be a satisfactory fit."

"Pah." He shook his head, chins wobbling in unison. "Do you think I have so little pride in my craft that I would allow you to leave here wearing any misfitting tunic you choose? Your Master has instructed me to dress you properly, and I shall do no less. Now, come with me."

I had no choice but to comply as he clamped a beefy paw about my wrist and dragged me back toward the center of the room. I gritted my teeth and let him stretch the cord across the narrow breadth of my back, and then from each shoulder to my wrist. From there, I stiffly held my ground while he awkwardly lowered his bulk into a kneeling position long enough to measure my legs from hip to ankle, and then groaned and puffed his way back to his feet again.

Between each stretching of that knotted cord, he paused to scratch a note on the paper sitting atop his workbench. As he did so, I waited in silent terror lest he finally realize from his poking and prodding that it was a maid and not a youth whose measure he was taking. But no frown of suspicion supplanted his expression of disdain, and the frantic pounding of my heart slowed to a more moderate beat. Indeed, I had begun to breathe quite easily when the tailor looked up from what I had hoped was his last scribbling to proclaim, "I have one final measurement to take. Lift your arms, boy, so I can measure about your chest."

For an instant, I considered bolting from the shop, never to return, but I knew Luigi would gleefully inform the Master of my transgression. Thus, I gingerly lifted my arms while attempting unobtrusively to slump so that my chest appeared less prominent. The tailor would have none of that, however, but jerked me upright like a recalcitrant colt and whipped his cord about my upper chest, pulling it tightly.

"What's this?"

Now came the suspicious frown, and he let the cord slide away as he poked a pudgy finger into my padded breastbone. "Have you something wrapped around your ribs, boy?"

"I-It's nothing," I stuttered as I dredged up the excuse I had concocted the first night I donned my disguise. "You see, my brothers always made fun of me because of my sunken chest, so I took to winding a bit of cloth about myself to look a bit more hearty. Please, signore, it is but a bit of vanity. You need not mention it to anyone else."

"Indeed."

His frown deepened, but he made no further comment as he turned to his worktable to note the final measurement. I lowered my arms, meanwhile, and resumed my slightly hunched posture. *Hurry and fit me with my clothes,* I silently demanded of him, relieved that the measuring was finally over, and that I apparently had passed this last obstacle with only a slight raising of doubt, now quashed. Once Luigi had settled on the appropriate style and size garb for me, I would insist upon taking my new clothes back to my quarters with me. There, I could don them in private and avoid any further handling by the tailor. In the meantime, all that remained was continuing to be patient for the remainder of this ordeal.

And then, quite without warning, the tailor turned and swung one pudgy arm like a pendulum so that his fist landed a blow squarely in my nether region.

"Ouch," I cried with equal parts surprise and pain, wondering what I had done to deserve such an ignominious assault. A heartbeat later, as a look of smug satisfaction flashed across his fleshy features, I realized my error. Mimicking a reaction I had seen numerous times from one or another of my brothers when they scuffled as children, I swiftly clutched myself between my thighs and dropped to my knees, moaning in feigned agony.

My attempt at playacting had come a few seconds too late. Even as I continued my calflike moans, Luigi seized me by the scruff of the neck and dragged me to my feet.

"Cease your pretense, boy . . . or should I call you girl?" he roared and gave me a shake.

"I-I don't know what you mean," I choked out. "My name is Dino, and I—"

"Silence! Do not insult my intelligence any further," he cut me short. "I have dressed women enough to know one when I see one, no matter if she is garbed as a male." He paused, puffing in anger, and then went on, "Is this a joke your master thinks to play upon me, to make a fool of Luigi? We shall see if Il Moro thinks it amusing."

"No, no, signore . . . please!" I gasped out, catching hold of his tunic sleeve when he turned as if to leave. "Leonardo knows nothing of this, I swear to you. And it is no joke."

He hesitated before turning back to face me, his fleshy arms crossed over his belly. "Pray, go on," he said coldly, his brows twisted down almost to his bulbous nose.

I took a deep breath, knowing I had but one opportunity to placate the man and bring him to my side; otherwise, my masquerade would soon be at an end.

"It is true . . . I am a female," I began in a halting tone. "My true name is Delfina della Fazia, and I am from a town not far from Milan. I hope one day to be a great painter . . . but without serving beneath an even greater master, I would not be able to learn what I must know."

I paused, recalling that Luigi had apprentices of his own, so that he surely understood role of both student and master. "You are a man of the world, Signore Luigi. You know that few masters would ever take on a female as an apprentice . . . surely none in a court such as this. But the opportunity to study with Leonardo was one that I could not easily let pass by. I had no choice but to pretend to be a boy so that he would allow me into his workshop."

"And that is the only reason you took on this disguise?" Luigi asked, raising one brow. "You are not one of those odd females who would prefer to be a man, and takes on male trappings to the point of even seeking out a wife?"

"Certainly not!" I felt a blush wash over my cheeks at the thought of assuming so unnatural a role . . . indeed, I had never heard of such a thing until this moment. Stoutly, I went on, "I am quite content with my gender, signore. My sole reason for this disguise is to further my art. Were I able to study as a woman, I would certainly prefer that to this masquerade."

"So you are certain our Signore Leonardo has no knowledge of your deception, then?" the tailor persisted.

I nodded vigorously. "Quite certain. Indeed, if he were to find out, I am sure he would be the first to call for my dismissal. And so I beg of you, signore, please do not reveal my secret to anyone!"

I stood before him, hands clasped in the manner of a supplicant, wondering what else I might do to convince him of my sincerity. Had our previous encounters been of a more pleasant nature, I would have held out greater hope for gaining an ally. As it was, I knew his opinion of me already was less than positive. This new revelation could well tip the scale against me.

Luigi gave a nod, as if affirming whatever decision he had made. Coolly, he said, "You realize what you have done could have grave consequences . . . not just for yourself, but for your beloved master. But whether or not this deception is revealed is up to me. I could be outraged by your boldness, meaning I must take some action against you for the good of all concerned. Or I could be amused at your initiative, which means I would keep your secret safe, at least, for the time being."

He paused again, tapping pursed lips with one fleshy

finger. Finally, he went on, "I believe I shall choose to be amused."

"Thank you . . . thank you, signore," I gasped out, grasping his pudgy hands in mine. "I promise, I shall never act in a manner that will cause you to regret your decision."

"I truly doubt that," he replied, pulling his hands from my grasp. "But now that this matter is settled, let us proceed with dressing you as your master wishes. First, however, you must remove those wrappings you wear about your chest. Go now. You may use that alcove to preserve your modesty."

He pointed to a curtain in the corner. Uncertain what would happen next, I did as instructed, and a few moments later had unwound the cloth that bound my breasts. Feeling oddly naked, though I still retained my tunic, I peeked out past the curtain to see what Signore Luigi was doing.

The tailor was not tarrying over his work, but moved more swiftly than one would guess for a man of his size as he pulled down jewel-toned bolts of cloth and piled them upon his worktable. Once he'd collected a dozen or so, I saw him sort through them, unraveling a portion of the velvet or silk for a closer look. Most of fabric he dismissed with a snort and put to one side, though three or four bolts seemed to meet with his approval. Sensing my regard, he gestured me toward him.

"Come here, er, boy . . . let us see which colors favor you."

One at a time, he held the fabric up to me, muttering to himself. For myself, I was hard-pressed not to gasp in pleasure with each new swath he tossed across my shoulder, for the material was far richer than any I'd ever before worn. Finally, Luigi appeared satisfied.

"I believe a deep blue and gold suit you best," he decreed with a nod. "Now, since your master is in a hurry, let us see what we might have already made that can be tailored to you. But first, we must do something about your, er, chest."

So saying, he trotted over to a wooden rod upon which hung several shirts of fine, bleached linen. He pulled the smallest of them from its hook and then rummaged about on the shelf beside it, pulling forth an odd article of clothing I did not recognize. "This should serve," he declared, returning to where I stood.

Handing me the shirt, he held up the second garment to me. It appeared to be a corset by the way it laced, save that the upper portion of it appeared padded across the front. He smirked at my look of confusion.

"This is a garment of my own design for gentlemen who, as you put it, are not so hearty. The horsehair padding gives them a more substantial chest and makes their clothing hang with greater grace. But for you"—he grinned more broadly as he flipped the corset upside down, so that the padding was at the bottom now—"we shall let it act in an opposite fashion. Try it on. I believe you shall find it far more comfortable than that crude cloth you are wearing."

Uncertainly, I returned to my curtained alcove and laced myself into the garment. "Come, come," I heard Luigi calling to me as I was tying off the strings, so I swiftly pulled on the new shirt over it and pushed aside the curtain.

He nodded and gestured me over to the far wall. "Indeed, this is a vast improvement," he said and pulled aside a cloth that covered a large glass mirror.

I stared in no little shock at my reflection. The corset flattened my breasts far more effectively than the length of cloth, while the padding below smoothed the line of my body. Covered by the softly draping shirt, my figure appeared slightly stocky but unmistakably boyish.

"Signore Luigi, you are a genius," I said in awe as I admired my new appearance.

He flicked his hands dismissively, though I could see he was pleased by my reaction. "It is but a trick that any competent tailor could perform. One must simply understand the lines of the body and how fabric clings and flows. Now, let us see what we can do about a tunic and new trunk hose."

More quickly than I could have imagined, he constructed a tunic from one of the partially made garments hanging on another rack, scissors and needle flying as he basted on fabric from the bolts he had earlier selected. When the design was to his satisfaction, he carefully removed it from me.

"My apprentices will finish the sewing," he explained. "While they are occupied, we shall put together the rest of your ensemble."

While I waited for the promised outfit to be completed, I amused myself by wandering about the tailor's shop. With our newfound understanding between us, Luigi allowed himself to take an interest now in my company, his sour manner sweetening slightly as he watched me exclaim over every fabric treasure that caught my eye. But what proved to me that his heart was not as curdled as he made it out to be was the lark sitting in a large woven cage hanging from his shop ceiling.

"Ah, yes, that is one of your master's finds," he reluctantly explained when I heard the bird's sweet song and wondered how he'd come to find it. "You must know by now his habit of buying creatures from the marketplace only to free them. He purchased this lark, intending to do the same, only to discover that it had a broken wing and could not fly."

"Poor thing," I murmured in sympathy, peering into its cage. The bird trilled a few more soft notes, making me smile. "But how did it come to stay in your shop?"

"He stopped by here on the way back from the marketplace to pick up one of his tunics and asked for my assistance. He had an idea for a small splint that might be stitched to its feathers to assist the bone in mending."

The tailor paused and gave me a wry look. "Of course, only Leonardo could have guessed what few others know, that I share his affection for dumb creatures. In fact, I would not be boasting to say I have some small talent for healing them when they are wounded. Unfortunately, in this case the wing healed well enough to restore the bird to health but not so completely that she was able to fly as she should. Sending her back to the wild would have meant a swift death, so I agreed to keep her here in my shop."

"How very good of you," I warmly approved, drawing a
sour look from him in return.

He wagged a finger at me. "I have agreed to keep your secret," he reminded me. "Now you shall keep mine. Let it not
be said that Luigi the tailor is softhearted, or my customers
will deluge me with excuses as to why they cannot pay."

We turned to other subjects, and time passed quickly. By
the promised hour, I was standing before the mirror again,
wearing my new page's outfit. My tunic was blue silk trimmed
with gold velvet over matching parti-colored trunk hose. My
new white linen shirt puffed artfully through the slashed
sleeves tied on with contrasting red laces that matched the
new red shoes and soft cap that I wore. The effect was under-
stated enough for someone of my station, yet rich enough so
that I would draw no undue comment when I accompanied
the Master as he questioned the nobles on his list. Certainly, it
was the most elegant apparel I had ever worn, for all that it
was male garb!

"I believe Signore Leonardo will be well pleased," Luigi
proclaimed in smug satisfaction as he made a final adjust-
ment to one sleeve. "But I pray you do refrain from wearing
my creation while you are mixing plaster or attending to
some other such messy endeavor."

"I shall take the greatest care of my new clothing," I assured him, grabbing up the sack in which he'd put my other
shabby garb. Then, glancing about to make sure I would
not be heard by one of his apprentices, I added, "And I am
in your debt for your silence in the matter that we discussed."

"As I said, I have chosen to be amused for, as there is little
mirth to be had in Il Moro's court, I welcome the change.
But should you be found out, I shall plead ignorance of the
situation. Now, return to your master . . . and you may carry
the bill for my services with you."

The clock tower was ringing out the noon hour when I
arrived back at Leonardo's private workshop. My fellow

apprentices had long since taken their morning meal, and my stomach rumbled to remind me that I had not. Tightening my belt in response, I sighed and knocked on Leonardo's door. "Enter," I heard him call, and I stepped inside.

No sign remained of the previous night's surgery, for the bloody blankets and basin were gone, the table appearing to have been scrubbed down with ash. In fact, the chamber was deserted, but this time the door leading to what I'd guessed was his workshop lay open. A rush of excitement swept me as I realized I might now have the chance to enter into that hitherto secret sanctum. But as I started eagerly toward it, Leonardo, dressed in his usual stained work clothes, appeared in the entry and closed the door behind him.

"Ah, very fine," he proclaimed as he took in my new garb, motioning me to turn about so that he could look from all sides. "I daresay Signore Luigi will make me pay dearly for this, though of course the duke shall foot the bill in the end."

Grinning slyly at that last, he made his way to the table and plucked two plump pears from the wooden bowl upon it. Tossing one to me, he gestured me to sit there, saying, "I fear I have once again made you miss your meal, but perhaps this will hold you until we return. Give me but a moment, my boy, and let me don something more presentable for our morning's visit to the archbishop."

While I gratefully crunched into the pear's juicy flesh, he went to the wooden chest at his bedside and threw it open. Carelessly, he examined and then tossed aside one after another tunic before settling upon one of sober black trimmed in brown. That decided, he pulled off his outer garment; then, with a rueful sniff at the shirt beneath, he added, "And perhaps a change of linen would not be amiss."

He stripped off the shirt, as well, and started searching through the box for a replacement. Taken aback, I quickly averted my gaze, but I was not swift enough to avoid a glimpse of his bare torso. The glance was sufficient to tell that his curious diet served him well, for his upper body appeared lean yet muscular. Indeed, partially clothed, he resembled the handsome young nudes he sketched, those depictions serving as part of our anatomy lessons in the workshop.

The sight was not at all displeasing.

Blushing furiously at my wayward thoughts, I applied myself to finishing off my pear and praying he would not feel the need to doff his brown trunk hose for a different set. Fortunately, he contented himself with the new shirt and tunic, which he quickly pulled on.

"Much better, do you not agree, Dino?" he asked, looking quite elegant now as he tied a matching brown belt around his tunic.

I mumbled an agreement through my final mouthful of fruit, hoping that my blush had subsided sufficiently not to draw undue notice. But the Master was not looking at me, for he was busy finishing off his own pear while he rummaged about in the pouch he'd left upon the table. He nodded as he pulled forth and then replaced the chess queen and the list of names before tying the pouch to his belt. Then he reached into another basket for two scraps of paper and two pieces of red chalk.

"There is one final thing we must do," he said, handing me one page and a bit of chalk. "I need you to sketch from memory the face of the second porter you encountered the other night . . . the one who is yet missing. For myself, I shall draw the unfortunate Lorenzo."

Though curious, I did not question why he made the request but applied myself to the task. It was not difficult, as the image of the red-haired young man with his bony face and full lips was still etched upon my mind. After a few tentative strokes, I confidently completed my sketch, satisfied I had captured the boy's youthful if worn visage and the cruel cast that overlaid his features.

"Well done," the Master said in approval, peering over my shoulder at my finished work. "Should I see him now, I could easily identify him from your drawing. Tell me," he added, showing me his own sketch, "does this sufficiently represent the other young man? I fear he was rather bloodied and bruised the one time I saw him."

I looked at the Master's work and shook my head in amazement, humbled as always at his skill. The dead Lorenzo's features he had captured flawlessly, but the drawing was far more than a simple depiction of his face. Something in the way he had sketched the boy's eyes conveyed a hint of silent desperation that overlaid his expression of belligerent youthfulness. Indeed, the drawing abruptly made me mourn the young porter's death in a way that even seeing him fatally injured the previous night had not.

"It is wonderful," I said sincerely. "But what shall we do with these sketches?"

"Quite simple, my boy. We shall show them to the persons we question in the matter of the conte's murder and see their reactions."

He carefully folded both drawings so that the chalk would not smudge and tucked them into his tunic. Then, tossing aside the remains of his pear, he gestured me to follow him. "The archbishop is expecting us, Dino, so let us not tarry."

11

The bee may be likened to deceit, for it has honey in its mouth and poison behind.

—Leonardo da Vinci, *Manuscript I*

We were fortunate in the fact that the archbishop—who was also the cardinal of Milan—was staying in Castle Sforza as Ludovico's guest. Otherwise, we would have had to travel to find him for, despite his appellation, he did not live in Milan. He had a sumptuous palace in Rome, as well as several smaller villas throughout the region, and he journeyed among them on a regular basis while seeing to Church affairs. This particular visit to the castle had been a courtesy because of the French ambassador's presence this past fortnight. Usually while in the region, he stayed in his own villa outside the city gates.

But the archbishop would soon be returning to Rome . . . that was, should he survive his stay in Milan. "For your theory is not without merit, Dino," the Master told me as we made our way to the elegant rooms where the archbishop was quartered. "If His Eminence was indeed the intended victim, then it is possible the assassin will make another attempt upon his life. At the very least, we must warn him of the danger."

But we soon saw that an assassin would be hard-pressed

to get close to the archbishop. Access to the wing of the castle in which he was housed was guarded by half a dozen armed men—papal guards, we later learned—who would not let us pass until the archbishop's secretary was summoned and approved our entry. Additionally, a staff of clerics roamed the connecting chambers and would have halted anyone not in their company.

Even Il Moro did not have as elaborate a system of protection within his own castle, I thought in surprise.

"Yes, indeed, His Eminence does have enemies," our tonsured guide replied in answer to the Master's query, while I walked behind them at a respectful distance. "You must understand that he holds a most powerful position within the Church. As both archbishop and then cardinal for more than twenty years, he has had the ear of no fewer than four popes; indeed, he could well be next in line for the papacy himself. But, while he is beloved by most, there are always some who are threatened by a man of God."

"And has an attempt been made recently upon his life?" Leonardo casually asked.

The cleric gave him a bland look. "I am sorry, signore, but I cannot discuss such matters with you."

Whether or not the Master would have persisted in his usual diplomatic manner, I did not find out, for we had halted before a set of ornate double doors that stretched almost to the ceiling. Our guide knocked, his knotted knuckles eliciting but a faint sound upon the carved and gilded wood; still, a voice from within answered, bidding him to enter. Gesturing us to remain where we were, the priest slipped silently through the entry and shut the heavy doors behind him.

We waited in patient silence for what seemed several minutes, before the doors opened again. "The archbishop will spare you a few minutes as a favor to his host, the duke," the cleric said and motioned him inside.

Of course, he made no mention of my presence. Still, I followed the master at a respectful distance, head slightly bowed as befitted a servant while I tried unobtrusively as possible to make note of my surroundings.

The room itself was designed for ostentation if not for comfort. Half a dozen tall, carved chairs of some gleaming dark wood unrelieved by any padding or cushion lined the walls on either side of us. Here, instead of the more modern frescoes of the dining hall, yards of tapestries that appeared far older than the castle hung from heavy rings and rods, draping the rough-hewn walls and muffling both sound and dampness. The stone tiles beneath our feet were uneven and unforgiving, and I could imagine how cold they would be upon a winter's day, unrelieved by a thick bed of rushes as they would have had in times past.

But the centerpiece of the room was an immense table with legs twice as thick as mine and with carvings as elaborate as those of the outer doors. Beneath lowered lashes I managed a good look at the old man seated on a thronelike chair behind it.

Close up, the archbishop of Milan was spare, his wrinkled face pale beneath the cardinal's red cap that he wore upon his balding head. Today, he was dressed in a white tunic trimmed in lace, over which he wore a hooded red cloak buttoned across his breast. Visible beneath that cloak hung a hand-sized gold cross upon a heavy chain. The cross was his only ornament, other than the gold ring upon his finger. The simple garb was a startling contrast to the elaborate vestments he had worn at the chess match and while presiding over the conte's funeral.

"Your Eminence, this is Leonardo the Florentine, currently employed as master engineer by the duke of Milan," the priest announced, and then stepped discreetly to one side, giving the appearance of privacy while remaining within earshot.

The archbishop did not gesture us to a chair. He did, however nod, indicating that Leonardo could approach, and he offered his be-ringed hand across the table for the traditional kiss. I held my breath, knowing the Master's disregard for religious convention and worrying what he might do. To my relief, however, he gracefully performed the customary gesture and waited for the archbishop to speak.

"So you are the great Leonardo," His Eminence pronounced in a firm if faint voice, so that I wondered at the state of his health. "Your talent is not unknown outside of Milan. As far away as Rome, word has spread of an artist of no little genius, for all that he is deemed a heretic. But I have seen your work, Leonardo, and I cannot believe one who paints such beautiful renditions of our Holy Mother cannot know God's word."

"I paint sinners as well as saints, Your Eminence," he mildly replied. "But I will concede that I do feel divine inspiration at times as I work."

"Then perhaps there is hope for you yet," the archbishop answered with a small smile. "So tell me, my son, what is the urgent matter you wish to discuss with me?"

Briefly, Leonardo described to him the circumstances of the conte's murder, and young Lorenzo's later mysterious death. "As the duke has charged me with discovering who is responsible for this crime," he went on, "I have been carefully studying the events of the past few days in hopes of solving that mystery. In the process, the possibility has arisen that it was you, Your Eminence, and not the conte, who was to have been the assassin's target. And so I am here to warn you of the potential danger you may face while here at the castle."

"My son, I have avoided murder more times than I can count," the archbishop replied in a calm voice. "No man reaches my station in the Church without gaining enemies . . . not if he does his job properly. But you can see that I am well-guarded, so that only the most determined of assassins might reach me. However, it distresses me greatly that another man might have died in my place. Do you have any proof of this claim?"

Leonardo shook his head. "As I said, it is but one possibility we are investigating." He paused and reached into his tunic, pulling forth the two drawings. Unfolding them, he laid them on the table. "Would you do me the kindness, Your Eminence, of looking at these sketches?"

The cleric squinted at them for a moment. "Very fine work, indeed," he said, then smiled a bit as he picked up the one of Renaldo. "But I must say I prefer this drawing, especially the way you have so expertly rendered the subject's expression of inner struggle. The young man appears to be a sinner quite in need of saving."

This unexpected praise for my small work made me blush in pleasure, the more so because the archbishop assumed that Leonardo himself had drawn it. As for the Master, I saw a flash of pique cross his handsome features. I had heard stories how once, while he was an apprentice, his own master had been outshone by the young Leonardo's brilliance with the brush and had vowed never to paint again. I wondered if he were recalling that incident, as well.

To my surprise, however, he told the cleric, "As it happens, Eminence, that particular sketch was drawn by my page. I agree that young Dino has some talent as an artist . . . but on to more important matters. Both these young men you see here are employed in the castle, and may have some connection to the Conte di Ferrara's murder. Do you recall seeing either of them during your stay here?"

The archbishop took another look and shook his head. "They are not familiar to me."

"And what of this?" the Master asked, plucking the chess queen from his pouch and setting it beside the drawings.

The archbishop nodded as he picked up the piece with an arthritic hand. "So you play chess as well, Leonardo? I fear I find it difficult these days to discover a worthy opponent, as those who are willing to play me lack either the skill or else the resolve to defeat me. Perhaps you are up to the challenge?"

"I would be honored to sit across from you," the Master replied with a slight bow. "But can you tell me, have you seen this particular piece before?"

"It is a queen, is it not?" The archbishop turned the figure in his hand, his gaze appreciative. "I would guess from the manner of carving that the set came from Arabia, perhaps, or else Spain. It is quite lovely in its simplicity . . . but, no, I do not recognize it."

He handed the chess queen back to Leonardo, who stowed away both it and the two drawings, and then bowed again. "I thank you for your time, Eminence. I will trouble you no further, save to ask that you do not leave your quarters unattended until we discover who is responsible for murdering the duke's cousin."

"I shall consider your advice, Leonardo . . . and I shall pray for a quick resolution to this sad business," the archbishop replied and held out his hand once more.

A moment later, his secretary was briskly escorting us back down the corridor, his expression distressed. "I assure you, my chess playing ability is quite adequate," he insisted. "If I lose to him on a regular basis, it is not for a lack of skill. It is simply God's will that His Eminence prevail."

"Indeed," Leonardo dryly replied, though I saw the flicker of amusement in his eyes. "But do assure the archbishop that I would be glad to accept his challenge at his convenience."

We left the priest still muttering and passed through the same connecting chambers and gauntlet of guards, finding ourselves back in the courtyard once more. The Master halted there and reached into his tunic for his list.

"We have done our duty and warned the archbishop of the possible danger he faces. It is unfortunate that he had no useful information as to likely suspects in the conte's assassination." He paused and added with a wry smile, "Unless you noticed something, Dino, that I overlooked since, according to His Eminence, you are an expert at recognizing inner struggle."

Blushing again, I thought for a moment and shook my head. "The archbishop seemed to me to be an honest and holy man. I am certain that he knows of no plot against him nor of any reason that someone would have murdered the duke's cousin."

"Then we must proceed with the next name on our list. The Contessa di Malvoral. Though she and her husband normally live in a villa outside of the city, as a member of the duke's family she does retain her own quarters here in the castle."

Something in my expression must have reflected my distress, for he gave me a keen look. "Ah, yes, she is the woman whom you most suspect of some unseemly mischief or another," he went on. "I pray you, put aside any fearful thoughts of her. We cannot allow our own emotions to sway us in the face of whatever evidence we uncover."

"I am not frightened of her, Master," I stoutly defended myself. "It's just that I am always swept by an uneasy sensation in her presence. Besides, what if she recognizes me from when I was costumed as the white bishop?"

He gave a dismissive flick of his fingers. "Do not let that concern you. People of her sort never pay heed to those below their own rank. And, even should she manage a good look at you, she likely could not tell you from any other servant in the castle. More to the point, she would never associate you with any of the courtiers who took part in the game."

I gave a doubtful nod. Despite his blithe assessment of the nobility, in general, I sensed the contessa was different from the rest. She would know the name and face of every servant around her, I felt certain. Moreover, I was sure that she could recall in minute detail her encounter with anyone not of her immediate circle . . . particularly, a noble who was not truly a noble and who was disguised as a bishop.

Thus, it was with some trepidation that I followed him to another wing where the duke's family were housed. As with the courtyard beyond, these chambers bustled with the restless activity of those forced by circumstances to remain somewhere well past their prescribed time. Voices were louder than usual, and manners appeared forced. And, as always, it was the servants who suffered the most, for they were the ones bearing the brunt of their masters' and mistresses' foul tempers.

We were provided with an unsettling demonstration of that reality as we approached the contessa's quarters. A servant girl little older than I abruptly fled through the door upon which we were poised to knock. Tears streamed from her swollen eyes, and her cap was knocked askew. The cause of her distress was apparent, for a red mark in the shape of a slim hand shone brightly against one plump, pale cheek.

The girl vanished down the hallway before we could offer assistance or even a word of comfort. I saw Leonardo's expression darken, and despite my own outrage I felt a momentary swell of relief. Here was proof before our eyes of the contessa's cruel nature. Surely, armed with this knowledge, the Master would be more willing to entertain the notion of the woman's possible guilt in the matter of the conte's murder.

Wordlessly, he knocked upon the door, and a sharp voice bade him enter. Taking a deep breath, I followed him into the chamber with the same sense of unease as I had felt when I followed him into the tomb the previous day.

The windowless room we entered was furnished somewhat less severely than the archbishop's outer chamber. Here, the carved wooden chairs were smaller and softened with gold brocade cushions, and they flanked but one side of the room. Opposite them lay a low table spilling with bowls of flowers and fruits . . . and, I saw in no little excitement, a chessboard, though its pieces were smaller and more ornate than the set from which our chess queen had come. Beside that table sat a broad, cushioned bench encircled by head-high gold curtains, where the room's occupant might find a moment's repose during the day.

The tapestries on these walls were brighter and of gayer subject matter than those allotted to the archbishop's quarters, and were trimmed in gold cording and tassels. Most of the far wall consisted of an immense stone fireplace, its yawning black mouth large enough that I could easily stand within, and likely a welcome addition during the winter months. A narrow door lay to one side of its hearth . . . leading, I presumed, to the sleeping chamber.

We waited expectantly for the contessa to make her appearance through that entry; thus, we were both taken by surprise when the curtains surrounding the bench fluttered, and a woman's pale, bare foot slid from beneath the tangle of drapery. The foot was followed by an equally naked leg, slim and white against the golden fabric. And then the curtains parted, revealing the Contessa di Malvoral, herself.

She was dressed still for slumber, wearing only a filmy white garment that seemed to cling to every curve of her womanly form, so that I blushed on her behalf. Her golden hair, shaved well back from her forehead, was uncovered and streamed in pale ribbons down her back, as if she were an unmarried girl. Yet despite this, she looked older, more faded than I recalled her, and I wondered if she had employed cosmetics or some other artifice upon her features to look younger.

The one thing unchanged about her appearance, however, were her eyes. A shade of blue so pale they could be ice, they gleamed with intelligence, and with more than a hint of malice. Nothing in them reflected any discomfiture at being seen in such a state of undress by an unknown man. Indeed, the way her pink tongue flicked at her full lips, it seemed that she actually relished the situation, I surmised in no little dismay.

Then she smiled, her pale gaze locked upon the Master. "This is an honor, the great Leonardo here in my chamber," she said, her cool voice seeming to wrap itself about us like the sleek serpent from the Sforza coat of arms. "Ludovico warned me that you might be paying a call. You must forgive such an informal greeting. I fear my servant is not here at the moment to properly announce you."

"Yes, we saw her leave," he replied in an equally chill manner. "It seems that she had suffered an injury."

The contessa assumed a look of distress, and her lips quivered. "It was quite an unpleasant incident, to be sure. She and my dressmaker got into a disagreement over one of my gowns, and poor Anna received the worst of it. I will, of course, be dismissing the dressmaker."

Despite the implication of innocence, I suspected that her tale of the dueling maidservants was a fabrication, and that the luckless Anna had been victim of no one save the contessa. Whether or not Leonardo believed her version of the incident, I could not tell from his expression. But no more was said regarding the matter, for she abruptly seated herself on the bench once more. "Tell me, what business does Ludovico's master engineer have with me?"

"I am here at the behest of the duke. He is determined to learn who murdered his cousin, and he has charged me with uncovering what information I can regarding the matter."

The contessa lifted a pale, narrow brow. "As you must know, Orlando was my cousin, as well. I, too, wish to see his assassin caught, but I fear I cannot guess who he may be."

"He . . . or she," the Master corrected her. "Perhaps, then, you can tell me a bit about the conte. Did he have any enemies? Were his actions secretive of late?"

"Every man has enemies. You should know that, my dear Leonardo." Then she shrugged, the motion sending her garment sliding perilously lower down her shoulders. "As for being secretive, Orlando was a remarkably simple man . . . rather stupid, in fact. He knew nothing of secrets, only how to smile and look pretty. I do not understand why Ludovico thought to make him his ambassador."

"Perhaps that is the very reason," the Master dryly replied. "I understand that your husband, the Conte di Malvoral, was to have taken that duty but was supplanted by Orlando. Did he resent losing this post, perhaps to the point that he would have risked anything regain it?"

The contessa's tinkling laugh held just the slightest note of sharpness. "Are you suggesting that my husband killed Orlando so that he could have the ambassadorship? You may rest assured that he had no desire to go to France. He would rather remain at his villa, or here at Ludovico's court . . . any place where he can keep an eye on me."

She stood again and gracefully padded to the table, reaching for a small cluster of grapes. "That is not to say that my husband's suspicions are not well-founded. I will confess I am not the faithful wife I should be, but it is a tedious fate being wed to a man of his advanced age. I prefer my men younger and more attractive. I am sure you can understand that," she added with a small smile, and took a languid bite of the dark red fruit.

At the sight of the wine-colored juice staining her pale lips, I felt an uncomfortable sensation low in my belly. I suspected that the contessa devoured men much as she did grapes . . . carelessly, and in great number. I only prayed that the Master was cleverer than most of his sex in such matters and would not fall prey to her obvious wiles.

With a small sound of satisfaction, she finished off the rest of the cluster and then advanced upon the Master, circling him. Now, she reminded me less of a serpent and more of a lioness challenging her mate. "Perhaps you would like to paint my portrait," she coyly continued, tracing a pale hand upon his sleeve while I watched in growing alarm. When he made no reply, she went on, "Of course, it would mean that you would spend time alone with me in my chamber, but my husband could hardly object if it were the great Leonardo who was painting me."

"The Master is quite busy with the duke's commissions," I blurted without thinking, and then gasped at my own boldness. Desperately, I wished that I could recall the words, but the damage had been done. No doubt I would be dismissed for such insolence, I thought as I stared at my shoes in misery.

Leonardo, however, merely shrugged. "I fear Dino is correct, for all he speaks out of turn, but be assured I am flattered by your interest in my work. Perhaps if the duke grows weary of my presence, my time will again be my own."

"Perhaps." The contessa's coy smile assumed a hard edge as she turned her attention to me. "And what a pretty young page you have," she said, her gaze sharp as she took me in from toe to cap. "I must say, he seems familiar to me. Tell me—Dino, is it?—do you perhaps have a brother who works in the castle?"

"No, Contessa," I replied in a soft voice, doing my best to appear bland and unassuming, though a sudden cold sensation gripped me. "I am the only one of my family here at the castle."

"Indeed? I am quite certain I have seen you before, though not in your Master's company." She moved closer, circling me in that same feline manner as she had approached Leonardo. It was all I could do not to flinch when she reached out a slim hand and stroked my hair. Instead, I kept my gaze resolutely lowered, hoping that my page's finery was sufficient to block from her mind any memory of the bishop's costume or else the borrowed porter's tunic.

"Contessa, if you would indulge me," the Master smoothly interrupted her stalking of me, "Can you tell me where you acquired this box?"

While the contessa had been plaguing me, he had apparently spotted something that I had not seen tucked amid the lush display upon the table: a gold casket little larger than a woman's hand and studded with pearls and colored stones. I forgot my discomfiture as I saw that its lid was held shut by a clasp into which was set a keyhole. That slot was quite small enough, I judged, to accommodate the key hidden inside the chess queen. Could this perhaps be the clue that pointed to her guilt?

He had casually picked up the tiny chest; the contessa retrieved it from him in an equally swift gesture, even though her words were carelessly dismissive. "Pah, it is but a trinket I received from Ludovico last Christmastide. It may have some value, but I had always considered it gaudy. Surely the great Leonardo does not find so common a bauble of interest?"

He gave a deprecating smile. "I thought I recognized the workmanship as that of a friend of mine from my youth. But let us not concern ourselves with such trifles, for more important matters are at stake here. Would you allow me to show you a few items that might have some bearing upon the conte's murder?"

"Very well." Her tone held unmistakable pique now, even as uncertainty flashed across her features. That emotion was gone as quickly as it appeared, however, and she returned to her platter of fruit and plucked another grape.

He reached into his pouch and pulled forth the chess queen, balancing it upon his palm. "I noticed, as well, that you play chess," he coolly remarked. "This piece but recently came into my possession. I believe that it may have been stolen, possibly from one of the duke's guests. Did it perchance come from a set of yours?"

"An unremarkable bit of art," she said with a dismissive shake of her head. "Had it been mine, I would have welcomed its loss . . . but, no, it does not belong to me."

Seemingly content with that answer, he tucked away the chess piece again and pulled forth the two drawings. Unfolding them before her, he went on, "These are sketches of two young men who work here in the castle. Do you recognize either of them?"

She gave the sketches but a cursory glance and again shook her head. "I fear I do not make a habit of speaking to porters, but I am certain that I do not know them." Then her pale eyes narrowed. "Why do you ask? Do you believe they are the ones who killed Orlando?"

"They have not been eliminated as suspects. In fact, they are both being held under lock and key by order of the duke, and it is only a matter of time before they confess all."

Had he hoped to trap her into some sort of admission by what he and I both knew was a lie, the ploy did not work, for she merely shrugged again. "Perhaps a bit of persuasion would not be amiss," she said with a small sneer, so that I shivered to guess at her definition of that word. "I do hope they confess quickly, so that cousin Ludovico allows us to leave this cursed place. Even staying at my husband's villa would be preferable to being kept a virtual prisoner here for much longer."

"I am certain all will be resolved in a matter of days, perhaps even hours," Leonardo blandly assured her as he refolded the drawings and slipped them back beneath his tunic. "And now, if there is nothing more you can add regarding your cousin's recent activities, we shall leave you. Perhaps our next conversation will be of matters far more pleasant than this."

"That, my dear Leonardo, is entirely up to you," she replied, resuming her earlier coy expression. "You are welcome to visit me at any time . . . day or night."

She followed us to the door, and I fancied I could feel her pale gaze fixed upon my back. Perhaps my intuition was not unfounded, for as she was shutting the door behind her, I heard her laugh. That cold sound of mirth held a note of sharpness, like glass shattering.

Softly, she called to me. "I am quite certain, my dear Dino, that I know you from somewhere else. But do not trouble yourself trying to remember. Be assured it will be but a matter of time before I recall where we met."

12

Do not be distracted by bright colors and flashing jewels, as is the magpie. Look beyond for what is steadfast, as does the raven.

—Leonardo da Vinci, *The Notebooks of Delfina della Fazia*

I had expected after the ill-fated visit with the Contessa di Malvoral that we would seek out the next noble on Leonardo's list. That is why I was surprised when, upon quitting her chamber, he instead led us back out into the main courtyard. After last evening's burst of rain, the sky hanging over the immense quadrangle was as brilliant as any in his frescoes, though the warm air held an unpleasant heaviness that hinted at more storms to come. I began to perspire gently in my page's garb, for all that I had been gripped by a chill while in the contessa's unsettling presence.

We halted at a stone bench distant enough from any open windows or doors that we could speak freely, and the Master gestured me to sit beside him. He did not break his silence for several moments but merely stared at the two drawings of the porters, so that I busied myself with recalling in as much detail as possible the conversations we'd thus far had.

The archbishop, I was certain, knew nothing of the recent murders. Whether he had been the intended victim instead of the conte was still a matter of conjecture. As for the contessa, an inner voice told me that she must somehow be connected to the crime. Unfortunately, it seemed our questioning of her had yielded nothing of value, save for the fact she owned a small box, which might or might not be unlocked by the chess queen's key.

Or so I thought. When the Master abruptly spoke, however, his first words were, "I am not yet sure if she had anything to do with the one boy's death and the other's disappearance, but the Contessa di Malvoral did indeed know them. That much is certain."

"But how can you be sure?" I asked in surprise.

He carefully refolded the drawings and slipped them back inside his tunic. "That is quite simple, my dear boy. If you will recall, when I showed their sketches to her, she referred to them as porters. Yet we had made no mention of their position, nor did the drawings show them wearing any distinctive clothing that would indicate the same. For all she knew, they could have been stableboys or my own apprentices. She could not have known their role unless she also had some personal knowledge of them."

"But what of the casket we saw . . . and the chess queen?"

"I do not believe the chess queen came from her household. I watched her quite closely as we talked, and her manner did not suggest that she was lying, nor that she found the piece of any inordinate interest." He paused and gave me a keen look. "I have become quite the student of human nature as well as human anatomy, particularly when it comes to dissecting the way in which men interact when they have something to hide. You do know, my boy, it is an irrefutable fact that those who are lying cannot help but evince certain physical signs that they are dissembling, no matter how expert they may be at controlling their expression. For example, there is the involuntary dilation of the pupils . . ."

He went on at some length explaining other such signs, while I outwardly nodded in interest and inwardly trembled. Was he also warning me that he knew I carried a secret? Had he guessed from some small action on my part that I had not always been truthful with him?

If so, he did not reveal his concern. Instead, concluding his impromptu lecture, he went on, "But the matter of the casket is something entirely different. It contains something that she does not wish revealed. I may have to return to her chamber tonight and try my key in her lock."

Uncertain if he were being literal or metaphorical in that last statement, and fervently praying it was the former, I muttered, "Just be careful lest your key prove to open something you might not wish to find."

The Master stared at me in surprise for a moment before bursting into laughter. "My dear boy, if I did not know better, I would say you were jealous. Fear not, I have no intention of letting that woman sway me by her wiles."

Then he sobered. "Come, Dino, there are others I must speak with before the day grows much later," he said, pushing back his sleeve to look at his wrist clock, while I contented myself with a glance at the sun to judge the time. "As for you, I have another task for you of even greater import that must be accomplished with haste."

While I waited breathlessly for my assignment of great import, Leonardo reached into his pouch. He pulled forth a handful of florins and a small scrap of paper, all of which he dropped into my open palm.

"I fear that with Il Moro's ban against leaving the castle grounds, we have grown short of supplies for our current projects," he said by way of explanation. "Here is a list of what we need and sufficient money to procure it. I have already sent word to the guards at the gate that you are allowed beyond the walls for the space of a few hours. Take Vittorio with you and go to the marketplace. When you return, I shall share with you anything I learn in your absence."

He did not give me time to protest but abruptly rose, leaving me to tuck away the coins in my pouch and stare quizzically at the triangle of paper torn from some discarded sketch.

Any other man might have jotted simple columns of items and quantities. The Master's list, however, consisted of various descriptive notations sprawled in several directions across the page, no doubt noted as they occurred to him. As usual, it was written in his customary reverse hand, so that it took me a few moments to make out what was needed.

"Lime, as large a sack as can be easily handled," I read aloud. "Hematite, one dozen pieces in as dark a shade as possible, each the size of a man's fist. Azurite, the same quantity and similar size, taking care that they are pure specimens." Those last two items would be ground upon the Master's marble slab to make pigment, and the lime mixed with the water to which those pigments would then be added.

"Animal skins, as many as can be carried." These, I knew, would be boiled to make the glue for the gesso.

A few other similar items with quantities equally as vague finished the list. We would need a large basket to carry it all; then I recalled the cart we had used to carry Lorenzo from the cemetery. Perhaps it could be used again for a far less grisly duty.

Sighing, I rose and started for the Master's workshop, where I had left my apprentice's garb. I would need to change to my workday clothing again before I went in search of Vittorio. I dared not appear before the others as richly garbed as I was now, for I would never hear the end of their questions and accusations!

Not many minutes later, I once more was clothed in my familiar brown tunic and green trunk hose. My fine new garments, I had carefully folded and hidden beneath my pallet. Now I was on my way to the dining hall, where I knew the apprentices would still be working on preparing the final wall for the fresco.

Constantin was directing his small army from atop the broad wooden scaffold they had erected the day before. I climbed the ladder to join him, careful as I did so to watch my step. I had heard tales of less-than-vigilant apprentices being injured or worse after falling from a similar high platform, and I did not care to join that number.

Constantin greeted me with eagerness, frowning only slightly as I explained my mission to him. "It is true, we do need more supplies," he agreed, "for all I would prefer to have both of you helping here, instead. But it is as the Master wishes."

He plucked Vittorio from the ranks of the boys busy sweeping the dirt and cobwebs from the existing plaster and turned him over to me. The young apprentice's joy at the opportunity to abandon his task and instead wander the marketplace, at least for a short time, was contagious. Thus, I was in a cheerful mood when, for a second time that same day, I made my way past the castle gate and into the city, itself.

"Do you think we will have time to watch the jugglers?" Vittorio asked in excitement. We were pushing our cart down the narrow cobbled lanes toward the main square where the market was held each day. It was all Vittorio could do to keep his side steady, for anticipation was causing him to jump about like a young colt at winter's first crisp wind.

Regretfully, I shook my head. "Not today," I told him. "The Master and Constantin both need us back to the workshop as quickly as possible. We have time only to purchase the items on this list, and then it is back to the castle for us."

When he looked crestfallen at the news, however, I relented just a little. "Perhaps you can stay with the cart and watch them for a few minutes while I go to the pharmacist," I offered, drawing a small cheer from the younger boy that made me smile in return.

The rumble of wooden wheels atop stone echoed loudly off the winding rows of shops and houses clustered one atop the other. Here, the buildings were so close and reached so high that one could barely see the sky above, save for a single slice of blue if you peered between the rows of laundry that stretched across the lane between buildings. But even the sound of our cart could barely be heard above the surrounding hubbub of merchants calling their wares, the men and women laughing and shouting, the occasional fretful child crying.

This meant that, even though Vittorio chattered away beside me, true conversation was nigh impossible. He seemed not to care if I made only the vaguest of answers, however, but appeared pleased simply to be free of his duties for an hour or two. Thus, while we walked, I let him prattle on while I held my peace and instead thought back on the Master's words to me when I warned him against the contessa.

"Jealous," he had suggested in an amused voice, the memory of which now made my cheeks burn. He made it sound as if something more lay behind my concern for him as my Master, I thought in indignation. I was certain she'd had a hand in the conte's murder; indeed, even Leonardo had suggested she had some knowledge of the two porters. What else could I conclude but that her interest in the Master would lead to no good? Surely he must understand that I was spurred by worry on his behalf. Jealousy implied some other, deeper feelings . . . certainly none of which I had for him!

Deliberately, I shoved such thoughts aside and concentrated on the clamor around me. Like a brisk ocean wave it engulfed me, allowing me to think of nothing else, for which fact I was grateful. The colors were as varied as an artist's palette—bright flags and crisp white linens flapping with equal abandon from balconies; dandified young men in their parti-colored hose and tunics of reds and yellows and greens; jewel-toned fruits and vegetables spilling from barrels and bins—that glorious rainbow set against a soothing backdrop of russets, tans, and browns of the surrounding structures.

I took a deep breath and let myself be equally overwhelmed by the pervasive aromas of fresh flowers and bread and woodsmoke . . . and the less pleasant stench of boiled onions and manure and rotting garbage. Odd, how every city and village had its own unique scent. I realized now that I missed life in town.

For it was rare that we apprentices left the castle grounds

at all, save for feast days. I could count upon a single hand the trips I had made to the marketplace since I had come to Milan. Those outings had always been in the company of Constantin or another of my fellows, and for the sole purpose of purchasing supplies at Leonardo's behest. But even though we were not free to wander about as we wished, each excursion was still an exciting adventure.

By the time we reached the market square, I had grown more accustomed to the din. Cupping one hand to my mouth, I called to Vittorio to follow me.

At the candle maker's shop, we found wax . . . "sufficient quantities to hang numerous stencils upon walls." The tanner's shop yielded a bundle of odorous skins of unknown origin, but which would serve our purpose. He also had a selection of fine hog's bristles—"white, for the best brushes"—which we purchased, as well. We loaded all this in our basket and pushed the cart toward the pharmacy.

"Look, there are the jugglers!" Vittorio exclaimed as we came upon a trio of dwarves in bright parti-colored costumes tossing all manner of objects before an appreciative crowd. "Please, Dino, you promised!"

Skilled as the trio was, I was hard-pressed not to stand and gawk, myself. Reluctantly, I left the boy with strict instructions to keep one eye on the cart and made my way into the pharmacist's dimly lit alcove just off the square. A balding man with blackened teeth, he counted Leonardo as one of his best customers . . . despite which, when it came to minerals, he attempted always to cheat him by offering the poorest specimens.

"I do not understand why you don't trust me," he whined piteously as I carried each rock into the sunlight to better inspect it.

Shutting out his pleas, I ruthlessly culled those samples with too many impurities. With a bit of final bargaining over the price—a skill I had learned from my mother—we concluded our business. Bundles in hand, I stepped back into the street to call for Vittorio.

At first glance, however, I saw neither him nor the hand-cart. My heart began a frantic pounding as frightening scenarios played through my mind. What if Vittorio had somehow suffered the same fate as the unfortunate Lorenzo . . . or what if he had gone missing like the second porter, Renaldo? Or perhaps he was lying dead in a nearby alleyway, a knife protruding from his young body, just like the conte?

Then the crowd parted momentarily, and I spied him a small distance from where I had left him. He was dutifully leaning against the cart as he laughed and clapped in response to the juggler's antics. Heaving a relieved sigh, I waved in his direction. He caught sight of me and pantomimed a plea to stay a few moments more; then, when I shook my head no, he responded with a despairing gesture, though he dutifully took hold of the cart and began pushing it toward where I waited.

It was while I watched his progress toward me that I felt a sensation of being spied upon in return. Neck prickling, I spun about in the direction from where that unsettling sensation seemed to originate. I saw nothing out of the ordinary at first, just the milling crowd, none of whom stood out in any particular way. And then, as I started to turn back, I glimpsed from the corner of my eye a familiar if unwelcome face.

I gasped and blinked. The face abruptly vanished, so that I wondered if I had imagined seeing it. But there could be no mistaking the red hair, bony face, and full lips, those features overlaid by that unmistakable hint of cruelty. It had to be Renaldo, I told myself. He was not dead, after all. Did that mean he somehow had escaped Lorenzo's killer? Or were he and Lorenzo the murderers, responsible for the conte's death? Had he attempted to conceal his guilt by bludgeoning the other youth and leaving him for dead, and then managing to flee the castle to avoid punishment?

No matter his role, his enmity toward me needed no explanation. But so intent was I on trying again to spot him amid the crowd, that I forgot about Vittorio until he caught me by the shoulder. I yelped and all but dropped the bundle of colored minerals for which I had bargained so fiercely.

"What are you looking at?" he curiously demanded, twisting his head back and forth in an attempt to spot something out of the ordinary among the press of people.

I rapidly debated whether or not I should take him into my confidence. Of course, I dared not tell him the entire truth, but as Renaldo would surely see him with me, perhaps it would be safer to let him know we were being watched . . . perhaps even followed. Saying nothing could possibly put Vittorio in danger, as well. On the other hand, there was no need to frighten the youth unnecessarily.

"It's nothing," I finally said. "I thought I saw someone from my hometown, but I'm sure I was mistaken."

Our return to the castle proved uneventful, though I could not help the occasional glance behind me every twenty paces or so to see if Renaldo reappeared. Vittorio was so preoccupied with relating all the various feats of the jugglers that he seemed not to notice my uneasiness, for which I was grateful. Had he questioned me again, I would have felt compelled to take him into my confidence.

Our only small bit of excitement occurred when we reached the castle gates, and one of the guards momentarily barred our passage. "Your cart was empty when you passed through here the first time," he barked out with a gesture at the bundles with which it was now laden. His manner one of importance, he went on, "I must check to see that you are not attempting to smuggle someone into the castle against the duke's orders."

I refrained from replying that our cart was so small that only one of the juggling dwarves could possibly be hiding beneath the collection of sacks. Instead, we dutifully stepped aside and allowed him to paw through our purchases. He made quick work of the search, however, cutting it short when he opened the bundle of skins, which had begun to ripen beneath the sun. With a sound of disgust, he waved us on, and it was with an effort that we held back our laughter until we were safely out of earshot.

Once back at the workshop, we began unloading the sacks and bundles and storing them safely away. Vittorio picked up the sack of lime and made as if to peer inside it. "Are you certain no one is hiding in here?" he asked with a snicker before plopping it onto a shelf.

I grinned at him in return, enjoying this respite from the business of searching out a murderer. I dared not admit it to Leonardo, but I was growing weary of stumbling over murdered men. More to the point, I was more than a bit fearful I might eventually find either him or myself added to their number. Once this gruesome business was resolved, I silently vowed, the only bodies I ever wanted to see again were in the Master's collection of anatomy drawings.

By the time we had organized all the newly purchased supplies, the rest of the apprentices were returning from their day's work in the dining hall, prepared to head for the kitchen for the evening meal. A few of them raised their brows in mock surprise when they saw I would be accompanying them.

"So the Master finally tired of your company?" Paulo asked with a sly grin, while Davide merely shook his head and smiled.

I accepted their mock rebukes with as much good humor as I could muster, but my earlier moment of lightheartedness had already begun to fade. I could not dismiss the memory of Renaldo's face and the feeling that our encounter had not been accidental. He'd seemed to be searching me out, though how he would have known I was to be in the marketplace that afternoon, I could not guess. But the knowledge that Il Moro's guards were searching for unauthorized people coming into the castle, and not only those attempting to slip out, served to calm my fears somewhat.

So occupied was I with my thoughts, however, that I barely noticed Marcella's bright greeting as she spooned out my evening's portion, nor her frown when I merely muttered a reply and moved on. Constantin tried to engage me in conversation, as well, but finally gave up when my responses were little more than shakes of my head.

When we finished our meal, I joined in the usual evening tasks that fell to us apprentices. I diligently applied myself to each, even while I kept expecting a summons from the Master. He had said, after all, that he would share with me anything he learned in my absence. But as one hour passed and then another, I wondered if I might be spared further investigation this night.

Once the last willow twig had been pulled from the fire to add to our pile of new charcoal sticks, Constantin gave us leave to stop for the night and pursue our traditional amusements. This night, however, everyone seemed more subdued than usual, and the workshop far more quiet without Tommaso's lute. No one objected when Constantin snuffed the candles well before they guttered, but all trailed off to their respective pallets with little comment.

I undressed in the darkness, sparing a moment's gratitude for Signore Luigi and his clever corset that made my boy's masquerade more tolerable. No longer would I be forced to secretly wind and unwind lengths of cloth around my chest to conceal my gender, I thought with a sigh of relief as I untied the simple lacing and crawled beneath my blanket. Visions of dead men and moldering crypts kept pressing upon me, however, so that in a fit of pique I finally tugged my blanket over my head in an attempt to block them from my thoughts.

Despite my agitated stated of mind, I drifted into a restless sleep. In my dreams, Vittorio and I were back in the marketplace watching the jugglers, but they were no longer the familiar trio of dwarves. Instead, it was Renaldo and Lorenzo who were performing there. And rather than brightly colored balls, they tossed dozens of knives back and forth while the crowd cheered, seemingly oblivious to the danger in such a feat. Only I cried at them to stop, but of course they did not heed me.

And then the inevitable came. First one knife, and then another, and another went astray, until each youth had half-a-dozen sharp blades buried in his throat. I screamed, waiting for the blood to come streaming from them, but the pair only smiled and continued to juggle their remaining knives.

Frantic now, I made my way through the spectators, tugging at one sleeve after another in hopes of finding someone—anyone—who would help them. My efforts, however, were for naught. When I turned back to the youths, they were lying upon the cobbles, bright red blood spurting from them as if from a fountain. I tried to run to them, but it suddenly seemed I made no progress, no matter how swiftly I put one foot before the other.

Then, across the square, I spotted the Master standing beside a chess queen as tall as he. No one else seemed to notice this oddity . . . nor did they see when the chess queen suddenly transformed into the Contessa di Malvoral, dressed in a porter's blue and white tunic and clinging to the Master's arm.

And only I saw the serpent that slid from her full lips as she locked her ice-blue gaze upon me and smiled.

I awoke from that dream with my heart pounding frantically and my fear fresh enough that I dared not stir nor open my eyes. After what seemed an eternity—though it was perhaps but a minute or two—the erratic hammering slowed to a more regular beat, and the tightness that had gripped my chest eased. It was as my breathing went from frantic gasps to the soft inhalations that heralded a welcome return to sleep that I realized someone was standing beside my bed.

At first, it was just that unsettling sensation of being observed by an unknown watcher. Then I heard a soft footstep nearby, felt the slightest movement of air about me. With an effort, I managed not to gasp aloud but feigned continued slumber, though a sudden chill had settled in my veins. My blanket was still pulled over my face so that, even if I dared open one eye a slit, I would not be able see this nocturnal intruder.

Perhaps it is just the Master, come to wake me for another night's adventure, I frantically told myself . . . but if it were indeed he, why had he not yet attempted to rouse me?

It was the hardest thing I had ever done, continuing to lie upon my pallet pretending sleep while I prayed for the intruder to leave without first thrusting a knife into my blanketed form. Only one other route was open to me besides that passive course. Rather than lying there, I could leap up in hopes of catching him by surprise. Even if the action did not immediately frighten him away, perhaps it would rouse my fellow apprentices in time for them to save me from whatever ill might otherwise befall me!

So, then, do it, I harshly told myself.

Gathering my courage, I took in a long, soft breath . . . and abruptly sprang from my bed with a shout.

13

The pen has necessary companionship with the penknife, and, moreover, useful companionship for the one without the other is ineffective.

—Leonardo da Vinci, *Manuscript L*

Hands raised to ward off any attack, I squinted into the darkness . . . and saw the room was empty, save for my fellow apprentices, who were stirring now around me, awakened by my cry. The only other sign of movement was my blanket, which I had set flying with my leap from the bed. Now, it fluttered to the ground like a threadbare night bird returning to its nest.

"What is it? Who's there?" came sleepy murmurs from all sides, while a tousled Constantin swiftly padded from his cot to check upon my welfare.

"Are you hurt? What has happened?" he softly demanded between yawns as he peered about the room. "Shall I light a candle?"

Still trembling with reaction, I managed to reach down beside me for my lost blanket. Wrapping it about me, I shook my head. "I-I awoke and thought someone was standing over me. It must have been part of the nightmare I was having," I miserably whispered in return. "I'm sorry I disturbed everyone else with my fright."

"Don't worry, no one will remember anything about this by morning," he consoled me. "So, would you like me to sit up with you and converse for a while?"

I shook my head even as I gave him a grateful smile. "I will be fine. Please, go back to sleep and do not worry about me."

Yawning more broadly, he needed no further prompting but returned to his bed. Within a few moments, the familiar soft breathing of my fellows filled the room again, signaling that everyone was once again asleep . . . save me.

I had insisted to Constantin that my fright was but the result of a nightmare but, in truth, I was not sure of that. As I had reached down for my lost blanket, I had noticed something out of place. Now that my eyes were better adjusted to the dark, I quietly crawled to the edge of my narrow bed and peered over the edge. The simple wood chest where I kept my belongings was not quite closed. Its lid was propped open by the sleeve of my best tunic, which hung over its edge, as if the garment had been pulled forth and then carelessly tossed back.

The sight sent a shiver through me. I knew with certainty that I had closed the lid of that box quite securely before I went to sleep. It had not been a dream, after all. Someone had indeed been beside my bed, searching through my belongings.

Anger swept away my fear, and I decided I would not let this invasion go unanswered. Scrubbing the sleep from my eyes, I swiftly pulled on my outer clothing. A few moments later, I was making my way through the darkened workshop. I paused long enough to take up a couple of sulphur matches and one of the candle stubs that had been left upon a table, prying it from its pool of cooled wax. Those items I tucked into my pouch lest I later need a bit of light.

I was grateful for that bit of foresight when I slipped through the door into the courtyard and saw that the previous night's clouds were returning. For now, however, I would take advantage of the darkness, which would cloak my movements while I conducted my investigation. But it was not until I was standing there in the cool night air that I began to wonder just what I intended to accomplish. Mud lingered outside the workshop, but the prints from our many feet going in and out that door would make it difficult to distinguish them from those of an intruder. And even should I find fresh tracks, how would I follow them in the dark?

So, think, Delfina. What would the Master do?

It had not been many minutes since my nighttime visitor fled the workshop, I reminded myself. Likely, he would be but little concerned with concealing his movements, not expecting me to follow. I would methodically make my way along the castle's outer walls, looking for a shadow that should not be there, that of someone else wandering in the middle of the night.

Treading carefully, I started along the wall running parallel to the parade grounds, moving in the direction of the castle's main quarters. The only movement I saw was that of the guards upon the battlement. At this hour, finally, it seemed the castle was asleep, save for the unknown person I sought, and me.

And what if I find someone . . . what then?

That last question gave me pause. This was no bloodless game of chess I was playing. Two people had already died at someone's hands, sturdy males both larger and stronger than I. And the murderer had shown that he knew how to wield a knife and cudgel with equal skill. How could I hope to confront such a person, unarmed as I was?

Uneasiness swept me now. Perhaps this had been a rash idea, wandering about in the night looking for someone who could be a murderer. Better I should wait until morning and tell the Master what happened, and wait for his advice on the matter.

I had reached the portico that ran the length of the guest wing of the castle, where Leonardo and I had been earlier in the day. I would conceal myself here for a few moments, I decided; then, if nothing drew my attention, I would return to the workshop and to my bed.

I squeezed myself into the shadow of one narrow pillar and waited. For once, I wished for a wrist clock like the Master's to know the time, for the clouds had further obscured both moon and stars, making it hard to judge the hour. Perhaps an inward count of the seconds would serve to track the passage of the next few minutes.

By the time two minutes had passed by my reckoning, I was yawning and more than ready to give up the chase. It seemed obvious now that, had the intruder meant me harm, he could have stabbed me as I slept. Seeing as I was still drawing breath, perhaps that person had not wished my death, after all, but had been nothing more than a thief.

Still, I could not shake my trepidation as I made my silent way back down the darkened portico. I paused once, certain I had heard a step behind me . . . but when the sound did not repeat itself, I continued walking.

And that was when someone seized me by the arm and clamped a hand over my mouth.

I gave a muffled cry and fought to break free, but the grip on me was unyielding. Just as I feared I would suffer the same fate as Lorenzo and the conte, I heard a familiar voice in my ear murmur, "Cease your struggles, my dear boy, or you are likely to injure me."

I froze, and the hand across my mouth and the grasp on my arm both fell away. "Saints' blood!" I softly gasped, swinging about to make certain. "Master, is that you?"

I could barely see him in the shadows, dressed as he still was in his black tunic, but a stray sliver of moonlight abruptly caught in his russet hair and confirmed his identity. Nodding, Leonardo put a finger to his lips indicating silence, and then gestured me to follow him. A few minutes later we were in his chambers, where he bade me take a seat as he turned up the lamp.

"My apologies for startling you, my dear Dino," he said with a smile as he took the bench across from me, "but I was not expecting to encounter you in the early hours of the morning. Neither would you have been expecting me, which is why I resorted to physical restraint. I feared you might cry out and awaken the castle if I simply appeared out of the shadows."

As likely I would have, I wryly thought. Indeed, the Master was fortunate that I was *not* proficient with a knife or cudgel . . . for had I been carrying either weapon, I would have attempted to use it.

His expression grew quizzical. "So tell me, why were you skulking about the castle grounds at this unnatural hour?"

I related what had happened when I awakened from my nightmare, my feeling of being watched and then finding evidence that the intruder had not been a figment of my dreams but apparently had even searched my belongings before vanishing into the night. I was relieved when he did not chide me for unwisely wandering the shadows for this phantom, for I was already berating myself for such folly.

Instead, nibbling a fig from the ever-present basket of fruit, he said, "You said you suspect this unknown person was searching in your chest for something. Is it perhaps as likely that he was instead leaving something behind in it?"

So unexpected yet so obvious was that possibility that I could do nothing for several moments but stare at him with my mouth hanging open. Then, abruptly snapping my jaws shut, I leaped to my feet. "Of course!" I exclaimed. "Quickly, let me return to the workshop, and I shall search through the box for something that does not belong there."

"Later," he said mildly, raising a restraining hand. "It is but two hours before dawn. I think it best that you stay here for what is left of the night, just in case I am mistaken in my assumptions. In the morning, you may go through your belongings and let me know if you find anything out of the ordinary concealed among them. But for now, you may take my bed."

"But where shall you sleep?" I asked as I unsuccessfully tried to subdue a yawn.

He shrugged. "You know that I do not require much in the way of rest. But should I feel the need for sleep, I have a pallet in my workshop where I can lay my head."

I did not protest for, in truth, memories of my recent fright made me reluctant to return to my own bed just then. Obediently, I climbed beneath the neatly tucked blanket and started to settle down; then, as a question occurred to me, I abruptly sat up.

"But why were you searching the grounds, Master?" I wanted to know. "Surely you were not looking for me?"

By way of reply, he reached into his pouch and withdrew a small metal object that caught the lamplight. "Do you not recall?" he asked with a small smile. "I vowed I would find out what was inside the casket that the Contessa di Malvoral was so jealously guarding."

My eyes widened at his words, and I spared a critical look at his appearance. Only now did I notice that he had a tousled air about him that our brief struggle did not justify, his tunic slightly askew and the laces of one sleeve untied. I recalled the contessa's coy invitation to visit her any time of the day or night. Surely he had not . . . he could not!

"You look disapproving, my dear boy," he went on, his smile widening into a grin. "Fear not, I escaped the contessa with my virtue still intact, but I did manage to distract her long enough to try out my duplicate key. It appears that, while the chess queen may not be hers, the key it holds belongs to her . . . or is perhaps yet another copy."

I was not sure which was greater, my relief that he had not fallen victim to the woman's wiles or my curiosity as to what the casket had contained. Curiosity swiftly won out, and I exclaimed, "Please, Master, can you not tell me what you found in it?"

"The casket contained but a single letter, appearing recent and well read." He hesitated, and what I could only describe as a flash of angry embarrassment darkened his features before he went on, "I had but a few moments to commit the words to memory before I had to return the missive to its hiding place. My intent while you sleep is to re-create that letter for further study. Unfortunately, we may still find some difficulty in reading it."

"But why?" I wanted to know, envisioning a page covered in a secret code known only to the contessa and her correspondent.

He frowned, and for a few heartbeats I thought he would divulge no more. Finally, he replied, "It happens that the letter is written in Latin, with which I have little familiarity."

The confession took me aback. Indeed, his breadth of knowledge was such that I simply assumed there was little beyond his scope. I would learn later that, as an illegitimate son, he'd had no formal education but instead had taught himself everything that he knew. For myself, my father had insisted I receive the same curricula as my brothers. That instruction had included a required proficiency in that tongue of the Mother Church.

Timidly, I offered, "If you can but reconstruct the letter from memory, I am well able to translate it for you."

"Then you will have earned your keep," he replied, his good humor seemingly revived just a little.

I nodded in return and started to settle into my blanket again, when another thought occurred to me. Sitting up once more, I said, "I almost forgot, Master. You did not tell me what you learned today while Vittorio and I were in the marketplace."

"I fear there is little to report," he replied with a dismissive shrug. "I was able to speak with most of the remaining people on our list, all of whom where able to account for their actions at the time of the conte's death. As far as motive, I was not able to uncover one. Most described the duke's cousin as genial and had nothing worse to say of him other than the fact he was not particularly effectual at handling either money or men."

"But what of the guards who carried his body into the crypt? We listened to them talk about bad blood between the conte and someone else," I reminded him . . . though, indeed, I had all but forgotten that bit of overheard gossip, myself, until this very moment.

He gave me an approving nod. "We did indeed hear an indication that the conte had been involved in some unpleasantness. Unfortunately, whatever quarrel he had with these unknown persons is either not common knowledge or else has long since been forgotten by those of higher rank. No one mentioned any recent outrages committed by him."

Then he gave the faintest of wry smiles. "However, there is one consensus among the local nobility regarding their late friend, Orlando. It seems that all of the courtiers would cheerfully kill the Conte di Ferrera a second time simply for the inconvenience that his original murder has caused them. I fear that if the duke does not relent in his current policy, people will soon be storming the castle gates to get out, and not in, as is the usual case with mass uprising."

With that, he snuffed the lamp on the wall, so that only a small stub of candle remained burning upon the table. "And now, my dear boy, I suggest you go to sleep, and I shall have your assignment waiting for you in the morning."

I awoke to the sound of a deafening crash, as if a tinsmith's cart of pots and pails and ladles were tumbling all at once onto a cobbled street.

For the second time in the space of a few hours, I leaped up from my cot in a tangle of blankets, uncertain for a moment where I was or what could possibly be happening. Memory returned in a swift measure, however, as I saw the familiar surroundings and recalled I had spent the night's waning hours in the Master's chambers. As for the din, it seemed to come from his private workshop, the door of which now stood slightly ajar.

I took a moment's alarm, fearful that he might have been injured in the course of whatever accident had just occurred.

Then I heard his voice above the fading clatter, and by his choice of colorful invectives was relieved to know that he'd suffered no harm. But perhaps I should take a look inside the workshop, anyhow . . . not just for curiosity's sake, I nobly told myself, but to make certain that the Master required no assistance. And surely he would not fault me for what was nothing more than common courtesy.

Before I could convince myself of the selflessness of my plan, Leonardo exited his workshop, shutting the door on whatever secrets that room contained.

"Forgive me if I woke you, dear boy," he said, brushing dirt from the same black tunic from the day before. Ruefully examining a long tear in one sleeve—now I understood Signore Luigi's laments over the Master's battered wardrobe—he added, "It appears I still have a few adjustments to make to one of my inventions before it can see the light of day."

Light of day? I forgot my curiosity as his words drew my attention to the midmorning sun streaming in through the window. "I have slept far too long," I cried in dismay, scrambling from the bed. "I must hurry off to the workshop. Constantin will be worried that I, too, have vanished along with Tommaso."

"Do not fear; I have already advised him you are assisting me with a project," Leonardo assured me. Gesturing to a sheet of parchment upon his table, he went on, "And so you shall. As soon as you finish your ablutions, you may begin work on that letter we discussed last night."

I was seated at the table a few minutes later, quill and pot of ink at hand. Like some minor patron saint, the familiar figure of the chess queen held court upon the table's gleaming surface, offering me a bit of inspiration. I gave her a smile and then, brow furrowed, began translating the missive in question into the common tongue.

I was not sure at first what to expect . . . a love letter, or perhaps a confession. The Master had warned me, however, not to let my excitement overrun my pen. "We may have uncovered naught but a list of the contessa's gowns or jewels, or perhaps her past lovers," he said with a dismissive shrug.

But within the first few words, I knew he had found something much more.

It was shorter than I had expected, barely half a page. I was relieved to find the Master had written out his version in a standard hand, rather than in his usual reverse writing. Here and there, I found a missing letter or misspelled word, but the error could be as easily attributable to the original author as to him. Indeed, I was amazed at how thoroughly he seemed to have recalled what he had read, the feat all the more amazing because it was in a language with which he was not conversant.

Perhaps not surprisingly, the note bore neither salutation nor signature, a fact I had pointed out to the Master before I began my work.

"Most unusual for a letter," he had agreed, and then went on to explain that it appeared the original page had traces of red wax remaining upon it. "Though I doubt the sender applied his usual seal, lest the stamped wax reveal his identity. I also suspect that it was delivered concealed within something else—a package, perhaps, or even another letter—which could be discarded so that no clue would remain as to the sender."

And the recipient would have been quite right to fear the letter's discovery by anyone else, I soon realized. By the time I translated the last word, I had no doubt that those few lines quite clearly detailed the final stages of a murderous plot.

Barely had I put down my pen when the Master was peering over my shoulder at the paper. "You look quite smug, my boy," he told me. "Should I assume the letter contained something of import?"

I nodded and handed my translated page to him. Taking the bench across from me, he read it aloud.

"All is proceeding as planned. The shepherd will be in Milan on the dates discussed. All that remains is finding an opportune time and place in which to carry out the deed. I will leave it to you to find a man or two willing to bloody his hands for coin, and I shall trust you to rid yourself of those men as soon as it is expedient. Be assured of the import of our mission. Forget not that the fate of our two countries depends upon our success in this matter. We must not fail."

He sat silent for a few moments after he had finished reading. Finally, I ventured, "This letter seems proof enough to me that the contessa was part of a murder plot. As for its writer, he must be the French ambassador, as he spoke of two countries . . . surely France and Milan. And it is obvious that Renaldo and Lorenzo were the two chosen to commit the actual murder."

"And the victim?" Leonardo prompted.

I shrugged. "If the motive had to do with affairs of state, it would seem the conte's death would indeed have some import. So perhaps we were right at the first, and he was the intended victim, all along."

While I silently congratulated myself on tying up the mystery into such a neat package, Leonardo merely raised a brow.

"Are you quite certain of your hypothesis, Dino?" he persisted. "Keep in mind that the writer surely knew his words could prove incriminating in the wrong hands. The use of the word *countries* might well be symbolic, perhaps referring to two different cities, or two different families. And recall that the letter writer referred to his quarry as the shepherd. Unless the Conte di Ferrara had recently taken up the pastoral life, such an appellation does not make much sense. It does, however, bring to mind a liturgical reference . . . a shepherd of men, perhaps?"

While I considered that, he went on, "And what does a shepherd carry but a crook, one similar to the traditional bent staff that is a bishop's sign of office. We could make an equally reasonable case for your previous theory, that the true victim was to be His Eminence Stefano, Cardinal Nardini, the arch-bishop of Milan. That would also make it likely that the conte's murder was indeed an error, for I suspect that neither Lorenzo nor Renaldo would have known His Eminence on sight, save by his vestments."

"But why murder a cardinal?" I asked in confusion. "Would not dispatching an ambassador make more sense, when the letter speaks to the possible fate of two countries?"

"My dear boy, surely you must know that the Church dabbles in politics as freely as any statesman or king. Recall the words of the archbishop's secretary, that His Eminence has had the ear of four popes and might be elected to that very post one day. The archbishop of Milan wields far more political power than the conte did as ambassador."

Propping my elbow on the table, I rested my chin upon my fist and considered his words. Though a bit disappointed that he had torn apart my neat scenario, with a bit of thought I was inclined to concur with his view of things. "But we are in agreement that the French ambassador and the Contessa di Malvoral are part of the scheme, are we not?"

"At this point, it is still but a guess," he replied. "Keep in mind that possessing this letter is not proof of the con-tessa's guilt, only a sign of possible complicity. It could be that she stole the incriminating letter from the true villain—perhaps the conte—and was keeping it under lock and key in order to blackmail him. For it is also possible that it was the conte who was involved in the plot with his French counterpart. We have already heard rumors that the duke's cousin has been involved in other unpleasant busi-ness before."

"So maybe his murder was deliberate," I said, taking up that line of thought. "Perhaps he plotted with the French am-bassador to assassinate the archbishop, but then had a change of heart . . . perhaps even threatened to make the scheme pub-lic. And when that happened, he was then stabbed by one of his compatriots."

"All within the realm of possibility," Leonardo agreed. Grabbing up a pear, he took a large bite and went on in a muffled voice, "As to the French ambassador, he does seem the likeliest candidate for writing the letter. But that begs the question of whether he was working on his own or at the behest of his king . . . which could have far greater implications than we have yet imagined. But we are hasty in assuming the note came from his pen. Do not forget that the city is filled with foreigners, any of whom could be its author."

"Saints' blood, but this is a tangled affair," I said with a sigh, my head suddenly throbbing as I realized just how many threads we would have to sort through in order to follow our way to the truth. "Surely the duke cannot expect us to unravel such a mystery in so short a time."

"Ah, but he does." The Master stared again at the translated letter, an unaccustomed look of worry creasing his features. "As it happens, I received word earlier that he wishes to speak with me at midafternoon. I suspect he will be pressing me for a resolution to his cousin's murder, and if he does not get it . . ."

He trailed off without finishing the thought aloud, but I feared I knew what he intended to say. If the duke did not soon get the answer he sought regarding the conte's assassination, he might well decide to dispense with Leonardo's services altogether.

My sudden alarm must have been apparent on my face, for he gave me a small smile. "Fear not, Dino, all is not yet lost. As the court's master of pageantry and master engineer, I still have a few tricks hidden in my tunic sleeve."

"But what will you tell Il Moro?" I asked in no little worry.

He shrugged and tossed the letter onto the table. "I will think of something. In the meantime, in light of what we have just learned, I think it is time that we question our friend, the French ambassador." He reached for the chess queen and gave her a thoughtful look before tucking her away into his waist pouch again. "But before we do so, there is one other person here at court who may be able to give us a greater insight into the conte's activities in the days before he was murdered."

14

What greater joy, and what greater sorrow, is there than to be joined to another for eternity?

—Leonardo da Vinci, *The Notebooks of Delfina della Fazia*

I had first seen the Contessa di Ferrara that night in the dining hall, when Il Moro had coldly announced the news of her husband's murder before the entire assemblage. The second time had been at the conte's funeral. Then, however, she had been swathed with veils, so that I had not been able to see her face. But both instances had left me with the impression of a wan and self-effacing woman who was but a victim of circumstances.

Had I expected to see the same sad, helpless woman this time, however, I would have been sadly disappointed. As her maidservant led us into her chamber, we found her making notations into a ledger. Like the Contessa di Malvoral the day before, the Contessa di Ferrara also appeared as if she had but recently awakened. The younger woman, however, was dressed in a far more modest fashion than her distant relative.

Rather than a scant few yards of linen, she wore a long, belted gown of dark blue velvet, with her feet in matching slippers and her hair tied back in a loose braid wrapped in ribbon the same azure shade. The sumptuous garb made her appear even younger than she had before, though the jewels at her ears and neck were those of a mature woman and not a girl.

I was glad to know that we were as presentably dressed. Before embarking upon this visit, I had returned to the workshop and donned my page's garb. As for the Master, he had changed out his battered black tunic for another of gold trimmed in green, which robe made him appear as elegant as any noble . . . at least, to my eyes. Surely, we were fit to visit a contessa.

"Signore Leonardo," she greeted the Master with a small smile, gesturing us forward. "Cousin Ludovico said you might wish to speak with me about Orlando. Have you had any success in finding the villain who struck him down?"

Leonardo bowed low before her. "I fear, Contessa, that there is much about your husband's death that remains a mystery. That is why I am here, to offer my condolences and to ask you a few questions."

"I assure you, signore, I have heard condolences enough that, were they indulgences, Orlando would long be gone from purgatory. As for questions, I fear the shock of my husband's death has left me ill-prepared to handle all but the most simple of tasks."

Looking at the stack of ledgers before her, I wondered at this last, but the Master made no comment. Instead, waiting for her to sit first, he took the seat she offered and reached into his tunic for the sketches.

"We suspect, Contessa, that two young men from the castle may have had a hand in the conte's murder. Would you be able to look at these drawings and tell us if you recognize either of them?"

She gave the portraits but a passing glance. "I fear, Signore Leonardo, that I keep to my quarters much of the time and see few people other than my personal servants and members of my husband's family. I do not recognize these men."

"And do you recall, Contessa, if your husband seemed worried or preoccupied in the days before his murder, perhaps even mentioning that he feared for his safety? Did he send or receive any mysterious missives, or was he unexpectedly absent at times?"

The woman gave a soft laugh. "My dear Signore Leonardo, my husband spent very little time with me, either recently or at any time during our marriage. Had his routine changed from the norm, I of all people would not have known it."

Her frank admission seemed to give him a moment's pause. For myself, I felt a sudden surge of sympathy for her. I recalled the intuition that had struck me as I watched her leave the churchyard after her husband's burial. Surely locked in what obviously was a sterile marriage, she could have felt little more than relief at being freed of it while she was still young. But, oddly enough, I heard an undercurrent of pain in her words now, and I sensed that she had indeed loved her husband, for all his apparent neglect of her.

It was then, as I glanced uncomfortably about, that a small casket upon the shelf caught my eye, and my gaze widened. It appeared identical to the one that belonged to the Contessa di Malvoral, down to the design of the inset pearls and colored stones. The Master had seen it as well, for he moved casually to the shelf and picked it up, then turned back to the conte's wife.

"An interesting trinket," he said as he examined it. "Was it a gift from your husband?"

"Certainly not."

She gave a dismissive snort, even as she swiftly rose to take it from his hands. The gesture reminded me of the Contessa di Malvoral's reaction, and I wondered what this woman hid from us.

All she said, however, was, "The casket was a present from Ludovico last Christmastide. It is nothing special. I believe that he gave a similar box to every noblewoman of the court."

"The duke is a generous man," the Master murmured, his words drawing another sound of derision from the widowed contessa. She did not elaborate upon her feelings for Il

Moro, however, but merely set the box back in its original spot.

"As I said, Signore Leonardo, I have no knowledge of anyone who might have wished my husband ill. Is there anything else you would ask me? I have much work to do."

"There is one last thing, Contessa," he smoothly replied. "One of the young men whom we suspect of involvement in your husband's death had this upon him. Do you perhaps recognize it?" he asked, withdrawing the chess queen from the pouch at his waist.

As with everyone who had seen it, I expected a bland dismissal of the small, carved figure. This time, however, the reaction was quite different. The blood rose in the contessa's wan features, and her smile as she beheld it was one of joyous relief.

"You have found her," she gasped as she took the piece from him, clutching it to her with a proprietary air. "I had thought her lost and had given up hope of ever seeing her again."

While we watched in no little surprise, she set the chess queen upon the table at which she had been seated when we entered and then rushed to a nearby cabinet. Opening it, she pulled forth a large chessboard with alternating squares of gleaming black and white stone set into a framework of dark wood. Atop the board sat a matching wooden box carved with an intricate if unfamiliar pattern. She carried both items to the table, carelessly sweeping aside the ledgers at which she had been so arduously working in order to clear a space.

"This set was a wedding gift from my husband," she explained as she began removing delicate stone figures—half of them a gleaming black, half of them an opalescent white—from their niches within that dark wood case.

"He found the set in his travels in Spain," she continued, "and he brought it home for me, just before we were married. He had been afraid I might have preferred something more ornate . . . but, of course, he was wrong about that, as he would be about many things."

Her large fingers handled the pieces as if they were the most precious of jewels. Eight small triangular shapes in each of the two colors represented the pawns. The remaining larger pieces of each color, while all different, had been carved with the same smooth, abstract lines as the chess queen. And, just like the queen, those pieces seemed to glow in the room's soft light.

Methodically, the contessa began lining them up on either side of the board, adding, "Chess was the one pasttime that we enjoyed together. Many nights, we stayed awake almost until dawn as we played. We had other chess pieces, it is true, but I always felt there was something quite special about this set, for all it appears quite plain."

She picked up the queen again and ran loving fingers across her smooth curves. "Perhaps it was the stone that the carver used, or maybe it was the skill of his hands, but the figures seem to possess an inner light, a life of their own." So saying, she gave a satisfied smile and set the white queen upon the remaining white square, completing the set.

I tore my gaze from the figures to glance at the Master, who was watching the contessa with cool interest. "I am pleased we could return something so precious to you, particularly in light of your other recent loss," he replied with a small bow. "Unless you have any request of me, we shall disturb you no longer."

I doubted the woman heard this last, for she had turned her attention to the chessboard. Deliberately, she moved first a white pawn, then a black, as if she were playing both sides of a game. I watched her in bewildered silence, wondering at this sudden obsession. Only when the Master jostled my arm did I tear my gaze from her and follow him to the door.

"And so now we know the identity of the chess queen's true owner," he said once we were safely out of earshot, "though the mystery is not entirely solved. How the piece came into Lorenzo's possession is something we may never learn."

"But you do believe she knows nothing of the motive behind her husband's murder?"

"I am not yet certain of that. Her reaction to recovering the chess queen was genuine, I do not doubt. But, for the rest, there is something in her manner that is unnatural, though I cannot quite put my finger upon it."

"She is angry," I said, surprising myself as much as him, though I felt sure as soon as I said it that my guess was correct.

The Master spared me a keen look. "Indeed, Dino, you seem to have some insight into the female manner of thought," he said. "But you may well be correct. Perhaps I need to pay a second visit to her and, just as with the Contessa di Malvoral, use my key to see what she is hiding in that casket."

I managed but a nod in reply, for I had not missed the question in his voice as he commented upon my supposed insight. From now on, I must be careful in my observations, for it seemed I was growing too bold. Most importantly, I warned myself, I must refrain from any similar undue sympathy in the future, lest the Master begin to suspect the true reason for my understanding of a woman's heart!

"Monsieur Villasse prays you forgive the long delay, Signore Leonardo, but he is at last able to speak with you."

So saying, the French ambassador's secretary gestured us toward the same heavy, carved door through which he had just returned. Upon leaving the Contessa di Ferrara's chamber, the Master and I had set out in search of Monsieur Villasse. We had been waiting in his antechamber for perhaps an hour while the secretary sat at his high table scribbling upon a page and directing the occasional severe glance at us.

Twice already, a muffled voice from beyond the door had summoned the man inside, so that we were certain the ambassador was within. Each time, however, the secretary had returned to his raised chair without looking our way. I'd barely been able to hide my growing impatience, though the Master had sat serenely waiting with the air of one quite enjoying this forced idleness. His manner might have fooled the secretary, but I had caught him glancing at his wrist clock more than once, so that I knew he had chafed as much as I at the imposed delay.

At first, the secretary had refused even to carry a message to his employer, claiming that Monsieur Villasse was quite unavailable. It was not until Leonardo had called the man over and whispered in his ear that his attitude had abruptly changed.

Whether it had been a bribe or a threat that roused him to action, I could not guess, but the secretary had practically run into the adjoining chamber. He had returned a few minutes later to announce that the ambassador could happily spare a moment or two for the great Leonardo if we had the goodness to wait.

And wait, we had. I suspected the delay was more the secretary's doing than the ambassador's, for all that man's insincere apologies as time continued to tick on. Indeed, he had seemed almost disappointed when he'd finally received word to usher us in. Now, leaving the secretary to stare sourly after us, we made our way into the inner chamber, where the French ambassador had set up his temporary offices.

This room was far larger and more opulent than any of the chambers we had entered thus far, no doubt reserved for heads of state and other important personages. Patterned rugs muffled the stone floors, while ornately carved and gilded wood trim surrounded the doors and windows. The furnishings were equally as grand: a long table, now strewn with books and papers, and two smaller square tables flanked by carved and padded chairs. Along one wall stood an oversized cabinet of dark wood inset with light, while the wall opposite consisted of an elaborate trompe l'oeil which offered in allegory a depiction of the triumph of the Church over man's baser instincts. At the room's far end, an elaborate four-poster draped in silk sat atop a tall platform and was partially concealed by a tapestry screen.

The man who occupied these quarters seemed quite at home in such grandeur, dressed as he was in a long pale blue and silver brocade gown trimmed in white fur along its hem. A black skullcap contrasted sharply with his faded gray hair and gave him an air of nobility.

"Welcome, Monsieur Leonardo," the ambassador exclaimed in his thickly accented Italian, his manner effusive as he rose from the table and rushed toward the Master. "It is indeed a privilege to see you again. I have not yet forgotten my disappointment at losing your beautiful portrait to the duke. I do not suppose you are here to offer me an opportunity to win it back?"

Leonardo gave a small bow, his smile polite. "I fear the duke had become quite attached to the painting of the lady with her ermine, though it is but a minor work. Still, if the treaty you are brokering holds between our two countries, it could be that I will have the opportunity to visit the court of France and ask some of your lovely women to pose for me. Perhaps Madame Villasse would make a charming subject?"

"Madame Villasse?" The ambassador gave a sly grin. "Ah, but why not? And afterwards, you may also paint a certain mademoiselle who happens to be my mistress."

The Master's gracious smile never wavered. "I will be sure to do both of them equal justice." He paused; then, as if the thought just occurred to him, he went on, "As you are an aficionado of the royal game, monsieur, would you be interested perhaps in playing a game with me, with another painting as the wager? Should you win, I shall give you a portrait of both your wife and mistress, and waive my usual patronage."

The ambassador's eyes took on a covetous gleam. "Ah, to own a painting by the great Leonardo, what I would not do for that? But what am I to wager, that I should give up should you win, monsieur?"

"I ask very little . . . just a letter of recommendation from you."

"That is no little request." The ambassador's gaze sharpened. "Are you asking me to help you obtain a position in the court of His Majesty, King Louis?"

"In a manner of speaking. You must understand, Monsieur Villasse, my position here in Milan continues solely at the duke's whim. Should he grow displeased with me—or should the political climate change—I might find myself in search of another wealthy patron." The Master gave a meaningful nod and added, "A patron such as the King of France."

"Ah, Monsieur Leonardo, you are a man after my own heart." The ambassador laughed and playfully shook his finger. "One must always assume that the future brings change, and not all of it pleasant. And so, I accept your challenge. Shall we play now? I have no other appointments for next hour or so."

Not waiting for the Master's reply, he rushed over to the tall cabinet and brought forth a large chessboard and wooden box. "But surely a game of chess was not the reason for your visit, monsieur," the ambassador went on, gesturing Leonardo toward one of the smaller tables. "Pray, what other business brings you to my quarters?"

"You are well aware, of course, of the unfortunate incident that occurred the day of the living chess match," the Master replied as he took the offered seat. When Monsieur Villase nodded, he continued, "As he deemed it a delicate matter beyond the abilities of his guard, the duke tasked me with discovering who murdered his cousin. Sadly, I have learned little as yet that will help solve the mystery. I hoped that you might be able to shed some light upon the matter."

"Me?"

The ambassador had settled the board upon the table and had opened the box containing the chess pieces. Now, he looked up from the painted wooden figures he was lovingly arranging and raised his gray brows in surprise.

"I fear I can be of no use to you," he said. "I had met the Conte di Ferrara but one time before, when he paid a visit to France last year. This was, of course, before his cousin the duke appointed him as ambassador to our country. As I recall, we spoke only briefly then, and not again until my visit here."

He paused and, with a fleeting glance at me, lowered his voice. "Forgive me," he added with a discreet nod, "but the rumor among the court is that he was killed by someone of his acquaintance over, shall we say, a personal matter."

"That is entirely possible; however, given his new position, we cannot dismiss the possibility that his was an assassination of a political nature."

"And you wonder if France was behind it?" His thin features suffused with blood, and his accent grew even thicker with indignation as the ambassador went on, "I assure you, Monsieur Leonardo, that His Majesty the king of France had nothing to do with the death of the duke of Milan's cousin."

"I never suspected that he did," Leonardo easily replied. "I merely raise the possibility that someone of a lower rank— perhaps a disgruntled noble of our own court—sought to cut short the negotiations between France and Lombardy in this manner. But, if such were the case, I am certain that a man of your resources would have long since heard whispers of such a scheme."

"I pledge that I know of no such plot against our countries."

"And I gladly accept your word. But you can understand that my duty to the duke compelled me to ask that question of you."

"Of course." With a seeming effort, the ambassador resurrected his earlier warm manner. "Now, if that ends your questions, let us put that unpleasantness behind us and begin our game. I am anxious to win the paintings you have promised."

Standing discreetly to the side, I had watched the men's exchange with some interest, trying to judge from the ambassador's expression if he spoke the truth. As always, in my servant's guise, I was safely ignored, save for the ambassador's one brief look at me. Thus, I was taken by surprise when Leonardo motioned me closer.

"I trust you do not mind," he told Monsieur Villasse, "but I am attempting to teach my page, Dino, the finer points of the game so that I have someone to play against. It would serve him well to watch someone of your skill."

"Certainly." The ambassador gave a magnanimous nod and then spun the board about so that the light pieces were on the Master's side. "As you are my guest, you shall take white and the first move."

The Master nodded and swiftly moved his queen's pawn—a stern-visaged little figure whose painted garb, I saw in some amusement, was similar to mine—ahead two spaces. The ambassador countered with a comparable move. With a small smile, Leonardo used his turn to move his queen's side bishop's pawn forward alongside his first pawn.

"You will note, Dino," he said with a gesture at the board, "that with this last play I have set up what is called a queen's gambit. I have demonstrated my willingness to sacrifice a pawn now in hopes of gaining a later advantage. My worthy opponent may choose to accept the gambit by using his pawn to capture mine, or he may decline."

"And it appears he has accepted the challenge," he added as the ambassador took the white piece and replaced it with his darker pawn. With a swift move, Leonardo answered by moving his queen diagonally. "And now, I have put the ambassador in check."

Frowning, Monsieur Villasse swiftly moved his knight to block the queen's path.

"He has forestalled my check," the Master explained to me, "and should I dare to capture his knight, I would then forfeit my queen. And so—" He slid his queen sideways and scooped up the ambassador's piece."—I have captured his pawn and temporarily evened the score."

From that point, the game proceeded at a far slower pace . . . at least, on the part of the ambassador. With each play, he squinted and frowned for several minutes before finally moving his piece. In stark contrast, Leonardo seemingly required no forethought as he swiftly completed his turn, occasionally capturing one of the black pieces while losing few of his own in the process. And, at least twice more, he mildly announced, "Check," causing the flustered ambassador to make a hurried move out of danger.

The game continued for the greater portion of an hour. By now, perhaps half the white pieces remained, and even fewer of the black. Through it all, Leonardo had remained relaxed, even jovial as he explained one strategy or another to me. In comparison, the ambassador grew increasingly morose, and sweat beaded on his brow, though the room was cool. I suspected, as well, that the Master's description of the play was beginning to wear on him. But as the ambassador had agreed to my presence, and most of the explanation came during the Master's own play, Villasse could hardly complain without appearing ungracious.

"You have begun to see, Dino," he commented while the ambassador puzzled over his next move, "that the game of chess is conducted much as a real-life war. One must always think several plays ahead and plan for winning the overall battle . . . and not simply triumphing in an individual skirmish," he added as Villasse, with a smile, swooped up Leonardo's queen.

While I watched that move in alarm, the Master merely shrugged. "As you know, my boy, the queen is perhaps the most powerful piece on the board. Her loss usually means defeat for her side. But sometimes, the queen deliberately sacrifices herself for the good of her king. And while the other side celebrates her capture, the distraction allows one of the lesser pieces to pick up the standard for her and win the day."

So saying, he slid his remaining pawn one space so that it

stood diagonally from the black king. Sitting back in his chair, he genially told the ambassador, "If I am not mistaken, monsieur, I believe that is checkmate."

The ambassador sputtered and gasped for a few moments as he stared at the board from every angle, as if hoping an alternate view would bring to light a route of escape he had not noticed. Finally, he shoved his chair back, as well, and lifted his hands with a sigh.

"I concede defeat, Monsieur Leonardo. You are indeed a fine player. I regret I will not have those paintings after all."

"It was a hard-fought match," the Master consoled him. "But with the letter you will write me, perhaps I shall be at King Louis' court in the future, so that you may yet obtain a portrait from me . . . at my usual fee, of course."

The ambassador chuckled. "Of course," he agreed, rising from his seat and heading for the table. Taking up a sheet of paper and a quill, he swiftly penned a few lines; then, dripping a bit of wax upon it, he stamped it with his seal. "Here is your letter, Monsieur Leonardo," Villasse proclaimed and handed it to him. "May it serve you well."

The Master read the letter with a satisfied smile, then carefully folded it and tucked it into his tunic. "I am sure it shall," he replied. "And now, we shall take our leave of you. But do send word to me should you recall anything regarding your dealing with the conte that might assist me in my investigation."

We departed the chamber, the ambassador's assurances ringing in our ears. The Master spared a cheery nod for the secretary, who abandoned his chair simply for the pleasure of closing the door to the antechamber after us. Once back in the main chamber again, I waited until I was certain no one nearby could hear and then asked with unbridled curiosity, "Please tell me, Master, whatever did you say to that unpleasant man to obtain his cooperation?"

Leonardo lifted a brow. "I merely told him I knew what he had done the night before and that I would take pains to inform the ambassador if he did not announce us."

"But whatever had he done that he feared it becoming common knowledge?" I persisted.

He shrugged. "I have no idea, my dear boy. But my long study of human nature suggested that someone of that man's disposition was prone to conducting himself poorly, so I gambled that he had behaved intemperately of late. As you saw, my intuition proved correct."

I shook my head in admiration. "And what of the chess match with the ambassador? Had you lost, would you have painted both his wife and his mistress?"

"Of course," he carelessly replied. "I am a man of my word. However, the ambassador might not have been pleased with the final work. For rather than giving him two portraits, I likely would have painted both women into the same one."

I could not help but laugh at the absurdity of what he had described: the painted images of both wife and mistress confronting each other. Perhaps he would have rendered one seated before a mirror, and the other one as the reflected image in that glass. Doubtless such a work would have been hailed as sly genius by all, save the ambassador and the two luckless women.

My amusement swiftly faded, however, as I thought back over the conversation with Monsieur Villasse. While I had been prepared to cast him as one of the villains in the plot, his manner had not reflected that of a guilty man.

"You didn't show him the drawings of the porters," I reminded him. "Should we go back and do so?"

"There is no need. The pair would have been hired by the contessa, or else Orlando, were he one of the conspirators. Villasse would have had no part of it."

I shook my head in disappointment. It seemed the ambassador had revealed little of use to us, and I told the master as much.

Leonardo halted abruptly and faced me. "Ah, my dear Dino, but this time you are quite wrong. The French ambassador revealed quite a bit, although he does not know it."

He reached into his tunic and pulled forth the letter. "I deliberately suggested the chess game for I knew he was still stinging over his loss to Il Moro. As for my choice of a prize in this wager, it was not an idle one . . . nor was it for my benefit. I sought only to obtain a legitimate sample of Monsieur Villasse's handwriting."

He unfolded the letter and glanced over it again, nodding in satisfaction. "And now my curiosity is satisfied. You see, if I were to place this letter side by side with the missive I found in the contessa's casket, it will be quite evident that both were written by the same hand."

Then, as I stared back at him in awe, he added, "Unfortunately, that means only that he is intent on arranging the archbishop's death. We still do not know with certainty who killed the Conte di Ferrara, or why. For that, it will take a queen's gambit to force the assassin's hand."

Recalling the explanation he had given of that particular chess strategy, I wondered aloud, "But whom will you sacrifice to open the way for the mystery to be solved?"

"That is quite easy, my dear boy," he said with a smile. "I shall sacrifice myself."

15

Experience is never at fault; it is only your judgment that is in error . . .

—Leonardo da Vinci, *Codex Atlanticus*

Following his last cryptic comment regarding the queen's gambit, Leonardo left me at the workshop to rejoin Constantin and the others . . . though first, he bade me carry his torn tunic to Signore Luigi to repair for him. This time, I was able to leave the castle grounds with little difficulty. One of the guards informed me that one of the scullery maids had told him that a valet had confided to her that Il Moro was about to end the ban on passage to and from Castle Sforza. I'd wondered whether the duke was revoking his decree on his own, or if the Master had somehow had a hand in that change of heart.

For once, the tailor seemed almost glad to see me as I entered his shop late that day. "Ah, my little friend, er, Dino," he greeted me as he raised his bulk from the tiny bench he was perched upon. He shooed his two young apprentices to the workshop next door and gestured me toward him. "And how have those elegant clothes I made served you?"

"Quite well," I told him most sincerely. "I appeared quite splendid in my role."

"And the other garment?" he wanted to know, waggling his brows meaningfully.

I blushed just a little. "I find it most comfortable, Signore, and far more suitable than what I had worn before."

"Ah, so then our masquerade continues undiscovered." He gave a satisfied nod and then shot a questioning glance at my bundle. "Do not tell me, Signore Leonardo has destroyed yet another tunic of his."

Ruefully, I nodded and showed him the torn sleeve. Luigi stared at it with pursed lips, then shrugged. "The damage is not so bad, not like the time your master brought me a tunic that he had been wearing when some experiment or another of his exploded. That garment was more holes than fabric and fit only for scrubbing pots in the scullery. This one, I can repair so that it looks like new."

Then he leaned closer and dropped his voice to a whisper. "I have heard rumors, my young Dino, that your Master is looking into the events surrounding the murder of Il Moro's cousin. Come, do not pretend not to know what I mean," he urged when I gave him a blank look. "It is common knowledge by now. In fact, I already have orders for new tunics to be worn to the upcoming execution. But I am surprised that the great Leonardo has not yet come to me for information in this affair."

"I don't understand," I said with a frown. "Do you know something about the murder that he should also know?"

"I know everything about everything. You must understand that people will gladly tell their tailor secrets that they will not reveal even to their confessors," Luigi said with a languid wave of his hand.

I purposefully plopped myself onto a bench and fixed my gaze upon him. "So you do know something. Please, you must tell me."

"Not so fast, my, er, boy." The tailor assumed a virtuous expression. "Like a priest, I cannot divulge what was said to me in confidence. But I can tell you that the conte was not the devoted husband he appeared to be. More than one woman of the court knew his favors, both before and after his marriage."

He shrugged and went on, "Of course, one cannot entirely blame him for looking elsewhere for companionship. You see, the Contessa di Ferrara is hardly the most placid of females, for all her mousy appearance. At any rate, I suspect it was a disgruntled spouse who had a hand in dispatching the charming Orlando," he finished with a smug nod.

I considered Luigi's revelations with no little interest. Though the Master and I had discussed other possibilities, to this point we had no cause to believe that the conte's death was anything but an assassination. Either Orlando had been the intended target because of his post as ambassador, or else he'd been killed by accident while costumed as the archbishop, against whom we were quite certain there was a death plot. But now a third possibility seemed to take equal precedence . . . that his murder was instead an impulsive crime committed by someone to avenge a personal outrage.

Luigi, however, tired of the subject just as quickly as he had seized upon it. He drifted off to other topics of gossip, apparently finding me a far better confidante than any of the youths who worked for him. I listened politely for several minutes longer, even while I yearned to hurry back to the workshop.

It was not just that this new information regarding the conte bore looking into, though indeed I would relay it to the Master as soon as I could find him. I had one other item to attend to, one which I had overlooked in the excitement of the day. As soon as I returned to the workshop, I would search my box of belongings to discover if last night's intruder had indeed left something behind, as the Master had guessed was possible.

By now, I suspected that my nocturnal visitor might well have been Renaldo, for I judged him audacious enough to make his way past the castle walls without being noticed. I also had begun to wonder whether his pursuit of me in the marketplace had been an attempt simply to talk to me, rather than to do me any harm. For if, as the ambassador's anonymous letter had instructed, the would-be assassins were to be eliminated, it could be that he had learned what happened to his fellow and feared now for his own life.

Of course, I could be wrong. Renaldo might have indeed killed his friend Lorenzo and was still intent on fulfilling his contract to murder the archbishop . . . and anyone else necessary!

I took my leave of Signore Luigi as soon as politeness allowed and made my way back to our sleeping quarters in the workshop. Both the main room and our alcove were empty for the moment, though I knew the other apprentices would soon be returning from their day's work on the fresco in the castle's dining hall. Once they'd assembled, it would be time to march over to the kitchen for the day's final meal. I would have to make my search quickly lest any of them arrive sooner than the rest and wonder what I was about.

The inventory of my belongings took but a few minutes. I was relieved to find that the florins my father had given me were still safely hidden in the toe of one well-worn slipper. Everything else was accounted for, as well, though the slight disorder of my garments assured me I had not imagined someone had shuffled them through without my leave. Neither did I find anything added to my modest collection of belongings . . . or so I thought at first glance. It was only as I refolded the tunic that had been left hanging from the box and was preparing to close the lid that I noticed a slight bulge in one arm of that garment.

I pulled it forth again and reached inside that sleeve, feeling what seemed to be a stiff bit of cloth rolled up inside. Frowning, I tugged the fabric free and stared at it in confusion, for it was not cloth but a piece of soft yellow leather. Moreover, it appeared to be a folded glove belonging to a woman, from the dainty construction of it. The leather seemed oddly stiff, so it was with no little trepidation that I unfolded it.

My first impression was that its owner must have inadvertently dropped it into a dish of fresh tempera, for some rust-colored liquid seemed to have soaked into a portion of the leather. Then I realized what I was seeing: a glove liberally splattered with blood. Perhaps the blood of a conte?

With a cry, I dropped the terrible object with the same thrill of horror as if the gore still dripped from it. Surely this must be the very glove worn by the person—no, the woman—who had murdered the Conte di Ferrara! My thoughts swiftly turned to the Contessa di Malvoral, whom I could readily tag as a murderess. Even if she'd not had a literal hand in the killing, here surely was proof she had been witness to it. But who had hidden this gruesome relic in my chest, and why?

Before I could guess at an answer, I heard my fellow apprentices entering the workshop, voices raised in eagerness and laughter. Acting hastily, I grabbed the gory object and wrapped it in that same length of cloth that I'd once worn beneath my tunic. Then I buried the bundle beneath my other garments and slammed the lid of the chest shut.

"There you are, Dino," Constantin called as I stood and brushed the dust from my knees. "If the Master does not need you tonight, why don't you come eat your meal with us?"

"Gladly," I replied.

In truth, I needed a bit of uncomplicated fellowship to help settle my mind, at least for the space of an hour. But my meal with Constantin and the others did not prove as straightforward as I had hoped. Even as we stood in line at the kitchen, word spread to us that the duke's rumored lifting of his curfew had indeed come to pass.

"They say all the visiting nobles are packing their trunks, preparing to depart at first light," Paulo reported, adding with a snicker, "I predict it will be an exodus of biblical proportions on the morrow."

"Who cares about them?" Vittorio piped up. "As soon as we finish eating, I intend to take a stroll outside the castle gates, just because I can. Oh, do not worry, Constantin," he added as the older apprentice stared sternly at him. "I shall only be a few minutes and then be back in plenty of time for the night's chores."

While the others added their voices to Constantin's, I strained my ears for news of a particular departure . . . that of the archbishop of Milan, who had made known he would leave for Rome two mornings hence. But it was the archbishop's intended parting gesture that had stirred interest among the castle residents. Barely had we seated ourselves with our bowls when Davide spoke up.

"Word is that His Eminence will go to the castle's hidden garden tomorrow night. He will spend the entire time kneeling in prayer for his people, just as the Lord did in Gethsemane," he exclaimed in admiration.

My emotion, however, was one of alarm. This was the same garden in which the Conte di Ferrara had been found murdered but a few days before. Was it merely coincidence that the cleric planned his night of prayer in that same place?

While the other youths discussed the virtues of kneeling for hours at a time, I puzzled over the archbishop's motives, especially in light of the warning that the Master and I had offered him only yesterday. Surely the archbishop must realize that any such public display of piety—particularly undertaken alone and at night—could leave him vulnerable to an attempt on his life. This likely would be the last opportunity the ambassador and his compatriots would have to complete their mission, for in Rome the archbishop would be carefully guarded.

Indeed, it was almost as if Cardinal Nardini hoped to be set upon by his enemies.

I frowned. Could this be the queen's gambit to which Leonardo had alluded . . . the sacrifice made in an attempt to gain the ultimate advantage over the opposition? Perhaps he meant to stand guard over the cleric and apprehend anyone who might attempt to harm him.

A cold knot formed in the pit of my stomach as I realized this must be the Master's plan. Doubtless he had made certain that the rumor spread quickly of the archbishop's planned devotion, so that the would-be killers would hear and have ample time to make their plans. With the court distracted by the conte's murder, these villains likely would feel confident of success. Thus deluded, Leonardo might easily be a match for them.

But it was not quite so simple anymore, I grimly reminded myself. Two men had already been killed, and a third was slated to die. The killers would be determined, even desperate. They would not be captured so easily, likely would not hesitate to claim yet another victim if they found their escape barred. Unless the Master planned to have Ludovico's guard at the ready with him, he might well fall victim to the killer along with Cardinal Nardini.

And I knew no guard would be waiting with him. Leonardo would disdain any assistance, but would attempt to thwart this crime on his own. I pictured the frightful scene in my mind as vividly as if I'd witnessed it. Frail as he was, the archbishop could be of little help in defending against an assailant. Should there be but a single assassin to confront, Leonardo might well defeat him. But if the ambassador's previous failure had caused him to recruit others to his scheme to guarantee success this time, there might be two knife-wielding men in the garden, or even more.

That was, of course, if the Master lived long enough to put his plan into works. For he had not yet seen the bloody evidence I had found or heard the rumors . . . did not understand as I did that the Contessa di Malvoral was indeed a dangerous woman. What if he returned to her chambers to question her further? Her suspicions could be sufficiently aroused that she might slip a knife into him before he realized what she was about.

"Dino, are you unwell?" Constantin asked me, the question abruptly bringing me back to the moment. "You look pale, as if you've seen a ghost."

"I am fine, just a bit tired," I assured him, wondering what he'd say if I told him of the ghosts I indeed had seen in my mind. There was but one way I could stop such a tragedy before it happened.

Determination promptly replaced my distress. Leonardo would not be alone in the garden tomorrow night, I vowed, for I would watch and wait with him. But first, I must find him and pass on the gossip I had learned from Signore Luigi and then show him my mysterious and quite grisly discovery: the bloodstained glove.

THE Master did not summon me later in the evening, as I'd hoped; nor, when I finally ventured from the workshop and tapped at his quarters did he answer. I could see a candle flickering within and guessed that he might be locked in his personal workshop, perhaps embroiled with the same invention he had been working on the night before. But I was not bold enough to march in and knock upon that particular sanctum demanding entrance. Thus, I had no choice but to retire to my bed with the day's events still roiling about my mind.

I slept but little that night. Dawn brought no relief; neither did it bring an appearance from the Master. Worry continued to grip me as I followed Constantin and the rest to the dining hall, where work continued in Leonardo's absence on this final fresco.

In the preceding days, the youths had applied the thick base layer of plaster and rough top coat. What I had not expected was that the Master had seemingly found time—perhaps within the last night—to sketch in the background of the fresco. Despite my sense of disquiet, I could not help but be impressed by the brilliance shown in even this most bare of renderings.

The fresco was to be a trompe l'oeil. To create that image, Leonardo had drawn over the stenciled outlines of rolling hills and distant battlements a series of draped windows and columned archways that gave the impression that the viewer was looking directly through the wall out into the countryside. Today, we would hang more stencils and pounce in the figures over that background, and then trace over the charcoal lines with red ink.

It was tedious work, for the wall was large and the charcoal easily smeared. By the day's end, however, we had completed our task and were making our weary way back to the workshop. Our spirits lifted when Constantin announced a small holiday for us. After the late-day meal, we need not return to the workshop for the usual evening's tasks but would have the entire night free to ourselves. The news brought a collective cheer from all of the apprentices . . . all, that is, save me.

"Why are you so glum, Dino?" Vittorio asked, splashing alongside me as I paused at the fountain to scrub away the charcoal and plaster dust before continuing to the kitchen portico.

I dried my hands and face on the hem of my tunic and turned to him. "I'm not glum. I am concerned about the Master. He's not been seen for a day now. Surely he should have been supervising today's work on the fresco."

"Ah, but you have not been his apprentice as long as I have," the younger boy said with an air of importance. "Sometimes he is gone for two or three days at a time working on one of his inventions. I am sure he will return tomorrow, never fear."

I returned the boy's encouraging smile, but I could not shake my sense of unease. It would be dark in another hour or so, meaning the archbishop would soon commence his vigil in the garden. If Leonardo did indeed have a plan, why had he not yet revealed it to me? Perhaps something else was wrong.

I thought again of the Contessa di Malvoral, wondering if she had a hand in his absence. Or perhaps the ambassador had grown suspicious and had sent Renaldo after him with his knife or cudgel! What if the Master had not sent for me because he could not?

My trepidation growing, I decided upon a plan of my own. I would wait until after the meal to return to his quarters. If he did not answer his door, I would find a way in, and then make my way into the workshop. I would gladly suffer his anger at my intrusion, just to know he was unharmed. If he was not within, however, I would then don my page's garments and search him out.

FORTIFIED by a portion of vegetable stew, I hurried back to the workshop. The other apprentices had remained behind, joining others of the castle servants in what had become a small celebration, so that none saw me as I made my stealthy way to Leonardo's quarters. As I feared, my knock was not answered, while the door appeared barred from within. The window, however, was propped slightly ajar, the opening just wide enough to allow someone of my agility and small stature to climb through. And so, with another quick glance around me, I did.

I dropped from the sill onto the floor, landing silently if rather ungracefully within the Master's chamber. By now the sun had almost set, so that the room was bathed in shadows, unlit save for the faintest glow from the hearth where a few coals lay buried. I could immediately see, however, that the Master was not inside. As for the door to his private workshop, it was closed, the gap between floor and door dark. Still, I gave a tentative knock.

When no voice called to me, I pounded with greater force. "Signore Leonardo, are you within? It is I, Dino."

Once more, there was no reply. A feeling of alarm swept me as I recalled the hellish clatter I'd heard from there two nights before, when something large within that chamber had fallen. That accident had left the Master with a torn tunic. What if a similar disaster had befallen him, but this time he had suffered some injury that had left him helpless, even senseless?

Cautiously, I tried the door and was surprised to find it was unlocked. The lamp was still on the same table where I had sat translating the ambassador's letter, so I swiftly lit it and carried it back to the workshop. The sharp scream of un-oiled hinges as I pushed the door open made me jump. I had to wait few moments for my heartbeat to return to normal before I crossed that threshold into the darkened workshop.

My first impression was of well-ordered chaos. Shelves and tables lined the walls, filled with all manner of items: pots of paint, lengths of metal rods, gears, bricks, sheets of parchment, half-finished sketches. A long table ran most of the length of the room, one end stacked with ledgers and books, while in its center were spread curling pages upon which devices both fanciful and practical were depicted. Had I the time, I could have spent a day wandering through there in amazement. My concern for now, however, was for the Master.

But, of course, he was not within, nor did his lifeless body lay sprawled beneath some toppled machine or sculpture. I could not guess how long it had been since he'd left the room, but the stubs of candles like squat mushrooms in the dark were cold, the puddles around them long since frozen into solid wax again. Should I wait here and hope that he returned, I wondered, or should I go in search of him?

Deciding on the second course, I pulled the workshop door closed behind me and snuffed my light. I exited his chamber the same way I had entered, making certain I left behind no overt sign of my unauthorized entry, and hurried the few short steps back to the main workshop.

A few minutes later, I had doffed my apprentice's tunic for my splendid page's garb, though my pleasure in such fine clothing was tempered this night by the gravity of my mission. Reluctantly, I reached into my wooden chest for the cloth bundle in which I had wrapped the single bloodied glove. Tearing off a piece of that fabric, I carefully folded the soiled item within it and tucked the small packet into my tunic.

It occurred to me that I should first check the garden to learn if the archbishop had begun his night of prayer. Thus, I started across the quadrangle in that direction. I found the garden gate closed but not barred, so I ventured a look inside.

The archbishop had not yet arrived, I saw in relief . . . neither did I glimpse any sign of the Master. Even had he already been hidden somewhere among the greenery, he surely would have made himself known had he seen my approach. They must both still be somewhere in the castle, I decided, which was where I would now go.

My stroll back across the open courtyard appeared far more casual, I hoped, than my true state of emotion this night. By the time I reached the castle's main buildings, however, my nervousness had begun to lessen. I remembered the lessons of the past few days, how servants drew little heed from the castle's more noble inhabitants, save if some manner of service were required. Dressed as I was, I should be able to wander most any public chamber with impunity.

I thought I'd had no definite plan of search in mind, until I realized my new red shoes were taking me toward the wing where the French ambassador was housed. Should a plot be in the making this night, surely Monsieur Villasse would have some hand in it. Perhaps Leonardo would have had the same idea, maybe even engaging the man in another game of chess to distract him from any such nefarious business.

It was still early enough in the evening that all manner of servants were about, so that my presence drew little notice from anyone I passed. Not so, however, when I reached the ambassador's rooms. The door to his antechamber was ajar, and I could see his secretary within, packing trunks with clothing and papers in apparent preparation for their morning departure. Of the Master and Monsieur Villasse, however, I glimpsed no sign.

Discouraged, I thought to slip away unseen, but my luck did not hold. To my dismay, the sour-faced clerk turned and immediately noticed my presence. His features grew even more pinched, if that were possible, and he stopped me in my tracks with an imperious gesture.

"You, boy," he exclaimed in a disagreeable tone, "what do you think you are doing here at the ambassador's private quarters?"

I gave a swift bow as I sought a reasonable explanation. "Begging your pardon, but my Master, Signore Leonardo, sent word I was to join him," I temporized. "I was given to understand that he was with Monsieur Villasse this night."

"Well, you understood wrongly," the secretary said with a sneer. "The ambassador has more important things to do before his departure than spend an evening with a minor artist such as your master. He is busy discussing matters of state with the duke. Now, off with you, lest I summon the guards."

Though stinging at the man's petty dismissal of Leonardo as an insignificant painter, I gratefully did as ordered. Hopefully, he would consider any further acknowledgment of my brief appearance to be beneath him, and thus would not bother mentioning it to the ambassador. But now there was another wing of the castle that I needed to investigate.

Having been taken unawares by the ambassador's secretary, I was far more wary in my approach to the contessa's rooms. I had not forgotten her insistence that she recognized me from somewhere; thus, I did not intend to give her another look at me that might then jog her memory of our first encounter. But I would find out if the Master was with her.

This time, my luck proved better. As I approached, the door to her chamber opened, and the same servant girl we'd seen rush crying from the room days earlier now slipped out into the corridor. Her expression was petulant, masking some of her youthful prettiness. But as her cheek still bore a dark bruise from the contessa's previous treatment of her, I could not fault the girl her bad humor and felt a stab of sympathy for her in the employ of so cruel a mistress.

She saw me then, and her expression brightened, restoring a bit of attractiveness to her plump features. I realized with my usual sense of discomfort that she properly viewed me as a boy. While I had always taken pains not to encourage any female attention, circumstances compelled me this one time to use the masquerade to my advantage.

"Good evening," I said and gave her a sweeping bow, the gesture drawing the expected giggle from her. "I fear I am in some difficulty and wondered if you might help me."

"Perhaps," she answered with another giggle. "What is the difficulty?"

"My Master, Signore Leonardo, instructed me to find him should a particular message he was waiting for arrive for him this night. I am not certain where he was to spend his evening, but he mentioned the Contessa di Malvoral's name. Can you tell me if she is within . . . or if my Master has been to see her?"

The girl's expression darkened. "There is a man in there with her now . . . that is why she has sent me away. I do not know his name, but I do not think he can be your master."

"Let me describe him for you," I urged. "He is tall and well formed, with russet hair and a handsome face. I cannot tell you how he is garbed, but his clothes could be those of a workman or a noble, depending on his mood."

She shrugged. "The man you describe could well be he," she replied, the admission filling me with equal parts relief and unease. Then she gave a sly smile that vanquished any prettiness. "If you like, I can let you inside, and you can peek into the bedchamber to see if it is your master atop her."

Her words were like a fist to my belly. Even in the privacy of my own thoughts, I had not dared give voice to my greatest fear . . . that, if Leonardo were indeed in her quarters, he might have gone there for some entirely different reason than to ask questions. Yet now it seemed that possibility confronted me.

"Do not worry," she added as I found myself momentarily speechless. "She always leaves that door open just a crack. I think she hopes that people will spy on her when she is with other men besides the conte. Come, watch with me. I do it all the time."

My first thought was to refuse, so eager did the girl seem for me to join in her lascivious game. I did not want to spy on the Master, I miserably told myself—certainly not if he were in the midst of bedding the woman—but I had to know for his sake if he was with the contessa.

I nodded silently, still unable to speak for the cold knot in my stomach that her words had left. The girl's smile broadened, and she put a finger to her lips. Wiping suddenly damp palms upon my tunic, I followed her into the contessa's antechamber.

The room looked the same as I remembered it, down to the overflowing bowls of flowers and fruit, save that the jeweled casket with its incriminating letter locked within was no longer on the table amid them. My soft shoes made little more sound than the girl's skirts upon the polished floors as we approached the far door. Now, I could hear the murmur coming from within . . . a woman's moans and soft laughter, interspersed with the low rumble of a man's voice, not loud enough for me to recognize it.

The girl gestured me forward. The heavy carved door opened outward perhaps the space of two fingers, the gap just wide enough for someone to stand to one side and peer in without being seen, or so I prayed. Pressing myself against the wall, I slowly eased my face toward that narrow opening. Then, taking a steadying breath, I peered inside.

The contessa apparently lacked any modesty in her coupling, for a dozen or more candles lit the chamber bright as day. I could see quite clearly the bed with its turned posts high upon a platform, and the lush spill of fine bedding, dyed gold and embroidered as finely as any gown. Entangled within those blankets were two half-naked forms.

I readily recognized the contessa, her pale limbs sprawled in abandon as she gave a soft, husky laugh to something her partner said. He was poised above her, his naked back to me, and for a sickening moment I was sure it was Leonardo. Then, in a rush of relief I saw that he was broader of girth, and his hair far redder than the Master's. Something about him was frighteningly familiar, however, and when he moved to one side to begin untying his hose, I caught a sufficient glimpse of his face to recognize him.

Renaldo!

I smothered a gasp, but before I could step back from the opening, I heard the echoing slam of a door behind me. Whipping about, I saw the servant girl had fled. The crash had likely been a deliberate action to announce my trespassing, and her abandonment of me a cruel trick that had been her devious plan from the start. Answering cries of outrage promptly spilled from the contessa's bedchamber, leaving little doubt that the servant girl's ploy had succeeded.

Not bothering with stealth, I took off at a run, knowing I might be recognized but praying I could escape the room without being caught. Behind me, I heard another thunderous slam as the chamber door flew open and crashed into the wall. *I am being chased.* The panicked thought flashed through my mind, though I could manage no other plan save to flee. But by then I was but a few steps from the door, and with a sob of relief I reached toward it, my fingers brushing the cold hammered iron of its latch.

And then a heavy fist slammed into my temple, dropping me to my knees only inches from the barred door.

16

A single candle may banish the darkness as readily as the sun.

—Leonardo da Vinci, *The Notebooks of Delfina della Fazia*

A rough hand jerked me to my feet. As I blinked away my dizziness, I saw a half-naked Renaldo glaring down at me. His eyes narrowing in recognition, he backed in the direction of the bedchamber and shoved me onto a nearby chair, snarling, "It's you. You're the porter who was eavesdropping on me and Lorenzo the night of the feast. Look, Elena, I've caught a spy here in your chamber."

"A spy, he may well be," the contessa replied with a cold laugh. She had pulled a long brocade gown over her chemise, though her bare legs were visible with every step she took in my direction. Pausing before me, she gripped me painfully by the chin.

"So we meet again, my pretty Dino," she purred, leaning forward so that her face was inches from mine.

Though my head still spun and fear now chilled me, I refused to flinch but boldly glared back at her. I could smell the wine on her breath and the musky scent of her body that was the result of her earlier exertions. I could see, as well, the fine pattern of lines about her eyes and mouth that, close up, betrayed her age despite the skillful layering of cosmetics. Her pale gaze still held traces of lust sharpened now by anger, and I suspected she enjoyed the discomfort she was inflicting upon me. Stubbornly, I vowed I would not give her the satisfaction of crying out or of answering her taunts.

Abruptly, she released me and gave Renaldo a sharp glance. "You may know him as another porter, but he also is page to Ludovico's pet artist, the great Leonardo. But those are not his only roles."

Her gaze even colder, she turned to me again. "I knew I had seen you somewhere before, my boy, and I told you I would eventually recall our meeting."

Her gaze still fixed on me, she addressed the young man beside her. "You recall how I told you, Renaldo, that when my dear cousin disappeared from the playing field the day of the chess match, another white bishop came to take his place. You can imagine my surprise when I first saw him and thought that Orlando had been miraculously resurrected. But, of course, it was none other than young Dino. Doubtless he had been put into the game by his master, so that no one would discover the Conte di Ferrara had gone missing until much later."

Her stiff smile returned as she ticked off on her fingers, "Porter . . . page . . . bishop. It seems that our dear Dino is a young man of many roles. And I fear that, with all the questions that Leonardo has been asking these past few days, both master and servant may now know more about certain secrets than they should. And that knowledge makes them very dangerous to us."

"So what do we do with him?" Renaldo asked.

By now, he had retrieved his dark green tunic and was belting it about him. I saw with no little alarm that a short dagger hung from the broad strip of leather. He followed my gaze and spared me a cruel grin as he lightly fingered the weapon. The contessa saw the gesture, however, and gave her head an imperious shake.

"Not that way. It is too messy . . . too difficult to clean

up all that blood. You must take care of him the way you handled your young friend, Lorenzo. Do you still have the key that I gave to you?"

Renaldo nodded, patting the pouch at his waist. "It's a good thing that Il Moro ended the curfew. It'll be easier getting him out of the castle than it was with Lorenzo. I can bribe one of the guards to open up the gate for me." His grinned widened. "I'll tell the guard that the boy had too much to drink, that I'm carrying him home to his mother. Too bad that his mother lives in the churchyard."

Despite myself, I choked on a gasp, the reaction drawing laughter from them both. Apparently satisfied that I understood what my fate was to be, the contessa abruptly turned her back on me and advanced on Renaldo. Her smile now was one of lazy desire as she trailed her fingers down his chest and then deliberately slid her hand under the hem of his short tunic.

"Take care of our young friend for me, and swiftly," she purred, pressing him back against the tapestry and moving her hand with slow, unmistakable purpose between his thighs. "When you are finished, come back here, and I shall finish with you . . . and then it will be time for you to complete the job for which you were hired."

"What about the painter?" he mumbled, his cruel expression growing slack now as he leaned back into the wall. "Do I kill him, too?"

"I'll decide that later. I have ways of guaranteeing a man's silence, and that might be a more interesting way of resolving the situation."

While this exchange was taking place between the pair, I had recovered my wits enough to realize that my only hope of not meeting my end at Renaldo's hands was to get out of that room. The door was farther from me than I would have liked, but the porter was sufficiently distracted so that it would take him a few moments to react. And I was almost certain that the door itself was only latched, and not locked, which would gain me a few seconds' more advantage. All I need do was run.

Run! a voice shrieked in my head, the command lifting me from my chair and sending me fleeing toward the door again. I could hear the contessa's shout, heard Renaldo's grunt of surprise before he came thundering after me. Once again, he caught hold of me just as I touched the door. This time, with a roar of outrage, he grabbed his dagger and wildly slashed at me.

My own senses equally inflamed, I was swift enough to spin out of range . . . almost. The dagger ripped lengthwise across my belly, tearing through my tunic and slicing the horsehair padding beneath. I felt the sharp sting of metal against my flesh and cried out, even as one corner of my mind assured me that the blade had but grazed me. My swift reaction and the padding beneath my clothes had spared me being sliced open like a marketplace sheep. But I could not stop myself from falling, nor could I avoid the stunning blow as my bruised temple connected with the stone floor at my feet.

I lay sprawled and half-conscious, aware that Renaldo had caught me by the hair and was pulling my head back to expose my throat. But even as his blade touched my flesh, I heard the contessa shriek at him to stop.

"No, you fool, don't slit his throat! The blood will be everywhere! He'll die of his other wound soon enough if you but leave him in that crypt."

I did not hear Renaldo's reply, but I felt the knife fall from my throat, felt the hard floor contact my face again as he let me drop. There was more conversation, but it seemed to come from very far away, as unintelligible as the buzzing of insects in a summer's field of grass.

They think I am mortally stabbed, I told myself, wanting to laugh at the way they had been fooled but unable to manage anything more than a whispered moan. *When I finally escape them, I shall have to thank Signore Luigi for his fine tailoring, which saved me.*

Vaguely, I was aware of being lifted onto Renaldo's shoulder, the throbbing in my head now a stabbing pain with each jarring step he took, so that I faded into senselessness. Sometime later, I roused enough to feel the cool night breeze upon my face. We must be outside the castle gates now, I realized, wondering if the guard had indeed laughed at the foolish boy who had imbibed more than his head could take. *Cold,* I tried to murmur, but my lips were not working.

My last thought before I slipped into unconsciousness a final time was that I had failed the Master. Surely by now the archbishop had begun his vigil, unaware of the danger that soon would come his way. I could only pray that Leonardo could manage on his own to stop Renaldo from killing Cardinal Nardini this night.

I also meant to pray that Leonardo would think to look for me when I was not to be found the next morning—assuming, of course, that he himself did not fall victim to Renaldo's blade—but darkness swallowed that thought long before it was finished.

I awoke tangled in my bedcovers, barely able to move, so tightly were they wrapped around me. Moreover, my head pounded with the same fury as it had following the ill-fated morning the previous year when, in defiance of my mother, I'd swallowed one too many cups of wine at the town's midsummer festival. The trouble was, I could not recall imbibing any spirits the previous night, nor could I even recall returning to my bed. But it had to be nighttime still, for the darkness I saw when I managed to open one eye just a slit was unrelieved by any light.

Slowly, bits of memory drifted back. I recalled being in the Contessa di Malvoral's chamber and my shock at seeing her and Renaldo entangled in an obscene embrace. And Renaldo had tried to stab me . . . but I felt no real pain other than my head, so perhaps it had all been a dream. If I could but rouse myself all the way, perhaps I might find a jug of water to rinse the grit from my mouth.

For, as I weakly struggled against my blankets, I became aware of the taste of dirt in my mouth and the cold, damp hardness beneath me and pressed against my one side. So strange, I thought in puzzlement, though the pounding of my head made it difficult to think logically. I was not in bed, at all, it seemed. But if not my own blanket, then what was wrapped around me, covering even my face?

I managed to kick one foot free and stretched my toes, bruising them upon more rock. It was then that, even through the cloth and the dust, my nostrils were assailed by the sickening odor of corruption, unmistakable in its sharp sweetness. Full memory of Renaldo's attack on me abruptly returned, and a horror such as I'd never before felt seized me.

Saints' blood, I was in the crypt, wrapped in cloth and shoved into a niche, trapped with the Sforza dead!

I screamed . . . or, at least, I tried, but my attempt was choked off by the cloth over my face and the dust that abruptly clogged my lungs. My fearful shriek ended in a coughing fit that as quickly turned into sobs.

Stop it! the remaining rational portion of my mind commanded me. *Think what the Master would do in this situation. Surely he would not lie here wailing in fear.*

Deliberately slowing my breath, I lay very still and took stock of my situation. Already, the cloth around me had begun to loosen with my movements, so I would surely be able to work myself free of the makeshift shroud once I managed to wriggle my way out of the niche. And once I was free, all I need do was manage a bit of light and then find my way to the door of the crypt. How I would get out, I did not yet know . . . but I would find some escape.

I searched my thoughts to re-create a mental image of the crypt's interior so I could determine where I was. Chances were I lay in a different niche from the one in which we'd found Lorenzo. For, unless Renaldo had checked on the state of his dead friend and found him gone, he would have known he must put me elsewhere. But in which one was I?

I recalled that the alcoves in the crypt's walls had been carved at no more than three levels. The lowest were but a few inches from the ground, while the highest were at head height for a man. A center row of niches lay somewhere between those two. Surely Renaldo would not have wanted to hoist my unconscious form into the topmost one; neither would he have troubled himself to drop to his knees and maneuver me into one of the lower alcoves. So that left me—

"In the middle one," I whispered to the rocks above me.

And if I could maneuver myself carefully, I should be able to slide my legs and torso out first and easily touch the crypt's rough stone floor. But maneuvering in such a manner would be difficult even unfettered. With my arms bound and unable to support me, if I were not careful I might roll from my rocky ledge and simply plunge to the ground. True, it was not much of a fall, but even a short drop onto the hard rock would be painful, at best. At worst, I could hit my head upon one of the stone sepulchers situated near the walls and kill myself that way.

Of course, I grimly told myself, I could just lie upon my rocky bed and wait for someone to find me . . . though chances were I'd die of hunger and thirst long before the Master thought to look for me here.

I blindly inched my feet toward the opening of the niche and felt them slide over its edge . . . but, for the moment, I could not tell if my toes were hanging over what might well be a vast chasm, or if they dangled but inches from safety. Carefully, I shifted at an angle so that my legs followed. Now my knees were bent, and by stretching my legs a bit more, I was able to touch the floor of the crypt. My guess had been correct, I thought with a relieved sigh.

Maneuvering the rest of my body from the narrow opening took even more dexterity, but a moment later, I managed to break free of my tomb to find myself poised somewhere between kneeling and lying upon the crypt's damp floor.

With a bit more struggle, I loosened the cloth around me so that my hands were free, and soon I had burst from that crude cocoon like a ragged moth born to the night. But even without the swathing cloth around my face, I could see nothing of my surroundings. The crypt was bathed in darkness so intense that, without any object to fix my gaze upon, I was seized by a sudden dizziness and would have fallen had I not already been crouched on the ground.

I slid backward so that I was seated against the wall now, my hands and feet firmly planted. As I rested there, I took a moment to assess my physical condition. True, Renaldo's knife had not split me open, but the blade must have pierced my would-be armor of cloth and horsehair enough to cut me, for I was now aware of a stinging pain across my belly.

Gingerly, I reached my hands beneath the cloth to find if I'd been slashed sufficiently to imperil my life. Though the cut burned to the touch, I was relieved that I'd seemingly bled but a little. As for the blow to my head, a painful lump bore testament to that injury, but it was unlikely that wound would prove fatal, either.

I wondered, however, if my surroundings might well do me in. The night's chill had sunk deeply into the crypt's stone, so that I found myself shivering as much from cold as from fear and pain. Furthermore, the smell of corruption was all but overwhelming, so that I worried at any moment that I might retch. And though all save I of the crypt's inhabitants were dead, the tomb seemed to faintly hum with some odd semblance of life, perhaps the echo of my ragged breathing, or maybe the ringing of my battered skull.

But as my previous lightheadedness began to ease, so did the sound seem to abate. And since it appeared I was sturdy enough of body to attempt my own rescue, I set myself to my next task, finding light.

I slid one hand to the belt on my tunic, and almost sobbed in relief to find that my pouch was still securely tied to it. Fingers shaking, I pulled forth what I had prayed was still there: the same stub of candle and two unused sulphur matches I had slipped inside the pouch the night I'd made my first nighttime foray.

But without a source of fire, how was I to light my match and, thus, my candle?

"Think," I whispered to the shadows. "What would Leonardo do if he were here?"

After a moment, it came to me . . . the memory of one the Master's demonstrations that he was wont to give during the occasional idle moments in the workshop. That time, he had showed us how one might light a match without benefit of ember or flame. He'd taken a hammer and repeatedly pounded an iron disk, each time hitting the metal in the same place. After a minute, he'd gestured Paulo over and bade him put a finger to that very spot. The youth had done so and promptly pulled his hand away with a yelp, complaining he'd been burned.

Grinning, Leonardo had commenced pounding again. After half a minute more, he'd set down the hammer and put the tip of a match to the same spot where Paulo had burned his finger. To our surprise, the match had sputtered to life as readily as if he'd touched it to a coal.

Of course, I had no hammer . . . but perhaps I could find something else to pound against the single florin I carried in my purse at my father's instruction!

Returning candle and matches to my pouch lest I lose them in the darkness, I carefully began feeling about me. Surely in such an aged crypt, I might find something of metal. A bit of chain, perhaps a rusted bracket, maybe even a breastplate.

It took a few minutes of frantic searching, but my fingers finally contacted what felt like a metal band. Praying it was a decorative piece of iron and not some bracelet fallen off a withered arm, I slipped it over a stone I'd found that must have worked itself loose from the wall. Now the metal circle had a bit of weight behind it, giving me my makeshift hammer.

I settled myself tailor-style upon the floor and pulled out the candle stub and matches again, carefully arranging them in the gap between my crossed legs. I reached back into the pouch and found the florin, which I set in front of my knees, keeping one hand protectively cupped around it. With the metal-wrapped rock in my other hand, I said a swift prayer and then began rhythmically pounding stone against coin.

It took only a few strikes for my hand to start aching, but I dutifully counted each blow until I reached the fiftieth one. Pausing with the stone still in my grip, I reached one finger to the coin. Its surface had indeed grown warm by this treatment, I discovered in satisfaction, but it was not yet hot enough to burn me, let alone ignite a match.

I started pounding again . . . faster this time. Bits of the stone began flaking off, but I did not stop until the sweat had begun beading on my brow, and my fingers screamed in pain. I touched the coin again, and promptly jerked my finger back. Hot! I snatched up one of the matches and put it to the metal.

Nothing.

Biting my lip, I resumed the blows against the coin again, wondering if I would flatten both pieces of metal into oblivion before the coin grew hot enough for me to accomplish my goal. But this was my only means of obtaining fire, I grimly reminded myself. Without light, I would simply flounder helplessly about the crypt until dawn, when perhaps a sliver of sun would penetrate the shadows. By then, however, the archbishop might be long dead . . . and perhaps Leonardo, as well. I dared not wait until morning to try to break free of my prison.

My arm was leaden now, each strike an agony. Yet still I persisted, losing count of the blows as I continued pounding. And then, when I could not raise my hand again, I reached for the match and put it to the coin's hot surface.

The match flared, blossoming into a tiny but glorious blaze that was almost blinding against the unrelenting darkness. With a cry of relief, I touched the match to my stub of a candle. It caught, as well, and for a moment twin flames lit this tiny netherworld in which I was trapped. All too quickly, however, the match shrank and smoldered perilously close to my fingers, so that I had to drop it lest I burn myself. That did not matter, though, for the dark veil around me had been pierced now.

Remembering the second match, I carefully tucked it and my battered coin back into my pouch and then gingerly took up my candle. The stub would not last long . . . certainly, not until dawn. Moreover, its meager if welcome glow would extend no more than an arm's length in front of me. With that candle as my only illumination, it would be difficult finding my way to the stairway and then up to the door. But, as the crypt saw visitors on a regular basis— those bringing in the dead and those visiting them—I knew there surely must be an unlit torch or two hanging upon the wall.

I stood and started my search along one side of the crypt. I could not see any of the bodies around me, for which small mercy I was grateful; still, I realized that I had begun to lose my earlier fear of what this place housed. For I had been locked here against my will, left to die by a villain who had no care that he desecrated a family's place of final rest. Surely the Sforza dead—if any of them still lingered here— would be sympathetic toward my plight. And, if they could, maybe they would help me escape so I might bring that man to justice.

I had taken only a few steps when my feeble light glinted against an iron bracket bolted to the wall, which held a torch that appeared never to have been lit. I touched my candle to it, and the torch ignited, illuminating a good portion of the crypt around me. I snuffed my candle, then pulled the torch from its holder and raised it high.

Odd how a tomb could become a familiar place, I thought as I recognized my surroundings. Indeed, I stood not far from where the Master and I had found Lorenzo. My torchlight caught a bit of white within the niche that I recognized as the dead porter's tunic we'd left behind. I glanced down at my page's costume to see that Renaldo's knife had left a large rent across its front, exposing the torn garment beneath, as well. Should I make my way out of the crypt and back to the castle, my appearance might draw undue questions that I would not have time to answer.

Impulsively, I pulled the crumpled blue and white garb from the niche and shook the dirt from it, then examined it beneath my light. Though wrinkled and somewhat soiled, none of Lorenzo's blood had spilled upon it, so that the tunic was still fit to be worn . . . more so than my own slashed garment. And it was heavy enough that it would provide some welcome warmth, for I had begun to feel the crypt's night chill now in earnest. Suppressing a shiver of distaste at the thought of wearing a dead man's clothes, I quickly pulled that tunic over my own.

But though I was warmer now, my earlier moment of optimism began to fade as I reached the familiar hewn stairway and carefully made my way up the rough-carved steps. Already, I could see what I had expected, that the heavy wooden doors above were shut. If they were locked, as well, how could I hope to make my way out unassisted?

Taking a deep breath, I leaned my shoulder against the spot where the two doors met and gave a fierce shove. I felt them move just a little before they caught and moved no farther, meaning that Renaldo had been thorough and relocked the crypt behind him. Of course, I also had anticipated this setback, but a wave of despair swept me, even so.

Summoning my resolve, I held the torch closer to the entry and peered through that narrow gap. I could see a glint of metal that must be the locked hasp that linked the two doors. If I could slide something between them, perhaps I could hammer upon that strip of iron with sufficient force to loosen it from its fittings. But what could I use as a tool?

Reluctantly, I made my way back down the steps and toward the raised stone platform upon which the Conte di Ferrara lay. Though I'd been closed up in the crypt long enough now to grow used to the stench of decay, the full impact washed over me as I drew closer to his rotting body. I felt my stomach roil again but managed to subdue it, though I had to pause to let a wave of dizziness pass.

With my free hand, I held the hem of my tunic over my mouth and moved to stand beside the dead man. I was grateful once more for the darkness and the shrouding length of linen that kept me from clearly seeing his dark, seeping body rotting there upon the stone. But it was not the conte that interested me.

"Such a waste, to leave so fine a blade to rust here in the dark."

Those words echoed now in my head as I recalled the brash banter of the guards who'd helped carry the conte into the crypt. As a noble, Orlando would have been laid to rest with a sword as befitted his position. If I dared pry it from his putrid hands, I might use it as a tool to break free from his tomb.

Cautiously, I raised the torch and managed a sideways look at his ghastly form just long enough to see the outline beneath the cloth of the sword clasped to his chest. The thought of having to touch him was by far the most horrifying event of this frightful night, but I could gain his weapon by no other means. Reminding myself that the archbishop's life—and even Leonardo's—might depend upon my stalwartness, I let the muffling tunic fall from my lower face. Holding my breath now lest I take in those unhealthy vapors, I caught hold of the cloth and pulled it from him.

But the job was only half done. Now, I used an unstained corner of that gruesome linen to shield my bare flesh and reached a trembling hand toward the sword. Half fearing the dead conte might contest this theft and hold tight to his blade, I grabbed it by the handle and gave a swift tug.

The sword came free more easily than I expected. I stumbled back a few paces, weapon in one hand and torch in the other, and all but tumbled over another of the Sforzas lying upon another slab. Thankfully, that body was long reduced to leathery flesh and bone, but even so I could not help a startled shriek. I scampered a safe distance away and leaned against the wall, waiting for my pounding heartbeat to settle to a more moderate pace. When it had, I set the torch in another bracket and made a quick examination of my prize.

The heavy garments in which the dead conte was dressed had preserved the sword against the noxious fluids that had seeped from his flesh. Even so, I used the cloth to carefully wipe down the jeweled sheath before I dared hold it in my bare hands. With an awkward move I pulled the sword free, examining its glinting surface in the torchlight. Surely this magnificent weapon could conquer the ancient hardware that held me captive!

With a whispered word of thanks in the conte's direction, I carried the sword up the steps, securing the torch in another bracket at the entry. As I had hoped, the heavy blade slipped readily through the gap between the doors. I positioned the sword over the hasp and, holding its handle in both hands, began attacking the metal strip with hard, sharp blows.

This task proved far harder than pounding the rock against the coin. With but a few strikes of metal upon metal, my shoulders began to ache and my breath became gasps. A few blows more, and I began to fear that my plan might fail. The sword had little effect upon the hasp . . . had not loosened it at all.

I managed but a few more strokes and then halted a moment to wipe my streaming brow. Indeed, it seemed more likely that I could hack through the doors, themselves, than defeat the hasp that held them shut, I thought in despair. Choking back a sob, I clutched the sword as I sank to my knees. Unless I could miraculously dig my way through the rocky walls, I would be trapped in this crypt until someone found me. And, unless the Master were alive to look for me—or else another member of Il Moro's family conveniently died in the next day or so—it would be a long time before these doors were ever unlocked again.

That realization sent a bolt of panic through me. Dropping the sword, I leaped to my feet and began pounding on the doors, crying for help.

How long I screamed and pounded, I do not know, but

finally I sank again to my knees, exhausted by fear and exertion. They would find me like this, I fatalistically told myself, kneeling with my head resting against the doors, my hands bloody from hammering upon the unyielding wood. And perhaps they would find a message scratched into the carved surface: my true name, Delfina della Fazia, and the year, 1483.

I scrubbed frightened tears from my face, summoning a bit of anger now. If I had time enough before death claimed me, I'd also write my parents' names and that of my town, so that someone could send word to them of my fate. More time, and I'd be sure to record my murderer's names, and the fact they had plotted against the archbishop. And maybe I would scratch out a farewell to my Master, Leonardo, and ask his forgiveness for failing him. Perhaps he would then record my name in his notebooks . . . that was, if he did not die as part of the contessa's plan.

So wrapped up was I in my misery, that it took a moment for me to realize that someone was faintly calling from outside the crypt.

17

The lion also covers over his tracks so as to leave nothing to indicate his course to his enemies.

—Leonardo da Vinci, *Manuscript H*

"Who's in there?" a frightened voice was demanding. "Are you dead or living? Do you need help?"

After my first moment of stunned paralysis, I leaped to my feet and began pounding again. "I'm here, inside the tomb of the Sforzas," I screamed. "I'm locked in! Let me out!"

"But who are you?" the voice cautiously asked. "Are you an angry spirit or a demon?"

"Of course not!" I shrieked back. "I am Delf—that is, I am Dino, apprentice to the painter Leonardo. Please, let me out!"

"Dino?" Now the voice, vaguely familiar, reflected astonishment. "Is that you? What are you doing in there?"

I ceased my pounding and put my eye to the crack between the doors. Someone stood without the crypt, and in the moonlight I spied a familiar face. "Tommaso?"

A blinking dark eye abruptly was plastered to the gap opposite me. "Dino?" he repeated. "It's me, Tommaso. How did you end up in there?"

"And how did you end up in the churchyard? Never

mind that," I interrupted myself, leaning weakly against the door in relief. "Free me first, and then I will explain."

"I don't suppose you have the key there with you?" he asked in a hopeful voice. "Very well, I'll have to find something to break the lock."

The blinking eye disappeared, leaving only moonlight, and I suppressed the panicked thought that perhaps he had abandoned me. A moment later, however, I felt a thud against the door, followed by a series of blows. The pounding stopped abruptly, and I heard a sound more glorious than a seraphims' chorus . . . the jingle of metal. The doors' thick hinges squealed in protest as he pulled them open, and I tumbled out into the moonlight.

Reflexively, I flung my arms around my dumbfounded rescuer. "Saints' blood, I thought I would die in there," I choked out. "I tried breaking the latch from within, but it was an impossible task. Had you not come by . . ."

"Yes, well." Embarrassed, he shoved me back and planted his fists on his hips. "You're lucky I was here, all right, and that the lock could be broken with a rock," he said, his foot nudging the small boulder he apparently had used to pound the lock into submission. Then he wrinkled his nose. "Fah, it smells horrible in there! Quick, let me close the doors."

"Not without this!"

I leaned back into the crypt—superstitiously, I dared not actually set foot inside lest the doors somehow shut after me—and caught up the conte's scabbard and sheathed the sword. Tommaso stared in awe at the weapon but said nothing as he grabbed the still-burning torch and helped me shove the crypt doors closed again.

"They'll have to send the smith to repair the lock and hasp," he remarked, sounding uneasy. "Don't tell Il Moro that I broke it."

"I shall tell him only if he vows first to reward you for rescuing me," I promised. Then I gave a quick glance at the night sky, noting the moon's position in relief. "It must not be much past midnight yet. Quickly, we must return to the castle and save the archbishop!"

Not waiting for his reply, I hid the sword beneath my borrowed tunic, tucking it through my belt so it would stay concealed. I knew the sight of an apprentice possessing such a weapon would draw unwanted questions—indeed, the guards might confiscate it—and I suspected I might need that sword before the night was over. That accomplished, I started back through the churchyard at as swift a pace as I could manage in the dark and in my battered state.

I heard the clattering of pebbles behind me that was Tommaso on my heels. Despite our onetime enmity, I was glad of his presence now, for he had demonstrated by my rescue that he was worthy of my trust. Once we were on the familiar path leading back the castle, I settled into a trot, Tommaso now at my side.

"What do you mean, we must save the archbishop?" he panted, torch lifted so that we could more easily see the trail ahead of us. "And you must tell me how you ended up in the tomb in the first place."

Between gasps, I related a brief version of the past days' events, including how I had come to be entombed with the Sforzas. Tommaso listened with the appropriate awe. When I finished, he shook his head. "Do not worry, Dino, I shall remain with you tonight. We will save the archbishop, and the Master, as well."

I shot him a grateful look for, even with the conte's sword, I would be hard-pressed to defeat Renaldo on my own should the Master be unable to defend himself. By now, I needed a moment to catch my breath, so I slowed to a purposeful walk. When I could speak again without panting, I asked him, "And what of you? How did you come to be in the churchyard, when we thought you had returned to your home?"

Tommaso ducked his head, and beneath the torchlight I could see his cheeks had reddened beyond the flush of exertion. He did not speak for a long moment, so that I feared he might refuse to say anything about his disappearance. Finally, he took a deep breath.

"After our fight, I thought the others would shun me, that they would laugh at me," he miserably began. "I thought I had failed at my apprenticeship, and that it would be best for me to return home. I waited until the guards were distracted, and then I climbed over the castle walls. But once I was on the road toward my village, I knew I had made a terrible mistake."

He paused, and I saw a single unheeded tear slip down his cheek. "My father had sold his horse to pay for my apprenticeship. I knew he would disown me if I returned in disgrace. My only hope was to appeal to the Master to take me back . . . but when I tried to return the next morning, the guards would not let me past the gate."

He shrugged. "They would only say that Il Moro might rescind his orders in another day or two, and that I would have to wait until then. I had no other place to go, so I slept in the chapel there at the churchyard at night, and in the day I wandered about the marketplace."

"But surely if you had sent word to Leonardo, he would have made arrangements for the guards to let you in."

Tommaso gave his head a violent shake. "He might have refused a message, and then all would have been lost. I knew I must wait to speak with him in person. That is why I stayed at the chapel."

We were almost to the castle gates, but despite my anxiety over the archbishop I could not suppress my curiosity. "What about me?" I wanted to know. "How could you have known I was locked in the crypt?"

"I spied someone in the churchyard after dark. It must have been that Renaldo you spoke of, but I . . . I was afraid to follow after him lest he be a bandit," he admitted, staring shamefacedly at the ground.

I gave him an understanding nod. Bandits were known to hide along the countryside's major roads, descending upon unsuspecting travelers and killing them for little more than a few coins. Even pilgrims roaming in large groups were not always safe from their assaults. The area near Milan was relatively free of their scourge, but one never knew.

Returning my nod with a grateful look, he went on, "But later, when I could not sleep for thinking of my fate, I thought I heard someone calling. I went outside to investigate, and it seemed to be coming from the churchyard."

He paused and puffed out his chest. "Of course, I am not afraid of spirits, so I went inside and looked around. The voice grew louder as I got closer to the crypt of the duke's family . . . and that is how I found you. But it was strange how that could have been, since surely I should not have been able to hear you from inside the tomb."

"The ear!" I exclaimed, and explained to him about Leonardo's invention, which still remained within the crypt. "If not for that, you would never have heard my cries," I finished on a shaky note.

Fortunately, I did not have time to think further on my fate had I not been found, for two of the castle guards stopped to block our way. One of them, whom I recognized from past forays, stared at me a moment beneath the torchlight, and then shook his head in disgust.

"Here he is yet again, the great Leonardo's apprentice," he said to the other guard, who tried to frown imposingly but merely looked bored. "It appears the duke's master engineer keeps busy both day and night . . . or at least his apprentices do."

"Maybe he can design a special gate just for them," the other replied and waved us through the doorway before I could explain our mission. The gate promptly slammed behind us, leaving us alone in the darkened expanse of the quadrangle.

"Should we not ask for their help?" Tommaso urged as he looked back at the gate. "If both the archbishop and the Master are in danger, we need someone to protect them."

"I cannot waste time trying to convince the guards of the

danger," I swiftly replied. "Besides, the Master has a plan, I am certain. Without his leave, we dare not frighten off Renaldo prematurely, or we will never be able to prove what the ambassador and the countessa intended to do."

I reached beneath my tunic and withdrew the conte's sword, noting in satisfaction how it glinted in the moonlight. "Come, we will make our way to the garden and watch over the archbishop. If need be, you can go for the guards later."

Tommaso gave me a doubtful look but nodded and followed after me. Of necessity, we had to skirt along the castle's outer walls to remain concealed as we crossed that expanse of lawn and walkways. I signaled him to slow as we drew closer to the garden. If Renaldo were already within, we must take him by surprise; if he were not, we would need to find a place that offered both a clear view and concealment without disturbing the archbishop at his prayer.

This time, the tall wooden gate to the garden hung ajar, though I could not guess whether the archbishop or his would-be assassin might have left it that way. Heart pounding with trepidation, I advanced upon that entry, even while expecting any moment for Renaldo to spring upon me from behind. But a quick look within the garden showed it empty save for the figure dressed in a bishop's white robes . . . a figure that, as far as I could tell, was still quite alive.

We were in time, after all!

I gave a soft sigh of relief. Though I had kept up a brave front before Tommaso, a part of me fully expected to find the archbishop sprawled lifeless in the grass just like the conte, a knife protruding from him. Instead, he sat in shadows atop the low rock at the garden's far end, his back to us. His cowled head was bowed in seeming prayer, propped upon his folded hands, his aspect such that I doubted he would hear an assassin's approach. Of Renaldo or the Master—or of anyone else—I saw no sign.

In the distance, I heard the tower clock strike twice. It was later than I'd thought. Likely after locking me away in the crypt, Renaldo had returned to the contessa to resume the coupling that I had interrupted. I would guess that they did not plan to make their final attempt upon the archbishop's life until the hours just before dawn. Earlier in the night, and someone might happen by and raise the alarm too soon for them either to flee or else craft a story that would seemingly prove their innocence. But wait longer, and likely the deed would not be discovered until daylight, at which point it was possible for almost anyone of the castle to have committed that foul crime.

Still crouched with Tommaso at the gate, I scanned the shadowed garden for a place where we might hide. But although numerous artfully placed trees and shrubs dotted the small enclave, none was large enough to hide two youths . . . at least, not at ground level. I gazed up to the tops of the garden's surrounding walls, which stood perhaps twice as tall as I. Along one side of the garden not far from where the cleric prayed, two olive trees stood like brothers together, their branches spreading well above the garden and serving as shelter to the turf seats below.

I nudged Tommaso, pointing toward the trees, and whispered to him the plan that came to me full-blown. He listened and then gave a swift nod of understanding. If we could scale the wall from the outside, we might hide within that canopy, unseen from below but with a full view of the garden. And, should the archbishop need our assistance, we could do as we'd agreed.

Securing the conte's sword beneath my tunic again, I spared another look along the open lawn to be certain no one else had approached. Satisfied we were still alone, we silently made our way around the garden wall to the place where the tree branches sprawled in leafy disarray over its top. In this, at least, we were in luck. The garden was an older creation of a long past duke, which meant its walls were more roughly hewn than those of more modern, sculpted terrains. Thus, we were able to find ample hand- and footholds with which to make our way to the trees above.

Once concealed within the branches, we each straddled the wall lest a careless move send us tumbling onto the turf below. Then, settled for the moment, I briefly shut my eyes. The fact that the archbishop was still safe had somewhat relieved my mind. But with that worry put aside came awareness of the physical trials I had suffered this night.

My belly, where Renaldo's knife had left its mark, now burned as if someone had passed a red-hot brand across it. My hands, which I had pounded near to a pulp upon the crypt doors, also ached, while my bruised temple throbbed as if it were a blacksmith's anvil beneath his hammer. Moreover, I was gripped with exhaustion that was as much a result of the day's events as it was the unholy hour. Even here upon our unwieldy perch, I was tempted to put my head down upon a tree limb and slumber for a time. Tommaso appeared to be contemplating similar thoughts, for his yawns now came as often as the night bird's call.

With an effort, I focused on the scene below. We had the owl's view of the garden, which retained its deliberately crafted wild beauty although it was draped in shadows. The archbishop was close enough to us that I could make out the velvet-wrapped book at his knee, though the cowl he'd pulled over his head served to shadow his features. He remained unmoving in prayer, and I marveled how a man of his advanced years could maintain so staunch a bearing despite the night chill.

Then I leaned a bit farther over the wall, and my admiration gave way to a thoughtful frown. From this angle, the archbishop appeared far more hearty a figure than the frail man I had encountered in Leonardo's company and had seen on two other occasions now. Perhaps it was but the shadows, or else the bundling of many capes and vestments.

Or perhaps he was not the archbishop, at all!

My thoughtful frown became one of suspicion, for it occurred to me now that maybe I'd not understood the queen's gambit that Leonardo meant to play this night. Not content to stand guard over the archbishop and intercept any attack upon him, he might have intended to take the cleric's place entirely. The Master likely had spread word of the archbishop's night of prayer himself, but only after first gaining Cardinal Nardini's assurance that he would remain safely in his quarters this night.

My eyes widened in dismay at the notion. If I were right, had Tommaso and I not come here, the Master would be facing the archbishop's assassin alone.

I raised back up to whisper to Tommaso of my conjecture, only to see that he had fallen asleep, snugly entangled in the tree branches. I dared not call to him lest Leonardo—or was it the archbishop?—hear us from below. And if I crawled over to him and shook him awake, he might start and tumble from his perch. I would have to keep watch alone until he roused again.

But as time marched on toward dawn, I found myself battling sleep as well. More than once, I closed my eyes long enough for fragments of dreams to take hold. How long I slept each time, I did not know, but each time I would shake myself awake with a frantic look down at the still figure below, which remained unmoving even as the stars above him continued their course.

One time when my eyes closed, I dreamed I was again traveling the road that first day to Milan, dressed in my brother's borrowed garb and making my first uncertain foray into this new life. As my father had instructed, I had aligned myself with others headed in that same direction . . . merchants, mostly, but also a few fellow travelers. In my dream, however, the dwarf jugglers from the marketplace had joined our number. But rather than colored balls and clubs, they tossed the bones and skulls of long-dead Sforzas, though I was the only one who noticed that oddity.

And it seemed in my dream that we traveled without getting anywhere, for the same rolling hills always remained the same distance ahead. Of course, progress with my newfound companions along my real journey had been much different. While we chatted amiably among ourselves, we had kept to a quick pace. Our motive had been twofold: to reach our destination sooner, and to avoid tempting any bandits who might prey upon those who lagged behind the others. One older wool merchant, in particular, had taken me under his wing and offered advice.

"You must understand, it is not so bad now, here in our northern country. But, years before, I made my home in Florence, where it seemed every nobleman had his own army of mercenaries. One dared not travel without armed escort, lest those mercenaries set upon you. Fah, it seemed that blood always flowed along the roads leading to Rome. It is better these days, but the prudent man who travels always keeps his gold well hidden and his dagger hanging from his belt."

Thus, in my dream I wore a collection of knives and swords dangling from the broad strip of leather tied at my waist. Of course, in reality I knew little of fighting with a blade, save what I'd seen of nobles practicing with their weapons at the castle. A time or two, I had joined with the other apprentices in mock jousts using sticks and done as well as any of them, but that was the extent of my training. Anyone with more than a bit of skill would be able to easily disarm me; still, asleep as well as awake, the weapons gave me a certain sense of invulnerability, knowing that I was not entirely helpless.

When night fell in this dream and we camped among the trees beside the road, I slept with the largest sword clutched to my chest, so that I resembled the conte upon his bier. But when I would have rejoined my fellow dream travelers at dawn, I found myself no longer stretched upon the damp grass; instead, I was once more locked inside the Sforza family crypt. I could peer through the gap to the road beyond and see the others journeying onward without me, the jugglers in the lead and dressed to resemble small bishops. Though I screamed and pounded upon the crypt

doors, none heard me nor turned to wonder where I'd
gone.

At this point, I jerked awake once again, heart drum-
ming at the imagined return to my ghastly prison. I scrubbed
the sleep from my eyes and hurriedly peered down into the
garden to assure myself that the lone form below remained
unharmed. Then I heard the sound of a distant cock,
awake long before all his fellows, and I gave a small sigh of
relief.

Though the night was still dark as lampblack, that familiar sound surely meant that dawn was not far away. Perhaps
the contessa and the ambassador had given further thought
to their scheme, and they had decided not to proceed with
their attempt upon the Church. With any luck, I need keep
watch but another hour or two, and then the danger would
be past.

It was as I began to relax my guard just a little that I
heard it: the faint squeal of hinges that was the garden gate
sliding slowly open. Fully awake now, I gazed in alarm from
Tommaso, who still slept, to the unmoving figure in white
vestments below. The sound had not roused the latter from
his contemplative posture.

Now, a sliver of shadow in the shape of a man spilled into
the garden. Not daring to breathe, I watched that shadow
shorten into a dark-robed figure who seemed to glide
through the gate. His hands were hidden within opposite
sleeves, so that I could not tell whether or not he carried a
weapon. Moving in silence, he threaded his way along the
path that led to where his would-be victim sat a short distance beneath me.

Anticipating this moment, I'd earlier retied my belt over
my porter's tunic and hung the conte's borrowed scabbard
and sword from it. It was an awkward arrangement, but it
meant the weapon would be swiftly at hand should I need
it. Now, as I shifted but an inch or two to keep the intruder
in view through the tangle of branches, the dangling scabbard lightly struck the edge of the wall on which I sat.

The gentle clang, though swiftly muffled, was still sufficient to catch the intruder's attention. He halted in seeming
confusion, his hooded head sweeping from side to side as
he tried to locate the sound's source. Breath lodged in my
throat, I shrank as deeply as I could into the leafy shadows
and prayed he'd not think to look skyward.

After a few endless moments, he relaxed his stance, apparently deciding the sound was of no import. He had removed
his hands from his sleeves, and I could see the metallic glint
of something in his grasp. A knife? That was what it had to
be, for such was Renaldo's seeming weapon of choice.

I gnawed my lower lip, trying to decide my next move.
He would soon pass beneath the tree and would then be but
a few lengths from the boulder. If I made my presence
known too soon, he might flee the garden before I could
clamber down the tree. If I waited too long, he might dis-
patch the man below before I could stop him.

I shot Tommaso a frantic look, willing him to open his
eyes. If he were awake, he could carry out the plan we had
decided upon. While I confronted the assassin, he would
hastily slip back down the wall and jam the gate shut from
the outside before running for the guard. That would leave
me locked in the garden with a knife-wielding Renaldo, but
I had a sword and could surely hold him off for as long as it
took to raise the alarm.

Something of my anxious determination must have pierced
his sleeping thoughts, for Tommaso abruptly sat up and
shook his head like a cur crawling out from a puddle. I
swiftly signaled him to silence and pointed downward. His
gaze followed that gesture, and then he snapped to attention, eyes wide as he stared back at me.

Go, I mouthed the word to him, pointing frantically toward the gate. He nodded and slid his leg back over the
wall, hanging by his fingers for a moment as his feet sought
purchase. The descent took far less time than the climb, and
a moment later he had touched the ground outside the garden and set off at a run toward the gate.

By now, the intruder had passed the tree and was slowly approaching his victim. With no need for silence any longer, I steeled myself and shimmied my way down the tree, half falling the last few feet to land on the turf with an unmistakable thud.

The intruder gave a guttural gasp and swung about to face me, robes swirling and knife held high, that blade glinting evilly in the moonlight. Swallowing back my fear, I drew my sword with something less than grace and wielded it before me, gripping it in both hands as I took a step back.

"Your plan has failed," I called in a shaking voice. "Even now, the guard is being summoned. And, lest you think to flee, know that the gate behind me is barred. You cannot hope to avoid capture."

The assassin's shadowy form seemed to waver a moment. I raised the sword higher, as if to redouble my threat, and wondered if he recognized me in the darkness. For surely Renaldo had thought me dead, or else clinging to life but doomed to remain in my prison crypt until I was nothing but bone. Perhaps he thought he was seeing a ghost . . . if not of me, then of Lorenzo in his blue and white tunic returned from the grave.

"Put down your knife, and the guards will not harm you when they arrest you," I urged. The archbishop—or was it Leonardo?—still sat upon that nearby rock, and I feared that even with capture imminent, Renaldo might still attempt to carry out his mission. If I could but keep him distracted, he might not have time to make that final desperate effort before the guard arrived.

Then I heard a soft laugh that seemed to cut the night like glass. The assassin lowered the knife and took a step forward, carelessly shoving back the concealing hood to reveal a familiar pale face framed by streaming locks of pale golden hair.

"So you have escaped the tomb, my pretty Dino," the Contessa di Malvoral spoke in a soft, chill voice. "I should have let

Renaldo finish you off with the knife, after all. But, no matter. Though you are quite brave, your efforts are for naught. Before the guard arrives, know that both you and the archbishop will be dead, and you shall be blamed for the deed."

18

Spirit is not limited to mortal flesh. Metal, properly cast, has a life of its own . . .

—Leonardo da Vinci, *The Notebooks of Delfina della Fazia*

I stared back at the contessa, almost dropping my sword in shock. I knew that she had planned the archbishop's death with the help of the French ambassador; still, I had assumed that Renaldo would carry out the foul deed. Yet it was the lapdog's mistress who had come to end the cleric's life. Then I recalled the bloody glove, designed for a woman's hand, which someone had hidden in my trunk. Likely the contessa *had* murdered the Conte di Ferrara. With one death to her credit—and at least one more upon her conscience—what was to stop her from wielding the knife now?

She advanced upon me, the knife moving in fluid gestures before her. "I recognize your weapon," she said with a small smile, her pale blue eyes oddly dark here in the night. "It belongs to my cousin, the conte. I see you have added grave robbing to your crimes."

Then the smile hardened. "It is apparent you know little of swordplay, though that is hardly surprising for one of your station. But I can assure you that I am as well-versed as any man in that art. My father insisted upon it. In my family, one never knew when it might be necessary to defend against an enemy's blade . . . or that of a friend."

"You will never get away with this," I insisted, trying to keep my voice from wavering like my sword. I glanced over at the still figure behind her, now certain he was Cardinal Nardini. Had it been the Master, surely he would have made himself known by now. "Even if you kill me and the archbishop," I went on, "Leonardo will see that you are punished."

"Do you think that I fear your beloved master? He is but a commoner, and an artist."

She all but spat that last word, as if it were the greater insult. "Ludovico will never take his word against mine. Besides, I am certain that the great Leonardo will quickly find other . . . diversions . . . that will distract him from the loss of a lowly apprentice. When all is done, he will agree with my account of events, never fear."

"Stay where you are," I choked out, though it was I who stumbled back a few paces. "I will do what I must to protect the archbishop."

"Indeed?" She laughed again and shrugged off her cape, dangling it from her free hand as she let her knife hand fall to her side. Now she stood dressed in nothing but a single white petticoat tied over a gold-trimmed white chemise that exposed much of her pale flesh.

"See, my pretty Dino, I have bared my breast to you. Quickly, before the guards come, I shall give you one chance to kill me . . . or disarm me, if you do not have the stomach for murder. If you succeed, you will have saved yourself and the esteemed archbishop. And if you fail . . ."

I did not need her to finish the thought. *Where is Tommaso?* I frantically wondered. And, more importantly, where was the Master? Surely I had not so dangerously misunderstood his intent. Gritting my teeth, I raised the conte's weapon, knowing this was my only chance. If I could frighten the woman into dropping her knife, perhaps I could hold her at sword point until the guard arrived.

I swung in a wide arc, intending to pass the blade within inches of her face. But even as the sword whistled toward her, she snapped her cape in a single swift, graceful move like a serpent's strike. The fabric caught the tip of my blade and jerked it from my grasp as easily as I had pulled that same sword from the dead conte's hands. Moonlight glinted upon it as it flew from me like some sleek, frightened night bird, landing far from me with its tip buried in the turf.

The contessa smiled and gave her head a pitying shake. "Poor, pretty Dino, you are not a master of the sword, are you? But perhaps you will accept a noble death."

"No, do not think to outrun me," she added as I poised myself for flight. Playfully, she flicked her cape again, its edge this time biting at my toes. "I can do the same trick with you as I did with the sword. But that would be so undignified, for us to wrestle about like that. Be a good boy and stay where you are. I promise you, I shall be swift as an adder's bite. You will hardly feel a thing."

It was then that we heard it, a sudden shriek and clang of metal that cut through the still night. And now the archbishop, who had sat so still for so many hours, began to stir, his movements oddly jerky as he slowly rose to his feet. But surely this was not the archbishop. Despite the flowing vestments, he was far too broad and tall . . . a far larger man even than the Master. And why did the harsh sound of gears and pumps accompany his movements?

The contessa had stopped at that first disquieting sound. Now she searched my face with a puzzled expression, seeming to debate whether or not this distraction was but some trick of mine. She must have seen my eyes widen in unfeigned shock, however, for she abruptly lowered her knife and turned to look behind her.

The white-robed figure slowly turned, as well, and the movement caused the concealing cowl to slip from his head. Moonlight glinted now on what appeared to be not flesh but rather some dark, burnished metal. He was no human, at all, but some manlike being perhaps twice as tall as we were, the mockery of his bishop's vestments only adding to his unworldly appearance.

Before either of us could do much more than gasp, the creature began to move with measured steps around the rock where he'd been seated. His movements continued disjointed, as if he were still learning how to walk, each heavy footfall accompanied by a tinny shriek of metal upon metal. His intent, however, appeared quite unhindered. With his sightless gaze unwavering, the being walked directly toward the contessa!

The vision of this metallic man did what my feeble attack with the sword could not do. With an answering scream, the contessa dropped her knife and began backing away from her pursuer. I scrambled out of her way, while my initial shock became a gaze of awe as I realized who was behind this man of brass.

This must have been the experiment that Leonardo had been secretly working on in his workshop, I realized in amazement. Though the creature was not his first foray into animating metal—I fondly recalled the brass lion he had created, which merely opened its mouth to roar—it was by far his most ambitious. How it worked, I could not guess, but such details did not matter for the moment. All that mattered was that it worked, and to frightening effect.

The contessa's pale face was white beneath the moonlight, her mouth now wide in a soundless scream as she continued to stumble backward in an attempt to elude the creature. And as she moved, the cape that dangled from her limp fingers began to wrap itself about her ankles, so that she faltered in mid step. Realizing what had happened, she tried to turn, but she now was hopelessly tangled in that garment. She tripped again and this time sprawled facedown upon the grass. Her breath was coming in ragged sobs now, and she tried to drag herself forward with her hands as the metallic man drew ever nearer.

Then he began to lurch and stumble as well, as if he'd been pulled back abruptly by some unseen hand. As for the contessa, she had given up her struggle and lay cowering on the ground, her white gown and pale, streaming hair like a beacon beneath the moonlight. The metallic being halted, then started to sway like a man who'd swallowed one too many cups of wine. Finally, with an ear-rending screech of metal, he slowly fell forward, landing squarely atop the prone contessa.

In the silence that followed, I heard behind me another screech of gears, and a sudden thud as if something metal had been pounded upon. That was followed by a soft bark of pain and then the sound of a familiar voice calmly cursing.

I turned slowly and sagged in relief at the sight that greeted me. Leonardo, dressed from head to toe in black so that he blended with the shadows, moved out from a con-cealing cluster of hedges growing opposite the boulder. As he moved closer, I could see that he carried a large metal box from which numerous thick wires trailed, fastened to that container by what appeared to be a series of large rings. He struggled a moment longer with one of them; then, with a sound of disgust, set down the box and started toward me.

"I assume there is good reason for your presence here," he mildly remarked, frowning as he drew close enough to take in my appearance in the fading moonlight. "If I am not mis-taken, you are wearing a tunic that greatly resembles the one belonging to the departed Lorenzo, down to the wine stains on the breast. And the smell emanating from it is re-markably similar to that of decaying flesh. And since you happened to have upon you a sword once belonging to the Conte di Ferrara, I would have to guess that you have paid another visit to his crypt."

"Not by choice," I replied, mortified to hear the sudden waver in my voice as relief now gave way to exhaustion. Blinking against the sudden sting of tears that threatened, I instead gestured toward the contessa's still form . . . or, rather, what I could see of it. The metallic man had landed in such a way that he pinned her lower legs and torso to the ground, though her head and arms were still visible. "Is she dead?"

With an expression of distaste, Leonardo knelt beside her and carefully checked her for signs of life. Finally, he shook his head.

"Sadly for the rest of us, she still lives. While I expect she is somewhat battered, it appears she was simply knocked insensible by the impact of my creation landing atop her." He rose and brushed the dirt from the knees of his black trunk hose. "I believe I hear the guard coming now," he went on as the sound of voices and running footsteps approached the gate. "We shall need their help in extracting her, I fear."

Barely had he finished those words when a frantic Tommaso, leading a dozen armed guards, rushed into the garden. The sight of a huge mechanical man garbed in white bishop's robes and sprawled across the half-dressed figure of the Contessa di Malvoral stopped them short, however. Indeed, the tableau was cause for several moments' consternation on the part of the duke's soldiers, but by now they had come to expect such odd happenings in connection with the court's master engineer.

At the Master's instructions, they surrounded the metallic creature and carefully lifted it from atop the unconscious woman, then propped it against the nearby stone wall. "We shall return for it after daylight," Leonardo assured them with a satisfied nod and then returned his attention to the contessa, who had begun to stir.

"Should we not aid the lady?" one of the men asked in confusion, taking a step forward as if to assist the half-conscious woman.

Leonardo blocked his way with an arm. "I recommend that you first bind her hands before she regains full use of her senses, lest she manage to gain your sword and run you through. The Contessa di Malvoral may appear to be a fragile noblewoman, but she is as dangerous as a poisonous serpent. She was apprehended attempting to murder the archbishop, so I fear that you will need to remove her to the castle dungeon until Il Moro decides what to do with her."

While two of the guards used a belt to tie the contessa's

wrists, the Master addressed the men's leader. "There are two others I would have you apprehend, in addition to the contessa. One is the porter, Renaldo. You will likely find him in the contessa's chamber, asleep. The other is Monsieur Villasse, the French ambassador."

"You are certain of this, Signore Leonardo?" the guard asked, doubt etched on his square, dark features. "The duke—"

"—has given me leave to handle this matter as I see fit," the Master cut him short with an impatient flick of his fingers. "Both of these men whose names I have given you are part of the plot to kill Cardinal Nardini. I suspect, as well, that one or more had a hand in the Conte di Ferrara's assassination several days before. I suggest you take both men into custody as swiftly as possible, lest you draw the duke's wrath when he learns his cousin's murderers still walk free. And know that the ambassador has plans to leave the city sometime before dawn."

As if at a signal, a distant cock gave a warning crow that the sun was stretching toward the horizon. The guard's leader snapped a few curt commands to half a dozen of his men, who promptly rushed for the open gate. "You two"— he pointed to the pair who had bound the contessa—"take the lady to her cell. The rest of you, follow me."

Within a few moments they were all gone, the cries of the outraged contessa echoing from the quadrangle beyond. Tommaso and I were now alone in the garden with Leonardo, who shot an enquiring look at that youth.

"I understood you to have abandoned your apprenticeship," the Master said to Tommaso, who dropped his gaze and stared miserably at the ground. "I shall be interested to hear why you left, as well as why you returned . . . but under the current circumstances, we shall proceed as if you were given proper leave for your absence."

When Tommaso glanced up in disbelief and began to stutter his thanks, however, Leonardo raised a hand to halt him. "Make no mistake, my dear boy, you shall find some punishment for your rash behavior. For a start, you will be in charge from here on out for boiling the animal skins to make glue for the gesso. I am certain I shall decide upon some other equally suitable tasks to occupy you for the next month, at least, so you might wish to restrain your joy for a bit longer."

Tommaso, however, merely grinned and nodded eagerly, and I suspected he would have accepted far worse punishment for his defection if it meant he could continue his apprenticeship. Then the Master turned to me, his expression stern.

"As for you, Dino, I gather you have some interesting tales to relate, as well," he dryly went on. "Perhaps you would like to begin with what you were doing here in the garden this night. For, unless I am quite mistaken, I do not recall requesting your presence in this matter."

Now it was my turn to stare at the ground, though not so much in shame as in dismay. Surely he did not think I would have come here to the garden and confronted a knife-wielding assailant had I not truly feared for his life? Nor had I requested being locked inside a moldering crypt, where I likely would have perished for not the good fortune of Tommaso's presence there. True, I had taken it upon myself to go looking for the Master without his leave, but only because of the bloody glove I had found hidden within my trunk.

Momentarily alarmed, I stripped off Lorenzo's borrowed tunic and searched inside mine, fearing I might have lost this incriminating bit of evidence. The glove was still tucked into the laced undergarment where I had hidden it, however, and I handed it to Leonardo.

"Remember, Master, how you suggested that my midnight intruder might have left something in my trunk, rather than stolen something from it? I searched through it the other morning after I left your workshop, and this is what I found."

The first hint of daylight was stealing over the garden walls now, so the bloodstains upon the pale leather were quite evident as he unfolded the glove and studied it. "It appears to be a woman's glove," he agreed, measuring against his own hand to demonstrate its small size, "and those stains do appear to be blood, though I do have certain chemicals in my workshop that can confirm that with certainty. As for its appearance among your belongings, it cannot be an accident that it was your trunk into which it was placed. Someone obviously meant it to be found, later if not sooner . . . and by someone who would know what it represented."

He turned the glove over again. "You will note the pattern of the stain—let us go with the presumption that it is blood—and how its heaviest concentration is along the sides and back of the glove. The palm is relatively untouched. Had the glove been sullied in some innocent fashion, perhaps in assisting an injured person, most of the blood would have soaked into its palm. But let us assume that the person wearing the glove been holding on to something . . . perhaps a knife."

By way of demonstration, he grabbed up the contessa's abandoned weapon from the grass and arranged the glove around its handle in the same way that a hand would have gripped it. Satisfied, he went on, "You can see how the palm and inner surfaces of the glove's fingers are pressed against metal. In this way, they would have been shielded from the spray of blood that apparently soaked the rest of the glove as the blade entered flesh."

"Do you mean that some lady wore that glove to kill someone?" Tommaso squeaked out, looking pale in the dawn light.

Leonardo nodded. "I think it quite likely . . . and I am certain that young Dino agrees, else he would not have guarded this clue so jealously despite his trials this night. Other than the unfortunate Lorenzo, the only person to meet a bloody end in recent days was the duke's cousin, the Conte di Ferrara. And, unless someone is cleverly diverting us from the truth, it now appears that his assassin was indeed a woman . . . more than likely, the Contessa di Malvoral."

So saying, he stuck the contessa's knife in his belt and

slipped the carefully folded glove into his pouch. "But the only way we shall resolve this mystery is to discover the glove's true owner," he added. "Of course, I intend to again question the contessa, as well as Renaldo and Monsieur Villasse, about the matter. I shall soon have an answer, never fear."

Then he shot a rueful glance back at the mechanical man, looking ludicrous now in its bishop's robes in the daylight.

"I fear I still have some adjustments to make on my automaton," he admitted. "While the theory is sound, the spring and pulley mechanisms did not act as swiftly as they should have when I pulled the various cords. And some of the counterweights appear to be off balance, which is likely why it toppled over. Believe me that I did not deliberately intend to stop the contessa by the crude expediency of dropping my invention upon her."

His gaze turned to me, and his expression was one now of concern. "And be assured, my dear Dino, that I did not mean to leave you unprotected for so long. Had the automaton performed as I'd hoped, the contessa would have been subdued immediately. You were indeed brave, challenging her as you did . . . and had that actually been the archbishop seated upon the rock, you would have saved his life."

Normally, I would have beamed upon hearing such a compliment from the Master. Instead, I merely stared dully back at him, aware that I'd begun to sway, and that my flesh felt both hot and chilled at the same time.

Through the buzzing in my ears, I heard Tommaso say, "You don't look so good, Dino. Is your wound bothering you?"

"Wound?" I heard Leonardo crisply ask him. "But the contessa's blade did not touch him. Tell me quickly, Tommaso, what is going on here?"

Vaguely, I was aware of Tommaso telling the Master the same story I had related after the youth had rescued me from my prison crypt. I would have elaborated on the tale, save that by now I had sagged to the grass. Sitting there, I squinted against the sudden flash of sunlight that poured into the garden. Dawn had at last arrived full-blown, and this past hellish night was over. Now, the morning's bright rays bathed the lush greenery in golden light far different from the cool half shadows that were the usual illumination. At least for the moment, the garden no longer resembled the same mysterious refuge where I had discovered a man's body only days before. It was instead a place of warm welcome, a cheery and inviting spot where one might comfortably stretch out upon the turf seats and dream quite happy dreams.

But the Master would not let me rest there, it seemed. He had lifted me into his arms and was carrying me . . . where, I did not know, nor did I care. I was content simply to float along, no longer in fear of knife-wielding contessas or brutal youths with red hair and cruel grins. Then I heard him telling Tommaso, "There's no time to be lost. We must get him to the surgeon."

That last word pierced my fog of feverish disinterest.

"Not the surgeon," I protested in alarm, returning to myself long enough to recall that such a decision put my disguise at risk, as that man would surely want to examine my wound. I could trust only one other person to care for me in this state. "Take me to Signore Luigi's shop," I told him . . . or so I hoped, for the words seemed to catch and stick upon my tongue.

Tommaso, however, managed to understand my request. "The tailor?" I heard him ask in disbelief as we passed through the garden gate. "You must be quite feverish. It is the surgeon you need."

"No, no. I do not trust the surgeon." I pried open my eyes to stare up at the Master. "Please, I beg you, do not take me to him." Then, using the only excuse that my fevered brain allowed, I added, "He let Lorenzo die . . . and surely I will die if he lays hands on me."

I saw a look of uncertainty upon Leonardo's face and knew he felt the same distrust of the surgeon's skill as I did. Rousing myself a bit more, I pressed my advantage and gasped out, "Please, take me to Signore Luigi, instead. He knows much about healing. Remember the lark? Besides, if I need my belly stitched, who better to do it than a tailor?"

Whether it was that last argument that resonated with him or simply my air of distress, I heard him curse beneath his breath before he nodded. "Do not distress yourself further, my dear boy," he told me. "I will take you to Luigi's shop. At least, it is much cleaner than the surgery."

I recalled very little for the next portion of time, rousing again only when I heard the tailor's words, "Pah, bring the boy in, and I will do what I can."

As they helped me onto the cot in the next room— Luigi's own bed, I would later learn—I could hear Tommaso's rather garbled explanation of my injuries followed by a more straightforward account from Leonardo. Through bleary eyes, I watched Luigi scribble a few notes upon a piece of paper, which he gave to Tommaso with orders to rush to the apothecary shop across the lane.

"Make sure he knows I need everything on this list, and with no delay," he insisted, shaking a couple of coins from his purse and then waving him away.

A bit more arguing sent Leonardo on his way, as well, with the promise from Luigi that he would send one of his apprentices around with word of my condition later in the day. I did not begrudge the Master's leave-taking, for I knew he still had much to do in resolving both the matter of the conte's murder and the plot against the archbishop. Besides, if he remained, he would surely want to assist the tailor.

I must have drifted off after that for, much later, I roused enough to hear Luigi warn me, "I fear this shall sting quite a bit."

I felt him slap what felt like burning coals upon the cut across my torso, and I managed a weak cry. Then he was pressing a cup filled with some foul-smelling liquid to my lips and urging me to drink. I did, but only because I was too tired to fight him.

Once, before sleep claimed me entirely, I struggled from

visions of crypts and swords and corpses to realize there was something about the bloody glove I'd found that I should have remembered and told the Master. The thought teased the edges of my brain, there but out of reach. It was as if I were grasping for one of those tame birds that Leonardo was wont to set free of its cage, but each attempt to recapture it merely sent it hopping just beyond my fingertips.

And finally, unlike the unfortunate lark held captive in Luigi's shop who never again would fly, that bird departed in a flutter of black wings, leaving me in equal darkness.

19

It is also a good plan every now and then to go away and have a little relaxation; for then when you come back to the work, your judgment will be surer . . .

—Leonardo da Vinci, *Manuscript 2038*

I slept through the entire day and into the night, gripped by a feverish exhaustion. Between ghastly nightmares of bloated corpses and a knife-wielding contessa, and pleasant dreams of life at home with my family, I drifted close enough to consciousness on occasion to overhear bits of conversation from a seeming distance.

". . . unseemly, to be dragging a young, er, boy out at all hours of the night and into harm's way," the faint voice of Signore Luigi was telling someone.

Someone who sounded much like the Master responded. I caught but a few phrases . . . "part of his duties" . . . "acquitted himself well enough" . . . "expand his horizons" . . . for me to guess Leonardo was defending his decision for putting me into danger.

Sometime later, a cool hand rested momentarily upon my burning forehead, and then I heard the Master's voice saying, "You must recover swiftly, my dear boy. I have grown accustomed to having a capable assistant at my side and would not care to lose you."

Other voices came, too. Once, I heard Tommaso and a
handful of the other apprentices asking leave to see me.
Their request was quashed by Luigi's sour demand that they
leave me to rest, though as they reluctantly departed he
gave them a few terse words of reassurance.

Or were all these voices simply more dreams? I could not
be certain, for the fever's grip on me had strengthened.
Now, I heard the icy tinkle of the Contessa di Malvoral's
laugh, and Renaldo's crude words as he threatened to finish
the job on me he had begun. Then came the dying Lorenzo's
doleful moans . . . or were they mine as I struggled in my
fever? Perhaps it was all a dream, I told myself at the height
of my shivering and sweating, and when I awakened, I
would be back in my own bed in my father's house.

But by the third morning, my fever was gone. I groggily
awakened to the sound of Luigi berating one of his young
apprentices for some transgression or another. The familiar
complaints made me smile shakily, even as I felt a welling of
gratitude toward him. Of course, my choice of him as my
physician had been primarily because I knew could trust
him to maintain my masquerade when I could not. But it
seemed that the tailor's knowledge of the healing arts extended to people, as well as to dumb beasts.

I put a tentative hand to the cut across my stomach and
realized that I was no longer dressed in my page's outfit. Instead, I wore a clean linen shift that hung loosely enough
but still could not adequately disguise my figure. Swiftly, I
pulled the blankets to my chin, recalling my dream of visitors looking in upon me during my illness. Surely he had
not allowed anyone to see me gowned this way!

A few minutes later, I heard heavy footsteps. The curtain
dividing the bedchamber from the shop abruptly parted, revealing the tailor's sour face. His expression brightened into
something resembling pleasure as he realized I was finally
awake again.

"By Saint Michael, perhaps you will live, after all," he said in dry satisfaction as he trudged into the small room. "I had begun to fear I might have to stitch a burial shroud for you."

He sat down on the edge of the bed, causing it to tilt precariously, and touched a pudgy hand to my face. "Aha, my tonic worked. Your fever appears to be gone, and your eyes are no longer rolling about in their sockets, as they were when you arrived. Here, let me see how your wound is healing."

Reluctantly, I rearranged the blankets around me and then cautiously raised the hem of my gown just enough to bare that portion of my torso. Seemingly unaware of my concern, he studied the gash, and then gave an approving nod as he picked up a small jar on the table beside the bed. "Much better . . . The inflammation is all but gone now, and it has begun to scab over. But you will want to apply this salve several times a day until the flesh is no longer raw. Tell me, how do you feel?"

"Hungry," I croaked out, "and thirsty . . . and in need of the piss pot."

After gaining my assurances that I was able to manage by myself that last mentioned item, he tactfully left me alone for several minutes. When he returned, he had with him a jug of water and a bit of broth and bread. "This should hold you for the time being, until you are a bit stronger," he decreed. "And do be careful moving about," he added as I settled myself higher against the pillows. "I was forced to stitch your wound with a bit of silk so that you would heal more readily."

In fact, I had already discovered his handiwork . . . a few tiny knotted threads along a surprisingly long cut just below my ribs.

"I fear you will still have a scar," he predicted, "but I am certain it will be less unsightly than what you would have been left with had the surgeon attended to it. Oh, now what is wrong?" he demanded in mild disgust as he saw my growing expression of alarm.

I gestured to my chemise. "While you were taking care

of me, did anyone else see . . . that is, did anyone guess that—"

"That your figure is not that of a boy?" he finished for me, assuming an offended mien. "Certainly, you must know me to be more clever than that. I made certain that only I attended to you, and only when no one else was in sight. And I was careful to keep the blankets pulled up around you whenever anyone visited. You should have no concerns in that regard."

I nodded, relieved. He poured me a cup of water, which I greedily drank, and settled me with a bowl of the soup.

"You were wounded more gravely than your Master realized," he went on in a disapproving voice while I swallowed down my sparse meal. "The blow to your head was worrisome enough, but your cut bled more than I'm sure even you knew. Fortunately, the corset you were wearing acted as padding so that the wound stanched itself. But I fear it must have been exposed to some unhealthy air while you were trapped in the crypt. It had begun to fester, and had I not applied the salves, it might have putrefied."

The word brought to mind memories of the conte's bloated and blackened body. My stomach roiled, so that I swiftly handed Luigi my bowl. "Th-That's all I can manage now," I weakly told him and leaned back against the pillows again. Saints' blood, would I ever scrub that frightful image from my mind?

To distract myself, I asked, "Has Leonardo brought you any news of the Contessa di Malvoral or the French ambassador? Do you know, is the archbishop safely on his way back to Rome? And what of Renaldo, and—"

"Stop," the tailor decreed in sour tones. "I have been stuck here caring for you, and out of the stream of the usual gossip. And rather than reward me for my good deeds by telling me all, your beloved Leonardo refuses to share with me any of this most interesting tale. I fear you will have to pry the story from him if you want any answers."

"And has he asked about me?" I wanted to know, trying

not to sound too eager. I still was not sure how much of what I had heard while I was ill was feverish imaginings, and how much had actually occurred. But I was certain I remembered Leonardo checking on me at least one time, as I lay racked with fever.

Luigi nodded. "He has been by half a dozen times to see you, as have several of the apprentices from the workshop. It appears our young Dino is popular among his fellows." He paused and gave a sly grin. "I was even told by Tommaso that there was a certain young woman from the kitchens—I believe her name is Marcella—who asked after your health."

"She's just a friend," I muttered, certain I would have blushed, had I the blood left for it. "I have given her no cause to have expectations of me . . . that is, the sort of expectations she might have if I were truly a boy."

"Ah, it is difficult, living a life of deception," he agreed, sounding as if he knew of what he spoke. "But you chose this masquerade of yours, when others might have been forced into it through no will of their own."

Curious now, I would have questioned him, save that I heard the shop door open, followed by the sound of women's voices admiring some garment or another. The tailor struggled to his feet and gave me a reassuring pat.

"Do not worry, I shall hold your secret tight. But for now, let me attend to my customers. And you might wish to make yourself presentable," he added, pulling from a shelf a wood comb and a bit of brightly polished brass. "I sent one of my boys to tell your Master that you were at last recovered from your fever. I'm sure he will be eager to see you."

I waited until he swept past the curtains to dare a glance in the mirror, gasping a little at the sight that met my bleary eyes. My face was pale as milk, and great hollows darkened the skin beneath my eyes. My hair—once my great vanity— now hung limply from my scalp, still dusty from when I lay captive within the crumbling stone of the niche in the crypt where Renaldo had locked me. Indeed, I looked a fitting bride for the grave.

Hastily, I poured a water into the basin beside the bed and used a bit of linen to scrub the dried sweat and tomb grime from my skin, then started in on my knotted locks. When I finished, I looked only slightly more presentable, but I comforted myself that I no longer appeared as if I had just crawled out from a crypt. The effort had sapped what energy I had, however, so that I sagged back against the pillows again.

It was some time later when I awakened again to hear the Master's voice within the shop. I snatched the covers to my chin just as Luigi popped his head past the curtains and gave me a questioning look. I nodded, and he drew the drapes aside to let Leonardo pass.

"My dear boy, I am glad to see you are mending," he greeted me. His expression was placid as he approached my bed, though I heard a genuine note of pleasure in his tone that gladdened my battered spirit. "We owe a debt of gratitude to Signore Luigi for so skillfully drawing you back from the brink. Had he not, I would have been forced to recruit another assistant to help me in my investigation."

"I am much better," I replied, ducking my head lest he see the sudden tears that welled in my eyes. For things could have ended much differently for me, I knew. By all rights, I should still be trapped in the conte's crypt, or else already dead from one blade or another. Instead, thanks to a series of good fortune, I was alive and would soon be hale again.

Gripping the blankets more tightly, I went on, "I am sorry, Master, to be such a burden to you. Tell me, did the guards find Renaldo and Monsieur Villasse? Is the archbishop safe, after all? And did the contessa confess to killing her cousin?"

"All very good questions," he dryly replied, taking a seat upon the bench at the far wall. "Are you certain you are well enough to hear the answers?"

At my nod, he went on, "First, to ease your mind, the archbishop is quite safe and should be traveling the road to Rome as we speak. As you might have guessed, his night of prayer in the garden was but a rumor started by me, though its success required his cooperation."

He cocked a wry brow. "His Eminence was reluctant, at first, to let me offer myself as the sacrificial lamb, saying he would have his guards posted at the gate. Fortunately, I convinced him that this would merely postpone a later attempt on his life. He finally agreed that the only way I could apprehend his would-be assassins was if they thought I—or rather, he—was alone in the garden."

"But how did you know it would be the contessa, and not Renaldo, who would try to kill you . . . or rather, the archbishop?"

Leonardo shrugged. "To be candid, I did not know which of them would wield the knife, though I was prepared for it to be any of them . . . even our friend, Monsieur Villasse."

Recalling the letters that pointed to that man's guilt in the plot, I persisted, "And what of the French ambassador? Is he in prison alongside the contessa?"

"I fear our Monsieur Villasse is a more clever strategist than one might guess from seeing him at the chessboard," he replied. "The guards stopped his entourage as they were leaving the castle grounds at dawn, not long after we took the contessa into custody. Unfortunately, the only one inside the wagon was his secretary . . . that agreeable gentleman who you and I had the pleasure of spending some time with a few days ago."

Agreeable, indeed, I thought with a snort, recalling the manner in which Villasse's secretary had treated us. "But what happened to the ambassador?"

"It seems the ambassador played a version of the queen's gambit upon us. With a bit of persuasion, his secretary—our captured pawn—confessed all."

Leonardo's gaze narrowed as he began to recount the tale. "Apparently, the same evening while Villasse's secretary was busy packing his employer's belongings, the ambassador managed to slip unnoticed through the castle gates and into the city. From there, he boarded a boat bound for France. The rest of his staff were left to make their way back to their home country as best they could. Of course, I sent our guards in pursuit along the river on horseback in hopes they might intercept the ambassador's vessel at one crossing or another. I suspect, however, that Monsieur Villasse will be over the border and out of our reach before they get to him," he finished with a shrug.

I stared back at him in dismay. "Surely Il Moro can send word to the king of France and demand his return. Why, he is guilty—"

"Of what?" the Master cut me short. "We have only a vague letter that names no names. True, it is incriminating, combined with other knowledge we have gained, and it appears to be written in the ambassador's hand, but he could easily claim that I forged that note using the letter he gave me as a model. As for any confession from the contessa or Renaldo, it is their word against his. The duke would not want to jeopardize the opportunity for an alliance with France over this matter, particularly when the archbishop escaped unharmed."

"That is not fair!"

"My dear Dino, it is time you learn the world as a whole is not fair," he mildly answered. "It was a lesson brought home to me when I was far younger than you, and I am long since resigned to it."

I did not wish to be resigned to that sort of inequity, but I bit my lip against further protest, instead asking, "Did the contessa confess to killing the conte or, at least, sending Renaldo to do her bidding?"

Leonardo rose and began pacing the small room. "Of that crime, both avow their innocence and claim someone else must have killed him."

He went on to describe how the guards had found Renaldo sprawled in a drunken stupor in the contessa's bed and locked him away in a cell deep within the bowels of the castle. Leonardo later had questioned him there and drawn the grudging admission that the porter had been part of the plan to kill both the archbishop of Milan and the Conte di Ferrara. He swore, however, that he had not been the one to murder the duke's cousin. He claimed instead that while he had gone to the garden with that intent, the conte was already dead when he found him.

I nodded in understanding. "That explains the conversation that I overheard in the hallway between him and Lorenzo, when he talked about blood. So surely what he told you must be the truth, for he'd have had no reason to lie to Lorenzo, especially not knowing until too late that I overheard the conversation."

"I agree with you, my dear boy. But there is much more to his confession . . . and Renaldo, for all his brutish ways, does not seem clever enough to concoct such a tale."

Still pacing, the Master went on. "It seems that, in the beginning, only the conte was in collusion with the ambassador to murder the archbishop. Rumor was that Cardinal Nardini was petitioning the pope to discourage the treaty between Ludovico and King Louis. Apparently, he was privy to the fact that Villasse and the conte were forging other secret pacts with certain unsavory parties from both countries, even as they negotiated the public alliance. Should the treaty between France and Milan be sealed, the pair would benefit monetarily . . . but the people of both countries might suffer as a result."

"So the conte agreed to the assassination to silence the archbishop but later changed his mind?" I asked in surprise.

Leonardo nodded. "Yes . . . that is, according to Renaldo's version of the story, which he says he heard directly from the contessa. The Conte di Ferrara's conscience got the better of him, and he told Monsieur Villase he would have no part of murdering someone of the Church. Villasse pretended to accept his change of heart, even as he decided to continue with his plans, though with another conspirator. Thus, he recruited the contessa to join in his plot."

"But how could he know that she would agree?"

"Our friend, Monsieur Villasse, is also a shrewd judge of character," he replied with a wry look. "He knew the contessa had raged over her cousin being given the ambassadorial post instead of her husband, and he rightly thought he could appeal to both her anger and her greed. Of course, the conte would have to die, too, lest he suspect the plot against the archbishop still existed and strive to stop it."

Once again, I felt a surge of pity for the duke's luckless cousin. True, he had conspired with the ambassador, even planned the archbishop's murder, but in the end he could not go through with so vile an act. Had the Conte di Ferrara been more valiant a gentleman—or else a greater villain—he likely would still be breathing.

While that thought flicked through my mind, Leonardo was continuing, "The contessa's task was to arrange the assassinations of the conte and the archbishop. In return, Villasse would give her a share of the wealth he would accumulate from his other agreements outside treaty. He also would press the duke to appoint her husband, the Conte di Malvoral, to the post vacated by her cousin's untimely death."

I frowned. "So Lorenzo and Renaldo were the two willing to bloody their hands for coin, as the ambassador's letter said. But how could Renaldo be convinced to kill his friend?"

"Ah, that is where the story grows more complicated." He paused and picked up the brass mirror I had been using, gazing into its dark, polished depths as if contemplating something beyond what he had thus far revealed.

"You will find, my dear Dino, that people tend to accept what they are told as the truth, especially when it benefits them to believe without looking deeper. As you have seen, the contessa has ways of persuading men of a certain sort to do her will in such a manner that they are happy to comply, no matter the task. Our friend, Renaldo, was quite smitten with her and readily believed her lies that she would protect him, even take him along with her to France."

With a sound of disgust, he set down the mirror again and resumed his pacing. "The contessa—Elena, she allowed him to call her—told him that all he and Lorenzo need do was carry out the murders of the conte and archbishop, and then it would be over with. When Lorenzo grew fearful of the consequences following the conte's assassination, the contessa convinced Renaldo he must kill Lorenzo. She told him that if he did not, the boy might throw himself upon the duke's mercy by implicating the contessa in the murder . . . this in return for himself escaping punishment. Renaldo willingly agreed, fearing the contessa would be lost to him if he refused. It never occurred to him that, once the archbishop was dead, he would be an equal liability."

"But I do not understand," I said in some confusion. "If Renaldo and Lorenzo were supposed to kill the conte, why did the contessa instead murder him, herself?"

"As I said, she joins Renaldo in insisting herself innocent of that crime."

Leonardo shook his head, a hint of a wry smile playing about his lips. "I paid a visit to her in her cell . . . a much more comfortable accommodation than allowed our friend Renaldo, but a cell, nonetheless. Fear not, my dear boy, I kept a good distance from her at all times and made sure a guard remained visible at the door. For she is truly a Sforza, a dangerous serpent able to slip in close without being noticed and silently strike."

His smile abruptly hardened, and the sudden chill expression in his eyes seemed a match for the contessa's cold gaze.

"She is a formidable enemy, that is clear . . . and quite clever. Of course, she also denied any acquaintanceship with the French ambassador or any knowledge of the plot against the archbishop. And when I confronted her with the letter I retrieved from her chambers, she claimed that someone else must have hidden it in her casket. Would you care to hear more?"

When I nodded, he went on, "As for her presence in the garden, she said she had gone there hoping for a private interview with the cardinal and that she always carried a knife for protection. Indeed, she even claimed that Renaldo's attack upon you was simply in defense of her, that you threatened her with a weapon of your own. Her manner is convincing enough that, if one did not know the truth, one could be persuaded to her side."

I could not help but shudder, wondering what my fate might have been had the Master not seen through her guile. "But what about the glove . . . did the contessa also pretend not to recognize it as hers?"

"Ah, yes, the glove."

He reached into his tunic and pulled forth the familiar bit of yellow leather with its gruesome pattern of blood. "It was Renaldo who originally found it, when he went into the garden and saw the conte dead already. He said he spied it lying in the grass not far from the gate. He assumed that its owner had stripped off the gloves following the murder and then accidentally dropped one of the pair while fleeing the scene. Like you, he was certain it belonged to the contessa, so he spirited away that bit of evidence lest she be blamed."

"And he put the glove in my trunk, hoping it would be found there," I finished in dismay.

He nodded. "Crude as the plan was, it would serve to point suspicion in another direction should the contessa be suspected. But her denials in this instance seem truthful. In fact, she had no qualms about trying on the glove in my presence. It was apparent even to me that it was made for a hand larger than hers."

"So, after all this effort, we still do not know for certain who killed the Conte di Ferrara?"

I sank back against my pillows and shut my eyes, my small bit of energy abruptly spent. For it seemed that, while the archbishop was safe, we had not accomplished the task that Il Moro had set for us. The duke's cousin had been dead for many days now, with no one yet brought to justice. And just as it seemed we had tied together every thread of this mystery, we were again back to where we had started. How would the duke react upon learning the killer likely was still on the loose?

"Do not trouble yourself, my dear Dino."

At those words, I opened my eyes once more to find Leonardo smiling down upon me. "All is not yet lost. The ambassador is distant enough now that he can do no harm, and the contessa and Renaldo are safely locked away. That should satisfy Ludovico for the moment. Let him think a while longer that one of them is responsible for Orlando's death."

"While you keep looking for the true murderer?" I weakly asked.

He nodded his head in assent. "We may be in check, but we are not yet checkmated. I shall ask Signore Luigi to share with me some of his gossip, and perhaps we will come upon the name of an offended woman . . . or perhaps the cuckolded husband of a wayward wife. But for now, you should rest and finish your recovery."

So saying, he turned and started for the outer chamber. I watched him go, only to call him back an instant later.

"The conte's sword," I remembered in some alarm. "I left it in the garden. I must find it and return it to the crypt."

"The sword is safe, never fear," he assured me. "When I returned for my mechanical man, I made certain to retrieve that noble weapon and bring it to my workshop, where it is safely locked in a trunk. I shall carry it back to the churchyard tomorrow."

"Please, let me go with you. I-I took it from the conte. It is only right that I return it to him, myself."

Leonardo eyed me silently for a few moments and then nodded. "As you wish. I shall check on your progress in the morning, and if you are well enough for travel, we shall make our final foray into the Sforza crypt."

20

The passage of time may dull the body but often sharpens the mind.

—Leonardo da Vinci, *The Notebooks of Delfina della Fazia*

I felt sufficiently recovered the next morning that Luigi grudgingly brought me another of his special corsets and helped bundle me into it before topping it with a plain white chemise and a jaunty brown jerkin.

"You should not be wandering the town in your condition," he muttered darkly, even as he slipped a pair of shoes onto my feet for me so that I did not have to stress my healing wound by bending. "For all my skills, I am not a miracle worker. Even our esteemed surgeon would likely tell you to keep to your bed for several more days."

"I shall be gone no more than an hour," I promised him. "Just long enough to go to the churchyard and then return. And, do not fear . . . I shall be with Leonardo."

"That is why I do fear," he sourly returned. "Your master seems to have a talent for stumbling into dangerous situations and taking you with him."

His muttering continued even as the shop door opened, and we heard Leonardo's voice calling. Luigi helped me from the bed, though I insisted upon walking unaided through the curtain and into the shop. While my legs still tended toward unsteadiness, my head no longer throbbed, and the cut across my stomach no longer burned but had begun to itch . . . a good sign, the tailor had assured me.

"Ah, there you are, Dino." The Master greeted me with a smile. "You are looking almost your old self again."

"Well, he won't for long, if you insist in dragging him about town," Luigi countered, pursing his lips. "Besides, I have spent long enough now playing nursemaid. If your apprentice falls ill again, I shall leave him to you to restore to health."

"Never fear, my dear Luigi," he countered. "I have taken measures to make certain that we do not tire him overly."

So saying, he pulled open the shop door and pointed to the lane beyond. Standing near the door was a small gray donkey, a blanket tied to her back, and the conte's sword securely strapped onto her side. "I have borrowed our four-legged friend from the chemist with a promise to bring her back unharmed before sunset. Come, my dear Dino . . . your fine steed awaits you."

Grinning, I made my way over to the beast, letting her nuzzle my palm with her soft nose a moment; then, mindful of the scabbarded sword that was almost as long as she, I gingerly climbed atop the gentle beast.

"Just be sure you don't let him topple off and break his head again," the tailor sourly called after us as Leonardo led us at a brisk pace down the cobbled lane.

He waited until we rounded a corner before stopping abruptly, the donkey halting obediently beside him. I stared at him, and he gave his head a wry shake. "I am simply trying to determine how you and Luigi have become such fast friends in so short a time. I can assure you that, if I were gravely ill, he would not spend a moment nursing me back to health, valued patron that I am of his."

"We simply found some common ground between us," I said with a shrug, hoping he would be satisfied by so simple an explanation.

But it seemed that the tailor was not his true cause of concern. Instead, he reached into his tunic and pulled forth the list that we had compiled days earlier. He frowned as he surveyed it once more.

"I have spent the past night considering the steps we have taken to resolve this mystery, and I fear that I am guilty of making assumptions and ignoring facts," he stated, crumpling the page and tossing it into the gutter. "For there is one name that was not upon our list . . . one person we did not question who might well possess information that no one else would have."

When I gave him a puzzled look, he went on, "You will remember the chess game and the brief conversation you had with the Marchesa d'Este while you were dressed as the white bishop. When you explained that the conte was unable to continue the game, remember that she told you, 'He brought this upon himself.' "

"But surely she thought he was ill," I protested. Wicked as her tongue seemingly was, she was but an old woman.

"And when Ludovico announced his cousin's death at the feast that night," the Master went on as if I'd not spoken, "the marchesa seemed quite unmoved, despite the fact the conte was her grandnephew. At the time, I simply dismissed her as an old woman who no longer had a grasp upon all of her senses. Recall, if you will, her other odd behavior during the chess match."

"But surely someone as old as she, and so frail . . ."

I trailed off, recalling that vestiges of the bruise from when she shoved me from my chess square still remained upon my arm. Old, she might be, but incapable of wielding a knife? I shook my head in dismay, not ready to consider such a possibility.

"Surely you cannot believe that the marchesa murdered her own grandnephew?"

"No, I do not think she committed the crime," he replied, gathering up the reins and urging the donkey to a trot alongside him, "but I suspect she might have an idea as to who did."

I clung tightly to the beast's stubby mane as we started off again . . . not toward the churchyard but back in the direction of the castle. As the Master seemed caught up in his thoughts, I used the time to puzzle over what the marchesa could know. Since the conte was her grand-nephew, it could be that he confided in her. Or maybe the fact that she would have watched him since birth meant that she saw things about him that others missed. Or per-haps age simply had given her a shrewdness that those who had lived far shorter lives than hers lacked.

Or perhaps she simply was an unpleasant old woman with no great love for her dead grandnephew, and that was that.

My thoughts on this subject were interrupted as we ap-proached the castle gates. This time, the guards were defer-ential, almost friendly, so that I suspected their fellows had told them of the events in the garden several mornings be-fore. One of them, whom I recognized from my many forays to and from the castle at the Master's behest, even gave me an approving nod as we passed through the man-sized gate and into the quadrangle.

Taking with us the conte's sword, which Leonardo tucked into his belt, we left the gentle donkey at the stables. From there, we started toward the ducal wing, where the Sforza family had their quarters.

Leonardo spared me a concerned look, slowing his usual brisk pace to match my slower step. "Are you certain you are well enough for this, my dear boy?" he asked, apparently noting how I kept my arms crossed over my wound as we walked.

I shrugged. "It is of no account, just a bit of soreness," I assured him, determined not to miss this conversation with the marchesa. If necessary, I would ask to be carried in on a litter. I had offered up too much blood, too much sweat in our attempts to solve this puzzle not to follow through with what could be a most important clue.

We found the marchesa's quarters the smallest and most

distant of the chambers, well removed from the rest of the household. I suspected she had been put there deliberately, far from sight as well as far from mind. Did she at least have a servant to attend her? Or, if she died in the night, as a woman her age was wont to do, would she lie there unnoticed for hours, even days, until someone thought to look for her?

After no little wait, her door finally opened a few inches. Peering out was a wizened female in servant's garb who looked even older than the marchesa. Her presence gave an answer to my first question. The woman made no response to the Master's request to speak with her mistress, but slammed the door again. I blinked in surprise and gave him an inquiring look.

"Patience, my dear Dino," was all he said.

Our wait this time was twice what it was the first. Eventually, however, the door reopened to reveal the same wizened servant. With an effort, she pulled open the heavy carved doors just wide enough for us to slip past. Leaving us to stand there, she wordlessly padded toward the room's far corner, disappearing behind a door there.

"I know, patience," I muttered under my breath, drawing a small smile from the Master.

As my stock of that particular virtue was all but exhausted, I amused myself by wandering about the small chamber. Unlike the more formal anterooms of the castle, with their few staid furnishings and requisite tapestries, this room more closely resembled a storeroom. I had to pick my way carefully as I walked lest I trip upon some furnishing or another.

Along one wall, a mismatched collection of chairs and benches of a style long past were scattered between carved and gilded tables in an assortment of sizes. Along the other side, I saw several wardrobes—some with open doors spilling their tattered contents—and a few decorative columns topped with minor sculptures. Brightly woven rugs in various states of disrepair layered themselves in splendid disarray over the cold stone floor. The wool provided a soft surface underfoot . . .

and, unless the old servant took pains to scatter the appropriate herbs on a regular basis, likely offered a warm breeding ground for all manner of biting vermin, as well.

It occurred to me that this room must hold the vestiges of the marchesa's life from when she was mistress of her own estate. Now, relegated to the farthest corner in which they could decently put her, she had stubbornly clung to as much of her outdated furnishings and clothing as she could, trying to retain the appearance of her previous opulent life. The realization made me regret my hasty dismissal of her.

And then she bustled into the room in a swirl of shabby black, looking little different than I recalled from the day of the chess match. Her first words, oddly enough, were for me.

"I recall you, boy," she exclaimed, poking a twiglike finger in my direction. "You were at the chess match pretending to be my grandnephew, Orlando. You know that he is dead, do you not?"

"Y-Yes, Marchesa," I choked out, for I'd not expected to be addressed while in my servant's garb.

I looked to the Master for direction, only to find that his attention had been caught by something else. I followed his gaze to see he was staring at yet another of the familiar jeweled caskets. Just as quickly, however, he turned his attention back to the old woman, sweeping her a dramatic bow.

"I trust you will forgive this intrusion, Marchesa," he began, "but it is vital that we speak with you. I am Leonardo, the duke's master engineer—"

"I know who you are, young man." She cut him short, her finger now poking in his direction. "You paint heretical pictures and design machines that have no practical use, and my fool nephew pays you far too much for such frippery."

At this dismissive response, a flicker of irritation passed over Leonardo's features. He quickly recovered himself, however, and continued, "That may be; however, he also has charged me with discovering who murdered the Conte di

Ferrara. You may not know this, Marchesa, but the conte became embroiled in some bad business shortly before he was killed . . . a scheme involving the proposed assassination of a church official. You will be glad to hear that he apparently had a change of heart and decided not to carry through with his portion of that plot."

"Bah, he never could finish anything, could Orlando," she exclaimed in disgust. "So you are telling me that you think his murder had something to do with this mysterious conspiracy?"

"That is what I suspected, at first . . . but I have reason now to believe that someone else killed him before his companions in that scheme had the chance to silence him. And that is the person we must find. As you seem to know everything that happens at court, I was hoping you might have some information that could be useful in solving the crime."

The marchesa cackled. "If it is information that you desire, you have done well coming to me, Signore Leonardo," she said, preening just a little as she took a seat upon one of the oversized carved chairs against the wall.

Her tiny feet dangled, childlike, well above the floor, but her dark eyes sparkled with an old woman's malicious glee. Dipping her nose at a regal angle, she went on, "People dismiss me because I am old and eccentric. It is as if I were invisible, and so they say and do things in my presence they'd not do with someone else." She cackled again. "Of course, being invisible can be useful sometimes."

"I quite agree, Marchesa. And so, can you tell me if you overheard your grandnephew recently mention anyone with a grudge against him?. Did he perhaps receive strange messages . . . meet with people far removed from his station . . . or perhaps did you see him leave the castle at unusual hours?"

"Do not coddle me," she snapped, her withered fingers gripping the arms of her chair. "If you truly wish my help, why do you not simply ask me if I know who killed Orlando."

"Very well, Marchesa. Do you know who killed the Conte di Ferrara?"

Leonardo's tone was one of polite patience, but I heard a thread of eagerness in his voice that reflected my own. I understood what the marchesa meant by being invisible . . . just like a servant, a woman of her age and forgotten station was easily overlooked. It could well be that someone in her presence mentioned a name or confessed to having a dark secret without being fully aware that the marchesa was listening.

She sat silent for a long while, the malicious spark in her dark eyes now a flame. Finally, she leaned forward and spoke one word.

"No."

I saw Leonardo's almost imperceptible sag of disappointment, while I could not help biting my lip in dismay. For all her evil cackling, it appeared the marchesa knew as little as anyone else about the matter.

Rallying himself, the Master gave her a polite bow. "Then I am sorry to have troubled you," came his smooth reply. "Please, do not summon your servant. We shall gladly see ourselves out."

We were at the door, when an imperious voice stopped us short. "Wait," the marchesa peevishly called. "You asked, Signore Leonardo, if I knew who killed Orlando. As I told you, I do not. But you've not yet asked me who I suspect his murderer is."

Leonardo had halted at her first word, hand on latch. Now he slowly turned, one brow wryly lifted as he rested a cool gaze upon her. "You make a good point, Marchesa. Is there perhaps someone you suspect of this crime?"

By way of reply, she hopped down from her chair and skittered with birdlike speed to the table on which the familiar jeweled box sat. Cradling it to her breast, she said, "This casket came from Ludovico, you know. Of course, he gave one just like it to all the court ladies, but it was a lovely gift, nonetheless. I keep certain small treasures safely locked in mine. You might ask Orlando's wife, the Contessa di Ferrara, what she keeps in hers."

I exchanged swift glances with the Master. He touched a hand to the pouch at his belt and gave a slight nod, indicating that he still had the key. "We shall do so," he told the old woman, sketching her another bow before turning back to me. "Come, Dino, it is time to pay the contessa another visit."

"And if you do not find her in her chambers, Master Engineer," the marchesa called after us, "perhaps you might visit her dear husband and see what you might learn."

"I should not have been so willing to dismiss the possibility that someone close to the conte was his assassin," Leonardo muttered as we stood outside the Contessa di Ferrara's chamber a few minutes later. "Who better to kill a wayward husband than his scorned wife?"

"But it could have as easily have been Renaldo's blade we found in the conte," I assured him in a low tone. "He admitted that he went to the garden with murder in mind. Had he arrived but a few minutes earlier, the situation would have been reversed. It would have been the Contessa di Ferrara who found her husband dead already before she could murder him, and Renaldo would have been the one we sought."

My argument seemed to mollify him, for he nodded in agreement as he knocked at the door. When, after several long moments, no one answered his summons, he tried the latch. The door swung readily open, revealing an empty room.

He pointed at the closed door beyond which led to her bedchamber. If she were within, we risked discovery should she rouse and hear us . . . yet we had no choice but to make the attempt. Signaling me to silence with a finger on his lips, he gestured me in, and then softly closed the door behind us.

A quick glance about showed that the casket was not where we had last seen it. Stealthily, we searched the room for its hiding place, but that small gold box was nowhere to be found. No doubt she had grown worried when the Master had picked it up and removed it to someplace safer . . . such as her bedchamber.

This time, it was I who pointed, first to myself, and then toward that door. He frowned for an instant, and then nodded. Should the contessa be within, I could manage some sort of excuse in my servant's guise. But the unexpected presence of the duke's master engineer in her chamber could not be as easily explained away.

Leonardo slipped to one side, hidden behind the tall cabinet where the contessa had kept her chess set. I moved softly to the door, my heart pounding so loudly that surely the woman could hear it were she indeed in the next room. I laid a careful hand upon the latch and twisted it, easing open the door but a few inches. Then I put an eye to the gap to see what—or who—was inside.

The dimly lit room was empty. I let out a small breath and softly called to the Master, who followed me in and closed the door after us. Then, cautiously, I looked around.

If the jeweled casket was in that room, it must have been hidden beneath a stone in the floor, I thought in surprise, for the bedchamber was sparse as a monk's cell. Other than a bed little larger than my own and a brightly painted cassone—a woman's traditional wedding chest— the room was empty.

"We'll try the trunk," Leonardo said softly, going to it and opening its lid with gay scenes of some mythical wedding day.

One after the other, he lifted the neatly folded garments, until he had emptied the cassone. The casket was not within. My heart still beating fast at the possibility of discovery, I helped him swiftly return the clothing to its place.

"Perhaps the bed," he suggested.

We made quick work of the linens, even checking beneath the thin mattress to see if it hid some secret there. Our efforts turned up nothing, however, and Leonardo gave his head a disgusted shake.

"She must have taken it elsewhere. Come, we have done all we can here. Let us leave before we are found out."

Once we were safely free of the rooms, he wasted no time but made his way back out into the daylight and headed toward the stables. I followed as quickly as I could, but by then my steps had begun to falter, and Signore Luigi's warnings were ringing in my ears. Grimly, I trudged on, determined not to give in to my weakened state.

The sight of the faithful donkey nearly set me weeping with relief, but when I would have climbed onto her narrow back, the master stopped me. "I fear we need a swifter steed than that if we are to reach the churchyard in time. True, we already were headed that way, but the contessa's absence and marchesa's words make our pilgrimage of greater urgency."

He left me with the donkey and stepped inside to converse with the stable master. A few moments later, he returned, leading a glistening black stallion already saddled for riding.

I had heard that among his many talents, the Master was a fine equestrian, though I had never before seen him on horseback. With his usual innate grace, he mounted the beast in a single fluid move and then reached a hand down to me. I could feel my eyes widen in dismay, but I dared not refuse the hand or admit that my brief ride upon the donkey was as close as I'd ever before come to riding a horse.

He lightly pulled me up onto the horse so that I was perched on the saddle behind him, and we set off across the quadrangle at a brisk walk. Once through the castle gate, however, he touched a light heel to the stallion. Not bothering with the rocky trail that we would have traversed if on foot, he instead directed his steed across the meadow toward the church beyond.

It was a journey I would never forget. Leonardo rode as if he'd somehow been transformed into that stallion, seeming to anticipate every twist and leap as we covered the short distance. At the first stamp of hoof, however, I forgot both pride and propriety to fling my arms about his waist. Now, as we galloped like one of the biblical horsemen, I shut my eyes and simply prayed that I could manage to hold on until we reached our destination.

To my great relief, it was but a few moments later when we reached the churchyard. He slowed the stallion a short distance from its gate, lest the sound of thundering hooves warn of our approach. Even so, I dared loosen my grip but a little, still fearful that I might slide down the horse's rump and tumble to the rocky ground.

We halted along the far side of the chapel. I clung to Leonardo's arm as he lowered me to the ground before he, too, dismounted. While I struggled to regain my balance, he tied the stallion to a nearby tree and then motioned me to join him at the corner of that small church. I knelt beside him and followed his gaze, looking into the churchyard toward the familiar crypt.

"The question," he murmured, "is whether we are too early or too late."

"I'm not sure I understand," I softly confessed.

Leonardo flicked his fingers in the familiar gesture, though I knew his impatience was not with me but with the situation. "The marchesa suggested that her nephew's wife had something to hide, and that we might find an answer in the conte's crypt. Do you recall, Dino, what I told you when we made our first foray here?"

I furrowed my brow for a moment, thinking. "You said that those who carry a burden of guilt cannot carry it for long, and that they require absolution." When he gave an approving nod, I stared at him in dismay. "Does that mean you think the Contessa di Ferrara is here now, inside the conte's tomb, asking him for forgiveness?"

"We shall soon find out," he softly replied, putting a hand to his borrowed sword as he rose and then pulled me to my feet. "Come, Dino, I believe it is time we return to the original plan that I devised. We shall make our way to the conte's crypt and once more listen to what is happening inside it."

21

Fire destroys all sophistry, that is deceit; and maintains truth alone, that is gold. Truth in the end cannot be concealed.

—Leonardo da Vinci, *Windsor Manuscript*

The crypt of the Sforzas yawned open, ready for anyone who cared to step inside . . . or to depart. But Leonardo gave the tomb entrance only a cursory look before gesturing me to follow him along its side, where the metal ear still listened for any sound that might come from within. Already as we approached it, we could hear murmured conversation drifting from that device. But as Leonardo held the ear between us, I realized that, though sound rose and fell in a discernable pattern, there was but a single voice inside the crypt.

Puzzled, I covered the ear with my hand, lest my words trickle back down to her. "It sounds as if the contessa is conversing," I whispered, "and yet no one answers her."

"He cannot answer," the Master replied in a low voice, "for it is her husband whom she addresses. Listen closely, and you shall see."

The woman's voice was soft, so that even with the mechanical ear I could make out only a handful of syllables from every sentence. It sounded to be a casual exchange, however, a woman telling a husband of her day. She would say a few words, ask a question, and then pause as if listening to a reply . . . though the other side of the conversation was audible to her alone.

She must be mad, I told myself in dismay. But had the madness always held her in its grasp, or did she only fall into its embrace after she had murdered her husband?

"Do we leave her there, to carry on a conversation with a dead man?" I softly asked, unable to bear being witness to such sorrow any longer. "Should we not bring her back into the daylight and try to help her?"

Leonardo laid down the metal ear and shook his head. "I fear, my dear boy, that even if we bring her out of that tomb, she will still be caught in darkness. But you are right, we cannot leave her there."

He quietly rose, and I followed him to the crypt's entrance. I could see torches flickering deep within, the circle of light they created stopped short by a wall of darkness that stretched back to the stairway leading out from the tomb's belly. Nothing, however, could halt the odor of corruption that belched from the crypt's depths like death's breath upon us.

The smell swept over us, and at the first gulp of it I had to swallow back the bile that rose in my throat. A step closer to the entry, and now a blade of panic sharper than Renaldo's knife pierced me. My feet seemed carved of that same rock upon which I stood, preventing me from moving. Indeed, I could not go inside the crypt again, not when its dreadful image still haunted my dreams.

My fear must have shown on my face, for the Master gave me an understanding nod. "You need not go in," he murmured. "Wait here, and I shall retrieve the contessa myself."

He might have said more, but at that moment a scream rent the still air of the crypt, the sound so raw with outrage that we both started. Now, the contessa's words were ringing up from the tomb, loud enough this time that we needed no amplification to hear them.

"You made me do this!" came the harsh cry that made the flesh quiver upon my bones. "I begged you to stay with me, to renounce all those other women, and all you could do was laugh at me. I was dying inside, and you laughed!"

The words trailed off into an anguished wail that made me wish to clap my hands atop my ears, though I knew that weak gesture would do little to block the unholy sound. Finally, the wailing ceased. When the contessa spoke again, her voice was strangely unemotional, as if she'd never given way to those moments of despair.

"I did not mean to do it, you know," came her calm voice, as if she were speaking of some trivial transgression. "I thought at first simply to frighten you, but you turned your back on me. And it was then that I knew things would never change, that you would always scorn me."

Now her voice rose, a thread of anger sharpening the words. "Tell me, beloved husband, did it hurt when my blade sank into your flesh? You were not laughing then. You simply looked . . . surprised."

She began to laugh all at once, the sound all the more chilling for its softness. *The Master is right,* I told myself. *The contessa has fallen into a darkness of the soul that cannot be cured.* Her quiet laughter continued even as Leonardo, his expression grim, began moving down the steps and into that ring of darkness.

As the shadows swallowed him, I knew I could not let him face this madwoman alone. It was not so much that I feared she would harm him, though she already had proved herself well able to kill. What I feared was for her madness to touch him, to leave a mark upon his being that no amount of prayer could wash away . . . just as a wine stain upon a white lace cloth never quite fades, no matter how long it may bleach in the sun.

And so, one trembling step at a time, I made my own way down into the tomb.

By the time I reached the bottommost step, the Master already stood at the edge of the shadows. Now I could see beyond him to the conte's stone platform, surrounded by lit torches that cast the dead man's bloated form into sharp relief. The contessa stood at his feet, staring down at him, seeming not to care that his flesh was blackened and almost bursting. Was she instead seeing him as she remembered him . . . young and handsome?

Or was she reveling in the destruction of his flesh that once had been so fair?

The sound of Leonardo's footsteps approaching her seemed to pierce the woman's veil of lunacy, for her laughter abruptly ceased.

"Who is there?" she demanded, fright and anger equally coloring her voice as she turned in his direction. She cupped a hand over her brow, trying to peer past the torchlight to the darkness beyond. "Answer me. Who are you?"

"Fear not, Contessa, I am not here to harm you," Leonardo mildly answered, taking a step into the light. I was close enough to him now that I could see him slowly unfasten the conte's sword from his belt to demonstrate his words. The ornate weapon flashed in the torchlight, its glittering richness seeming to catch the woman's attention.

She took a step nearer, one hand clutching at her breast, and the other hidden at her side. "That is the sword I gave my husband as a wedding gift," she said, her voice now tight with suspicion. "Who are you? What are you doing with Orlando's sword?"

Before the Master could reply, her eyes widened, and she swayed as if struck by some unseen hand. "Orlando, can that be you?" she asked in fearful wonder, sinking to her knees. "Have you returned to me, my husband?"

"No, Contessa," he replied, laying down the sword and taking another slow step toward her. "I am—"

"No!" Her shriek would have shattered all about us had the tomb been made of glass. She leaped to her feet, an answering flash of metal coming from the knife she gripped in one hand as she raged at Leonardo.

"You always ruin everything! I came to die here with

you, so that we could be together in the grave, but you had to come back to me." Her pale mouth twisted into an ugly scar across her white face, and she waved the knife wildly. "But I don't want you alive now, do you not see? And so the only solution is to kill you one more time!"

That last word rose on an unworldly shriek. I screamed, as well, when I saw the flash of metal that was her knife arcing toward him.

He stepped to one side and raised an arm to block the blow. I watched in anguish as her blade slashed through the sleeve of his tunic with a fury that surely must have cleaved his flesh. But by then I was already rushing toward the contessa, heedless of the knife and thinking only to subdue her before she could stab Leonardo again.

By accident or by some greater design, I stumbled as I came in reach of her. The fortunate misstep sent me flying toward her feet and well below the second furious swing of her knife as she turned her attention now to me. In a move eerily reminiscent of the lurching attack from the Master's mechanical man, I crashed into her with a force that sent her sprawling. I heard a scream, and then a sickening thud as her head connected with the crypt's stone floor.

Whether she lived or died, I did not care, for my only concern now was for Leonardo. I scooped up the knife she'd dropped and scrambled to my feet, ignoring my earlier wound that burned in protest at this rough treatment. Then, trepidation gripping me, I started toward him.

He stood just inside the circle of light, holding his arm and staring at me with a look of bemusement. Fearing the worst, I asked in a trembling voice, "How badly are you injured?"

By way of response, he tugged the ruined sleeve up to his elbow and raised his arm so I could see it. I bit my lip, expecting torn flesh and flowing blood, waiting for him to grimace in pain. To my surprise, however, the smooth flesh of his well-muscled forearm seemed untouched by the contessa's blade. Yet how could that be, when I'd seen the knife slash him?

He shrugged. "I appear to be uninjured . . . but I fear my wrist clock may be past repair."

I let out a sigh of relief and said a silent prayer of thanks for the metal box strapped to his arm that seemed to have borne the brunt of the attack. As for Leonardo, he studied his invention in obvious dismay for a moment before returning his attention to me.

"I am in your debt, my dear Dino," he said with an approving nod. "While I managed to avoid the contessa's first blow, it is very possible that she might have succeeded with her second, had you not hurled her to the ground. Once again, you have shown uncommon bravery in the face of danger. I am quite proud of you . . . and I forbid you ever again to do such a thing on my behalf," he finished with a stern look.

I gave a trembling smile in return and meekly replied, "Certainly, Master . . . the next time I see you in the process of being murdered, I vow I shall do nothing to stop it."

"And why do I not believe that promise?" came his wry reply.

Letting the tattered fabric fall back into place, he reached for the conte's sword that still rested against the bier. He carefully placed the handsome weapon atop that nobleman's distorted corpse once more; then he rearranged the shroud I had pulled aside during my frightful confinement inside the tomb. I waited for some irreverent observation from him—perhaps a quick lecture on the dissolution of flesh—but for once his attitude was appropriately respectful in the face of this sad example of man's mortality.

A moan from the prostrate contessa promptly recalled to us our reason for being there. Leonardo grabbed up one of the nearby torches and walked over to where the woman lay, then knelt beside her.

"It seems she was merely rendered senseless for a few minutes," he determined after a brief look. "Quickly, Dino, take the light while I bind her hands. We cannot risk another incident, even if she is now unarmed."

While I held the torch, the Master tugged a lace panel from her gown and used it to bind her wrists before her. She was stirring in earnest now and, once he assured himself that the bonds were secure, he helped her sit upright.

She blinked, as if awakening from a long sleep. Then her gaze slowly focused on the Master, and she gave him a puzzled smile. "I-I know you. You are Ludovico's master engineer, Signore Leonardo. But where are we?" Her eyes widened in fright as she stared down at her bound hands. "And why am I tied in such a fashion?"

"My apologies, Contessa, but this is for your own good," he replied in a soothing tone. "Let me help you from here and return you to the castle."

But when he would have lifted her from the cold stone, she shoved away his hands. By now, recognition had dawned, followed by a look of horror. "Dear God, we are in the crypt, are we not?" she gasped out, staring wildly about her. "I have dreamt of being here before, but I never thought . . ."

She trailed off on a sob, and her features crumpled for a moment as she strove to control her emotions. Finally, she managed in a hoarse whisper, "Tell me, signore, did I come here of my own will?"

"I fear that you did, but I am certain it was grief that drove you to such an act. Now, please, let us go."

Gently, he eased her to her feet . . . taking care, I saw, to stand between her and her husband's corpse but a few feet from us. Once she'd gained her footing, she straightened her shoulders and allowed herself a brief, humorless laugh. "Yes, it was grief," she agreed in a harsh tone. "Please, Signore Leonardo, take me from this place now."

When we set foot in daylight again a short while later, it was as if we had been born again. Leonardo doused the final torch and then closed the crypt doors behind us, those simple actions powerful as any ritual in dismissing the shroud of death and decay that had wrapped us. Never had the sun felt warmer or the air smelled sweeter, I thought with a welcoming smile for this all-but-forgotten world.

We left the churchyard in silence, returning to the spot where the stallion waited impatiently for us. Docile now, the contessa let him help her up onto the steed's broad back. Once she was settled, he turned to me. "I'll want you to ride pillion with the contessa," he told me. "Do not fear, she is of no danger to anyone in her current state."

At his words, the contessa seemed to notice me for the first time. She stared down at me, her smile wistful, though she spoke to Leonardo. "What a beautiful child you have, signore," she softly exclaimed, "and how fortunate for you. I had always wished for a daughter of my own, but now it shall never be."

Then her smile took on a fond note as she addressed me. "Tell me, child, do you know how to play chess?"

22

Truth and justice are not always the same beast; yet it matters not, if all wrongs are finally made right.

—Leonardo da Vinci, *The Notebooks of Delfina della Fazia*

I was not privy to the conversation Leonardo had with His Excellency, the duke of Milan, later that same day. Instead, the Master had returned me to Signore Luigi's shop, but not without first extracting from me a vow of silence regarding what had happened in the crypt.

"We shall let the duke decide if anyone will know of the Contessa di Ferrara's involvement in her husband's murder," he had decreed. "Until then, neither you nor I shall breathe a word of this day's events. I must have your promise, Dino, before I leave you."

When I solemnly agreed, he turned me over to the tailor with instructions for that man to keep me confined at his shop until the following morning. For once, I was not inclined to protest, as the morning's adventures had taken their toll upon my battered form. And so I enjoyed a rare day of leisure, bundled in my borrowed bed and listening to Luigi bemoan the latest casualty among Leonardo's wardrobe.

"Such fine workmanship," he muttered, examining the long tear in the tunic sleeve from the Contessa di Ferrara's blade, "and yet your master treats the clothes I make for him as if they were rags. Pah, what do you think he would say if I were to stomp upon one of his portraits, or piss against one of his frescoes?"

"I imagine he would be most distressed," I replied, smothering a small smile while reclining upon several plump, brocaded pillows. "But the damage was not the Master's fault. There was an accident"—I could think of no other explanation and still keep my word to Leonardo—"and it is only by the greatest good fortune that he escaped unharmed."

"And you are following in his footsteps," Luigi went on, still sounding aggrieved. "Your undercorset was slashed beyond repair, and your tunic required extensive work to make it a wearable garment again. I will have to charge your master a pretty coin for my efforts."

"Do not worry, Signore Luigi, it shall never happen again," I assured him. "My days of combating knife-wielding assailants are done."

But rather than bringing relief, the realization left me unaccountably depressed. Had I not been woozy still from overtaxing myself, I might have concocted any number of explanations for this. I would miss the excitement of the chase, the fanciful disguises, the opportunity to mingle with people of high station and low whom I might not otherwise encounter. And though I'd had my fill of moldering crypts and cruel murderers, the fact I had survived both had instilled in me a sense of pride beyond simple vanity . . . an intoxicating draught which, once tasted, was not easily forgotten.

None of these, however, was the true reason for my dismay. The simple fact was that, with the mystery of the conte's brutal murder solved, I would no longer be spending my days side by side with Leonardo.

As for why this mattered, I dared not examine my feelings any more deeply than that.

"Aha, there it is, that look," the tailor proclaimed in knowing glee, fixing me with a keen gaze. "I have seen it many times before. Your Signore Leonardo will choose one of his apprentices as his particular pet, to assist him with special projects or simply to amuse him. The boy follows his master about, eagerly doing his bidding, staring at him with calf eyes . . . for what young man could resist the attentions of so talented a genius as the great Leonardo?"

Luigi paused and pursed his lips, his expression growing sour. "But, of course, it never lasts. He eventually tires of the boy's company and sends him back to his regular duties. The boy who has felt so special now must be content with being but one of many once again. And when that happens, they all wear that same expression, like pups tossed out of the stables and into the streets." Then he dropped his voice to a murmur, adding, "I wonder, would things have been any different for you had he known your true sex?"

"I think you exaggerate the situation, signore," I said in an offended tone, even as visions of a distraught Tommaso flashed through my mind. "Of course the apprentices admire him . . . else why would they chose to study under him? And surely there is no harm in his showing one or another some special attention on occasion. As for me, I merely helped him as he requested . . . just as your apprentices assist you."

"Ah, but I cannot envision any of my apprentices risking their lives for me," the tailor dryly countered.

Then, unexpectedly, Luigi's smug expression softened into one of concern. "He cannot help it, your master. Handsome and accomplished as he is, Leonardo is a glorious flame to you tiny young moths, and it is little wonder that you find yourself burned at the end of the day. Just try not to care too deeply, my dear Delfina, when he no longer pays you the same regard that he has of late."

I had no opportunity to make a reply, for the door to his shop opened, and Luigi bustled out to attend to his customers. Silently, I sank back against my pillows and pulled the blankets to my chin as I considered his words.

Of course, such an ending would be all for the best, I told myself. It was difficult enough keeping up my masquerade among the other apprentices. Maintaining my secret before

Leonardo, whose keen powers of observation were matched by few, would eventually become impossible. Better that I fade into his background now, before any seed of suspicion took root, and concentrate on learning my craft.

Satisfied I had won this argument with myself, I closed my eyes for a welcome bit of rest. It was with an effort that I ignored the voice within that refused sleep . . . the voice not afraid to declare that I would gladly risk discovery if I could but spend such time with Leonardo again.

By the next morning, Signore Luigi deemed me well enough to return to the workshop. In truth, I did feel much recovered after another night; still, I suspected his haste to rid himself of my presence was influenced in no little measure by his eagerness to regain his own bed again.

The other apprentices greeted my return with eagerness. Tommaso, especially, was relieved by my swift recovery, feeling that my well-being was now his responsibility by virtue of his having rescued me from the crypt. Mindful of my promise to Leonardo, I left Tommaso to regale the others with that story and his version of the confrontation in the garden. I pleaded lingering weakness as an excuse to save my own account of events for another time.

The day passed quietly, with my hours spent at the table making new brushes . . . that simple chore a concession to my injured state. But no matter how deliberately I focused my attention on my work, I could not help glancing back toward the workshop door more often than usual in hopes of seeing the Master standing there. For surely he would not forget me after all that had happened, no matter Luigi's warning to the contrary.

But as the hour of the evening meal approached with no sign of him, I resigned myself to again being but one of many, as the tailor had put it. Grimly, I focused all my attention on separating clumps of weasel hair into smaller bundles, which would in turn become the bristles on the more delicate sets of brushes I was making. So intent was I upon this task that it was not until I heard a voice speaking that I realized someone was standing before me.

"Ah, there you are, my boy," a familiar voice said. I looked up to find Leonardo staring down at me expectantly. "Perhaps you would care to stop by my quarters after you sup, and I can tell you what transpired since I left you."

"Certainly, Master," I managed in response, ruthlessly squelching my reflective grin until after he had quit the workshop.

How I was able to maintain a placid demeanor during that meal, I could not say. All I know is that, as soon as I finished the final bite, I slipped away from the table and hurried back toward the workshop.

A few moments later, I was knocking on Leonardo's door. I found him seated at his table, a familiar chessboard before him. As the Contessa di Ferrara had done, he appeared to be playing a game himself, moving first a white piece, and then a black. He waved me to the bench opposite him while he contemplated his next move; then, sliding the white bishop a few squares on the diagonal, he pushed back from the table and turned his attention to me.

"That is the contessa's chess set," I exclaimed in curiosity.

He nodded. "The contessa herself gave it to me when I returned her to her chambers. She said she could never again enjoy the sight of it but wished it to find a place with someone who would appreciate its beauty."

"So what is to happen to her? Will she be punished for her crime?"

As well she should be, I told myself, even though a part of me argued it was her madness that was to blame . . . and that perhaps her husband's neglect and infidelities had somehow driven her deeper into that frightening state.

To my surprise, Leonardo shook his head. "Ludovico has decided that there is not sufficient proof to point to her guilt, that her claims of culpability are but a result of her madness.

He has decreed that she shall be sent to her family in Florence, never to return here."

I shook my head in exasperation. "But then whom shall he claim was his cousin's murderer? Surely not the Contessa di Malvoral?"

"Ah, yes . . . the Contessa di Malvoral." A wry smile played about his lips. "It appears that the lady has achieved what she sought from the first. Her husband has been appointed ambassador to France in Orlando's stead, with the understanding that he takes his wife with him to live in that fair kingdom. While the conte may return home to Milan whenever the duke requires his services, the contessa may not . . . that is, not until it is her turn to be carried into the Sforza crypt."

"But what if she and Monsieur Villasse join forces again? Next time, they might succeed in killing the archbishop . . . or perhaps even Il Moro himself."

"Do not worry yourself on that account," the Master replied. "I predict that the French ambassador will soon find himself without a post . . . and perhaps without a head."

I shuddered a little, picturing the man upon the executioner's block and falling victim to an expertly wielded blade. But Monsieur Villasse had brought such a fate upon himself for daring to orchestrate, no matter how poorly, the archbishop's death.

"So that leaves only Renaldo. What shall happen to him?"

"I fear that he will not be joining his mistress in France," Leonardo said. "After hearing all the evidence, the duke has decided Renaldo's claims that the conte was already dead when he found him are lies. As no one can prove otherwise— and as Renaldo has already admitted his guilt in young Lorenzo's murder—that leaves him the logical person to have killed the Conte di Ferrara. Thus, he shall suffer the consequences of his villainy on the morrow."

Renaldo, I would not mourn, given that I had almost become his second victim. "I suppose it matters not that he dies for two murders, when he is only responsible for one," I mused. "Or could the conte perhaps be right? Is it possible it was only the madness speaking, and the contessa did not kill her husband, after all?"

Leonardo shook his head. "You will recall the casket that we could not find in her chamber? On a hunch, I returned to the crypt and discovered it there. She'd left it upon his resting place as an offering of sorts. Since I suspected that it concealed something other than jewelry, I opened it."

I knew all at once what that small gold box must have held. Still, the words sent a shiver through me as he went on, "The casket that she had so jealously guarded contained the missing yellow glove, also covered with blood. I rejoined that one with its mate and locked them both back inside, and then left the casket with the conte. As for the key, I tossed it into the well when I returned to the castle."

Thus the final piece of the puzzle had been put into place. I sighed and propped my chin in my hand, glumly studying the chessboard. I would never be able to look at a chess queen again without picturing the tragic contessa and wondering at the happiness that never had been hers . . . and likely never would be.

Thinking of the contessa recalled to mind her words outside the crypt. Leonardo had not made mention of them, doubtless concerned with far more important matters, but I knew I must address the issue or else raise suspicion.

"There is still one thing I cannot understand. How could the contessa have mistaken me for a girl?" I demanded, doing my best to sound as offended as a boy of my supposed age surely would be.

Leonardo stared at me for a long moment, and I feared all at once that I had made a mistake. What if his artist's keen eye had finally discerned the truth I had kept hidden for so long? But to my surprise, he instead told me, "I understand your concern, my dear Dino. I, too, was accounted quite pretty when I was a boy. Unfortunately, people tend to make certain . . . assumptions . . . when one is far more fair than his fellows. But I emerged from that particular misfortune relatively unscathed, as shall you."

Then he smiled a little. "And it is I who should have been offended, that the contessa judged me to be old enough to have sired a child your age. Obviously, I am no longer that same pretty young boy I was."

"But you are quite the most handsome man at court," I protested, and then blushed as I realized how my words must have sounded.

The compliment seemed to please him, however, for he made no protest. Instead, he picked up the red chalk sketches of the two porters that we had drawn, which were lying now on the table beside the chessboard. Unfolding them, he gave mine a critical look.

"I fear, my dear boy, that you need to refine your manner of rendering hair. It should twist and flow with the same pattern as an ocean wave. Your effort more closely resembles a hedge of fallen brambles. But for the rest, it is a passable attempt. Perhaps you might care to keep the sketch."

I accepted the paper from him, shyly asking, "Perhaps I might have your drawing, as well, to use as an example?"

"An excellent idea, my dear boy. Take them both, and apply yourself to that lesson this very night."

With these words, he dismissed me, turning his attention back to the chessboard again. I carefully refolded both drawings and tucked them into my tunic, then stood. "I shall take my leave now," I softly said. "Good night, Master."

"Good night, my dear boy," he absently murmured, moving the familiar white queen to a distant black square.

I had reached the door, hand on handle, when he abruptly called to me. "Tell me, Dino, would you be interested in learning how to play the royal game in earnest?" he asked with a gesture toward the chessboard.

My heart began thrumming far faster than it should have at so casual a question. Trying not to appear too anxious, I shrugged and answered, "Of course."

"Very good," he answered with a nod of approval. "You

may come by tomorrow at this same hour, and we shall set ourselves to a game or two."

My step as I returned the short distance back to the main workshop was far lighter than it had been in days. The other apprentices had already returned and begun the evening's final tasks, so I joined them in some of the less demanding chores. But when time came for our hour or two of amusement before we slept, I instead took up a candle and retired to my bed, pleading my injuries as an excuse.

Alone in my small alcove, I retrieved my notebook from my trunk, where I'd left it hidden the past few days. As I had yet to record any of the most recent events that had happened, I spent several minutes jotting thoughts and impressions. I even added a few quick drawings in the margins, as the Master was wont to do. By the time I finished, I realized I had filled the small notebook completely. I would have to steal away to the marketplace and procure another sheaf of papers to begin a second volume.

But before I closed the final page, I reached into my tunic for the two drawings that Leonardo had given me. His, I would keep in my trunk where I could readily retrieve it and study it, as he had instructed. But as for the one I had drawn . . .

I carefully unfolded it and again studied the image of the brutal Renaldo. Reduced to a series of red chalked lines, he was now but a tragic figure. Perhaps someday someone would find the drawing and wonder who the raging young man was . . . and wonder, as well, what artist had rendered him into eternity.

A few moments later, I refolded that page and tucked it into my notebook, which I then tied shut with the same cord that had bound it. I would begin another notebook soon, but this one would remain hidden away, never to be seen again by anyone save myself . . . maybe in a few months, or maybe when I was old and wished to recall my life at Ludovico's court as apprentice to the great Leonardo.

Or perhaps it would be found by some scholar years after

my death. Or it could instead end up in the hands of another rag seller, who might be curious enough to open its pages to see what they contained. Doubtless whoever read it would discover the red chalk drawing of Renaldo. If so, the person might also notice a tiny scrawl that was the artist's signature in one corner, upside down and added in ink, as if in afterthought.

And if that person looked carefully enough, she might even be able make out the artist's name: Delfina della Fazia.

Author's Note

Born in 1452 in Tuscany, he was known variously in his life-time as Leonardo the Florentine, or Leonardo da Vinci, or simply Leonardo (never by the foreshortened name da Vinci, no matter what a blockbuster best seller may claim to the contrary). But by whatever name he was called, Leonardo was the embodiment of the Renaissance man. His famous notebooks literally and figuratively illustrate the breadth of his knowledge and interests, which ranged from anatomy to zoology.

In addition to his paintings, Leonardo was renowned for his myriad inventions, many of which foretold later innovations such as the airplane and the submarine. He also dabbled quite successfully in architecture and mapmaking, and was a lute player of no little talent. To the consternation of many, he was a vegetarian and an animal rights activist, as well as a fervent student of both human and animal physiology. Though an opponent of war, in general, Leonardo was opportunistic enough to offer his services as a military engineer to several nobles and kings, including Ludovico Sforza, duke of Milan. Ludovico took him up on that offer, and Leonardo served as the duke's military engineer, artist, sculptor, and court jack-of-all-trades from approximately 1482 until sometime around 1499.

Those modern readers who know Leonardo simply as the old man who painted the *Mona Lisa* (and then carried about that portrait over the years like an oversized wallet photo), might be astounded to know that the artist was considered quite a handsome figure in his youth. In more recent times, it has become fashionable to speculate upon Leonardo's sexual orientation. The debate gained credibility primarily thanks to Sigmund Freud, whose theories as to Leonardo's homosexual nature until recently were the accepted word. Records from the artist's time do show that, while in his early twenties, Leonardo—along with several other young men—was accused and then acquitted of a homosexual encounter with a presumed male prostitute.

Much has been made of the fact that he was not married, nor do his notebooks contain any specific references to female lovers. He did seemingly have an obsession with the naked male form, though how much of that is attributable to his artist's eye and how much to any more prurient interests remains a matter of speculation. But he also painted female subjects of astounding grace and beauty, so that it is apparent he had an appreciation for women on some level or another. Thus, with theories abounding but lacking definitive proof either way, I have chosen to leave the subject of Leonardo's sexual proclivities unresolved.

A few other notes. The keen Renaissance scholar might observe that Ludovico Sforza, known as Il Moro, was not technically duke of Milan during the period of this novel. In fact, from the time he wrested power from his infant nephew around 1480 until formally designated as duke by the pope in 1494, Ludovico's true title was more accurately governor. However, for ease of address, and because Il Moro held that office in all but name, I have elected in my story to use that ducal appellation.

Castle Sforza went through equal changes during this time. First built in the mid-fourteenth century as a fortress by the previous reign of rulers, the Viscontis, the castle endured a major transformation before and during Ludovico's administration. For my own purposes, I took a page from Il Moro and did a bit of castle remodeling of my own. Leonardo's workshops, the garden where the unfortunate conte met his end, as well as the churchyard and infamous Sforza family crypt, are all my own inventions.

In fact, Ludovico and his kin did not have a formal familial burial place until the duke designated the monastery of Santa Maria delle Grazie as such in 1495. Any existing tombs might well have belonged to the Sforza's predecessors and relatives by marriage, the Viscontis. But Ludovico's future resting place would one day gain a prominence that even he could not have foretold. For it was his court artist, Leonardo, who won the commission for a new fresco to adorn the walls of the monastery's refectory. And the subject he chose for the monks' viewing pleasure as they dined was that of another, more famous meal: the Last Supper.